**Praise for *New York Times* bestselling author William Kent
Krueger and his award-winning Cork O'Connor series**

WINDIGO ISLAND

"As blistering and crucial in its indictments of contemporary evil
as *The Jungle*."

—*Booklist* (starred review)

"Krueger paints a vivid picture of the sordid cycle of poverty, abuse,
alcoholism, and runaway (or throwaway) children on the reservation."
—*Publishers Weekly* (starred review)

"Krueger at his page-turning best—but this time with a higher
purpose."

—*Duluth News Tribune*

"Krueger demonstrates his penchant and ability for finding deep,
rich and new veins of stories from the seemingly inexhaustive mine
of the rural and deceptively peaceful northern Minnesota and its
surrounding environs."

—*Bookreporter*

"Krueger juggles a large cast of characters deftly and doles out clues
to the mystery judiciously. More important, he recognizes the com-
plexity of this place and its people."

—*Columbus Dispatch*

TAMARACK COUNTY

"A winter's tale that will both break and warm the reader's heart."

—*Publishers Weekly* (starred review)

"Hold-your-breath suspense. . . . Exceptionally scary."

—*Booklist* (starred review)

TRICKSTER'S POINT

"Contains some of Krueger's best prose to date in what is perhaps his strongest, most intriguing novel yet."

—*Bookreporter*

"Unlike many series, Cork and company age and evolve with each book."

—*Crimespree Magazine*

NORTHWEST ANGLE

"Krueger never writes the same book twice."

—*Publishers Weekly* (starred review)

VERMILION DRIFT

"Krueger is one of those rare writers who manage to keep the suspense alive until the final page."

—*Kirkus Reviews* (starred review)

"This book succeeds on every level."

—*Publishers Weekly* (starred review)

HEAVEN'S KEEP

"Every aspect of this novel is unreservedly convincing."

—*Deadly Pleasures*

RED KNIFE

"One of those hometown heroes you rarely see . . . someone so decent and true, he might restore his town's battered faith in the old values."

—*The New York Times Book Review*

THUNDER BAY

"Clean writing and deeply felt sense of place make this novel a standout."

—Rocky Mountain News (Denver, CO)

COPPER RIVER

"This series gets darker and more elegantly written with every book."

—Booklist

MERCY FALLS

"A novel that will keep the reader guessing through the final pages of the tale."

—The Denver Post

BLOOD HOLLOW

"Krueger has moved to the head of the crime fiction class. . . . The prose is so good and the plotting so deft that readers will be hard put to stop reading."

—Chicago Sun-Times

PURGATORY RIDGE

"Combines a first-class plot with excellent writing."

—The Denver Post

BOUNDARY WATERS

"Krueger's writing, strong and bold yet with the mature mark of restraint, pulls this exciting search-and-rescue through with a hard yank."

—Publishers Weekly

IRON LAKE

"Wildly intelligent."

—St. Paul Pioneer Press

WINDIGO ISLAND

WINDIGO ISLAND

A NOVEL

WILLIAM KENT KRUEGER

ATRIA PAPERBACK

New York   London   Toronto   Sydney   New Delhi

ATRIA
PAPERBACK

An Imprint of Simon & Schuster, Inc.
1230 Avenue of the Americas
New York, NY 10020

First Atria Paperback edition May 2015

ATRIA PAPERBACK and colophon are trademarks of Simon & Schuster, Inc.

For information about special discounts for bulk purchases, please contact Simon & Schuster Special Sales at 1-866-506-1949 or business@simonandschuster.com.

The Simon & Schuster Speakers Bureau can bring authors to your live event. For more information or to book an event contact the Simon & Schuster Speakers Bureau at 1-866-248-3049 or visit our website at www.simonspeakers.com.

Manufactured in the United States of America

20 19 18 17 16

The Library of Congress has cataloged the hardcover edition as follows:

Krueger, William Kent.
  Windigo Island : a novel / William Kent Krueger.—First Atria Books hardcover edition.
    pages cm
1. Private investigators—Fiction. I. Title.
  PS3561.R766W57 2014
  813'.54—dc23

                                                                                            2014013083

ISBN 978-1-4767-4923-5
ISBN 978-1-4767-4924-2 (pbk)
ISBN 978-1-4767-4925-9 (ebook)

For my publicist, David Brown,
who manages to do the impossible on my behalf,

and

for Sue Trowbridge,
the angel without whom I would be faceless to so many

AUTHOR'S NOTE AND ACKNOWLEDGMENTS

The Nishiime House in this story does not exist, but places like it do. For desperate Native women and for young, homeless Native youths, they provide shelter in a harsh world. All of us, regardless of our ancestry, need to support these organizations, which do nothing less than save lives.

I am indebted to the generosity of the staff at Saint Paul's Ain Dah Yung Center, particularly its director, Deb Foster. These are people who, every day, find a way to work miracles with lost Native kids. *Chi migwech* also to the friends of Ain Dah Yung, Eileen Hudon and Christine Stark, who helped open my eyes to the cold realities of being a Native woman in a White world.

Another thank-you goes to Suzanne Koepplinger and Linda Eagle Speaker of the Minnesota Indian Women's Resource Center in Minneapolis. Without their guidance, wisdom, and support, I probably wouldn't have written this story.

To Sergeant Grant Snyder of the Minneapolis Police Department's Child Abuse Unit I owe a big debt of gratitude for his clear-eyed but compassionate understanding of the heartbreaking situation of sexually trafficked women and children in Minnesota.

And finally, my thanks to the Anishinaabe people, who are among the strongest and most generous human beings I know.

In 2009 the Minnesota Indian Women's Resource Center

published a report they'd commissioned, which is called *Shattered Hearts: The Commercial Sexual Exploitation of American Indian Women and Girls in Minnesota*. In 2011 the Minnesota Indian Women's Sexual Assault Coalition in conjunction with Prostitution Research and Education published their own report, titled *Garden of Truth: The Prostitution and Trafficking of Native Women in Minnesota*. These groundbreaking documentations of the appalling reality of life for many Native women and girls are must reading for anyone with a social conscience. Our willing blindness to the truth is the greatest enemy of change.

PART I

CORCORAN O'CONNOR:

"Something Wicked This Way Comes"

CHAPTER 1

Fear is who we are.

Cork's old friend Henry Meloux had told him that. Though not quite in that way. And it was only part of what the ancient Ojibwe Mide had said. These were his exact words: *In every human being, there are two wolves constantly fighting. One is fear, and the other is love.* When Cork had asked which of the wolves won the battle, Meloux's answer had been: *The one you feed. Always the one you feed.*

In his own life, Cork had known more than his share of fear. He carried scars from multiple gunshot wounds and was scarred, too, in ways that never showed on skin. He'd lost his wife to violence, lost friends in the same manner. More than once, men whose hearts were black holes of hate had targeted his children, and he'd come close to losing them as well. In all this, fear had sometimes been the wolf he'd fed. But as Meloux had wisely observed, love also shaped the human spirit, and it was this element of his being that Cork had consciously done his best to feed. In far more ways than fear, this wolf had shaped the man he was.

There were different kinds of fear, Cork knew, and some had nothing to do with violence. They were sought out purposely, sought for the sake of excitement, an adrenaline rush—a roller-coaster ride, for example, or a ghost story. When he finally began his investigation, Cork discovered that it was the desire for this kind of fear that had brought the three boys to the cursed place the Anishinaabeg called Windigo Island.

When they set out that moonlit night, this was what the boys knew, what all the local kids knew: On Windigo Island, death came in the dark. It came in the form of an awful spirit, a cannibal beast with an insatiable craving for human flesh. Sometimes the beast swept in with the foul odor of carnage pouring off its huge body and a bone-chilling scream leaping from its maw. Sometimes it approached with stealth and wile, and in the moment before it ripped your heart from your chest, it cried your name in a high, keening voice. It could be unpredictable, but one thing was certain: to set foot on Windigo Island in the dead of night was to call forth the worst of what the darkness there held.

They'd shoved off in their kayaks a few minutes before midnight from the marina on the shore of Lake Superior. It was late July, hot, and there was not a breath of wind. A gibbous moon had risen over the Apostle Islands. The water of Kitchigami was black satin, smooth and shiny. Behind them, the lights of the reservation town of Bad Bluff curved along the shoreline of that greatest of the Great Lakes, and the three boys paused in their paddling and turned back to admire the sequined hills. Then wordless, because it was night and an excursion that called for silence, they pushed on, following the path the moonlight burned in silver across the water.

Ahead of them rose the island. It wasn't much to look at in daylight. A rough circle a couple of dozen yards in diameter, all of it broken rock, an island so tiny it appeared only on detailed nautical charts. From its center rose a tall, ragged pine, a tree that had somehow managed to put down roots in that humping of stone and had held to it tenaciously through season after season of November gales. The Ojibwe believed the pine was a lightning rod of sorts, a beacon attracting the evil spirits of Kitchigami to that cursed island. Not just the windigo but Michi Peshu, too, a monster that lived in the depths, a creature with horns and the face of a panther and razor-sharp spikes down its back and, some said, the body of a serpent. To the boys on that night, the tree looked like a black feather rising stiffly from the head of a skull almost completely submerged. They approached in silence, the only sound the dip of their double-bladed paddles and the burble of water as they stroked. They came at the island from the west and eased their kayaks up to the rocky shoreline. They disembarked one at a time, drew their crafts out of the water, and laid them carefully across the broken stone. The moonlight was intense, casting shadows of the ragged pine boughs across the boys like a black net, and they stood a moment, caught in the eerie mystique of the island.

Then one of the boys farted. The long, low growl broke the spell, and they laughed, released from the grip of their own fear.

"Dude," one of them said. "You let the windigo know we're here."

"Dude," the offending boy replied, "that was to keep him away."

The third boy waved a hand in front of his face. "If that smell doesn't drive him off, nothing will."

"Okay, what now?" the first asked.

The third boy reached into the opening of his kayak and brought out a knapsack. From it he pulled a can of white spray paint. "We find the biggest rock that faces town."

Which they did. It stood a good four feet high and had a nice flat vertical surface. In the daylight, it would have been dull gray, but in the shadow of the pine that night, it was as black as char.

The third boy knelt in front of the rock, as if praying, gave the can a good shake, then carefully sprayed his message: KYLE B + LORI D.

"How's she going to see it?" the second boy asked.

"Binoculars, dude, binoculars. I told her I was going to come out here to do this thing and the hell with the windigo."

The first boy stood back and admired the other's work. "Awesome. Totally."

And that's when the wind hit.

On a lake like Superior, weather can develop suddenly. That night the wind came out of nowhere, sweeping in from the vast open water. The limbs of the pine began flailing wildly, and waves rose up and crashed against Windigo Island and ate the rocks. No storm cloud obscured the stars or the unblinking eye of the moon, nothing to account for the phantom torrent of air that carried with it a frigid cold churned up from the depths. There was something in this wind that was terrible, something unnatural, and the boys could feel it. They stood frozen, feeding the wolf of fear suddenly prowling inside them.

"Hey, you guys," the first boy hollered over the cry of wind. "Did you hear that?"

"What?" the third boy shouted.

"I heard it," the second boy called back. His voice was a high screech because, in his terror, his throat had closed nearly shut. He stared wide-eyed at the third boy. "Your name. It called your name."

The third boy turned from his companions, turned his face into that furious wind, and listened. He didn't hear what they'd heard, but he saw something that made his blood run cold. In the black roil of the lake, just beneath the surface, a figure, luminescent white under the glare of the moon, swam toward them.

"Oh, God," the first boy cried. "Michi Peshu!"

He spun and fled, stumbling over the broken rocks toward his kayak. The second boy was close on his heels. The third boy turned, too, but caught his foot in a crevice between two stones and his ankle gave in an agonizing twist. He went down with a cry of pain that was snatched away by the wind. His companions didn't hear. They were already on the water, already digging the blades of their paddles into the swells. The boy cried out for them, but they didn't look back.

Then he heard it. What they'd heard. *His name.* His name called in a high, keening voice that was carried inside the howl of wind. And he saw the white form sliding toward him in the black water, the monster Michi Peshu coming, and he watched it slither onto the rocks, and he knew a fear such as he'd never known before.

The wolf inside him opened its hungry mouth and prepared to feed.

CHAPTER 2

The storm had knocked out power, and Sam's Place lay in the dark, lit only by frequent flashes of lightning. It was two o'clock on a Sunday afternoon, but it felt like evening. There were no customers waiting at the serving windows. The violent weather had driven folks to shelter, in their homes or their hotel rooms or their rented summer cabins. Iron Lake was an empty shiver of restless gray water deserted by fishing boats and pleasure boats alike. Aurora, Minnesota, deep in the great Northwoods, hunkered down and watched and waited for the storm to pass.

Heavy rain hammered the metal roof of the old Quonset hut called Sam's Place, and inside, the O'Connors readied for a period without electricity that could, they knew from experience, last hours or even into the next day. Cork had hauled the gas generator from the cellar, filled it, and got it running. It powered the essentials: the freezer, the refrigerator, the ice milk machine, the lights and outlets of the prep and serving areas. Cork didn't think there would be many customers until after this weather had passed, but he wanted to be ready, just in case. And God forbid that any of the perishables should go bad. In a small town like Aurora, in a close-knit area like Tamarack County, any hint of food poisoning could sink a food enterprise for good. It may have been only a burger joint, but Sam's Place had a sterling reputation, and Cork intended to keep it that way.

When they'd prepared for the worst, Jenny O'Connor, Cork's older daughter and officially in charge that day, brought out her notebook and sat at one of the serving windows. While rain cascaded down the awning outside, she wrote. Judy Madsen, a retired school administrator who'd just come on and would close up Sam's Place that night, worked the day's crossword puzzle in the *Duluth News Tribune*. Cork stood near Jenny, looking out at the dismal sheets of rain. He had paperwork waiting in the back section of the Quonset hut, which was the office for his business as a private investigator, but without lights or power to his computer, there wasn't much he could do.

Marlee Daychild, one of their teenage summer help, sat on a stool near the freezer, talking on her cell phone. She was seventeen, pretty, Ojibwe. She laughed and said into the phone, "No way." She listened and said, "You want to talk to them?" Then she said, "I love you."

She hung up and said, "Stephen says hello. He says he'll call you tomorrow. He has a surprise."

Stephen was Cork's son, also seventeen, and Marlee was his girlfriend. At the moment, Stephen was in the Twin Cities, where in recent weeks, he'd been working with physical therapists at the Courage Center. A bullet fired by a madman last winter had damaged his spine. The folks at the Courage Center believed they could help him walk again. Anne, Cork's younger daughter, had gone with him as company, cheerleader, and liaison with the folks back home. Cork would have chosen to be there himself, but because of the way the tragedy had occurred and because her own particular spiritual journey had prepared her, Anne believed this was a responsibility that lay on her shoulders. Her reports to Cork and the others in Aurora had been full of hope.

"No hints?" Jenny asked.

"He wants to tell you himself."

"He's walking?" Cork said.

"I can't tell you. He made me promise. But it's good," she said.

Even though the day was bleak, Cork felt a profound glimmer of hope.

They went back to what they'd been doing before. Jenny was

working on the manuscript for a novel. Her second attempt at a manuscript. The first, she insisted, was "a total piece of crap," and it gathered dust bunnies on a shelf in her bedroom closet. Jenny was twenty-seven. She had a BA in journalism and an MFA from the renowned Writers' Workshop at the University of Iowa. She was the mother of an energetic three-year-old and was also the managing force behind Sam's Place these days. Cork and Judy Madsen also took turns running things, but for all intents and purposes, the operation was Jenny's. She was terrific at it, yet Cork knew a career in food service, even if it was the family business, wasn't where her heart lay. Every free moment she was able to carve out for herself, she bent to her writing.

"Have you called home, Jenny?" Cork asked.

She didn't answer, so deep into her writing now that she didn't hear. Cork made the call to home himself from his cell phone. Rose, his sister-in-law, answered.

"Yes," she said, responding to his question. "The power's out here, too. Waaboo and I both have flashlights and we're making sure all our stuffed animals know that there's nothing to be afraid of."

Waaboo was Jenny's child, Cork's grandson. His real name was Aaron Smalldog O'Connor. His Ojibwe name was Waaboozoons, which meant "little rabbit," but everyone called him Waaboo. He'd been adopted, and the heart of every O'Connor held a special place for the little rabbit. They'd all, every one of them, put their lives on the line for him.

"If the outage lasts until dinner, come on up to Sam's Place," Cork suggested. "I'll put something together up here."

"A Sam's Special and a milk shake," Rose said. "Heck, we might do that even if we get power." She turned away from the receiver and said, "It's your grandpa."

"Baa-baa," Cork heard his grandson say. Which was what Waaboo had always called him.

"Thanks, Rose," Cork said.

"You know it's no problem. We'll see you later."

Cork ended the call, and Jenny finally looked up from her notebook. "How's my guy?" she asked.

"Giving comfort to all his stuffed animals."

"Very nurturing," she said.

"How's it going?" Cork nodded toward her notebook.

"It goes," she replied. Which, when it came to her writing, was how she always answered him.

His cell phone was still in his hand, and the ringtone played the first few notes of the chorus from "I'm a Believer" by the Monkees. He glanced at the number on the screen, smiled, and took the call.

"Hey, gorgeous," he said.

At the other end of the line, Rainy Bisonette said, "Flattery will get you almost anywhere. But right now, I need you here." Her voice was stern and urgent. Also a little broken up because reception where she was, a remote spot called Crow Point, could be spotty.

"What's wrong?" Cork said. "Is it Meloux?"

Her next few words were lost in static, then Cork heard her say, clearly and definitely, "Just get out here and you'll understand."

"I'm on my way." Cork slipped the phone back into the holster on his belt. "Hold down the fort. I'm heading out to Crow Point."

"What is it?" Jenny asked. "Is everything okay? Henry?"

"I'm not sure, but it sounds serious. I'll let you know."

Jenny studied the rain outside, which fell without any sign of letup. She closed her notebook. "I'm going with you." She looked toward Judy Madsen. "Okay?"

"We'll be fine," Judy said. "Marlee and me, we'll handle the hordes, won't we?"

The teenager gave a *whatever* kind of shrug and went back to playing a game on her cell phone.

Henry Meloux lived at the end of a long finger of meadowland called Crow Point that jutted into Iron Lake several miles north of

Aurora. Meloux was old. Exactly how old no one, not even Meloux himself, really knew. Somewhere in his nineties was Cork's best guess. Since he was a boy, Meloux had lived in a one-room cabin he'd built with his uncle, and for most of those years, he'd lived alone. He was a Mide, a member of the Grand Medicine Society, a healer of body and spirit. In his youth, he'd been a hunter of great renown. He'd also been a fierce warrior in defense of those who sought his protection. Many of them had been Anishinaabe, his own people. But Meloux's eyes were color-blind when it came to skin. Cork was one of those who owed their lives to Meloux, and even more important, his children were among them, too. Whatever Meloux needed from him, Cork was prepared to give.

Cork drove a red Ford Explorer. He'd bought the vehicle slightly used a couple months earlier after a huge buck had leaped in front of the Land Rover he'd been driving. The collision had killed the buck and totaled the Land Rover. All things considered, Cork was content to be driving an American-made vehicle again. He parked at the edge of a gravel county road, near a double-trunk birch that marked the beginning of the two-mile trail through thick boreal forest to Crow Point. His wasn't the only vehicle parked there. A mud-spattered green pickup sat among the weeds at the roadside. Cork put on his rain poncho and got out. Jenny did the same, while her father walked around the pickup. The plates were Wisconsin.

"What are you looking for?" Jenny asked.

"Maybe nothing." Cork peered through the rain-streaked window on the passenger side. "On the other hand, the gun rack's empty. Maybe whoever drove here didn't bring a rifle, but maybe they did. If so, they've got it with them. And it's not hunting season, Jenny."

"You're scaring me, Dad," she said.

He pulled out his cell phone and tried calling Rainy but got no answer. He looked at the trail that threaded through the dark pines. "Let's go. But keep your eyes peeled."

"For what?"

"We'll know when we see it."

The trail to Henry Meloux's cabin on Crow Point cut through national forest land for a mile or so, then crossed onto the reservation of the Iron Lake Ojibwe, or as they preferred to be called, the Iron Lake Anishinaabeg. In the wet air, the smell of pine was sharp and cleansing. Normally, the trail would have buzzed with insects, but the storm had driven them to shelter. Same with the birds. The only sounds were the rain cascading among the branches of the evergreens and poplars all around them, the crinkle of their ponchos as they walked, and the suck of mud on their boots where the ground was bare.

"He's big," Cork said.

"Who?" Jenny glanced at him from beneath her dripping poncho hood.

"Whoever got to Crow Point ahead of us." He poked a finger at tracks in the muddy ground ahead of them.

"You make it sound so sinister," she said. "Lots of people visit Henry."

"Carrying rifles?"

"You don't know that he's carrying a rifle."

"And I don't know that he isn't. Remember Waaboo and the Church of the Seven Trumpets?"

He was making reference to people who'd tried to kill his grandson when Waaboo was only a baby. That confrontation had taken place on Crow Point. Several people had died that day. Jenny, Stephen, Rainy, and Meloux had almost been among them. So Cork's concern was not unfounded.

"Given the urgency in Rainy's voice and the fact that she's not answering her cell phone, it seems prudent to err on the side of caution, don't you think?"

"I guess it makes sense. So what do we do?"

They'd crossed Wine Creek, a freshet that was well inside reservation land. Crow Point was another quarter mile ahead.

"One thing we're not going to do is come at Henry's cabin directly, in case someone's watching the trail. Follow me," Cork said.

He cut into the woods and began making his way through the undergrowth, which the thick bed of fallen pine needles and the acidic nature of the soil beneath kept sparse. He angled east, Jenny behind him, until he came to Iron Lake. The shore was lined with aspens and was a favorite roost of crows, the reason for the point's name. He slipped among the dripping trees and followed the shoreline until he could see three man-made structures: Meloux's ancient cabin built of cedar logs; the cabin of his great-niece Rainy Bisonette, which was much newer; and the little outhouse that serviced them both.

The sky above the lake and the point was an oppressive ceiling of charcoal-colored clouds from which rain poured relentlessly. Cork's boots were soaked, and each step made a squishing noise in the wet ground and the mud. He moved more slowly now, easing his way toward the rear of Meloux's cabin. He signaled Jenny to hang back while he crept to the structure. A single window faced the lake, and Cork slipped up beside it. The windowpane was lifted a few inches, enough for air to circulate but not enough to let in rain. He could hear the murmur of voices inside but could make out no words. He glanced back to where Jenny remained crouched among the aspens in her olive green poncho. She held up her hands signaling, Cork supposed, *So, what's up?*

He was about to hazard a glance through the window when the pane slid up fully and a familiar old voice inside said, "You come like a thief, Corcoran O'Connor. My front door has no lock. You are welcome to enter as a friend."

There had come a time, finally, when Henry Meloux accepted the reality of his situation, which was that he could no longer live alone. It had come to him as the result of a strange illness that had made him weak for a long while. That's when Rainy Bisonette, his great-niece and also a public health nurse, had come to Crow Point. Her purpose was not only to minister to Meloux but to learn from him the healing ways of the Grand Medicine Society. When little Waaboozoons had been given to them—by the hand of Kitchimanidoo, the Great Spirit, Meloux was certain—the dangerous circumstances of that gifting had forced the old Mide to confront his mortality, to put his life on the line for the little guy, and this, in the incomprehensible way of the Great Spirit, had been his own healing. Rainy had stayed on, even after Meloux's recovery, both to learn and to help the old man who was, after all, somewhere near a century old. Two summers ago, Cork had helped build the one-room cabin that was Rainy's. And since then, he'd often spent the night with her, sharing her bed and blanket and the blessing of her warm body.

Rainy stood in Meloux's cabin, a cup of coffee in her hand, listening as her great-uncle made the introductions.

"Daniel English," the old man said, indicating his guest with a nod of his head.

As Cork had surmised from the boot prints on the trail, Daniel English was a big man, well over six feet tall. Cork judged him to be in his late twenties. English was quite clearly Indian, though Cork couldn't have said what his tribal affiliation might have been. His hair was raven-wing black, his eyes almond, his nose like a hatchet blade set in a broad face. He wore jeans and a blue work shirt with the sleeves rolled up to expose his powerful biceps. There was one other thing that Cork noticed about him from the get-go: those dark eyes took in everything, and in a way that made Cork think, *Cop.*

"Daniel English," Cork said. "That name's familiar to me."

English said, "We've met before."

"Oh?"

"I was ten," English said. "Visiting Uncle Henry with my mother. You dropped by."

"Eudora English," Cork said, remembering. "You were Danny then, and smaller."

"You were in a sheriff's uniform and wore a gun. I was afraid of you."

"The uniform went a while ago. Same with the gun," Cork told him. "This is my daughter Jenny."

English hesitated when Cork's daughter reached out, an awkward move. When he finally took her hand, which was small in his own, he did it with care, as if afraid he might break her fingers.

"Henry's really your uncle?" Jenny asked. Because on the rez, sometimes familial titles were bestowed though no blood connection was involved. People of a certain age were all cousins, and to them the next generation were uncles or aunts, and above them were grandmothers and grandfathers. To the Ojibwe, traditionally, the community *was* family.

Meloux spoke up to clarify. "He is the son of my sister's granddaughter."

"My nephew," Rainy said.

Cork noted that the clothing English wore was dry, but he could see no rain gear, which made him think that the man had been there awhile, before the storm broke. A good deal of talking had probably gone on, and whatever it was they'd discussed was probably the reason for Rainy's call. Cork was deeply interested in that reason and in why Rainy's voice had been so urgent. But the Anishinaabeg never rushed anything, and so he resigned himself to patience.

Rainy poured coffee for the two new visitors, and Meloux suggested they smoke together. From a cupboard, he pulled a cedar box that held a small leather pouch and a pipe that was, Cork knew, carved from stone quarried at a site in southwestern Minnesota sacred to many tribes in the upper Midwest. Henry filled the bowl, but before he lit the tobacco, he took a pinch and made an offering of gratitude to the spirits of each cardinal direction. They passed the pipe and smoked in silence and listened to the rain, and then Henry said, "There is trouble, Corcoran O'Connor. Trouble in my family."

CHAPTER 3

Henry Meloux sat at the table he'd made himself from birch-wood long, long ago. Cork sat across from him. The chairs were birchwood, too, also of Meloux's construction. The old man slid a photograph across the tabletop. Cork lifted and studied it. A shot of a body, a girl's body, naked except for a pair of pale blue panties. She lay facedown on a rocky shoreline, her torso draped over broken rock. Everything below her waist was in water so clear it obscured nothing. Her arms were thrust out above her, as if she'd clawed her way to that place, crawled as far out of the water as she possibly could before she gave up the ghost. Her dark hair lay splayed across her shoulders and back. There were dark discolorations along her ribs—bruises. She was small. And young. There was no perspective, really, that told Cork her age. He simply sensed it. What he was looking at, he knew, was the body of girl still not quite a woman. Now she would never be.

"Her name," Daniel English said, "is Carrie Verga. She's Bad Bluff Chippewa, from near Bayfield in Wisconsin. Ran away from home a year ago. No one's seen her since. Then last week, her body washed up on a small island in Lake Superior near the Bad Bluff Reservation. Some boys who were out there to paint graffiti found her."

"I read about that in the *News Tribune*," Cork said. "Is she family?"

"No," English replied. "But when she left Bayfield, she didn't leave alone. A girl named Mariah Arceneaux went with her. She's family. My cousin."

And so kin to both Rainy and Meloux. Cork understood Rainy well, and understood now the urgency in her voice when she'd called him to come to Crow Point. But the ancient Mide was an enigma in so many ways. He was a man whose life was dedicated to the healing of others, yet he'd chosen to spend it in solitude far from any community. People sought him out, but he seldom went seeking others. He had family, but they'd been scattered to the winds long ago. When they were children, he and his two sisters had been taken from the Iron Lake Reservation and forced to go to Indian schools, odd nomenclature for places whose primary purpose was to drive everything Native out of their charges. Meloux had been sent to Flandreau, South Dakota. His sisters went to the government boarding school on the Lac du Flambeau Reservation in Wisconsin. Meloux had simply walked away from the Flandreau school one day and returned to Iron Lake. His sisters had stayed in Wisconsin, married, and created many additional branches in the family tree. As far as Cork knew, Meloux seldom saw them. But Cork also knew that Meloux's idea of family had nothing to do with blood or tribal affiliation or skin color. Anyone who came to him in need and with an honest heart was kin. Still, looking at the old man's face, Cork could see nothing there. Not concern, compassion, even interest.

Jenny stared over her father's shoulder at the photograph. "She's just a kid."

"Fourteen now," English said. "Same age as my cousin."

"Has anyone heard from your cousin?" Cork asked.

English shook his head.

Cork looked at the photograph again. "How did she die?"

"Drowned. But the medical examiner found heroin in her system."

"She didn't OD?"

"No. Her lungs were full of lake water. A drowning."

"Whose jurisdiction?" Cork asked.

"Bayfield County. The sheriff's department there is in charge of the investigation. They're calling it an accidental drowning, saying the heroin was a contributing factor."

Cork heard the stone in English's voice. "You don't buy that."

"There's more to it."

"What would that be?"

"I don't know. I just know there is."

"And you know this how?"

"Call it instinct."

Cork couldn't keep the smile from his lips. "You're a cop."

"Game warden. Wisconsin DNR."

"Guess my uniform didn't scare you too much," Cork said.

Jenny broke in. "So, what exactly are you doing here, Daniel?"

She stood in the gray light that came through the west window of the little cabin, her blond hair damp and dismal-looking.

Daniel English eyed her a long time before answering. "Louise—that's my mother's cousin—is all torn up. She asked to see Uncle Henry, but she can't come to him. She's diabetic, lost a leg. I'm here to bring my uncle to her. And she would like you to come, too, Cork."

"Me? Why?" Then Cork understood the reason for Rainy's call. He shot her an accusing glance.

She gave him a small, helpless shrug. "Family," she said.

English went on, but not with great enthusiasm, "The authorities have been no help. You were a cop once. You're a private investigator now. Louise knows about you, knows that you have Ojibwe blood and that Uncle Henry trusts you. She hopes you can find her daughter." He paused, then added, "Before it's too late."

Cork stood and paced a little, considering. On the cabin walls hung items that came from Meloux's long life: a bearskin, a bow with string made from the skin of a snapping turtle, a deer-prong pipe, a toboggan, other things.

"Do you have a photo of your cousin?" he asked.

From the pocket of his shirt, English pulled a couple of

photographs. He handed one of them to Cork. "That was her seventh-grade class photo, taken a little over a year ago."

It showed a pretty girl with long black hair, dark eyes, a Mona Lisa–kind of smile that might have been demure or shy. Or maybe it was simply an element unfamiliar to the girl's face. It was hard to say. She was young. So heartbreakingly young.

"And here's the other."

English handed him the second photo. At first glance, Cork would have sworn it was not the same person. This girl's face was layered in makeup. Her eyelashes were clearly false and absurdly long. The look struck Cork as a harlequin attempt at sexy and alluring, the work of someone who had no real idea of what she was about.

"I got that from her Facebook page," English said.

Cork handed the photos back. There was a hollow feeling in his gut, the kind he had when he was facing what he suspected was an assignment doomed from the outset.

"I suppose there's no harm in talking to her mother," he said. "But I don't want to give her a lot of false hope. Indian kids run away all the time. You know that, Daniel."

English nodded. "And if they don't want to be found, there's no finding them."

"But maybe she wants to be found," Jenny threw in. "Maybe she needs to be found before she ends up in a lake somewhere."

Rain fell outside, dripping off the roof onto the ground with a relentless drumming. The quiet inside the cabin had become uncomfortable, made so by Jenny's words, which were really a rejection of any choice but to help.

Meloux finally spoke, and what he said surprised them all. "I will not go."

Cork looked at him with astonishment and saw the same reaction on the faces of the others in the room.

"I am an old man," Meloux said. "The mother of this girl is still young. If there is something she wants from me, she will come here to receive it."

English said, "She has only one leg, Uncle."

"And I have no patience with guilt that wears the face of grief."

Cork wasn't sure he'd ever heard such harsh words from his old friend.

Clearly Rainy hadn't. "Uncle Henry," she said, "that's about as heartless a thing as I've ever heard you say."

Meloux lifted his dark eyes to English and there was nothing in them. The old man was absolutely unreadable. "Tell her this. I will help, but my help comes at a price. She must bring me her daughter's most precious possession, and she must bring it herself. When she has done this, I will do what I can for her."

"Uncle Henry—" Rainy began.

"I have said all I am going to say, Niece."

"Henry," Jenny said, feeling the rise of heat inside her. "Forget about the girl's mother. How can you turn your back on the girl herself? She's just a child."

"You want to help this girl?" He stared at Jenny with profound disinterest. "You save her."

Jenny reacted as if the old man had touched her with fire. She looked shocked, and Cork had a sense that her reaction was about more than just the old man's callous resistance.

"All right," she said. "All right, then. If you won't help, I will."

"It is settled." The old man stood and went to the doorway. "Now I am going to take a walk." Without further ado, he stepped into the driving rain, neglecting even to put on a hat or jacket against the downpour.

What he left behind was a stunned silence. Cork, in all the years he'd known the old Mide, had never known him to turn away someone who needed his help.

Daniel English was the first to speak. "I didn't expect that."

Jenny went to the opened door and stared at the old man's back as he walked away. "*Bring me her daughter's most precious possession. Who does he think he is? The Wizard of Oz?*" She turned to her father, fire in her eyes. "You're going, right?"

Cork said, "You're the one who volunteered."

"Cork," Rainy said. "Please. This is my family we're talking about."

Cork smiled. "Like Oz said to Dorothy, I have every intention of granting your wish. But I'll do this alone."

"I'm going with you, Dad."

"You don't even know this woman or her girl, Jenny."

"I told Henry I would go. I'm going."

"What about Waaboo?" Cork said. "And who'll mind Sam's Place?"

"Aunt Rose will be fine with Waaboo. And you know as well as I do that Judy can run Sam's Place for a couple of days without us."

"All right," he said, although he still had his doubts. "We'll leave tomorrow morning."

Jenny looked displeased. "You always say the earlier an investigation begins the better."

"If she'd gone missing yesterday, I'd leap on it today. But she's been gone a year."

"Her friend hasn't been dead a year."

"A week. So that trail is already cold. This won't be easy, Jenny. If we're going to do it, I want to be prepared. We go tomorrow." To English, he said, "Are you staying here with Henry and Rainy tonight?"

"No, I'll shoot back home to Wisconsin."

"Are you free tomorrow?"

"I can make myself free. I've got lots of personal leave saved."

"Let's plan on meeting somewhere in the morning. You can take us to Mariah's mother. Talking to her would be a good place to start."

"What about the sheriff's people?" Jenny said.

"We'll talk to them, of course. But I want to start with the family."

"There's a café in Bayfield," English suggested. "It's in the Bayfield Inn. On Rittenhouse Avenue. Why don't we meet there?"

"Sounds good. Eight?"

"That'll work. Thanks, Cork." He glanced at Jenny. "And thank you."

Cork and his daughter prepared to leave, but English said he wanted to stick around awhile and talk a bit more with Meloux, if the old man was willing. Cork kissed Rainy good-bye, and he and Jenny put on their ponchos and stepped outside. They began down the path that cut through the meadow on Crow Point. The tall grasses and the wildflowers stood bent under the relentless rain. He caught sight of Meloux standing alone on the shoreline of Iron Lake. The old man seemed small against that vast expanse of gray water and gray sky. To Cork he looked bent, too, burdened like all the other living things on Crow Point by the weight of what had fallen on them that day.

CHAPTER 4

They walked the long trail back to the county road where Cork had parked his Explorer. The entire way, Jenny held to her silence. Cork didn't try to break in on whatever internal dialogue she was having. When she was ready, she would tell him exactly what was on her mind. They reached the vehicle, shed their dripping ponchos, and got in. Cork swung a U-turn and headed south back toward Aurora.

The wipers slapped relentlessly at the rain. The tires crunched over wet gravel. Jenny stared out her window and finally said quietly, "Damn."

"So talk to me," her father said. "You were pretty emotional back there. What's going on? Why so invested in this lost girl?"

She didn't answer right away. The gray fall of the rain seemed to mesmerize her. Finally she said, "Henry's words."

"Which words?" He couldn't remember exactly what the old man had said, but he remembered the look on his daughter's face, as if she'd been touched by fire.

Jenny was quiet way too long, but Cork was nothing if not a patient man.

"Okay," she said at last, carefully, "we both know Stephen has visions."

Cork's youngest child had, indeed, been visited on occasion by visions, remarkable occurrences that had been confirmed by Henry Meloux.

"All right," Cork said.

"I know I don't have the Anishinaabe spirit in me like Stephen does, but ever since we found Waaboo, I've been having this dream. It's so real, Dad, I've always believed it was a vision."

"Tell me about it."

"I'm back there on the island where we found Waaboo and his mother. She's standing in that destroyed place, among all those shattered trees. You remember her? Just a kid, really. Not much older than this missing girl. She's looking straight at me, and she says one thing. Only one. She says, 'You save her.'"

"You save *her*? Not *him*? Not Waaboo?"

"No. She's very clear. Whoever she's talking about it's a *her*."

"And that's what Henry said, wasn't it? 'You save her.' It could have been just a coincidence."

She scowled at him. They both knew that with Henry Meloux coincidence wasn't likely.

"Okay," Cork said. "Have you told anybody about this vision, tried to understand what it means?"

"Stephen, because I figured he would understand."

"What did he say?"

"That when the time was right, the meaning would be clear to me."

"So now you're thinking that this vision is about Louise's girl?"

"I don't, Dad. But this is the first thing that's made sense to me. I'd have asked Henry today, but he was such an asshole." She looked out the window at the persistent storm. "Waaboo's the child of a child. Vision or no, it breaks my heart to think about any child abandoned."

"I understand."

"Do you? Because back there you seemed pretty lukewarm about this missing girl."

"I've been involved in this kind of thing my whole life, Jenny. If I've learned anything at all, it's that no matter how hard you try, you can't save everyone who needs saving. You do your best, but you're always prepared for the worst."

"So you keep your heart out of it?"

"No, you just make sure that your head is always out in front. Think of it like a boxer keeping his left up to protect himself until it's time for that sweet right hook to come into play."

"Or," she countered, "think of it like a girl alone somewhere, mistreated and scared and hopeless while people come up with metaphors for not caring."

Cork pulled onto the paved road that paralleled the western shoreline of Iron Lake. The cabins sheltered among the pines were full of summer people. On a sunny day, these folks would have been on the water or splashing on a beach, but the rain had driven them inside, and the lake was deserted, and Tamarack County felt empty.

"Think of it however you want," he said. "Just believe that I'll do my best, okay?"

He felt her ice-blue eyes considering him; then she said, "I'm sorry."

"You don't need to apologize, but you have to understand that an investigation like this will probably take time. You may be away from Aurora for a while, away from Waaboo. Since he came to us, you haven't been gone from him for more than a few hours in any day. Are you okay with that?"

"If it's what's necessary. Dad, I've never had this sense before that I'm supposed to do a thing, that I've been chosen for it. I know you've been here before. And I know Stephen has, but not me. I want to honor this. I have to. Do you understand?"

"I do." He shot her a smile, though one on the grim side. "So tell you what. In this partnership, I'll be the head, and you be the heart. Deal?"

He offered his hand. Jenny looked at it, then at her father. She returned his smile, one not so grim as his, and accepted his offering.

At Sam's Place, the power had been restored. Except for Judy Madsen's blue sedan and Marlee Daychild's old Toyota 4Runner, the parking lot was still empty. Jenny explained the new situation and asked if Judy felt comfortable taking over for a couple of days.

Judy snapped her fingers. "I could run this place blind and with both hands tied behind my back. You two go off and save the world. We'll be fine."

The house on Gooseberry Lane was an old two-story clapboard construction, well cared for, with a roofed porch across the front and a great elm in the yard. Cork had grown up in this house, and his children, too. If a man could have two hearts and one could exist outside his body, then that house on Gooseberry Lane was Cork's second heart. Everything he loved was in or had passed through there.

On the way home, the stoplights had come back on, and Cork could see lights in windows. Power had been restored in Tamarack County. But when he and Jenny pulled up to the house, they found that it was still dark. Inside, Waaboo was sound asleep on the living room sofa, clutching a stuffed orangutan he called Bart, one of his favorite toys. He had half a dozen other stuffed animals around him as well. Rose was in the kitchen, forming a meat loaf in a pan. She put a finger to her lips, and they talked quietly.

"He held the flashlight and I read stories to him," she said. "He drifted off a while ago. I left the lights off. It felt kind of right with the rain outside."

Rose Thorne was a remarkable human being. When Cork had first known his sister-in-law, she'd been a large, plain-looking, good-hearted woman who read tabloids. She'd helped raise the O'Connor children, and had the idea that when she was no longer needed in that way, she might enter a convent. As that time had approached, she'd had an amazing change of heart. She'd fallen in love with a man who was sliding away from his faith and out of the priesthood. Mal Thorne had, indeed, put aside his collar and his vows, but in a way, Rose had saved his faith. They'd married, and both of them looked at the love they shared as the blessing

God had always intended for them. Rose had slimmed down a good deal, dressed smartly these days, and wore her hair in a fashionable cut. But some things never changed. Her heart was huge, and her love for her sister's family was depthless.

Rose and Mal now lived in Evanston, Illinois. But that summer, Rose had agreed to return to Aurora and, in a way, to her former life. She took care of Waaboo while Jenny oversaw Sam's Place and Cork went about his business as a private investigator. She had no children of her own and seemed to relish every moment she had with the little guy. Every other weekend or so, Mal drove up from Evanston for a visit.

In the gray light through the windows, Jenny crossed her arms and leaned against the kitchen counter. "Aunt Rose," she said, "I need a favor." She laid out the situation, and it was clear from the look on Rose's face that she shared Jenny's concern for the missing girl. Without a moment of hesitation, Jenny's aunt agreed to give whatever was needed of her.

That night Jenny put Waaboo to bed. Cork stood in the doorway of his grandson's room and listened while Jenny sat in the rocker with Waaboo on her lap and explained that she would have to be gone for a little while.

"To help find a little girl who's lost," she told him.

"Is she scared?" Waaboo asked.

"Would you be scared if you were lost?"

"Not if I had Bart wiff me." He clutched his stuffed orangutan.

"She doesn't have Bart. She doesn't have anyone."

Waaboo was full-blood Anishinaabe. His hair was black, his eyes like cherrywood. He'd been born with a cleft lip and still bore a small scar where surgery had closed that split. He thought about what Jenny said and asked, "No mommy?"

"Her mommy can't help her. That's why she needs me."

"Aunt Rose will be here?"

"Yes. And I'll be back very soon."

"'Kay," he said, his concerns put to rest. He snuggled more firmly against Jenny. "Tell me a story, Mommy."

* * *

Later, they sat around the kitchen table—Cork, Jenny, and Rose—and talked about what might be ahead. Trixie, the O'Connors' mutt, lay in the corner near her food dish, looking bored or tired.

"Do you think she's still alive, Dad?"

"I don't know, Jenny. But once you ask yourself that question, you've got to do your best to find the answer."

Jenny held a mug of decaf coffee in her hands. She took a sip and frowned, as if the brew were distasteful. But Cork suspected it was not the coffee that displeased her.

"How do we do that?" she asked.

Cork got up from the table, walked to the coffeemaker on the counter, and poured a little more from the pot into his own mug. The rain had stopped and the clouds had passed, and the darkness beyond the kitchen window was night, plain and simple.

He turned back to the table. "We talk to her family, her friends, her teachers, anyone who knew her. And we do the same for Carrie Verga. We talk to the officers in charge of the investigation of the girl's death. We talk to anyone who might have some piece of information that leads to another piece of information. And, if we're lucky, we put the puzzle together that way, piece by piece."

"That sounds awfully slow," Jenny said. "Do we have that kind of time?"

"I don't know. But I also don't know another way."

Jenny stared into her mug. "She was only thirteen when she ran away. What was she thinking?"

"You used to run away all the time," Rose told her gently. "Whenever I scolded you or your mom did or Cork, you'd run away across the street to the O'Loughlins' house. Sue would let you in and give you milk and cookies, and after a while you'd decide to come back home."

"That was a different kind of running," Cork said, returning to his chair at the table. "Kids who really run away are usually running from a bad situation. But most of them, like you, Jenny, come back eventually. Being alone on the street is incredibly hard. Home is still home, bad as that might be. It's familiar. For a kid to stay away, the situation has to be really awful."

"Or someone's preventing them from going home," Jenny said.

"That, too." Cork looked at his watch. "If we're going to meet Daniel in Bayfield at eight tomorrow morning, we'll have to get off by four. I'm going to call it a day, get myself ready for bed, pack a few things in an overnight bag."

"I should do the same," Jenny said. But she didn't move.

"You go on, Cork," Rose said. "Jenny and I have some more talking to do, I think."

Cork rinsed out his mug and set it on the counter next to the sink. He said good night and headed upstairs, wondering what the two women still had to discuss. He was used to being in the minority in his house and sometimes excluded from the conversations of the women in his life. He didn't like it, but he had no choice.

He lay in bed that night thinking about Mariah and Carrie Verga and about the families they'd left behind. He didn't know these people, not yet. He tried not to be disposed against them. But when he wore the badge—in Chicago as a cop and in Tamarack County as a deputy and as Sheriff—he'd seen all too often the horrific results of child abuse. That got him to thinking about Meloux's statement when Daniel English had asked for his help. *I have no patience with guilt that wears the face of grief.* It sounded callous, but Cork thought he understood. Sometimes the tears that parents shed over their lost children couldn't be trusted. For some, children were not a blessing but a burden. A child gone was just one less thing to worry about.

Cork hoped that he would discover he was wrong in his thinking. But he fell asleep prepared for the worst.

CHAPTER 5

It was four hours to Bayfield, Wisconsin, which lay near the tip of a squat peninsula that jutted north into Lake Superior and at whose end lay the exquisite archipelago of the Apostle Islands. Cork and Jenny left at first light, driving the Explorer, a thermos of hot coffee between them. Almost two hours later, they passed through Duluth and crossed the harbor of the Twin Ports on the Bong Bridge. They entered Superior, Wisconsin, under a heavy ceiling of overcast that completely blocked the morning sun. They took U.S. Highway 2 east and after another hour, turned north onto Wisconsin 13, a road that followed the outline of the peninsula and that was, at that early hour, nearly deserted.

Cork thought Jenny might sleep. It had been a brief night, an early rising. But she was alert and talkative the whole way, and there was an excitement in her voice. She was a woman on a mission. For Cork, the day already held the gloomy feel of failure.

They found the Bayfield Inn and, inside, the café Daniel English had told them about the night before. When Cork and Jenny walked in, they found the place was three-quarters full and noisy. English sat at a table on the far side of the room, next to a window that looked out toward Lake Superior. He wasn't alone. A man as big as English himself sat with him. An Indian. English stood as they approached. The other man stayed seated and watched them without expression.

"Thanks for coming," English said. He shook their hands and nodded toward his companion. "This is Red Arceneaux, Mariah's uncle. Red, these are the folks I told you about. Cork O'Connor and his daughter Jenny."

Arceneaux was broad across the chest, heavy around the middle. His hands on the table were meaty and powerful. His face was hard, his eyes black iron. He didn't rise to greet Cork, and there was no welcoming energy in the handshake he offered from his chair. He didn't bother to shake Jenny's hand at all, simply nodded when English introduced her. Beyond an Indian's usual reserve around white people and strangers, Cork wondered what more was at work in this man's thinking.

They sat down, and Arceneaux said in a flat, deep voice, "I understand you're a blood." Which was the term sometimes used to designate a person of mixed racial heritage.

"My grandmother was true-blood Iron Lake Anishinaabe," Cork said.

"And you're a cop, too."

"Was a cop. Not anymore. I do private investigations now."

Arceneaux gave a small, dismissive grunt.

A waitress came to the table and dropped additional menus in front of Cork and Jenny. "Coffee?" she asked with no great interest.

They both said thanks, and she spun away, wordless.

Arceneaux had been sizing up Cork since English introduced them. "You think you can find Mariah," he said. It wasn't a statement but a challenge.

"I told Daniel I'd do my best to help."

"Help. You mean like my great-uncle Meloux?"

"I can't speak for Henry," Cork replied.

"Daniel told me what he said. I haven't seen him since I was a kid, but he sounds like he's turned into one heartless asshole."

"In my experience, Henry Meloux always has good reason for what he says and does."

"My sister's got one leg. How does he expect her to get to him out there in the middle of nowhere?"

"I can't answer that."

"Okay, answer me this. How do you expect to find my niece?"

The waitress came with mugs and a pot she set on the table. "Ready to order?"

Cork and Jenny asked for oatmeal. The other two stuck with just the coffee.

"I don't expect to find your niece," Cork answered when the waitress had gone. He poured coffee for himself and Jenny.

Arceneaux sat back, and his bulk made the chair he sat in squeak. He crossed his thick arms. "Then what the hell are you doing here?"

"My best," Cork said. "But my gut feeling is that it won't be enough."

Jenny gave him a harsh glance, which he did his best to ignore.

"I'll give it to you straight, Red. Either she's dead, like Carrie, and she'll wash up onshore one day or, more likely, she'll stay on the bottom of Lake Superior forever. That lake's so cold it seldom gives up its dead."

"Dad," Jenny tried to cut in.

"Or," Cork went on, "she's somewhere she's chosen to be, for whatever reason, and she doesn't want to come back and she doesn't want to be found."

"Or," Jenny said in a voice loud enough to be heard easily above the clatter of utensils and dishes, "she's being held somewhere against her will and unspeakable things are being done to her."

Arceneaux looked at Jenny. The iron left his eyes, and he said quietly, "My sister's all tore up. Has been ever since Mariah took off." Now he looked a little lost. "We did everything we could to find her."

"Did you report her as a runaway?" Cork asked.

"Yeah. But kids, they run away all the time. And the cops, they didn't much care. She's an Indian kid."

Cork said, "How do you know she ran away?"

Arceneaux shrugged. "She was there one day, gone the next."

"Maybe she was abducted."

"Some of her friends, they told us Mariah'd been planning on leaving for a while. Her and Carrie."

"Did these friends know where the two girls were headed?"

"Nope, just that they were getting out of Dodge. Seems they had it up to here with living at the edge of nowhere."

"Does Mariah have any relatives in Duluth or Superior?"

"None close."

"But some?"

"Got a cousin there somewhere, but we don't never see him."

"What's Mariah like?" Jenny asked.

"A girl. Likes girl things, I guess."

"Basketball," English said. "She's a good basketball player. Played for her junior high team."

"Did she have a boyfriend?" Jenny asked.

"Nobody special," Arceneaux replied. "Least not that I know of. Real closed mouth, she is. Keeps things to herself pretty good." He eyed Cork again. "You want to write any of this down?"

"Why?" Cork asked.

"That's what they do in the movies, private investigators."

"I've got it, don't worry, Red. Does Mariah have any brothers or sisters?"

"An older half brother, Tobias. We call him Toby. And two half brothers younger than her, Denny and Cal."

"The fathers?"

"Louise was never too certain about her first two kids. Denny and Cal's dad, he's doing a dime over in Boscobel for an armed robbery beef. Louise, she was pretty wild when she was young. Never bothered getting a wedding ring from anyone."

"Tell me about Tobias."

"What's Toby got to do with this?"

"Probably nothing. But it's the kind of question a private investigator asks."

"Trouble, that one. Smokes weed all day, gets drunk nights. No help to my sister at all."

"How old?"

"Seventeen."

"Is he close to Mariah?"

Arceneaux shook his head. "Close to what he calls his home-boys, that's it."

"Is he in a gang?"

"Nuthin organized on the rez. Just a bunch a kids with nuthin to do all day except get into trouble." He fell silent for a few moments and stared out the café window, where the overcast sky made the lake water look charcoal. "There's something you should know," he finally said. "Something Mariah told me before her and Carrie took off."

Their food came. While they ate, Arceneaux told them a story.

First, he said he wanted them to know that he was a modern Shinnob, so what he was going to tell them didn't have anything to do with believing in old myths. He asked if they knew about the windigo. Cork and Jenny said they did. Arceneaux said he'd first heard about the monster when he was a kid. It was told to him like one of those scary stories kids tell each other around a campfire or on a sleepover. He never believed it. Then Mariah told him something he'd been chewing on for a long time.

"She told me that Carrie heard a windigo call her name."

"How'd she hear it? I mean, what were the circumstances, do you know?"

"Mariah and Carrie and some of her friends were doing some partying out on the lakeshore, a place called Point Detour. They'd been drinking, smoking weed. She told me it was one of those nights when the moon was full. She said it was like this big eye looking down on 'em. It was real calm, then this strange wind come up out of nowhere. Hell, that happens all the time up here, the big lake and all. But she tells me that Carrie goes real pale, and says, 'Did you hear that?' And Mariah says, 'Hear what?' And Carrie says, 'Somebody out there on the lake. They called me.' And Mariah says she didn't hear nuthin. And then one of the other girls tells her, 'Must've been the windigo.' But Carrie, she's never heard of it. So the girl tells her about the windigo and how it's this giant cannibal beast that pulls the heart right out of your chest and eats it. And she says that when it's coming for you, it calls your name. Mariah told me that Carrie freaked out, and they had to leave. I didn't think nuthin about it until they found Carrie's body on Windigo Island. Now I can't think about anything else."

His dark eyes had been downcast the whole time he told the story. Now he looked up, glanced briefly at Cork, who kept his own face neutral, then settled his gaze on Jenny, who was clearly full of sympathy.

"You got a job, Red?" Cork asked.

"Yeah. Working at the restaurant at the casino. Dishwasher. Not a lot of money, but I also get some disability payment from the government. Vet, wounded in the first Iraq war. Enough between 'em so I make ends meet. And I usually got a little left over to help out Louise. Missing a leg and trying to make it on welfare, things don't never quite stretch enough." He squinted at Cork, and distrust was there again in his dark eyes. "You chargin' for your services?"

"At the moment, I'm working on what you might call spec," Cork said. "Before I charge you, I'll let you know. I'd like to talk to your sister."

"I figured. I wanted to check you out first. You understand?"

"Sure."

"And you go easy on Louise. That woman's already had more than her share of misery."

Jenny reached out but didn't quite touch Arceneaux. "We're here to help."

For a long time, he stared directly into her eyes, an odd thing for a Shinnob. And then he gave a nod, slight and simple. "I believe you."

CHAPTER 6

Daniel English followed Red Arceneaux. Cork and Jenny followed English. They drove north out of Bayfield and followed the shoreline. Across a mile of gray water lay the great green bodies of the Apostle Islands. Although the hour was still early and the day still gloomy, there were already sailboats cutting across the lake. In Cork's present mood, the sails reminded him of the fins of great white sharks.

"I liked him," Jenny said.

"Arceneaux?"

"Yeah."

"Unless I'm greatly mistaken, he's a man who's spent time inside."

"Inside what?" Jenny asked.

"Prison."

"Really? How can you tell?"

"Prison changes a man. If you know what to look for, you see it."

"So what did you see in Red?"

"I saw what his eyes saw."

"Which was what?"

"Mostly he watched our hands."

"No, he didn't."

"Yes, he did."

Jenny thought a moment. "Okay, what of it?"

"In prison, in the blink of an eye, a man's hands can hold something that'll kill you. So you always have to know where his hands are and what's in them. Gets to be habit. Also, manipulation is something men in prison get good at. I saw him manipulate you."

"Me?"

"As soon as he knew he had a sympathetic audience, he addressed everything he could to you."

"No," she said disbelieving.

"Yes," Cork said. "I also saw a great deal of distrust in him."

"We're strangers," she said with exasperation. "There's no reason for him to trust us. And yet, in the end, he did."

"That's what he said."

"Look, Dad, if there's a problem with trust here, you're just as responsible for it as you say Red is."

Cork smiled. "Fair enough."

A few miles outside Bayfield they entered the Bad Bluff Reservation and then passed through the town of Bad Bluff itself, mostly a scattered gathering of prefabs and mobile homes. They passed the Shining Waters casino and hotel complex and turned onto a road that ran west into second- or third-growth timber. Set back among the trees were more prefabs and trailers and some actual houses, these often surrounded by yards full of discard— old appliances, vehicles without tires, mattresses, playground equipment, bicycles, sheets of rusting, corrugated metal. It was reservation life in its worst depiction, Cork thought, evidence of a people whose whole way of being had been attacked a century earlier and who were still reeling. It made him angry, and because the blood of the Anishinaabeg ran through his own veins, it made him determined.

Arceneaux turned up a short unpaved drive that ended at a small, single-story house, which seemed cobbled together. The walls were weathered plywood, and the pale blue paint on them was scant and mildewed. The yard was less cluttered with debris than many they'd passed, but it was worrisome nonetheless. A couple of suspect-looking ATVs sat under a makeshift shelter of scavenged two-by-fours and canvas. A basketball backboard and netless hoop hung atop a metal pole set in a slab of concrete patched with tar. A big black and white mutt on a chain went crazy barking as Arceneaux led the caravan up to the house.

Arceneaux parked and got out of his truck and said harshly to the dog, "Shut up, Bruiser."

Much to Cork's surprise, the dog did. It sat on its haunches and simply watched the procession as they entered the house.

Inside something had exploded. Or more probably it only looked that way. Debris lay everywhere—clothing, magazines, plates and dishes, empty bottles, bottles not empty but filled with liquids only a trained scientist could identify, toys, blankets, newspaper sections. There was a couch and maybe more furniture, too, Cork suspected, somewhere under all those layers of crap.

In the middle of the chaos sat a woman in a wheelchair. She had long black hair and wore a gray sweatshirt and gray sweatpants. The right pant leg was folded under her at the knee. Her loose clothing disguised not at all the fact that she was a heavy woman. Cork could see that it wasn't just her flesh that weighed her down; there was a heaviness to her spirit as well. She was probably in her early forties and may have been pretty once, but now she was old beyond her years, and years beyond her beauty.

The living room was cramped, small to begin with and smaller because of all that filled it. Through an opened doorway, Cork saw a bedroom. He also saw two kids with video game controllers in their hands, facing a television screen where, judging from the din of battle, every war that had ever been fought was being fought again.

Arceneaux spoke first to the boys. "Denny, Cal, turn that game down a couple hundred notches." He waited for the boys to respond. When they didn't, he stepped into the room and in front of the screen. "Turn it down," he said.

The boys seemed to notice him for the first time, and they did as he asked.

Arceneaux came back and spoke to the woman in the wheelchair. "Louise, this here's the man Daniel told us about."

"*Boozhoo. Anish na*, Louise," Cork said, offering her a greeting in Ojibwemowin.

"Morning," she said in reply.

"Good morning, Louise," Jenny said. "I'm his daughter. Jenny's my name."

Louise nodded and studied her. Cork thought she was going to say something, some warm word of greeting. Instead, she yelled toward the bedroom, "Denny, go get your momma a blanket. I'm cold."

Neither one of the boys moved, but Arceneaux went to the couch, grabbed a ragged afghan, brought it to his sister, and arranged it across her lap.

Louise looked at Daniel English. "Where's Henry Meloux?"

"He didn't come," Daniel replied. "He said he wants you to come to him."

"How?" She lifted the afghan to expose the pant leg folded under the stump of her leg. "How am I supposed to do that?"

"I don't know, but it's what he wants. And if you go to him, he wants you to bring something."

"What?"

"Mariah's most precious possession."

Louise Arceneaux seemed completely bewildered. Cork didn't know if it was because the request itself was so outlandish or because she simply didn't have the slightest idea what that possession might be. Her next response was to become heavier, if that was possible. She seemed to sink further under that great weight Cork had felt from the moment he came into her presence.

She looked at him, her eyes dark, hostile. "Do you want something from me, too?"

"Only information, Louise. I need to know everything you can tell me about Mariah."

She relaxed a little, settled back into her wheelchair, and folded her hands on the afghan that covered her ample lap. "She was my hope. She was smart. She was helpful. She was sunshine."

"Did you have any inkling that she was thinking of running away?"

"No. She seemed happy."

"You haven't heard from her at all since she left?"

"Not a word."

"The girl she left with, Carrie, did you know her?"

"Not well. She came over sometimes, but not much. Usually, they hung out somewhere else. It can get kind of crazy around here."

As nearly as Cork could tell, it was a household of males. Considering the din of battle, the dirt, the disarray, he thought he could understand why a young girl would want to be somewhere else.

"Other friends?" he asked.

Louise squeezed her eyes in thought, then shook her head. "It was her and Carrie mostly. But maybe there were others. You could ask Toby. Cal," she called toward the room. "Go get your brother."

"He's sleeping," one of the boys yelled back.

"Wake him up."

"He'll get mad."

"Do it anyway."

The boy dropped his controller. He got up, came out, threw his mother a surly look, and went to a closed door off the living room near the back of the house. He opened the door and went in. Cork could see the end of a bed to the left and, against a far wall, an empty mattress, where surprisingly, the bedding had been neatly put in place.

Louise looked up at English. "I haven't seen Henry Meloux in thirty years. Did he remember me?"

"Yes," English said.

She nodded. "He helped me," she said, more to herself than anyone in the room. "But he didn't ask me for anything back then."

Cork wondered in what way she'd been helped by the old

Mide. Because what he saw of her life now made him believe she'd always been troubled or in trouble.

The boy came out. "I tried," he said. "He told me to go 'f' myself." He headed back to his idled controller.

"I'll wake him up," Arceneaux said. He disappeared through the opened doorway and turned left. Cork saw half his big body lean down, and when he straightened, he held a teenager in the grasp of his huge hands.

"Jesus," the kid cried out. "What the—"

"Your mother wants you," Arceneaux said and shoved the kid through the doorway into the living room.

He wore black boxer shorts and nothing else. He was licorice-stick thin, and his black hair was a mess. He was a good-looking seventeen-year-old, and he rubbed the sleep from his eyes and gave his mother a killing look. Then he gave the same look to the others. Except Daniel English, to whom he said, "'Sup, cuz?"

English said, "This man wants to ask you some questions, Toby."

Toby eyed Cork as if he had his number. "Cop."

"No."

He seemed surprised that he was wrong. "What kind of questions?"

"About your sister, Mariah."

"What about her?"

"I'd like to find her, if I can."

"Well, good luck with that."

"Any idea where she is?"

"Nope."

"Any idea why she ran off?"

"Nope."

"Any idea who her friends were?"

Toby yawned, maybe from lack of sleep or maybe from boredom. "Nope."

"Do you care if she ever comes back?"

His lips formed the word again, but he stopped himself and

actually considered the question. In the end, all he offered was a shrug. Then he yawned again and scratched his belly.

"Did you know Carrie Verga?" Cork asked.

"Not really. Saw her around."

"What about Mariah's other friends? Know any of them?"

"I never paid much attention." He sounded truly bored now.

It was clear to Cork he would get nowhere with the kid. "Could I see her room?" he asked Louise.

"Her room?" A look that Cork couldn't quite interpret crossed the woman's face. It may have been fear or guilt or some combination thereof. "Why?"

"It might give me a better feel for Mariah."

Louise's hands rose from her lap and gripped the arms of her wheelchair. "Not much left. We're kinda crowded here, so that's Toby and Puck's room now."

"Puck?" Cork asked. Because Arceneaux had neglected to mention anyone named Puck.

"My son," Arceneaux said. "Him and me, we're staying here with Louise. Temporarily."

Which was another detail Arceneaux had neglected to mention. Cork could see only two bedrooms—the one where the boys played their video game and the one from which Toby had just emerged. He wondered where Louise and Arceneaux slept.

"Puck?" Jenny asked. "Like in *A Midsummer Night's Dream*?"

"No," Arceneaux said. "Like in the little round thing hockey players hit. His real name's Paul. When he was a kid, he was short and round and loved watching hockey on television. So I called him Puck. It stuck."

"How long have you been living with Louise?" Cork asked.

"Little over a year. But I have a line on another place. Puck graduated from high school in the spring. He'll be leaving soon. Going to college. I'll be moving out then."

"Is Puck here now?" Cork asked.

Arceneaux shook his head. "He's working. Got himself a summer job on one of the fishing boats out of Bayfield."

"You need me for anything else?" Toby asked.

"No," his mother said, her voice flat and hopeless. "Go on back to bed."

In departing, the kid said nothing else to anyone. The door, when he closed it behind him, did not close gently.

Louise fell silent, stared at the floor in front of her. When she looked up, her eyes glistened with tears. "I miss her so much," she said. "And I swear if she comes back everything will be different."

Different how? Cork wanted to ask. Was it more than just the dirt and the disarray and the dysfunction? Which, clearly, this family could abide.

Jenny, who'd been oddly quiet, said, "Go see Henry Meloux, Louise. Whatever that takes. I think he can help."

Louise reached out and impulsively took Jenny's hands. "But I don't know what he wants from me."

"Mariah's most precious possession," Jenny said. "Think about it. Take some time. My dad and I have some more people to see, but we'll be back."

"All right." Louise seemed stronger now, as if she'd taken some of Jenny's strength, the strength of another woman who understood, into herself. "All right," she said again and released her hold on Jenny's hands.

Cork said, "We're going to talk with Carrie Verga's family. And also the Bayfield County Sheriff's Office. And I'd like to talk to Puck. Louise, is there anyone else you think we should see?"

"Mariah talked about her basketball coach a lot."

"I know her," English said. "We'll talk to her, Louise."

The woman lifted her dark eyes, and Cork saw something that hadn't been there when he'd first come in. It was something that worried him. Because what he saw was hope. And it worried him because so far he could see no reason to hope. He thought false hope was a far crueler thing than no hope at all.

"Thank you," Louise said to them all.

Red Arceneaux said to them, "*Migwech*," which meant "thank you."

Once outside, they gathered at English's pickup. "Why don't we leave one of the vehicles here?" he suggested. "No reason to take two. You okay driving, Cork?"

"I'd rather we used yours," Cork said. He put his hand on the mud-spattered old pickup. "It'll stand out less on the rez. And if folks here see you driving up, well, a guy who's clearly Shinnob has a better chance of getting a reasonable reception. You okay with that?"

"Sure," English said. "Makes sense." He looked back at the little, thrown-together house. "When I was a kid, if we saw Louise it was because she came down to Hayward to visit us. We never came up here. Pretty clear why."

"Yeah," Jenny said. "I think this visit told us a lot."

"Oh?" Cork said. "What exactly did it tell us?"

"It's awfully late for her to worry about being a good mother, don't you think, Dad? I mean, Christ, if I were Mariah, I'd've run away from that."

"I doubt it. That's home," Cork said. "That's what she grew up with. Dirt and noise and crowding. She was used to it. No, I think something else made her run."

"What?"

"Let's keep talking to people. Maybe we'll find out."

He opened the door of English's pickup and gestured for Jenny to get in.

CHAPTER 7

They drove south out of Bad Bluff. The road ran beside Chequamegon Bay, a long, broad inlet of Kitchigami. The landscape was hills covered with a mix of deciduous and evergreen, checkered here and there with orchards and meadowland. The gloomy overcast had finally broken. Although there seemed to be no wind, the clouds were fast becoming dwindling islands of gray afloat in a vast ocean of blue sky. Below, the water of the bay lay flat and silver-blue in the morning sun.

English was at the wheel of his pickup. Cork sat on the far passenger side. Jenny straddled the middle.

"What exactly do you do as a game warden, Daniel?" she asked.

"Mostly deal with guys trying to take what they're not supposed to take or taking something when they're not supposed to take it. Pretty straightforward."

"Is it dangerous?"

"You have to be careful. Most men'll be unhappy with a citation, but a few get outright hostile. I carry a sidearm. Never had to use it."

"You like your job?"

"I like that I get paid to be outside, in the woods or on a lake. And I think what I do is important."

"What do you do when you're not patrolling? Or whatever you call it."

"We call it patrolling. My time off, mostly I relax. Sit on the porch of my cabin. Read maybe."

"Read what?"

"Whatever."

"Hunting and fishing magazines?"

Cork suspected his daughter said this in a deliberate attempt to get English to be more forthcoming. If so, she seemed to have failed. The big Shinnob was silent and seemed deadly intent on the road ahead. But after half a mile and a good half minute had slipped by, he replied, "Billy Collins. James Welch. David Foster Wallace. Sherman Alexie. Hemingway."

"Whoa," Jenny said. "Impressive. But Hemingway?"

Daniel gave his huge shoulders a small shrug. "Flawed human being, but he's always seemed to me a guy who understood the profound impact the natural world can have on the human spirit." Then he asked in a flat voice that, to anyone who didn't know the Ojibwe well, might have sounded devoid of any real interest, "Aunt Rainy says you write."

"Not really," Jenny replied too quickly. "When I'm not being a mom, I pretty much run Sam's Place. Keeps me plenty busy."

Her tone was easy to interpret, and the conversation took a fatal nosedive.

They entered Washburn, a pretty little town perched on hills above the lake. They found the sheriff's department, part of a new-looking county government complex. At the public contact desk inside, they asked to speak with the sheriff and were told that he was out at the moment. The young woman on duty, who wore no uniform or name badge and was, Cork suspected, simply a clerical employee, asked if there was something she could do for them. They explained their situation. She told them to take a seat and she'd get the officer who'd been in charge of investigating Carrie Verga's death.

They sat in black plastic chairs in the small public waiting area. In a couple of minutes, a man who looked like an NFL linebacker stepped into the waiting area. He wore a short-sleeved white shirt, blue tie, and khakis.

"Lieutenant Joe Hammer," he said, offering his hand.

Cork introduced them all and once again explained their presence.

"Why don't you folks come on back, and we'll talk."

They followed Hammer down a short corridor to his office. It was little more than a cubbyhole, but neatly kept. On the desk sat three stacks of file folders, like watchtowers. On one of the walls hung two framed photographs. One was of a younger Hammer with a woman in a yellow bikini on a beach that might have been Hawaii. In the other, Hammer stood with the same woman, this time on a lakeshore, both of them older and each holding the hand of a young child. Hammer took the chair at his desk. With a wave of his huge hand, he indicated that Jenny should take the only other chair. Cork stood behind his daughter, and English leaned against a tall green file cabinet with a stuffed owl atop it that looked down on the gathering with an indifferent, glassy eye.

After he'd ascertained their interest in the case, Hammer gave them some of the pertinent details.

"Cold-water immersion and drowning," he explained. "That's the official probable cause of death. There was a high level of alcohol and also traces of heroin in the girl's bloodstream. I haven't come up with any witnesses, anybody at all who'd seen Carrie Verga in the last year. So it's puzzling."

"There were bruises on her body," Cork said, recalling the photograph English had shown him the day before.

"Yes. She was treated pretty badly before she died. And lacerations, too, although our coroner concluded those were postmortem and probably occurred when the body washed onto the rocks of the island."

"Any indication of sexual assault?"

"Our coroner didn't find any, no. Of course, the body had been in the lake, so a lot of evidence could have been washed away."

"How long was she in the water?" English asked.

"That's a tough one. The frigid temperature of the lake tends to preserve a body. So it could have been a week or it could have been a month."

"A year?" Cork asked.

"I thought about that and asked the coroner. He said he didn't think so. Thought it was much more recent, although he couldn't really say how recent."

Cork said, "Carrie and Mariah Arceneaux disappeared at the same time, probably together. Who investigated that disappearance?"

"That would be me. But it wasn't a disappearance, as such. When their families reported them gone, I looked into the situation. Became clear pretty quick that the girls had run away. They'd been talking about it for a while, and they didn't leave empty-handed. They packed suitcases. May have got a ride out of town with a friend."

"What friend?"

"Never was able to get a name. You ever try getting information from folks on a reservation? They close ranks."

"Any idea where they were headed?"

Hammer shrugged. "Indian kids when they run off generally go to a relative's place. I checked and that's not where these kids went. So I notified Ashland and Duluth PD and all the shelters in the area. Also in the Twin Cities. Those are the places where kids up here usually run to if they're serious about running. I gave their information to the National Center for Missing and Exploited Children. I questioned the kids' parents. I continued to ask around at their school and on the reservation. I didn't come up with anything useful except that the girls had talked to some of their friends about getting out of here, going somewhere more exciting. If I'd been concerned that Carrie and Mariah were abducted, that would be one thing. But like I say, it was pretty clear they'd just taken off on their own. It's been my experience that, more often than not, runaways come home eventually. It's a hard life out there on the street."

Cork nodded his agreement with that last statement. "When her body washed up on Windigo Island, what did you think then?"

"Honestly, I've been wondering if she'd been around here somewhere the whole time, just didn't want to be seen. Runaway and all. I mean, the home life of some of these kids is pretty bad. They want to get away from it, but not away completely from what's familiar, you understand?"

"Is that possible up here?" English asked. "To hide for a year without being spotted? Seems to me like an area where people would recognize each other."

"Generally speaking, I think that's true. But with Indian kids . . ." Again, Hammer shrugged. "The autopsy showed that the girl had been using. Dressed as she was when we found her, it's not hard to guess what she might've been up to."

"Which was?" Jenny asked.

"In my experience, a young Indian girl who's into drugs and who doesn't have a lot of money also doesn't have a lot of choice in how she gets those drugs."

Jenny leaned forward, and Cork was afraid she was going to spring at the detective. "Prostitution? That's what you're saying? It could only be prostitution?"

"Pretty much that's what I'm saying, yes."

"Because she's Ojibwe."

"Okay," Cork jumped in quickly, "how does a kid prostitute herself up here? I mean, without being seen and recognized? Even an Indian kid."

"We're not on the moon. We have the Internet. So, Craigslist, for example."

"Did you check Craigslist?"

"Yes. And Backpage. That's another way they do this kind of thing."

"And?"

"I didn't find anything, but that doesn't mean it wasn't there. She probably used information that wouldn't identify her. Look, it's upsetting, I know," Hammer said, addressing his comment directly to Jenny. "Think it doesn't bother me? I'm supposed to be the one keeping kids like her safe. Even Indian kids."

"I'm sorry," Jenny said. "I wasn't suggesting—"

"That's okay."

"Considering what's happened to Carrie, how are you proceeding with Mariah?" Cork asked.

"We're not. We have no information, no new leads, no nothing."

"If Carrie could hide up here for a year, couldn't Mariah?" English said.

"Of course. But if nobody saw Carrie, who'd see Mariah? We don't really have anything to go on. Look, one of our big problems is that nobody on the reservation is eager to talk to a cop, even one who's wearing a Bad Bluff uniform." He eyed English. "Are you Chippewa?"

"Yes."

"Bad Bluff?"

"Lac Courte Oreilles, down near Hayward."

Hammer didn't look hopeful. "Maybe they'll open up to you, but I doubt it. You're not Bad Bluff. It's a close community, the reservation."

"I understand," English said.

"But look, promise me this. When you're poking around, if you find information that ought to change my thinking or that'll give us something substantial to go on, you'll let me know."

"We'll do that," English told him.

Hammer opened his empty hands toward them all. "We're not uncaring here. We're just human and limited."

CHAPTER 8

Lieutenant Hammer had given them Carrie Verga's home address, as well as the telephone number. He also gave them the cell phone number of the girl's stepfather. He'd told them Demetrius Verga was a widower. His wife had died in a boating accident a couple of years earlier. If they didn't find him at home, he advised them to check the Port Superior Marina. Verga was an avid sailor and was often on the water.

They tried calling the house but got only voice mail. Same result with the cell phone number. Jenny keyed in the address on the Garmin app of her smart phone. The home, they discovered, was situated south of Bayfield, high on a hill with a gorgeous view of some old apple orchards and, beyond them, the broad water of Chequamegon Bay. A lovely gazebo stood on the sloping front lawn. A little way above the gazebo was a swimming pool filled with water so clear it looked like air and on which there was not a leaf or a ripple. The home sat against a great stand of hardwoods and was old and grand and beautifully maintained. In an elegant and inviting way, everything about it said *money*.

English pulled up the long drive and parked in front of a multi-car garage. Cork got out, walked to the door, and rang the bell. He expected no one to answer and was surprised when the door swung open. A big-boned blonde filled the doorway, a woman who was clearly descended from Vikings and who looked as if pillaging might be second nature to her. She was probably in her forties, but her sour expression added a decade to her looks. She said nothing in greeting, just gave Cork a blue-eyed glare that might have sent a lesser man packing.

"Good morning," he said in the cheeriest tone he could manage. "I'm wondering if I could speak with Demetrius Verga."

"He's not here." Flat and hard.

"Do you have any idea when he might be home?"

"None."

"And you are?"

"Not Mr. Verga."

"I don't suppose you'd be willing to tell me where I might find him."

She pointed toward the lake. "Out there."

"When he returns, would you mind giving him my card?"

From his wallet, he took one of the business cards he carried for his private investigation work.

She studied it, then looked at him, and there was interest in the hard blue marbles that were her eyes. "You're a private detective?"

"I do private investigations and security consulting."

"What do you want with Mr. Verga?"

"If you were him, I'd tell you. But you've already made it clear to me that you're not." He smiled pleasantly. "On the other hand, if I knew who you were, I might trust you with that information."

"Bibi Gunnarsdottir. I'm Mr. Verga's housekeeper and cook."

"Cork O'Connor. It's a pleasure, Bibi."

He offered his hand. She took it with no great enthusiasm and continued to eye him as if he might yet be after the family's heirloom silver.

"I'm looking into the disappearance of Mariah Arceneaux, on behalf of the Arceneaux family."

"Bad Bluff." She said it with such distaste that she might as well have simply spit.

"I just came from speaking with Joe Hammer. He's the Bayfield County sheriff's officer who's in charge of investigating both Mariah's disappearance and Carrie's death. I understand that the two girls were friends and that they both disappeared at the same time."

She shut down, went cold. "You're right. You should be talking to Mr. Verga."

"And I know. You're not him. But would you deliver my card?"

She considered him and the card and finally gave a slight nod. "Is that all?"

"Yes, thank you." He started to turn away but swung back. "One more thing, Bibi. Does it hurt much?"

"Does what hurt much?"

"That big chunk of ice up your ass."

As he headed back to the pickup, Cork heard the door slam behind him.

"Anything?" English asked when Cork got in.

He shook his head. "And they say the glaciers are melting."

Before they pulled away, Jenny gave a final look at the home that Carrie Verga had apparently run from. "I can understand why Mariah would want to get away from her life on the rez, but why would a girl who had all this turn her back on it?"

"And the questions continue to mount," her father replied.

They found Port Superior Marina south of Bayfield, asked about Verga, and were directed to an empty slip. Cork tried the man's cell phone again. Still no answer.

"What now?" Jenny asked.

Cork looked at English. "You said you know Mariah's basketball coach."

"Her name. I don't know where she lives."

Cork said, "If Bayfield's anything like Aurora, somebody here does."

And that proved to be true. They found Leslie Littlejohn in the swimming pool at the Bayfield Area Recreation Center, leading a dozen senior women in water aerobics. Although it was ungodly humid in the pool area, they stood waiting fifteen minutes until the session ended. When Littlejohn climbed from the water, they introduced themselves.

She wore a black bathing suit, was tall and slender, and kept her dark hair short. Her eyes were a startling auburn. She appeared to Cork to be in her late twenties or early thirties. And clearly, there was Native blood in her.

Cork explained their business, that Mariah's family had asked them to look into her disappearance.

"Kind of late for that, isn't it?" Littlejohn said.

"What do you mean?"

She grabbed a white towel from a webbed chair at poolside and began to dry off. "Somebody should have been looking for that girl a year ago."

"Maybe so," Cork said. "But we're here now and doing our best. Mariah apparently talked about you a good deal. We're wondering if there's anything you can tell us about her that might help."

"Why don't we go to the lounge and sit down?" Littlejohn suggested.

They followed her to a bright little room with a couple of tables and chairs and a narrow view of one of the streets of Bayfield that ran toward the commercial fishing docks on the lake.

"Nobody pays teachers a living wage these days," Littlejohn said, sweeping her hand the length of her suit. "I supplement my income by working at the rec center, full-time in the summer, part-time the rest of the year. Fortunately, I love what I do."

Cork said, "What can you tell us about Mariah?"

"A great kid. Despite everything."

"What do you mean by that?"

"She's Bad Bluff Chippewa. Strike one. She attended a school that, despite the fact that eighty-five percent of the students are Native, I'm one of only two Indian teachers. There are significant challenges in that environment, for staff and kids alike. Expectations, resources, prejudices, you name it, it's a challenge."

"Are you Bad Bluff?" Cork asked.

She shook her head. "Ho-Chunk from Baraboo." She ran her fingers through her hair, which was still wet and reminded Cork of sleek otter's fur. "The message Native kids here get too often is that their situation is hopeless. They have no future, no reason to strive, to learn, to try to make a difference. They frequently come from homes where no one values education, probably because the parents grew up hearing the same messages their children still hear today, or worse."

"What about Mariah?"

Littlejohn smiled in a sad way. "She had such potential. You've been to her home?"

"Yeah."

"A lot to overcome, but I really believed she had it in her. You should have seen her on the basketball court. A natural. Where did that come from? Who knows? But it was there. The ability, the passion. At least for a while. Then something happened. She just . . . changed."

"What? Overnight?"

"Not quite. I saw it first in her play on court toward the end of the season. She lost something. That's how it felt. A part of her just fell away. She didn't bring the drive she had before, the passion. Distracted, I thought at first. You know, that age, boys and all. But there was more to it, I'm sure. She missed her last two games. Just didn't show. And the next thing I heard, she'd run away."

"Did she talk to you about what might be going on?"

"Believe me, I asked her. She said nothing was going on. Said she just wasn't interested in playing basketball anymore. This from a kid who used to show up early to practice and stay a long time after to shoot hoops. You don't have that kind of passion and then just lose it like you might your cell phone."

"There was a change on her Facebook page," Jenny said. "Not long before she disappeared, she posted an entirely different kind of picture than she'd had up before. A disturbing picture for a thirteen-year-old kid."

"Yeah, I saw that. And when I cleaned out her basketball locker after she stopped showing up, I found some pretty disturbing items of clothing. Thong underwear, for one thing. And a bustier. They weren't cheaply made garments."

"Did you ask her about them?" Jenny said.

"Of course. She said no big deal. A lot of girls wore them."

"Is that true?"

"A lot of girls wear underthings they think are sexy, but usually not at thirteen and usually not expensive items. Not like what I found in Mariah's locker."

"What did you think?"

"Honestly? I thought she was involved in something way beyond what a thirteen-year-old kid should be involved in."

"What did you do?"

"I talked to our school social worker. She talked to Mariah and to Mariah's mother. Nothing came of it. And then Mariah was gone."

Cork asked, "Did you know Carrie Verga?"

"Yes. She played basketball, too. She was good, athletic. But nobody on the team played like Mariah."

"What did you think of Carrie?"

"A beautiful girl. No trouble. She was Bad Bluff, like Mariah, but her family has money. Her mother was killed in a boating accident a couple of years ago. Carrie was a real quiet girl, and I always wondered if that tragedy might have had something to do with it. And then Carrie runs away and ends up drowning." She shook her head as if the situation was inexplicable to her.

"The two girls disappeared at the same time. Folks seem to think they ran away together. What do you think?"

"They were pretty tight. So, yeah, I'd say it's a real possibility." Her face darkened, and she seemed to be looking inside herself for an answer to a question she had voiced. "You know, I honestly believed they'd come back. I've seen kids run off before, and almost always they come back. And now that Carrie's dead, I've got to say, I'm really scared for Mariah."

"Was there anyone else that Mariah and Carrie hung out with

who might be able help us? Another teacher, another teammate? The school social worker?"

"You'll have trouble talking to Liz. That's our social worker. She spends her summers working for some kind of camp for troubled kids out in Wyoming. I can't recall where. But there was a girl Mariah mentioned a lot, another girl from the rez, someone I didn't know, someone older. I've only been teaching a couple of years, and this girl dropped out of school before I arrived. Went off and became a model or something. Her name was Raven"—she thought a moment—"Raven something. I can't remember exactly. Mariah was all gaga because she had great clothes and a nice car. It's the kind of thing that impresses kids."

Cork took out his notepad and pen and wrote *Raven Something*. He said, "It seems strange that Carrie Verga would be gone for a whole year, and then suddenly wash ashore so near to Bayfield. We spoke with the investigator in charge of the case. He told us he thought Carrie might have been involved in prostitution and had been hiding out here somewhere. Do you think that's possible?"

"I suppose anything's possible. But hiding out here?" Littlejohn shook her head. "Not unless she'd been locked up in an attic somewhere." It didn't sound like a joke.

"Did the investigator or anyone else in law enforcement talk to you?"

"No. No one's talked to me officially. This is the first, if this is really official."

"I used to be the sheriff of Tamarack County, Minnesota. I've retired, and this is what I do now. I can't arrest anyone, but I can still track them down."

She opened her hands in a show of complete cooperation. "Anything you think might help you find Mariah, you just ask."

Cork took a business card from his wallet and handed it to the woman. "I think we're okay for now, but if you remember anything that might be helpful, would you give me a call?"

"Sure." She read the information on the card; then her attention swung suddenly to Daniel English, and she offered him an engaging smile. "You look awfully familiar. Do I know you?"

English said, "We never actually met before this."

Littlejohn's startling auburn eyes spent a moment assessing Jenny, and Cork had the sense that she was trying to get the lay of the land and if there was anything between his daughter and the game warden.

"Are you from around here?" she asked English, with more than casual interest.

"Hayward. Lac Courte Oreilles Ojibwe."

"Ah. I'll bet you came to one of Mariah's basketball games when we played down there, right?"

"That's right."

"Odd that I didn't notice you then." She smiled and said, "Well, *boozhoo*."

CHAPTER 9

Bayfield sat on hills on the lee side of the peninsula, with a view looking east toward Madeline Island and south across Chequamegon Bay. It was a small town full of lovely old buildings that in winter held a population of only a few hundred permanent residents. But at the height of the summer season, the streets were choked with tourist traffic. The day had turned hot. When Cork and Jenny and English left the rec center, they walked into a world that wore shorts and tank tops and cheesy T-shirts and shady hats and sunglasses. It was well past noon, and they were hungry. They found a cozy little place called Maggie's but had to wait for a table. When they were finally seated, Jenny stared at her menu with a troubled look on her face.

"Don't see anything you like?" Cork asked.

"I see a lot I don't like," she replied.

"You're not talking about the food, I suspect."

"I'm talking about Mariah. Who is she?" She gave English a penetrating stare.

English responded with a puzzled look, as if the question didn't seem to make sense to him. "My cousin."

"No. I mean, who is she? Nobody seems to know, really. All we hear is that she's an Indian girl who had potential. Then she changed. How does that make her any different from any other thirteen-year-old girl? We all change when we become teenagers, change dramatically."

"We don't all run away," English said.

Jenny ignored him. "I'm wondering what she dreamed, what she feared, what she loved, what she read, what made her laugh. I'm wondering who she is—here." She made a fist and thumped her breast above her heart. "I'm wondering what the answer to Henry's question is."

"Henry's question?"

"What's Mariah's most precious possession?"

"The key to why she ran away?" English asked.

"I don't know. But I still want the answer."

Cork said quietly, "The deeper you go, the more personal it becomes, Jenny. Henry gave me a fine piece of advice once. He told me that anger blinds. That to hunt, you need a clear eye, and for that you need a clear mind."

"I'm not angry."

"Not yet maybe. But if you allow this to become deeply personal, you will be. And in the end, you won't only be blind, you'll be hurt."

"So your answer is not to care."

"My answer is to keep a clear mind and a clear eye. It seems to me the best way to help Mariah, if she can be helped."

"And I think you ought to be able to care, care deeply, about someone, and still think clearly."

"All right," he said.

"All right?" She seemed surprised that he'd given in so easily.

"So how do we do this?" Cork said. "How do we find out who Mariah is? How do we find out the answer to Henry's question? Because it was obvious that her mother didn't have a clue." He glanced at English. "Any idea?"

English shook his head. "The Arceneauxs are blood relatives, but I know my next-door neighbors better. Between the government boarding schools and all the relocation policies, Indian families have been torn apart. With us there's more to it than that. See, my great-grandmother married a good man, Lac Courte Oreilles Anishinaabe. Veteran of World War One and proud of it. Owned a gas station. Great mechanic. Still alive when I was born.

I remember him fondly. My great-grandmother's sister, things were different for her. Married a Bad Bluff Shinnob, a fisherman. What they called a herring choker. Knew how to handle a herring net, but couldn't handle the booze. Been a battle for them up here. Don't get me wrong. We've had our struggles, too. Wouldn't be an Indian's life if things came easy. But we've always been strong on family where I live. The battles we've fought have been against governments, bureaucracies, stupid prejudices, not against each other. We're some of the lucky ones. We know that. I think the Arceneaux bunch know it, too, and there's always been a little bad blood there. So Mariah?" He shrugged, clueless.

Jenny said, "Girls sometimes keep diaries or journals." She thought a moment and then said with a sudden epiphany, "Or they post their lives on Facebook."

"But don't you need to friend her or something to see her Facebook page?" Cork said.

"I'm one of her friends," English said.

Jenny said, "I thought you didn't keep track of the Arceneaux branch of the family."

"Don't really follow anyone on Facebook, but I do have a page. Mariah shot me a friend request a couple of years ago. I accepted."

"Let's take a look at Mariah's Facebook page." Jenny pulled her smart phone from her purse. "Damn it. Battery's dead."

"There's probably a computer at the public library," English suggested.

"Let's go see." Jenny got up.

"You haven't eaten," Cork said. "You need to eat. Keeps the mind clear."

Jenny gave a little growl of grudging consent and sat back down.

They all ordered fish sandwiches. Cork requested the Lake Superior whitefish. English and Jenny both had the lake trout. Despite the crowd in the little restaurant, the food came quickly.

Between bites, English said, "So what's the trained mind of a private investigator think at this point?"

Cork wiped his mouth with a napkin. "It's clear that something was going on with Mariah that was way beyond what a kid ought to be dealing with."

"Prostitution, you think?"

"Despite Hammer's and Littlejohn's concern, I think it would be hard to engage in outright prostitution in a town this size without a lot of people knowing about it. All we've heard is conjecture. So I'm not ready to jump on that bandwagon yet. But there was clearly something disturbing going on. Maybe it involved Carrie Verga, too. I'd love to get hold of Demetrius Verga, but at the moment that's up to him. I'd also like to talk to Puck Arceneaux, but that'll have to wait until his fishing boat docks."

English said, "What about the other girl Leslie mentioned? The older one who'd dropped out? Raven something."

"Worth a try, but we'll have to figure out who to ask. Someone on the rez must know her."

Cork's cell phone vibrated. He checked the number on the display. "Demetrius Verga. Finally." He stood up. "I'm going to take this outside."

On his way into the sunlight in front of Maggie's, Cork answered the call with "This is O'Connor."

"Yeah, Demetrius Verga here. You called."

Although Cork had never seen Verga, the voice told him this was a big man. Not necessarily in his size but certainly in his own thinking. There was also something foreign in the accent, a little hint of the Mediterranean.

"I've been asked by the family of Mariah Arceneaux to look into her disappearance. I'm wondering if I could talk with you."

"I don't know what help I could be."

"I'd still like to talk. I know this must be a difficult time, so soon after your daughter's death, but it's important, Mr. Verga."

From the other end of the connection came only the sound of wind, and Cork wasn't sure if it was from a breeze running past a man standing at the wheel of his sailboat or was simple static across air into which no one spoke.

Verga's voice finally returned. "I'm on the lake right now. I'll probably come back in around four. You want, I'll meet you at Port Superior Marina. Know where that is?"

"I do," Cork said. "If your plans change, I'd appreciate a call."

"Good-bye, Mr. O'Connor," Verga said without making any promises.

Back at the table, Jenny and English had finished their food. Jenny said, "Well?"

"He'll talk to me when he comes in from sailing. That'll be around four down at the Port Superior Marina."

Jenny looked at her watch. "A lot to do this afternoon. We should get going."

Cork's sandwich was only half eaten. He reached into his pocket and pulled out his car keys. "Why don't you go get the Explorer and bring it back to me while I finish eating? Then you and Daniel go do your research at the library."

"What about you?"

"I'm going to make a call on the Bad Bluff police, see if they can shed some light on any of this."

"Okay," Jenny said, clearly eager to be off.

Daniel English reached toward the wallet in his back pocket, but Cork stopped him. "Lunch is on me."

English said, "*Migwech*," and followed Jenny out the door.

Cork finished his sandwich slowly, appreciating the quiet time to himself to think. Jenny was right. All they had at the moment was a fairly generic picture of Mariah Arceneaux. But for him, that was enough. What happened to her, whatever it was, didn't necessarily depend on who she was at heart. The world often did things to people that they never saw coming and that they would never have called down on themselves. Mariah may have opened a door on her own, but what came through that door might well have been a monster she could never have imagined.

About Carrie Verga, he knew next to nothing, but he couldn't help believing that the fates of the two girls were entwined. It seemed not at all coincidental that they'd been friends and then had disappeared at the same time. Runaways? But for the fact of Carrie Verga's body washing up onshore so near to Bayfield, he would have said yes. Her death, however, and all the uncertainty of how she came to be in the lake cast a lethal shadow over every question, every consideration.

He scanned the patrons of Maggie's, enjoying their lunches and their conversations and their summer day in this little resort community. They all looked typical and normal. And that was, Cork knew, the advantage of real evil. On the surface, it often looked so ordinary. It was only when you'd finally cut your way to the heart of the darkness that you saw the ugly thing the ordinary smile masked.

CHAPTER 10

At a convenience store in Bad Bluff, Cork was directed to the tribal police department, which shared space on the main highway with the tribal fire department. There was a single cruiser parked in the lot. The place seemed deserted at first, but as soon as Cork entered, a uniformed officer stepped from a doorway along one wall. Behind him was a large garage area, and Cork could see the cab of a fire engine. The officer was tall, with brown hair and green eyes, and if he was Indian, not much of that blood showed in his features. The name badge above the right breast pocket of his uniform read CAPT. BIGBOY.

"Afternoon, Captain," Cork said.

"Afternoon." The officer came forward, using a rag to wipe what looked like engine grease from his hands. "What can I do for you?"

"My name's Cork O'Connor." He held out his business card. The officer took it, read it, seemed just as underwhelmed as most cops were in the presence of a private investigator. "I've been asked by the family of Mariah Arceneaux to look into her disappearance."

"That was a year ago." Bigboy handed the card back. There was a greasy, black thumbprint across most of Cork's name. "The trail on Mariah's pretty cold."

"With the discovery of Carrie Verga's body, the family's quite concerned."

"They shoulda been concerned a year ago."

"They weren't?"

"First I heard of it was when the Bayfield County sheriff's investigator paid me a call. He was looking into the disappearance of Carrie Verga. Told me she'd vanished along with the Arceneaux girl."

"The Arceneaux family didn't report her gone?"

"Nope. After I spoke with the sheriff's investigator, I checked around and found out Mariah had been talking about quitting the rez for a while. Pretty clear what we were dealing with. Kids here run away all the time. They wouldn't be Indian if they didn't." He smiled as if it were a small joke. Very small. "The rez isn't a place many kids want to spend their lives."

"Ambition drives them away?"

"That. A bad home life. Money. Sometimes just for kicks they run off. So I figured it was one of those. But I also figured Mariah'd come back. More often than not they do."

"Now that Carrie Verga's body has washed up, any other ideas?"

"She's not the first unusual thing to wash up on that island. We've seen boat wreckage wash ashore there. Found an arm a few years back, a human arm. Never figured out where it came from. If you're inclined to believe old stories, that island's kind of a magnet for evil."

"You believe that?"

"What I know is that there are strong currents that run between these islands, and Windigo Island is smack in the middle of one. Makes perfect sense things are going to wash up there."

"From where? Where would a body have to go into the lake to end up here?"

"I couldn't say."

"Did you investigate at all?"

He shook his head. "Bayfield sheriff's jurisdiction." He said it as if he were speaking about some kind of line demarcated by razor wire. Cork figured relations between the two jurisdictions weren't as copacetic as Joe Hammer had painted them. Which was often the case in those instances where reservation law enforcement interacted with other jurisdictions whose officers were predominantly white. "Any other island, it would have been a federal problem. National lakeshore and all. But Windigo Island is part of the rez. Major crimes on the rez get investigated by the Bayfield County sheriff. So I've stayed out of it."

"Not even a little something unofficial?"

"I've asked around. Haven't come up with anything helpful. And I don't think it's because folks on the rez have something to hide. I really think they're in the dark, too. Carrie Verga's body out there on Windigo Island? That's the biggest mystery we've had here in a good long while."

"Joe Hammer down at the Bayfield County Sheriff's Office thinks Carrie Verga might have been drawn into trafficking. If that's true, do you think Mariah might have been involved as well?"

The captain's dark eyes narrowed in deep offense. "You're talking child prostitution. I don't know about Carrie Verga. She lived in Bayfield, and I can't say one way or the other about what goes on there. But we don't have that kind of problem on the Bad Bluff Reservation."

"You'd know about it if you did?"

"This is a small community. It's not hard to know what goes on and what doesn't. We've got our share of problems, sure, but I'm here to tell you child prostitution ain't on the list."

Cork was tempted to point out that Bigboy didn't know Mariah Arceneaux had disappeared until the Bayfield County sheriff's investigator told him. Instead he said, "The kids who found Carrie Verga's body. They were Bad Bluff kids, right?"

"That's right. Three boys. Took off to Windigo Island in the dead of night. Nothing worse in mind than mischief, but they ended up getting a lot more than they bargained for. The kid who actually found her body got the wits scared out of him. He swears he heard a monster call his name."

"Monster?"

"The island's called Windigo Island." Again, the small-joke grin.

"He heard a windigo?"

"Not only that, he believes he saw Michi Peshu swim up and crawl onto the rocks."

"No wonder he was scared out of his wits."

"Pretty clear that what he saw was the body of Carrie Verga washing up in those waves, which were big at that point. The two boys who made it off the island were lucky to get back safe."

"And the other boy?"

"Broke his ankle, had to stay there. After we got the call, we went out in our boat to get him. That's when we found the girl's body."

"What about a windigo calling his name?"

Bigboy shrugged. "The wind. His imagination. Like you said, scared out of his wits."

"Mind if I talk to this boy?"

"What for?"

"Whenever possible, I like to get things from the horse's mouth. You understand."

Bigboy thought it over a couple of moments and finally responded with a nod. "I'll give you his folks' address, and then I'll give them a call. Let 'em know you're coming."

"Appreciate it, Captain. One other question. You know a girl named Raven? A little older than Mariah Arceneaux?"

"That would be Raven Duvall. Don't see her much anymore. Last I heard, she'd gone to live with some relative down south. Duluth or the Twin Cities, maybe. Got herself a modeling job, I guess. Doing well, seems like. Why?"

"I heard she might have been a friend of both Carrie and Mariah."

"On the rez, all the kids know each other. They're friends or they're relatives. Like I said, small, close-knit community here."

"Are you Bad Bluff?" Cork asked.

"On my father's side. Bad Bluff Ojibwe and German. On my mother's side, Winnebago and Irish."

"Lived here long?"

"Most of my life."

"Like it?"

"It's home," Bigboy said, as if that was the obvious answer to a stupid question.

Cork found the home of Kyle Buffalo off Raspberry Road just outside Bad Bluff. It was a nicely kept two-story house, wood siding newly painted pale green. The mowed lawn held a swing set instead of a rusting, wheelless vehicle. It stood against a backdrop of poplars, and not far beyond that, though out of sight, lay Kitchigami. When he pulled into the drive, Cork spotted a man on a stepladder sliding a brush across the trim above the front door. Cork parked behind a Ford Bronco, and the man climbed down to greet him.

"*Boozhoo*," the man said. "You must be the private investigator Tom Bigboy called about."

"Cork O'Connor."

"Brian Buffalo." He offered Cork a paint-spattered hand. As they shook, he apologized. "Sorry. I teach down at Northland College in Ashland. Native studies. But summers I earn a little extra money painting houses. This year I'm doing my own as well."

"I appreciate your time."

"Would you like to come inside?"

"I'd really like to speak with your son."

"I'll get him in a minute. I think we ought to talk first."

"Of course," Cork said.

Inside he found a house that reminded him in some ways of his own in Aurora. The disarray was comfortable. Buffalo led him to the kitchen and indicated a chair at the dinette there.

"Can I get you something to drink? My wife makes a mean sun tea."

"Sounds good," Cork said.

After he'd poured them both glasses and sat down, Buffalo said, "Tom told me you're looking into what happened to Carrie Verga."

"Actually, I'm trying to find Mariah Arceneaux."

"Ah," he said, as if that was adequate answer for many questions. "Did you know the girls?"

"Sure. Everybody knows everybody here."

"What did you think when they disappeared?"

"They didn't just disappear, Mr. O'Connor. They ran away."

"Any idea where?"

"Duluth is usually where our kids go when they light out. It's the closest big city and has a strong Native presence."

"Kids who run away generally come back, and they come back alive. But Carrie's dead and Mariah's still missing. Does that change your thinking?"

"Of course it does. I know Louise is worried, and she has a right to be."

"There's been some speculation that Carrie Verga may have been lured into sex trafficking. Would that surprise you?"

Buffalo may have been a college instructor, but he was also Shinnob. His face gave away nothing. "Carrie was a very pretty girl. But she was just a kid."

"A kid who, when she washed ashore up here, may have been hooked on heroin and was brutalized before she died."

Cork had the feeling that Buffalo wanted to respond to this, but instead he said, "Why exactly do you want to talk to Kyle?"

"He found Carrie's body."

"That was totally accidental. And I don't see how anything he might tell you could help you find Mariah."

"I won't know that either until I've talked to him."

Buffalo said carefully and clearly, "I want you to stay away from any suggestion of prostitution and drugs where Carrie and Mariah are concerned."

"Fair enough. I just want to hear your son's story."

Buffalo stood up. "I'll get Kyle. He's in the den, reading."

"That's pretty admirable."

"Not really. Because of that outing to Windigo Island, he's lost all his electronic access. No television, video games, cell phone for a month. He's already gone through *The Count of Monte Cristo.* He's working on *The Three Musketeers* now. In a way, it's been a blessing in disguise for him. He's realized he likes reading. You'll remember your promise?"

"Yes."

A minute or two later, Buffalo returned with his son. Kyle was on crutches, his right foot strapped into a big black walking boot. He was a tall kid, good-looking, and there was a little fire in his eyes. Whether it was a flame of resistance because of Cork's presence, or had to do with the constriction of his freedom because of his current situation, or was simply the smoldering defiance of a thirteen-year-old boy, Cork couldn't have said. But he thought to himself that this was a kid with heart, and he liked him immediately.

"This is Mr. O'Connor," Buffalo said.

"*Boozhoo. Anish na?*" Cork said.

The kid replied politely, "*Anin,*" and they shook hands.

Kyle took a chair at the table with the men. "Dad said you wanted to know about Windigo Island."

"You took a big chance going out there at that time of night. Lori must be pretty special."

"You know about Lori?"

"I think everyone in Bad Bluff knows about Lori now. Has she seen what you spray-painted on that rock?"

"I don't know. Since I've been stuck here I haven't talked to her." He gave his father an unhappy glance.

"Can you tell me exactly what happened out there, Kyle?"

The kid related a pretty good story, but he left out two important details.

When Kyle had finished, Cork said, "I've been told that you heard a windigo call your name."

For a moment, the smoldering fire in the kid's eyes seemed about to die, and what Cork saw there instead was fear.

"It was just the wind," the kid said.

"Do you know what it means when a windigo calls your name?" Cork asked.

"Yeah, I know. But it was just the wind, like I said."

Cork sipped his sun tea. "I heard a windigo call my name once."

The kid studied him, gauging his seriousness.

"It was a long time ago. I knew what it meant, and I tried to tell myself it was just the wind. But a wise friend of mine, a Mide, told me that a man knows the difference between a windigo and the wind. What I heard, Kyle, wasn't the wind. And yet I'm still here. So what I've come to believe is that there's a way to defeat a windigo. Do you know what that is?"

The boy didn't reply, but Cork knew he had his profound attention.

"Courage. The windigo can't stand up against a strong heart. And do you know what I believe to be the most courageous thing a man can do? Be truthful. That takes real courage. Face the windigo with a true and courageous heart, and that monster, well, it just gives up and goes away."

"All that's just a story," Kyle said.

"My story's true. What about yours?"

The kid sat stone still, staring straight ahead, contemplating something only he could see. Cork wondered if he'd crossed a line in bringing up the windigo and if Brian Buffalo might be ready to pull the plug on the interview. But Buffalo said nothing.

"I did hear a windigo." Kyle sounded relieved to confess it. Then he told Cork the second salient detail he'd left out of his story. "Not only that. I saw Michi Peshu. I swear I did."

"I believe you," Cork said.

He looked at Buffalo, wondering how the man would react. The father put his arm around his son and said, "I do, too."

The kid's face opened up, bright with hope. "Does that mean I can play video games again?"

"No," his father said. "Going out there when you did was still a bad idea. Are we finished here, Mr. O'Connor?"

"I think so."

"Kyle, go on back to your reading," Buffalo said.

The kid got up, slid the crutches under his arms, and started to leave. Then he turned back. *"Migwech,"* he said and hobbled away.

Buffalo remained seated. He folded his paint-speckled hands on the tabletop and leaned toward Cork. "I've got a PhD, but I'm still Anishinaabe. I've lived on the shore of Kitchigami most of my life. I know there's more to that great lake than I can ever imagine. If Kyle says he heard a windigo, he heard a windigo. If he says he saw Michi Peshu, he saw Michi Peshu."

"Watch your son, Mr. Buffalo," Cork warned. "Carrie Verga also heard a windigo call her name."

For a long moment, the two men, two fathers, sat in the silence of that kitchen, knowing absolutely that there were monsters in the world, and knowing as well that they could not possibly protect their children from them all.

CHAPTER 11

The *Argos* came into the marina with its sails furled, moving smoothly under the power of its engine. Cork knew little about sailboats. This one looked to be about forty feet long, with a single mast and two sails. The hull was sleek white, and he suspected it was constructed of fiberglass but couldn't say for sure. What he could say without doubt was that it cost a hell of a lot more than he would ever dream of paying for a boat. It eased into its slip. A young woman jumped lithely to the dock with rope in hand and tied off the bow to a cleat, then moved to the stern, where she was tossed a rope and did the same there. The engine died. A minute later, a compact, tanned man wearing a white ball cap and white shorts, a dark blue Polo shirt, blue boat shoes, and black Ray-Bans joined the young woman on the dock. Young woman? That was stretching it. Cork judged her to have been just out of high school, if that. She had long blond hair and wore dungarees and a beige linen shirt, unbuttoned, over a yellow bikini top. They kissed, and the man patted her behind and said something. She laughed and went back aboard the sailboat. The man walked the dock toward Cork.

"O'Connor?" he asked, his eyes invisible behind his sunglasses.

"Mr. Verga?"

"Call me Demetri." They shook hands. "Why don't we go into the bar? I could use something cold."

Inside, Verga took a table next to a window that overlooked the marina, where the masts of the sailboats stood white as bare aspen trunks against the silvery blue of Chequamegon Bay. He finally removed his sunglasses, and Cork saw that his eyes were algae green. His face was broad and weathered, and the dark stubble of his cheeks made his skin there look charred. Cork put him at maybe fifty.

A waitress came immediately.

Verga said to Cork, "You want something?" As it had on the phone earlier, the man's voice carried the hint of a Mediterranean accent.

"You have Leinenkugel's?"

"We do," the waitress said.

"I'll take a Leinie's."

"Two, Mitzi," Verga said, and the waitress vanished.

"Thank you for agreeing to talk to me, Demetri."

Verga waved it away. "No big deal."

"I hope I didn't take you off the lake."

"I'll go back out later."

"You seem to spend a good deal of time on that sailboat of yours."

Verga held up his hands. The palms carried long scars that looked as if they may have been from rope burns. "I'm Greek. Sailing's in my blood." He leaned his forearms, muscled and knotted with veins, on the table. "So you're trying to find Mariah Arceneaux. Good luck."

"I'm sorry about Carrie."

"Thanks. Except I kind of figured something terrible had happened, so I had time to prepare myself."

"Why so sure something terrible?"

"Everybody I talked to when Carrie ran away told me kids come back. She never did."

The beers were delivered, bottled and cold and dripping with condensation. Verga took a long draw, and when he'd swallowed, Cork asked him, "Did you have any sense at all where Carrie might have gone?"

Verga wiped his mouth with the back of his hand. "None.

Clueless. I kept thinking I'd get a call from her when she ran out of money. She never called. Like she dropped off the face of the earth."

Cork drank from his own bottle. The beer went down with a satisfying chill. "What did you think when Carrie's body washed ashore?" he asked.

"I still don't know what to think. I ask myself, Where the hell has she been all this time? Up here somewhere? Where would she hide, and why?"

"What was she like?"

"A terrific kid." Verga took another long draw, belched, and didn't bother to apologize. "Her mom used to waitress here. Lot of times while she was working, she didn't have anybody to watch Carrie, so she brought her to the marina. Carrie was real good, real helpful. Used to hang out on the docks, always asking about sailing. So I started taking her and her mom out on the water occasionally. Carrie was a natural. A born sailor. Her mom, not so much. Prone to seasickness, real nervous about falling in. One thing led to another, and Christine and me got married. I adopted Carrie. We became a family."

"How long ago was that?"

"Three years."

"I understand your wife drowned in the lake."

"Yeah. Terrible, terrible thing. We'd sailed out to Cat Island, all of us. Anchored there for the night. Christine never drank while we were sailing, but once I lowered the canvas, she usually made up for lost time. That night, she really put it away. We went to bed, woke up in the morning, and she was gone. Just gone. Me and Carrie looked all over for her. Finally radioed the Coast Guard. They found her on the bottom of the lake not far from the boat, wearing what she was wearing when we went to bed. As near as I can figure, she got up in the night, went up on deck, God knows why, and stumbled overboard. She wasn't much of a swimmer. And with all that alcohol in her . . ." He finished with a fatalistic shrug and another draw from his beer.

"You never heard her call out?" Cork asked.

"Never heard a thing. Neither did Carrie."

"That must've been quite a blow."

"It was tough on both of us."

"You're still sailing, I see. What about Carrie? I mean before she ran away."

"Didn't keep her off the lake at all. Affected her in other ways, though. She got real quiet."

Cork sipped his Leinie's. Verga's eyes had shifted away from the table, and Cork saw that he was watching the waitress, Mitzi, who was a redhead, tattooed and big-breasted and no more than twenty-one.

"Were you surprised when she ran away?"

Verga brought his attention back to the table. "Yeah, it hit me hard."

"Any idea why she ran?"

"Anyone who says they understand teenagers, Mr. O'Connor, is a damn liar."

"Did you try to find her?"

"Of course I did. I pushed the sheriff's people down in Washburn to look into it. I talked to everybody I could think of who knew her. Went over to the reservation and asked around. That's when I learned that Mariah was gone, too. That's all I learned. Those people wouldn't say shit to me."

"How did you know she ran away? Couldn't she have been abducted?"

"She packed up. Took everything with her that meant anything. My housekeeper, Bibi, told me another girl picked her up in a car."

"What girl?"

"Bibi couldn't say. Never saw her before."

"Mariah Arceneaux?"

"Not her. Bibi knew Mariah. She'd been to my house before and had gone sailing with Carrie and me. This was someone else."

"What did she look like? Did your housekeeper give any description?"

"Indian. That's about it."

"Young? Old?"

"A kid, like Carrie. But Bibi did say she was driving a nice set of wheels. Kind of unusual for a kid from Bad Bluff. I told all this to Joe Hammer, the investigator from the sheriff's office. He didn't get anywhere with it."

Cork's statement was a tough one, and he was quiet while he considered how to couch it.

"I talked to Hammer, too. Considering the state in which Carrie was found, one of his speculations is that she might have been involved in sex traffic."

"You mean like a prostitute? Carrie?" Verga's eyebrows came together, storm clouds colliding. Anger stirred in the algae-green eyes beneath. "He never said that to me."

"You think he's wrong," Cork said, stating it as fact.

"I think when I see him next, I may have to put my fist down his throat. Spreading garbage like that about Carrie. Who the hell does he think he is?"

"Does the name Raven Duvall mean anything to you?"

"Nothing. Why? Should it?"

"It's possible that's the name of the girl who drove off with Carrie."

"And you know this how?"

"It's the kind of thing I get paid to find out."

"You said you're working for Mariah's family, yes?"

"I said I was investigating on their behalf."

Verga eyed him a long time and with suspicion. "Someone else footing the bill?"

"Client confidentiality," Cork replied.

"What does it cost to hire you?"

Cork told him.

Verga said, "I hire you, you'll share anything you find out with me?"

"I already have a client."

"Yeah, yeah, I know. The Arceneaux family. For them, you're finding Mariah. But for me, you'll be looking for someone else."

"Who?"

"The son of a bitch who killed Carrie."

"Officially, her death was an accident."

"You believe that?"

"At this point, I don't really know what to believe."

"So what about it? You'll work for me?"

"Let me think on it, okay? The ethics might be tricky."

"Ethics." Verga finished his beer, set it hard on the tabletop with a crack of glass against wood, and said, "Fuck ethics."

CHAPTER 12

As Cork drove into Bayfield, his cell phone rang. He pulled off the road, but not in time. He checked the display. The call had come from Jenny.

"Charged your battery?" Cork said.

"At the library," Jenny confirmed. "We finished there a while ago. Where are you?"

"Just coming into town. Where do you want to meet?"

"We should think about a place to stay for the night."

"How about the casino hotel?" Cork suggested.

"Meet you there."

The Shining Waters casino and hotel complex was modest compared to many of the Indian casinos Cork had seen in Minnesota. It sat on the shore of Kitchigami with a broad, lovely view of Basswood Island across West Channel. The parking lot wasn't particularly full, and when they asked at the reception desk inside, they had no trouble securing accommodations. Cork and his daughter took a lake-facing room with two queen beds. English took a room with a king, same view. They carried their bags up and agreed to meet at the hotel bar to share information. Jenny wanted to call home and check on Waaboo, so Cork went down ahead of her and found English sitting at a table next to a window.

"Got a call from Red," English told him. "Invited us to dinner at Louise's place." He was quiet a long few moments, then said, "It's an important gesture."

"Did he give you a time?"

"In an hour. Said Louise had something important she wanted to tell us."

"He didn't say what?"

"Not a word."

"Maybe she's finally figured out the answer to Henry's riddle."

"Good luck to her," English said, "because we didn't get much."

"What did you find?"

The bar wasn't hopping, and the noise of the casino machines was distant enough that it masked nothing they said, so English spoke quietly. "She was just a kid. Just a regular kid. Her earliest Facebook postings were about Justin Bieber. And horses. That was three years ago, when she was turning eleven. She posted some poetry about wolves. Pretty good, I thought. She talked a little about being Shinnob, but not much. She wasn't very proud of her heritage, I think. I would love to have had a chance to work with her on that."

"But you almost never saw her."

"And I'm regretting it. I feel like we deserted her. Like we deserted all of them up here. They're family, but they're also so much of what the white world expects of Indians."

"What the white world made of Indians," Cork said.

"Some Indians," English replied, and Cork acknowledged that truth with a nod.

Jenny appeared and sat down with them, and a barmaid finally came and took their drink orders. Cork thought his daughter seemed subdued. In fact, he thought she might have been crying.

"Everything okay at home?" he asked.

"Waaboo and Aunt Rose are getting along just fine."

"So why the long face?"

"How do you do it, Dad?"

"Do what?"

"Get all tangled up in people's lives and people's problems without it tearing you apart."

"Who says it doesn't?"

"You always seem so unemotional about an investigation."

"And that's hard for you?"

"Jesus, I spent the last couple of hours steeped in Mariah's life. I feel like she's my little sister."

"*Nishiime*," Cork said.

Jenny shot him a questioning look.

English said to her, "Means 'little sister' in Ojibwe. I get what you're saying, Jenny. I was just telling Cork the same thing."

That made her nod, in agreement or sympathy or alliance. Whatever it was, Cork felt she saw herself—and maybe English—on one side of a line of behavior and he was on the other. He decided not to push it.

"What did you learn?" he asked her.

"I was hoping she might have posted what it was she loves most. You know, so we can help Louise answer Henry's riddle. It's the kind of thing kids put on Facebook."

"But she didn't?"

Jenny shook her head.

"Did you find out anything?"

Her gloom continued. "That she's a reader. She liked *The Hunger Games*. That she got a guitar for her twelfth birthday and was learning to play. Home was too noisy and confused, so she would go down to the lakeshore to practice. The first day she did that, she saw an eagle soaring overhead. She thought maybe it was a good sign, but didn't really know what it meant. She doesn't understand the place of eagles in her culture. She said she knew they're important and wanted to know more. She has a friend who's really into being Anishinaabe and who's learning the jingle dance. She envies her because she's proud of being Indian. She hates her big brother, Toby. She thinks he's mean and doesn't do anything and hangs out with mean boys. But she really likes her cousin Puck. He's more a big brother to her than her real big brother. And she likes her uncle Red. He's kind of mean sometimes, too, but not to her. She understands that's because he was in jail, and things are hard for him. When she goes into Bayfield, people treat her cold sometimes, just because she's Indian."

Jenny spoke as if Mariah were still in their midst, still present in Bad Bluff. Still alive.

"Then around a year ago, a little while before she ran away, her posts began to change. Listen to this, Dad." From her purse, she pulled a slip of paper on which she'd written, " 'Dogs wander the woods along the lake north of my town. I think they used to be pets but got abandoned or something. They don't belong to anybody, and they always have this hungry look. I don't know if they'll attack or not, so I try to stay away from them. Old guys look at me the same way.' " Jenny set the paper down and lifted her sad, blue eyes to her father. "It wasn't long after that she changed the picture on her Facebook page to the one that's so scary. And then she stopped posting altogether. I think something very bad happened to her before she ran away."

"Any clue what that was?"

She balled her right fist and cupped it in her left hand, and it reminded Cork of a sheathed weapon. "If I had to guess, I'd say someone abused her. After I saw the dramatic change in her Facebook picture and her posts, I had my suspicions, so I Googled symptoms of sexual abuse. From everything we've heard, it seems clear to me she was exhibiting a lot of that behavior before she left. The sudden disinterest in her studies, in basketball. The change in her appearance. Those expensive, sexy underthings Leslie Little-john found in her locker."

"If that's true, any clue about the abuser?"

Jenny glanced at English. Apologetic, accusatory, Cork couldn't say. "Family is usually the first place you look."

English replied, "If we need to turn over rocks, we turn them over. Red's invited us to dinner at Louise's house. Maybe it's time we asked the hard questions. But I can tell you this. If there are shameful secrets, getting anyone to talk about them will be like asking a tree to speak."

Cork leaned nearer and said quietly, "If she was abused, it might not have been by her family. I just talked with Demetri Verga, Carrie's father. There's a man I'm not much inclined to like. And I heard and saw things that make me think digging deeper into the dynamic of that particular family would be a good idea."

Their drinks arrived. When the barmaid had gone, Cork related his interview with Verga.

After he'd finished, Jenny said, "Her mother drowned and only Verga and Carrie were around? Only their word about what happened? But if there was something fishy about her death, wouldn't Carrie have said so?"

"Maybe she didn't know anything. Or maybe she had reasons of her own for not coming forward. But I find it uncomfortably coincidental that both Carrie and her mother died in the same lake in the same way."

Lines of concern cut across English's broad smooth brow. "You think Demetri Verga is a man capable of killing? Maybe killing twice?"

"What I believe is that, under the right circumstances, anyone is capable of anything. Verga told me quite a lot, but what of it was true I couldn't say for sure. It all sounded rehearsed. He got mad when I told him that Hammer thinks Carrie might have been trafficked, but even that didn't ring true. He tried to hire me, ostensibly to find who killed Carrie. I'm thinking it was more a question of trying to keep track of what I discover. So I'd like to know more about Demetrius Verga. Particularly in light of Mariah's post about old guys looking at her hungrily."

"Where do we go from here?" Jenny asked.

"Dinner with Red and Louise," Cork said. "And I'd like to talk to Puck Arceneaux, if he's around. I'd also like to see if we can track down the family of Raven Duvall."

"Raven? The girl Mariah and Carrie were hanging with toward the end here? You found out her last name?" Jenny finally sounded a hopeful note.

"They weren't just hanging around with her. I think she might have been their way out. According to Verga, a girl picked up Carrie the day she disappeared."

"Hammer didn't say anything about that when we talked to him this morning," English said.

"Maybe he didn't investigate as thoroughly as he tried to make us believe," Cork replied.

Jenny said, "Verga told you Raven's last name?"

Cork shook his head. "He claimed not to know who it was that had picked up Carrie. But like I said, I don't know what was true and what was bullshit. The chief of the Bad Bluff police told me Raven's last name. I thought it might be a good lead, so I made a call to Tamarack County and asked Marsha Dross—our sheriff and a good friend of mine," he explained to English, "to check on a driver's license. She got back to me pretty quick. Said no license had been issued in that name in either Wisconsin or Minnesota. So a dead end there. But I keep coming back to Bigboy, the Bad Bluff police chief. In the end, he didn't really give me much. Seemed awfully protective of his town."

"What do you mean?" Jenny asked.

"In my experience, a small town is like a family," Cork said. "Nobody wants to air the dirty laundry in public. And although they may all know the dirty secrets, even among themselves they don't talk about it. But, you know, I got a bad feeling from Bigboy that didn't necessarily have anything do with being protective, so there may be more to dig into on that front."

Jenny looked perplexed. "If nobody talks, how do you get your questions answered?"

"Two ways. You find the right arms and you twist really hard."

"Or?" English said.

"In a place like this, you get Henry Meloux to ask the questions."

CHAPTER 13

The table, at least, was clean. Or cleared of debris anyway. There were enough chairs for the adults. The two boys—Denny and Cal—ate on TV trays in their bedroom and played a video game, this one full of the sounds of car racing, muted just a little because Red Arceneaux had threatened to smash the controllers if they didn't turn the damn sound down. Tobias wasn't present. Off somewhere, Louise told them, with his friends. When Cork asked about Puck, Arceneaux said his son had come home from working the fishing boat, cleaned up, and gone to listen to a group playing at the Bad Bluff community center that evening. He didn't know when Puck would be home.

Dinner was macaroni and cheese. The real thing, not from a Kraft box. Arceneaux and Louise had worked on it together. There were canned peas to go with it. Bud Light, Diet Pepsi, and water were the drink choices. They all took water, except Arceneaux, who drank a couple of Buds in the course of things. Louise sat at the head of the table in her wheelchair. She listened closely as Cork and Jenny and Daniel English told what they'd all discovered in that long day. There'd been a change in her since the morning. Cork could see it. She took in everything, absorbed it without reacting. It didn't seem to Cork a showing of courage; it felt more like fatalism. She didn't seem shocked or offended when he raised the possibility that Carrie Verga had been drawn into the sex traffic and, because of Mariah's association with the girl, her potential involvement as well.

Instead she said, "I want to talk to Henry Meloux."

Jenny said, "You've figured out the thing Mariah loves most?"

"No," Louise said. "But if I go to him, he has to see me."

Cork said, "When do you want to go?"

"Tomorrow."

"What about your children?" There was a sharpness to Jenny's words.

"I'll watch the kids," Arceneaux told her. "They'll be fine."

"Tomorrow?" Cork shook his head. "I still have people here I need to talk to."

"Who?" Arceneaux asked.

"The family of Raven Duvall for one."

Arceneaux said, "You want to talk to Lindy Duvall, I'll take you over tonight."

"I'd like to talk to Puck, too."

"Him you can find at the community center. The music'll go on there until late."

Cork had mixed his peas and macaroni and cheese, something he always did with this particular meal offering. He hadn't quite finished, but he put down his fork and asked Louise, "Did Mariah ever say anything to you about Carrie's father, Demetrius Verga?"

Louise said, "She talked about how much stuff he had. What a nice house he lived in and what nice cars he had, the big sailboat. You know, everything we don't have. That was at first. After a while, she didn't talk about him at all."

"Do you know Verga?"

"He dropped Mariah off sometimes after she spent time with Carrie at his place. I never actually met him. Knew his wife. She was Bad Bluff."

"She died in a boating accident."

"Drowned. That girl couldn't swim to save her soul."

"Carrie drowned, too."

"So?"

"I'm just thinking that's quite a coincidence."

Arceneaux said, "You think her old man had something to do with both those deaths?"

"I'm not saying anything except that I don't put much stock in coincidence."

"Maybe he knows something about what's happened to Mariah?"

"I don't know that. But he's another reason I'd like to stick around awhile."

Louise said, "I want to see Henry Meloux. I have to see him."

"A day, Dad," Jenny said quietly. "Mariah's been gone a year. What difference can another day make?"

On the surface, the argument was sound. But Cork felt like he was getting somewhere in Bad Bluff, and he didn't want to leave the investigation hanging, even for a day. On the other hand, he wanted something from Meloux, too. So maybe it would be best to return to Tamarack County. For a day.

"All right," he said. "We'll leave first thing in the morning."

Jenny offered to help with the dishes, but Louise said that if they wanted to talk to Lindy Duvall, they should go. She'd make sure things got cleaned up. Cork had his doubts.

Arceneaux rode with English. Cork and Jenny followed in the Explorer. The sun was still up, but just barely. The shadows were long, and the day had a tired feel to it. They passed through Bad Bluff, passed the community center, where the doors were open and Cork could hear bluegrass music coming from inside. He wanted to get back to Puck before things there wrapped up.

They pulled up in front of a duplex that looked like an old BIA construction. The paint was flaking and the grass of the yard needed cutting. But there was no junk despoiling the property. Cork didn't want to overwhelm Lindy Duvall with a lot of strangers descending on her, so he and Arceneaux approached the house together while Jenny and English stayed in their vehicles. Arceneaux knocked on the door, and it was opened by a kid no more than ten years old.

"Your mama home, Wade?"

The boy had big dark eyes and a mop of black hair and a streak of what looked like chocolate ice cream across his cheek. He shook his head and said, "Unh-uh."

"Know where she is or when she'll be back?"

"Unh-uh."

The television was on inside, and Cork thought he heard *SpongeBob SquarePants*, a cartoon he sometimes watched with Waaboo, which, to his chagrin, he kind of liked. He also heard a baby crying somewhere in the house.

"Anybody here with you?" Cork asked.

"Unh-uh." The boy squinted at him and asked, "You from the county?"

"No," Cork said. "Is your sister Raven around?"

"Unh-uh. She never is."

"Where is she?"

"Dunno." He gave a little shrug. Inside, the baby went on wailing.

"Is that your little brother or sister I hear?" Cork asked.

"Sister."

"Sounds like she needs something."

"She always cries."

"Could I see her?"

"My mother says not to let strangers in."

Arceneaux said, "I'm no stranger, Wade."

The boy thought this over, gave a shrug, and let them pass.

The house was clean, at least compared to the home they'd just left. The furniture was in good shape, the curtains new-looking, the television a big flat-screen. The crying child was in a corner of the living room, holding on to the side of her playpen. Cork thought she was maybe ten or twelve months old. He lifted her and could smell immediately what her problem was.

"What's her name, Wade?"

"Shannon."

"Hey, Shannon," Cork cooed. "We're going to take care of you. Wade, do you know where your mother keeps her diapers?"

Without a word, the boy disappeared down a hallway and came back a moment later with a disposable Huggie.

"Would you get me a towel, too, and a wet washcloth?"

The boy did, and Cork laid the towel on the carpet, the child atop the towel, and did what needed to be done. By the time he'd finished, Shannon had stopped crying. He gave the dirtied diaper to Wade to put in the garbage. The soiled washcloth he wrapped in the towel and left them both on the floor next to the playpen. He'd only just accomplished all this when they heard the back door open, and a few moments later a woman walked in, carrying a couple of grocery sacks in her arms. She pulled up, startled, and then shot Arceneaux a killing look.

"What the hell's this all about, Red? Who's that holding my baby girl?"

"Take it easy, Lindy," Arceneaux said. "Came to talk to you about Raven. Cork here just helped Wade out a little, changing your daughter's diaper. That's the whole of it."

"You got no right coming in unasked. Wade, you let these men in?"

In the face of his mother's anger, the boy's eyes had grown huge, and he'd become mute.

"We invited ourselves in, Ms. Duvall," Cork said. "Your son did his best to keep us out."

She pushed between Cork and Arceneaux and brushed past her son on her way to the kitchen. Cork heard the grocery sacks set heavily down, then Lindy Duvall swept back in and whisked her daughter from his arms. She stepped away a safe, protective distance and snapped, "What about Raven?"

"When was the last time you saw her?" Cork asked.

"Who are you? Why do you want to know?"

"He's a private investigator, Lindy," Red said. "We asked him to help us find Mariah."

Tall and tired-looking, she stood studying both men silently. Her hair was long and black and in need of a good brushing. She was a pretty woman now, but in her youth, which was a good two decades behind her, she'd probably been stunning.

"What's Raven got to do with that?" she finally asked. She was still guarded, but the anger seemed to have drained.

Cork said, "I have reason to believe that Raven may have been the last person here to see both Carrie Verga and Mariah before they ran away last year. Raven was in Bad Bluff at the time, wasn't she?"

"She comes, she goes. I don't keep track."

"She's a model, I understand," Cork said.

"Yes," Lindy Duvall replied, much too quickly and emphatically.

"In Duluth?"

"I thought this was about the other girls."

"If it's true that Raven was the last to see them here, I'd like to find out if she has any idea where they went when they left Bad Bluff. I need to talk to her."

"I'm sure she doesn't know."

"Why?"

"She just doesn't." The anger was returning.

"She does pretty well as a model, I understand."

"What of it?"

"Does she send money home?"

The woman nodded. "She's good that way."

The child in her arms had begun to squirm, and she returned Shannon to the playpen. Wade went back to watching SpongeBob.

"Do you know the name of the agency she models for in Duluth?"

"No." She turned her attention to her daughter, gave Shannon a toy, a plush, purple octopus that, when the child hugged it, played a soft little melody, "London Bridge Is Falling Down."

"I made a call today to some folks I know in law enforcement, Lindy. I asked them to check on a driver's license for Raven Duvall. They couldn't find anything, not here in Wisconsin or in Minnesota. Are you sure she's working in Duluth?"

"I'm sure."

"Do you have any recent pictures of Raven, from a photo shoot maybe?"

"No."

Cork was getting nowhere, and he decided to try a different tack.

"I've been told that Raven took Mariah and Carrie Verga with her when she left Bad Bluff to return to Duluth a year ago. Drove off with them in that nice car of hers. Now Carrie's dead—I'm guessing you know that—and Louise is afraid for Mariah. And rightly so. Is it possible that Raven's in trouble, Lindy? Is there something we can do to help her, too?"

"No." She kept her back to the men, leaning over the playpen, squeezing the octopus so that it played its soft little tune. "We've talked enough. I want you to go."

"All right." Cork pulled one of his cards from his wallet and held it out toward her. "If you think of anything I ought to know, I'd appreciate a call."

She turned her head, saw the card, considered, and finally accepted it.

"I'm sorry for intruding," Cork said. "It's just that Louise is so worried about her little girl. I'm sure you can understand."

Lindy Duvall gently touched the top of her own daughter's head, as if in benediction. "Around here," she said, "they don't stay little very long."

"Night, Lindy," Arceneaux said, and they left the way they'd come.

CHAPTER 14

The community center was a newer, whitewashed cinder-block construction at the edge of a circular, bleacher-flanked field that, Cork figured, was the Bad Bluff powwow ground. The sun had set, and the cool of the lake was like a wave washing the air clean. What light was left in the sky was a thin, powdery blue. Music poured from the open doors of the community center, the same kind of bluegrass that had been playing when they'd passed on their way to the Duvall home. A number of people stood gathered outside the doorway, all smoking cigarettes under the entrance light. English pulled into the parking lot, which was nearly full, and Cork pulled in beside him. Red Arceneaux got out of English's truck and came over to the Explorer to speak to Cork through the open window.

"You wait here. I'll go in, find Puck, bring him out."

Arceneaux walked toward the light and the music.

Daniel English left his truck and came to Jenny's window. The pale, late evening glow fell on him and softened his broad face. "I heard things didn't go so well."

Cork leaned his arms and weight on the steering wheel and studied the amber sky in the west. "Lindy Duvall wasn't at all inclined to talk about Raven. But we didn't come away completely empty-handed. I think we know more than we did going in."

"What do we know?" Jenny asked.

"Lindy was defensive. She knows more than she's willing to say. Maybe she's protecting Raven. Maybe she's just afraid. I'm not sure which. But Red was right. It was clear we weren't going to get answers from her. I didn't want to push her too hard. Not at this point anyway."

"Maybe Henry?" Jenny suggested.

"Maybe Henry," Cork agreed. "If he's willing to come here."

Arceneaux exited the building, and the gathered smokers made way for him. He looked unhappy as he approached the Explorer. "Puck's not inside," he said. "Appears he's gone off with a couple of friends, down to the campgrounds on the lake. Drinking beer or smoking weed most likely. We can walk from here, if you want."

Bad Bluff was a small community. The campgrounds turned out to be just north of the casino, which was a stone's throw from the community center. It was dark enough by then that the halogen lamps of the complex's parking lot had come on, and they walked in that harsh neon glare.

The campgrounds appeared to be nearly empty. A tent occupied one of the spaces along the lakeshore. A low fire burned in the pit there, but Cork saw no one around it. A few spaces south was an RV with a canopy spread above the site's picnic table. The lights were on inside the RV, and Cork heard a radio tuned to a ball game. Arceneaux kept walking as if he could sense, even in the gathering dark, exactly where to find his son. And he did.

It was the last site south in the campgrounds. Possibly because it was the site nearest the casino and hotel, it looked barely used. The fire pit contained no char, no ash, no evidence of a recent blaze. Tall grass had grown in the tent pad area. Just beyond, the ground sloped steeply to the lake. Arceneaux stood in the tall grass at the crest of the rise. Below him, a little fire had been kindled on a flat rock jutting into Superior. Three figures sat silhouetted there. A tiny orange spark traveled among them, and Cork caught the unmistakable aroma of burning pot.

"Thought you were going to be listening to music, Puck." Arceneaux slowly descended a path that was faint in the deepening dark.

"Aw, shit. Busted." The voice didn't sound at all concerned.

Arceneaux continued until he was close enough to distinguish faces in the firelight. "George, Connie," he said.

"Hey, Red." The voice of a young man.

"Evening, Mr. Arceneaux." A young woman's voice.

"The music wasn't good?" Arceneaux said.

"It was fine, Red. We're just taking a break." This came from the first voice that had spoken, which Cork figured belonged to Arceneaux's son. Cork found it interesting that he addressed his father by his given name. The kid turned, and Cork saw a face cut in half by firelight and the dark. "Who'd you bring with you?"

"Those are the folks I told you about," Arceneaux replied. "Mind going for a walk with us?"

"I'm kind of occupied here, Red."

Cork said, "It'll only take a minute, Puck. And it's important."

Puck reached for the joint that was being passed. He took a hit, held it, and blew out the smoke. "Chill, guys. I'll be back real soon." He leaned over and kissed the girl, whose hair was gold in the firelight. He stood and climbed the slope.

He was no longer the size and shape that had been the reason for the nickname he'd been given as a child. He was tall and slender and fit. The pupils of his eyes were large and dark. His hair was as black as a starless night. He wore a clean white T-shirt and clean jeans and new-looking, neon red, high-top sneakers. Although he'd worked a fishing boat all day, he didn't smell of fish. He smelled of smoke, both wood and weed. He studied Cork, then English, and finally Jenny. He said "Hey" to them all in general.

"*Boozhoo,*" Cork replied.

Puck said, "Right."

"Mind if we take a little walk? Not long, I promise," Cork told him.

"This is about Mariah?"

"It's about Mariah."

He gave a *whatever* shrug and said, "Lead the way."

They didn't walk far, just enough to be out of hearing range from the kids still by the fire, or anyone else who might be interested in listening to their conversation.

"So what do you want to know?" Puck asked when they stopped. He shoved his hands into the back pockets of his jeans and stood tall, with his chest out.

"Tell me about her," Cork said.

"Hell, I'm guessing everyone in Bad Bluff's already told you about Mariah. What do you want from me that you didn't get from them?"

"What did you think of her?"

"I liked her," Puck replied without hesitation. "She was a good kid."

"Any idea why she ran away?"

"Yeah."

Cork waited, then waited some more.

Jenny broke the silence. "She was a good kid, then she changed. Do you know what I mean, Puck?"

"I know exactly what you mean. When Red and me came here, Mariah was just a kid. Really pretty, you know, but a kid. Then, like you say, she changed. Started wearing all kinds of makeup, dressing slutty, trying to look older. I told her it wasn't her. She told me it wasn't any of my business."

"When did that change happen?"

"A while before she ran off."

"What changed in her life?"

"She began hanging with Carrie Verga for one thing."

"What did you think of Carrie?" Cork asked.

"Trouble."

"How so?"

"Like a festering boil. She kept it all in, whatever was bothering her, but you could see it was going to blow up sooner or later."

"You're pretty sensitive to that kind of thing, are you?" Cork said.

"That's how I spent my life, mister."

"What do you mean?" Jenny asked.

The young man looked at his father, those dark eyes bottom-less. He spoke in a flat voice. "Being Indian's never been much of a leg up for me. I don't go in for all that powwow and drums and spirits in the lake shit. The truth is that this is a white man's world. If you're going to succeed, it's going to be on the white man's terms. I got that a long time ago.

"When my dad was in prison, the county placed me with a foster family. White people. Very religious. I was their salvation project. They used to lock me in a closet. Never beat me. That's something a social worker or somebody at a clinic could see. But they'd hold off feeding me for a while and beat me in other ways. In the name of God and for the sake of my eternal soul. You know what? I learned to play along. I learned to say whatever it took to get out of that closet, to get fed, to get clothed. I learned that it's a white man's world and the only God is the white man's God. I learned to take all that crap they dished out with a smile, because one day I was going to be better than them. Richer than them. I was going to beat them at their own game. So I know about keeping stuff inside and what to look for. I saw it in Carrie Verga, in spades."

Daniel English spoke up for the first time. "How're you going to beat them at their own game, Puck?"

"I've been working my ass off, saving money for college," the young man told him. "I'm going to UW–Superior in the fall. I'm going to major in business. You know who Dave Anderson is?"

"The Dave Anderson who started up Famous Dave's barbecue?"

"Yeah, that's him. He's Ojibwe. I'm going to make it like he did. Do the white man's thing in the white man's world."

"With a white man's heart?" English asked.

Puck said, "The white man's got no heart. And that's his secret."

Cork was afraid of losing the kid to his bitterness. To bring the conversation back to what was necessary he said, "Carrie and Mariah may have run off with the help of another girl. Raven Duvall. You know her?"

"I didn't really know her, just knew about her from what Mariah said. Drove a nice car. A model down in Duluth or the Twin Cities. Somewhere."

"Is that when the changes you talked about seeing in Mariah occurred?"

"Naw, that happened before. In fact, she got better after she started hanging with Raven. I figured Raven, being a model and all, maybe showed her how to use makeup and how to dress nice, but not slutty."

"Know where we can find Raven?"

"Nope. Haven't seen her since Mariah took off."

"Puck," Jenny said carefully, "what do you think of Mariah's brother, Toby?"

"Worthless, that one. And if you're looking for reasons why Mariah might have run off, you should talk to him."

"Why?"

"Because he was hitting on her, him and those worthless shits he hangs out with."

"Hitting on his own sister?" Jenny said.

Puck gave her a long look. "Welcome to the party. I threatened to beat the crap out of him if he didn't lay off her."

"Did it work?"

"She ran away," Puck said. Then he addressed Cork: "I've been thinking about Carrie, about her washing up on Windigo Island after all this time. That hump of rock out there's too far to swim to, especially in this cold lake water, and it's too small to party on."

"And?" Cork encouraged.

"One thing I know because of the work I do: you want to get rid of something, you take it out and drop it in the lake."

"You think somebody dumped Carrie in Lake Superior?"

"Every day we go out on the fishing boat, I see lots of other boats out there. Big sailboats, big powerboats, yachts, you know? Belong to guys from the Twin Cities, Chicago, places like that. Lots of money. I run across them sometimes when we come into dock. A lot of them seem to me like the kind of people who'd buy something, use it awhile, and when they're tired of it, they just throw it away. Worth thinking about, you know. We done here?"

Cork said, "If we wanted to talk to you again, Puck, would that be all right?"

Arceneaux said, "He'll talk to you."

Puck shook his head. "You're just like a white man, Red. Always trying to tell me what to do." To Cork he said, "You really think you can find Mariah, I'll talk some more. But I don't know anything I haven't already told you. See you around."

The young man turned, and as he walked toward the little fire where his friends were waiting, his back was lit with the dull glow of the casino neon.

Arceneaux watched him go, his face stone. "Let's get out of here," he said.

They dropped Arceneaux at his sister's house, returned to the hotel, and went to the casino bar for a beer and to talk things over. Daniel English reported that the big Shinnob had said almost nothing on the way home.

"Like hauling a rock. A big, heavy rock," he said.

"A lot on his shoulders." Cork sipped the Leinie's that the barmaid had brought him. His mind was working fast and hard. "I keep thinking about something Puck said. People throw things from their boats when they're done with them."

"You think that's what happened to Carrie Verga?" Jenny asked. She'd ordered a Diet Coke, but it sat untouched on the table in front of her.

"I've been trying to figure how someone might operate a prostitution business from up here. There are half a dozen marinas on the Bayfield Peninsula. It seems to me that catering to the men who dock their expensive boats here wouldn't be a bad way to go about it."

"So," Jenny said, "assuming circumstances had forced Carrie to be a part of something like that, then what? The john just got tired of her and threw her overboard?"

"In that kind of situation, anything's possible. Who knows

what might have happened? But Kitchigami's an ideal place to drop a body. That lake almost never gives up its dead."

"It gave up Carrie," Jenny pointed out.

English said, "I suppose prostitution might work in season, but it's a short season up here. What about the rest of the year? Things slow to a crawl, I imagine. And we come back to the question of how Carrie could continue to be here and not be seen."

Cork lifted his beer. "I'm still working on that."

It was late when they climbed the stairs to their rooms. English said good night and closed his door. In their own room, Jenny went to the window and looked at the black water of the lake.

Cork joined her and spoke to her reflection in the glass. "How come you didn't tell Daniel that you're a writer?"

Jenny said, "The first question people ask you is, Have you published? Like that's the be-all and end-all."

"You asked him what he read, and he was honest. Couple of those guys I never even heard of."

"Hemingway, Dad. He likes Hemingway."

Whatever that meant. Cork wasn't a writer, and had never been much of a reader, and so had no idea. He said, "I'm going for a walk."

Jenny turned from her window reflection. "Not tired?"

"A lot of snarls in my thinking. If I go to bed now, I'll just lie there trying to pull them apart. Better if I walk. I won't keep you awake that way."

"I won't be lying down for a while. Aunt Rose promised to call before she went to bed and give me an update on her day with Waaboo."

Cork left the hotel and walked down to the lakeshore. He couldn't see the campgrounds because of the dark, and he wondered if Puck and his friends were still there. He liked the kid. There was anger in Puck, which he'd channeled in a way that would drive him for a while. At some point, the anger wouldn't be enough. He might well accomplish what he intended to do, outwhite the white man, but the cost would be great, Cork suspected. Then again, what did he know? He ran a burger joint and a second-rate detective business and had no ambition beyond that. Still, he considered himself a happy man, and who could put a dollar sign to that?

Although the moon hung almost directly above him, everything to the east seemed oddly dark. Yet Cork discerned gradations in that darkness. The water of the West Channel was a soft, shifting black, like liquid ink. The sky, with its billions of stars, was a great piece of charcoal dusted with ash. Basswood Island, solid as coal, rose out of one of those blacknesses and stood silhouetted against the other. In a way, Cork thought, this was exactly where he was in his investigation, trying to sort out one dark from another.

People were lying to him. Or maybe simply not telling him the truth of everything, which was different from lying, he supposed, but equally unhelpful in his investigation. Louise had not told him everything, he was certain. It was the same with Lindy Duvall. Captain Bigboy, in his assurances that child prostitution couldn't possibly be occurring on the rez, may have simply been fooling himself about the community he was responsible for policing. Or maybe he had something to hide. And Demetrius Verga? He was a man clearly used to dishing up crap and calling it caviar.

Even in the night, boats still cruised smoothly across the lake, their lights reflected in the liquid black of the water. Cork watched a big, gaudily lit power launch glide down the West Channel, and as he studied it, the lights winked out for a moment in succession, as if, one after the other, they were being turned off and then on again. For a moment, he was confused. Then he realized what he was seeing. Between him and the launch stood Windigo Island. Now he could discern the tall, solitary pine tree a couple of hundred yards offshore, rising out of that small humping of rock. He hadn't noticed it in daylight, had been too intent on other things. But there it was, a couple of hundred yards from shore, the beacon for the spirits of the lake—the windigo and Michi Peshu. In a way, the heart of all this darkness.

Kyle Buffalo was right to be afraid, as was his father. There were monsters in the world. They preyed on the vulnerable, so many of whom were children, and their greatest ally was fear. Whatever the truth that Louise Arceneaux and Lindy Duvall and everyone else was afraid to speak, Cork knew he had to get to the heart of it. Not only for Mariah, if she was still alive, but for the nameless others just like her.

He started to turn away from the lake, and as he did, a wind came up out of nowhere, a torrent so cold, so sudden, so powerful that it almost knocked him over. Caught off balance and stumbling, he heard, or thought he heard, what had made Kyle Buffalo's blood freeze in his veins. For the second time in his life, Corcoran O'Connor heard, or thought he heard, a windigo call his name.

"O'Connor." A human voice this time, male, coming from the shadow of a small shed at the edge of the parking lot near the water.

The wind that had brought the windigo's voice died as quickly and mysteriously as it had come.

Cork tried to see into the shadow from which the human voice had spoken. "Who's there?"

"You want to know about the girl, right?"

"Are you talking about Mariah Arceneaux?"

"Her, yeah. I got information."

"Tell me."

"I don't want nobody to see me. You come over here."

Cork moved toward the shed and its shadow. He was almost there when the blow caught him. It might have been a baseball bat; the impact came too quickly for him to see. Whoever wielded it used it like a cop would a nightstick and rammed the tip hard into his solar plexus. All the breath went out of him, and Cork went down. The next blow fell across his shoulder. He tried to curl into a ball to protect himself against more battering.

"Hey! What's going on over there?" The cry came from the direction where Puck Arceneaux and his friends had gathered.

The man in the shadow leaned close to Cork's ear. His breath smelled of beer and barbecued potato chips. "Get out of Bad Bluff, O'Connor. We don't like *chimooks* who're too interested in our girls."

Cork heard the slap of footsteps approaching across the parking lot pavement. The man in the shadow disappeared without a sound.

Cork felt a hand on his back. "Hey, you okay?"

He recognized Puck Arceneaux's voice.

"I think so." Cork rolled over and found the three kids he'd met earlier staring down at him.

"It's you," Puck said. He glanced down the shoreline, where the shadow man had gone. "Who was that?"

"Don't know."

"Figures."

"How so?" Cork thought about standing, decided to give it another minute.

"White man comes to the rez, asks insinuating questions, thinks nothing of it. We have problems here, Mr. O'Connor, but they're our problems."

"I'll keep that in mind."

He started to push himself up. Puck and his friend gave a hand.

"You want an escort back to the hotel?" Puck asked.

"I'll be fine, thanks."

Cork made his way across the parking lot, trying to walk upright so that the kids who watched him wouldn't see just how much he hurt.

CHAPTER 15

"Called you a *chimook*, huh?" Daniel English sipped his morning coffee at the breakfast table in the hotel and considered what Cork had told him about the attack the night before. *Chimook* was an unkind Ojibwe reference to white people. "Bad Bluff Shinnob, you think?"

"Or somebody who knows enough to sound Shinnob."

"Demetrius Verga?" Jenny asked. "He was married to an Anishinaabe woman. And from what you told us, he could be a man with a lot of skeletons in his closet."

"Whatever this guy used on me, he knew what he was doing."

"A cop?" English asked.

"Or a veteran maybe," Cork said.

"Or a sailor," Jenny threw in.

Cork looked at his watch. "We'd best get going. Got a long drive ahead of us."

Jenny said, "So we just forget about what happened to you last night?"

"I've got the bruises. I won't forget. But right now we have other business to attend to."

It was a little after first light when they headed off. A heavy mist had rolled in from the lake, and they drove to the Arceneaux home through a wet gray that obscured most of Bad Bluff. Louise was ready, sitting in her wheelchair near the front door. She'd brushed her hair and put on a little makeup. She wore a loose-fitting white blouse and jeans, the right pant leg folded under her stump and held in place with what looked like an embroidered elastic headband. A small overnight bag sat in her lap. She looked frightened.

Red Arceneaux wheeled her out to English's pickup and helped her in. He collapsed the wheelchair and laid it in the truck bed. He went back into the house and brought out a couple of old wooden crutches and a long khaki-colored canvas bag two feet in length that looked to Cork as if it might contain a rolled tent. These he laid in the pickup bed alongside the flattened wheelchair. He went back into the house and returned with another bag.

"Louise's insulin stuff," he explained to Cork. "Special carrying case. Keeps the medicine cooled."

He kissed his sister good-bye, told her not to worry about anything and that he'd take care of the kids. Then he shook hands all around and said, *"Migwech. Chi migwech."* When they drove away, he was still standing in the drive in the cluttered yard, a big, solid, hopeful man eaten, in less than a minute, by the shifting mist.

The thick mist hid sun and just about everything else. Daniel English, in the lead, went slowly. Cork and Jenny followed at a distance that was safe but not so great that they would lose sight of the pickup's taillights. The road was mostly empty. Cork kept an eye on his rearview mirror. In this pea soup, he didn't want a careless driver screaming up on him from behind and colliding with the rear end of his Explorer. A couple of miles outside of Bayfield, he noticed a pair of headlights, dim through the fog, keeping pace. It could just have been a cautious driver, but after Cork's encounter with the man in the shadow the night before, his radar was on high alert.

After several miles, he flashed his headlights at Daniel English and pulled to the side of the road. Behind him, the trailing vehicle did the same.

"What's up, Dad?" Jenny asked.

"Stay here." Cork got out.

English had stopped, too. He left his truck and walked back to the Explorer. "Anything wrong?"

Cork nodded toward the phantom vehicle behind them. "Being followed."

"Know who it is?"

"Fog's too thick."

"Should we find out?"

"Yeah, let's do that."

The two men began toward the headlights. As soon as they approached, the lights retreated. They stopped, and the lights held steady.

"Whoever it is, they don't care that we know about them," English said.

"Maybe they just want to make sure we're actually leaving town."

"I think we should ask," English said.

"I'm with you," Cork said. "Now."

Together, they broke into a run. The vehicle swung a quick one-eighty and headed back the way they'd all come.

"You get make or model?" Cork asked breathlessly when they finally stopped running.

English breathed hard and fast and said, "Too foggy."

As they stood on the gravel of the shoulder, staring in the direction the vehicle had gone, a pair of headlights broke through the gray curtain of mist and came straight at them. They leaped off the road into the drainage ditch, which, fortunately, was dry at the moment. The vehicle sped past and vanished back into the fog ahead of them.

They stood in the wild grass, looking where the vehicle had gone.

"Pickup truck," Cork said. "White. That's all I got."

"Same here," English said. "Think he'll be waiting up the road?"

"Only one way to find out. You carrying?"

"My service firearm. A Glock. It's in my truck."

"Maybe you should have it handy."

"Ten-four," English said.

They drove carefully, every pair of eyes in the vehicles scanning the gray murk ahead, behind, to the side. But whoever it was had apparently accomplished whatever they'd set out to do, and the rest of the drive to Superior was uneventful.

They stopped at a Perkins for breakfast. They didn't talk much. The pea-soup fog had not thinned, and they watched headlights on the highway creep out of the gray only to disappear again.

"Does he know I'm coming?" Louise asked.

"Henry? I haven't called, but I suspect he does. Henry has a way," Cork said.

"I met him once," Louise said. "I was just a kid, ten years old. My mama was sick, and the doctors couldn't seem to figure out what was wrong with her. She went to see him, and I went with her. He was old, I remember. He had white hair."

"He told me it's been that color since he was twenty," Cork said. "He fought a windigo, and the battle turned his hair white."

"A windigo?" Louise said. "That's just something out of stories."

"Many unbelievable stories have a basis in fact."

"You believe in windigos?" she asked.

In answer, Cork said, "Henry once told me that there are more things in the woods than a man can ever see with his eyes, more than he can ever hope to understand. So I'm willing to consider the possibility of almost anything. Also, I once heard a preacher say that the devil's best defense is a person's disbelief in his existence. So it's always seemed to me prudent to be ready for the worst of what you can imagine."

"The worst," Louise echoed, and her face puckered into worried creases.

"Did he help her?" Jenny asked.

Louise seemed confused for a moment, as if she'd lost the thread of the conversation. Then she understood. "Henry Meloux?" She looked at the gray outside and thought before she answered. "He told her he couldn't cure what was wrong with her. He told her no one could. But he did help. He taught her how to die. And when the time came, she wasn't afraid. It was hard to lose her, but I remember it as a good death."

They left Superior and crossed the Blatnik Bridge into Duluth, which was all fog and dim lights. It wasn't until they were out of the city that they finally saw blue sky. At Two Harbors, they turned due north up Highway 2, and Cork's heart gave a little kick of happiness to be heading toward Tamarack County and home.

They came into Aurora under a blazing noon sun and stopped at the house on Gooseberry Lane. Jenny seemed desperate to see her son. Little Waaboo didn't disappoint. He burst from the front door, bounded down the porch steps, and ran through the shadow of the front yard elm calling, "Mommy!"

Trixie was right behind him, and behind the dog came Rose, all of them moving as if in a race. "He saw you," Rose puffed, "and wild horses couldn't hold him back."

Jenny lifted him, and he wrapped his little arms around her neck and squeezed so hard Cork thought he might end up choking her. But she made no complaint. Waaboo pushed himself free, and Jenny put him down and he gave his grandfather the same welcome. Then he put his face a couple of inches from Cork's and said, "We fished."

"Did you catch a whale?"

"We saw a snake. In the water. I didn't know snakes could swim."

"Well, now you do, kiddo. Was it a scary snake?"

"Snakes aren't scary. Just wiggly."

Introductions were made. Jenny had called ahead, and Rose had lunch prepared and waiting on the patio in the backyard. English pushed Louise's wheelchair along the flagstones, and they gathered around the table in the shade of an umbrella and ate chicken salad sandwiches and potato chips and drank lemonade. Waaboo sat between his mother and his grandfather. He spent much of his time stealing the potato chips from Cork's plate and feeding them to Trixie under the table and pretending innocence.

Louise seemed subdued at first, but Rose could put anyone at ease. Soon the two were talking as if they'd known each other all their lives.

"Diabetes," Louise said. "They tell me I may lose my other leg, too."

"I'm so sorry." Rose put her hand over the other woman's.

"Do you want to know something?" Louise said to her.

"If you want to tell me."

"I sometimes pray and tell God he can have my other leg if he just gives me back my Mariah."

"You know what I think, Louise? I think God wouldn't ask that of you. And you know what I'm going to do? Until you find her, and I believe that you will, every hour that I'm awake, no matter what I'm doing, I'm going to say a prayer for you and your daughter. Every hour, that's a promise."

"Thank you," Louise said, and she began to cry.

"Why is she sad?" Waaboo asked his mother.

"Her little girl is lost."

Waaboo said, "Grandpa can find her."

And Cork thought that, in that regard, he could probably use a prayer every hour, too.

Jenny stayed at the house. Waaboo had missed her and wanted her, and she could not say no. Once again, Cork followed English, and they headed north out of Aurora to the gravel county road where the double-trunk birch marked the path to Crow Point. English prepared to lift the wheelchair from the bed of his pickup, but Louise stopped him.

"I'm going to walk," she said.

English glanced at Cork, his look full of surprise and question.

Cork said, "It's a couple of miles, Louise. And there are some pretty rough patches."

Louise turned herself on the seat toward the open cab door. She handed her overnight case to Cork and said to English, "Get my crutches, my insulin, and that tent bag Red tossed in back."

English did as she asked. He shouldered the insulin bag, propped the crutches against the side of the truck, and handed her the canvas tent bag. She undid the tie and drew out an object that made Cork stare in amazement.

It was a peg leg. A wooden peg leg. The wood was polished, fitted at the top with a kind of padded leather saddle and straps. Designs had been scrolled into the peg itself, so that, all in all, it was a lovely piece of woodwork.

"They wanted to give me a plastic leg at the hospital," Louise said. "I didn't want a plastic leg. So Red made this for me, carved it out of a piece of driftwood he found on the lakeshore. He said the spirit in it was good and strong." She strapped it on by herself and stood next to the truck. "Okay, I'm ready."

"What about the crutches?" English asked.

"Best bring them along, just in case."

"You don't have to do it this way, Louise," Cork said.

"Yeah, I do. When my mama came, she could barely hold herself up, but she walked all the way to that old man's cabin. She didn't have nothing to pay him with, but she figured if she did that, he couldn't say no to her."

"Henry doesn't expect payment," Cork said.

"No, but he expects me to be bringing something I don't have. I'm hoping this'll help. Let's go."

Walking alone, Cork could make the two miles to Meloux's cabin in half an hour. In the company of Louise Arceneaux, he took that long to go less than a quarter of the distance. The day was hot. The woman was heavy and worked hard. Sweat poured down her face and soaked her clothing. Her breath came in gasps, and Cork was worried about things like heatstroke or a heart attack. But Louise Arceneaux did not give up. She stopped often to rest, sitting on a fallen tree trunk or a big rock in the shade of a tree along the way. Cork wished he'd brought a water bottle, and chided himself for the stupid oversight, but he'd had no inkling that this would be the scenario he'd deal with on the way to Meloux's cabin. The path to Crow Point had always been such a simple walk for him, and he'd figured the hardest thing he and English would have to deal with was maneuvering the wheelchair across Wine Creek.

When, after nearly an hour and a half, they reached that clear, clean stream, Louise finally asked for help. Cork and English both gave her a hand as she knelt and splashed her flushed face, and then, before Cork could stop her, cupped her hands and drank. He was going to warn her about giardia, the pernicious parasite that might be found in untreated water of the North Country and that could result in disaster for a person's digestive tract. But given the circumstances and the revitalizing effect the cool water seemed to have on her, he held his tongue.

By the time they broke from the trees and Crow Point was revealed to them, the sun had dropped low in the sky. The shadows were growing long. Where meadow met forest, Louise Arceneaux paused, leaning on the crutches she'd been using for the past forty-five minutes. The light was the color of lemon peel, and the meadow was deep green, and the wildflowers were like colorful confetti caught in the tall grass. After the arduous walk from the double-trunk birch, even to Cork, who'd been there more times than he could remember, it looked like the land of Oz. Louise was clearly exhausted, but in the lemon light, her eyes burned incandescent with hope. She looked toward Meloux's cabin not more than two hundred yards distant, small and sturdy, and she said, nearly breathless, "I remember this."

As they walked the final distance through the meadow, Rainy came to meet them. She put her arms around Louise and said, "*Boozhoo*, cousin."

Louise leaned into her, and Cork was afraid the weight of the woman's body and weariness would tumble them both. But Rainy held her up and said, "He's expecting you."

That was enough. Louise walked on her own to the door of his cabin, where Henry Meloux stood waiting. The woman stopped short of him. They faced each other in a long silence.

Meloux finally said, "Did you bring it?"

Louise looked ready to collapse and cry. "I only brought me."

Meloux nodded, then he smiled and said gently, "Welcome, Niece."

CHAPTER 16

Meloux's sacred fire ring lay just beyond a rock outcropping on the west side of Crow Point. It was an area bared of ground cover by the tread of countless feet during countless gatherings. The aspen-lined shore of Iron Lake edged the area to the north and west. South was the meadow and east the rocks. The fire ring lay at the heart of it all, a circle of stones that held a bed of ash and char and that was circumscribed by sawed sections of tree trunk, which served as seating. That night Meloux sat near the fire, his lined face a ripple of reflected flame. Cork was there and Rainy and Daniel English. Louise Arceneaux, a woman who'd exhausted all her strength in the pilgrimage to Crow Point, was not. She was sound asleep in the bed in Rainy's cabin.

Cork appreciated that Meloux had not turned the woman away, even though she'd come empty-handed, without bringing to him Mariah's most precious possession. That bespoke the kindness of the old Mide. But it also puzzled Cork in a way, because Meloux, once he'd set down a requirement, insisted that it be followed, even if the point of it was a mystery to everyone except Meloux. Cork figured that Louise had been right: if Meloux saw what it took out of her to come to him, the old Mide couldn't refuse her.

They'd shared tobacco, all of them, in Meloux's pipe, and now they sat in a semicircle around the fire, while the embers drifted toward the night sky and were lost among the stars. Cork had related everything that took place on the Bayfield Peninsula, and the old man had listened without comment. Finally Cork said, "Louise believes that with your help, we'll find the answers."

"She has worked hard today," Meloux said. "Tomorrow, she will work hard in a different way."

"Will you guide her in a sweat?" Rainy asked.

"No, Niece. You will guide her."

"Me?" Just as quickly as it had come, the look of surprise on Rainy's face vanished. She nodded and said, "Of course."

"And you, Nephew," he said to English, "and you, Corcoran O'Connor, will see to the sacred fire and to the care of the Grand-fathers."

"What will you do, Henry?" Cork asked.

"Nothing," the old man said.

"Nothing?"

"I told you. If she wanted my help, she had to bring me her daughter's most sacred possession."

"But I thought—"

"Sometimes that is a real problem with you, Corcoran O'Con-nor. You think too much."

Cork couldn't help feeling disturbed by this sudden turn in what he'd thought was the positive direction events had taken. And then his cell phone rang, startling and further disturbing him because it was so late. When he checked the display he saw that it was Stephen calling from the Courage Center in the Twin Cities. He rose quickly and stepped away from the others.

"Stephen," he answered. "Is something wrong?"

"Didn't Marlee tell you I'd call?"

"She didn't say when. And it's late now. What's up?"

"I just got off the phone from a long talk with Jenny. She filled me in on your current undertaking."

"Oh, checking up on the old man, are you? Is Annie there with you?"

"She is."

"Say hello to your sister for me."

Cork heard his son do just that. Then he heard his daughter's voice, though he couldn't make out the words.

Stephen said, "She says give her best to Rainy."

"Of course. Marlee said you had news you wanted to share."

"I walked a half dozen steps today, on my own. No support."

Cork closed his eyes, as if he'd just received a blessing. He said, "Way to go, guy. I knew you'd do it."

"I'm feeling stronger and stronger every day. I think I'll be home before too much longer."

"I miss you, kiddo."

"I miss you, too, Dad. And everybody up there. And . . ."

Stephen's voice trailed off, and Cork thought maybe his cell service had dropped, as it sometimes did out on Crow Point. But he glanced at the display and still had two bars.

"Stephen? You there?" he said.

"Yeah, Dad. It's just that I've been having this feeling, and it's not a good one."

"Your legs?"

"No, nothing to do with that. I've been really fearful the last day or so, and I haven't known why. But since Jenny told me what you guys are up to, I think I understand. I think I'm picking up danger. And since I'm doing fine down here, I'm thinking it's you and Jenny I ought to be concerned about."

Seventeen-year-old Stephen was the O'Connor child in whom the family's Anishinaabe genetic heritage showed most strongly. Like Henry Meloux, with whom Stephen felt a strong kinship, he was gifted with visions. Long before the tragic event, he'd foreseen his mother's death. And in advance of his own violent encounter with a madman, which had left him with a damaged spinal cord, he'd seen the danger coming. Cork respected his son's sensitivity well enough not to dismiss Stephen's fear. And, too, the voice of the windigo was still fresh in his own mind. "Believe me, I'll be careful, Stephen, especially where your sister's involved."

"I hope you find her, the missing girl."

"I hope so, too."

"You'll keep me—us—in the loop?"

"Will do, guy."

"All right, then. Say *boozhoo* to Henry and Rainy for me."

"Give your sister a hug on my behalf. Night, buddy."

Cork ended the call and returned to the fire.

"How is Stephen?" Meloux asked.

"Walking, Henry. Walking on his own."

"You sound surprised, Corcoran O'Connor. Strong, that one." Meloux stood. "But this old man needs his sleep. Nephew?" He eyed English.

The young man got up from his seat. "I'm coming, Uncle Henry."

"Rest, Niece," Meloux said to Rainy. "And you, too, Corcoran O'Connor. Tomorrow is an important day."

The two men headed away from the fire. Guided by moonlight, they would walk the path that threaded between the rocks and led across the meadow to Meloux's cabin. There, English would spend the night on a mattress of straw laid out on the old man's floor. Because her own bed was already occupied, Rainy would spend the night with Cork on a blanket under the stars.

"What do you think he meant?" Cork asked.

"You mean about tomorrow being an important day?"

"No. I think he's right there. But he said to rest. What did he think we're going to do?"

"My guess," Rainy said, leaning toward him, "is this." She took his face in her hands and kissed him long and languidly. Then she stood and, with slow deliberation, began to unbutton her blouse.

They lay together, naked on the blanket in the meadow grass. Above them, the moon was a soft, watching eye in the star-dusted face of heaven. Crickets chirred around them, and from the aspens along the shore of Iron Lake came the trill of tree frogs. The scent of the night was a warm mix of the wildflowers and the distant evergreens and the vast, clean water of the lake. Rainy lay with her head on Cork's chest, her fingers idly tracing the line of one of his ribs.

"We deserted them, Cork," she said.

"Louise and Mariah?"

"The whole family. It was easiest for the rest of us not to think about them. They weren't like us. They were the kind of Ojibwe that seemed to prove the prejudices. Now I wonder if we were just afraid."

"Of what?"

"A kind of there-but-for-the-grace-of-God thing, you know." She was quiet a long time, staring up at the stars. "I want to help Louise. And I will, in my way, if she'll let me. I believe I can do that. I can't find Mariah, though. I don't know how. But you can."

"Find her? Or save her? Two different things, Rainy. It might already be too late to save her."

"But if she can be saved, you'll do that. I know you will."

Now it was Cork's turn for quiet and star-staring. Each one of those lights was a giant, he knew, but they all looked so tiny, and there was such a vast distance between them that all he could think of was their loneliness. He loved Rainy, longed for those moments when, after they'd made love, he felt so wonderfully close to her. They were often times when he was vulnerable and was willing to share with her things he might otherwise keep locked inside. But this night, despite all that Rainy had done to open his heart, there was a truth he couldn't tell her. And it was simply this: he was afraid.

If he'd spoken, he'd have talked about his failures. How he'd tried to save Jo—God how he'd tried to save his beloved wife from those bastards who killed her simply because of their greed—but he'd failed. And last year, when a crazed man had stalked his family, Cork had been able to do nothing to shield Stephen from the bullet that had lodged against his spine.

He'd agreed, reluctantly, to try to find Mariah Arceneaux. Only that. Not to save her. But that really was the whole point of what he was being asked to do. By Louise and Red Arceneaux. By Daniel English and Jenny. Now by Rainy. Save this child. As he lay beside Rainy, he wanted to confess that he was afraid. Afraid that, even if it were possible to save the girl, he wasn't the man for the job.

Instead, he said, "It's late. We should both get some sleep."

He rolled to his side and put his back to the woman he loved.

CHAPTER 17

Every spring, Cork and others from the Iron Lake Reservation helped Henry Meloux construct a sweat lodge. Until last winter, the site had always been on the east shoreline of Crow Point, about a hundred yards from Meloux's cabin. But after the madman's attack on Stephen, which had occurred during a sweat in that location, Meloux directed the lodge be constructed on the opposite side of the point, well north of the fire ring. It was round, ten feet in diameter and five feet high. It had been built of aspen boughs bound together with rawhide strips. This skeleton structure had been covered with blankets and tarps. There was a single opening, flapped with a blanket and facing east. Three feet directly in front of the lodge but a safe distance away was the pit for the sacred fire where the Grandfathers, the stones that would be used in the sweat, were heated.

Cork and Daniel English were up early that Wednesday morning building the fire and banking the coals upon which they would set the Grandfathers. Not far away, Meloux sat on the trunk of an aspen that had long ago fallen among the tall grass and wildflowers of the meadow. He watched and occasionally gave a word of direction, but for the most part, he stayed clear of the work. Cork wasn't certain if the issue was Meloux's age or the line that the old Mide had drawn and would not cross in this business with his great-niece Louise Arceneaux. Rainy spent the morning with Louise, preparing her for the ceremony, which was about cleansing and healing and asking and, if so blessed, receiving.

They came when the sun had completed a quarter of its arc. The day was cool for late July, but there seemed to Cork to be a promise in the morning air, a particular purity in the blue of the sky, a profound tranquillity that had settled over Crow Point. Meloux, from his seat on the fallen aspen, watched the women approach. His face was an old weathered rock fractured by time and the elements. His hair was the fluff of milkweed, long and soft and white. His eyes were darkness, absolutely unreadable.

Seeing the women come, Cork took up the old wood-handle pitchfork, which Meloux had always used for the Grandfathers, and scooped the first of the stones from the red coals. With the needles of a freshly cut pine branch, English swept the rock clean of ash and char. Cork bent and crawled into the sweat lodge and laid the first Grandfather in the shallow depression in the center. He backed out, and he and English repeated this process until there were ten large stones heating the air inside the lodge.

Louise wore a loose-fitting dress and a big white T-shirt. She sat on a sawed section of tree trunk near the fire, removed the sandal she wore on her left foot, and then unstrapped the peg from the stump on her right leg. Rainy, who wore a blue tank top and shorts, gave Louise the crutches she'd carried from the cabin. Louise stood and leaned on the crutches. From a small deerhide medicine bag, Rainy took sage and a little clay dish. She placed the sage in the dish and lit it and waved the cleansing smoke over Louise and herself as she said a prayer in Anishinaabemowin. When the smudging was complete, she let the sage ash fall to the earth and put the dish back into her medicine bag.

"You're ready," she said to the other woman.

Louise looked a little fearful but nodded and hobbled to the sweat lodge entrance, where she discarded her crutches. Rainy helped her down on hands and knees, and Louise disappeared inside. Without a word to the men, Rainy followed, with her medicine bag over her shoulder. Cork knew that among other things it contained tobacco, which Rainy would offer in advance of her prayers. Cork dropped the blanket flap over the opening behind them. Then he and English returned to tending the fire, where additional Grandfathers were heating. If all went well, there would be several rounds of sweat and prayer.

Meloux, who'd kept his distance, rose from the meadow and walked slowly to where Cork and English had perched themselves on sawed sections of tree trunk beside the sacred fire. He sat his old, bony butt on the ground near them and stared into the coals awhile.

"What is the question you want to ask, Corcoran O'Connor?" he finally said.

"I don't have a question, Henry."

The old man looked up at him calmly. "That's not what I have seen in your eyes since you came back from the Bad Bluff Reservation."

Cork glanced at English, who kept his own eyes averted, intent on the fire. If what transpired between the Mide and Cork was of any interest to him, he showed it not at all.

Cork said, "All right, Henry. Carrie Verga heard a windigo call her name. And now she's dead."

The old man waited.

"The boy who found her body, he also heard a windigo call his name."

"What did you do about that?"

"I told him to be courageous. And I told his father to watch him carefully. But I'm not sure that was enough, Henry."

"What more could you do, Corcoran O'Connor, except battle the windigo yourself?"

Cork said, "A windigo called my name, too, Henry."

Meloux sat with his back toward the risen sun, his face darkened by the overcast of his own shadow. For a long time, he studied Cork's face, his eyes unblinking.

"I think that is a good thing," the old man finally said.

"A good thing?" Cork didn't hide his surprise.

"The windigo is a terrible creature, but it is a stupid one. It is only concerned with feeding its hunger. Courage is needed, you are right there. But a quick mind, that is a good thing, too." The old man smiled slyly. "Sometimes, Corcoran O'Connor, you are as dumb as an old shoe, but I still think you are smarter than the windigo."

Daniel English laughed quietly. Meloux swung his gaze away from Cork. "And you, Nephew, you are a turtle chasing the moon."

"Me?" English looked completely baffled.

"She will not be in your sky forever."

"What are you talking about, Uncle Henry?"

The old man made a gesture of dismissal. "Just like a turtle. When you are afraid, you pull your head in."

Cork could see from the look on the young man's face that he had no clue what Meloux was referring to. Cork was pretty sure he knew, but he held his tongue. When dispensing advice, the old Mide often spoke in riddles. This riddle was English's to solve.

In half an hour, the first round of the sweat came to an end. Rainy lifted the blanket over the entrance and crawled out. Behind her came Louise Arceneaux. The clothing each wore was soaked with sweat, and their faces carried a high flush. Rainy took the crutches from where she'd laid them near the entrance and helped Louise stand. English gave them water from a metal bucket, and they drank in silence.

"Let's cool off now," Rainy said.

She and Louise walked together to the lake, where there was a little area of sand bordered by rocks. Louise waded in, crutches and all, and let herself slide completely under the surface of the cold, crystal water. Rainy dipped herself, too, but mostly she stood ready to help Louise, should the woman require it.

In the meantime, Cork removed the cooled Grandfathers from the sweat lodge and replaced them with stones fresh from the fire.

The women returned and once again entered the sweat lodge.

They'd endured four rounds when Rainy declared the sweat complete. Louise looked exhausted, even more worn out from the sweat than from the long walk to Crow Point the day before. Rainy helped her back to the cabin, while Cork and English did the work of cleaning the lodge and taking care of the Grandfathers so that everything would be in readiness for the next sweat that would be held there.

Meloux said, "My stomach is empty, and my curiosity is satisfied."

He stood and headed toward his own cabin. Cork and Daniel English followed.

Long ago, Meloux had constructed a larder beneath the floor of his cabin. He'd built the little box of maple, and even on the hottest summer day, the food he stored there was kept cool. He directed Cork to pull some ham and cheese from the larder, told English to get bread from the cupboard, and asked them both to make sandwiches. Then he left with a small embroidered bag over his arm. He came back in fifteen minutes bringing greens from the meadow for a salad. When all was ready, he directed Cork to fetch the women from Rainy's cabin.

Cork wasn't certain what, if anything, the sweat had accomplished. Louise had fasted before the ceremony, and she had to be hungry. But she chewed absently during the meal, as if not tasting the food at all. She looked ready to drop, so perhaps she was simply exhausted. Finally she put down the half-eaten sandwich, looked at them all intently, and began to cry. She wept deep sobs that shook all her loose flesh. Cork had no idea what to make of this. Rainy's face, as she looked on, was a perfect portrait of sympathy. For his part, Daniel English seemed clueless about what to do. Henry Meloux, the old Mide, simply watched, his brown eyes hard as walnut shells.

"What did you bring me, Niece?" he finally asked.

"I have nothing," she cried.

"That is not true. What did you bring me?"

"I thought and I thought and I couldn't think what it could be."

"And still you came." The old man's voice, which had been like the edge of a stone ax, grew soft and became gentle. "And you brought me something."

Two waterfalls of tears cascaded down the mounds of her

cheeks and pooled before her on the rough tabletop. Cork wasn't certain he'd ever seen a woman more desperate, more lost. And his heart broke for her.

"I . . ." she tried, then shook her head angrily because she couldn't finish.

"You know what you brought me," Meloux coaxed.

"I . . . didn't . . ." Between her sobs, she gasped for air.

"In your heart, you brought me something."

She looked long and deeply into the eyes of the old Mide. She gathered her breath and said, "Only me. That's all I have. Only me, and that I love my Mariah."

The old man reached across the table. His hands were brown and bony and spotted, and they held the hands of Louise Arceneaux as if cradling a newborn child. "In her heart, Niece, when she looks there, she knows this is what matters. You and your love for her. That is what is most precious." He drew himself up, erect and strong, and in a voice as young and powerful as Cork had ever heard, Henry Meloux said, "Now, we will find your daughter."

CHAPTER 18

Once the wolf of fear inside her was gone, Louise Arceneaux told them everything, the whole truth of the boats and the sailors and the humiliations and the abuse.

"We all did it," she said. "Me, Lindy Duvall, Carrie's mom. Others I could name. Our mothers did it, too. Even some of our grandmothers when they were kids. And it wasn't just us. I met girls from other reservations. None of us had money. Nobody would give us jobs. We didn't have casinos back then. Working the boats down in Duluth, we made enough that we could send money home. For a lot of girls, what those sailors did wasn't any worse than what had already been done to us by other men, even some in our families. And the sailors, they paid us for it."

"Did Mariah know this?" Rainy asked.

Louise shook her head. "I never told nobody till now. It was shameful stuff. And I wanted it to be different for my girl."

"Will you tell us how it happened for you, Louise?" Cork said.

The day was hot, but a breeze came off the lake, blew in through the windows of Meloux's small cabin, and exited through the open door. Louise sat with her back to one of the windows, her face silhouetted against the sunlit aspens of the lakeshore. She drank cool water and, despite the awful things she related, seemed calmer than Cork had seen her since his association with her had first begun.

"My dad was a drunk," she said. "Couldn't keep a job. Beat my mom pretty regular. And Red. Dad was merciless with Red. My brother got out of there as soon as he could, ran away young. I didn't blame him. My dad started in on me, you know, molesting me, when I was nine or ten. When I was twelve, he gave me over to a cousin who handled girls on the boats in Duluth. I did that work till I was fifteen, sixteen. Got pregnant then and went back to Bad Bluff. That baby, I lost. I was wild in those days, drinking, doing drugs. I took up with anybody who'd take care of me. Some pretty lousy men, let me tell you. No idea, really, who Toby's father is, and only a guess at Mariah's. Had 'em both taken away by social services when they were real little. That woke me up. I got sober. Had help with that from Oscar. That's Cal and Denny's dad. He's got problems of his own, but he was real good about helping me get off the booze. He's in prison, sure, but there are men in there lots worse than him.

"For a long time, I worked at a hotel in Bayfield, cleaning rooms. Pretty tough cuz I been diabetic for years. Lots of trouble with my feet. They finally had to take my leg. It's been real rough since then. Red's been a big help, 'specially with the boys. I've tried real hard to be a good mom, to keep my kids from all the crap that screwed me up. But I see the gang Toby hangs out with, a bad bunch, and now Mariah's gone. I feel like I failed 'em all."

She'd cried herself out earlier, and she told this sad history without tears.

"Are you thinking that maybe Mariah and Carrie ended up working the boats in Duluth?" Cork asked.

"If they went off with Raven Duvall, I'd bet on it."

"Why?"

"Lindy tells everybody that Raven's got a job as a model. My ass. I never saw one picture of her in any magazine. She was my daughter and she really was a model, I'd give out those magazines to everybody. Raven? She went off with a relative, some cousin, years ago. Now when she comes back, she comes back wearing nice clothes and driving a nice car. The only way I ever knew for an Indian girl to get that kind of money is spending all your time on your back. She's seventeen, eighteen now. That's old to be working the boats. You ask me, I'd say she's hooked up with somebody who handles girls, and maybe part of her job is making friends with kids like Carrie and Mariah, getting them into the business."

"Why didn't you tell anyone this when she disappeared?" Rainy asked.

"I couldn't be sure. And I'd have to tell the truth about me. I kept hoping I was wrong and that Mariah'd show up one day, just come back home. Then Carrie washed up on Windigo Island. You know, when I worked the boats, I heard stories of girls getting so beat up and so mistreated by those sailors that they jumped overboard. Gave themselves up to that big lake. I got so scared, I knew I had to do something. That's when I asked my family for help."

She looked gratefully at Rainy and Daniel English and Henry Meloux.

"When you worked the boats, Louise, how was that done?" Cork said. "I mean, did you have somebody who arranged it for you?"

"Yeah. Back then there was this Fond du Lac Shinnob. His name was Smiley. Easy to see why. Big-toothed grin all the time, and all the time he was figuring how to screw you. He got us the jobs on the boats and took most of what we made. But he also got us rooms to live in and made sure we didn't starve. And somehow, he was able to keep the cops off our backs. That's part of what we were paying for, I suppose."

"Think he's still around?"

Louise looked doubtful. "That was years ago. Probably everything's different now. For all I know, they set things up through the Internet."

"Do you have any cop connections in Duluth?" Rainy asked Cork.

"Nobody in vice, but with somebody like Smiley, maybe all the cops know him. I'll see what I can find out. But it seems to me, our best lead is Lindy Duvall. I'm thinking she probably knows how to contact Raven."

"She wasn't helpful the first time we talked to her," Daniel English said. "Why would she help us now?"

Cork turned to Meloux. "Would you be willing to go with us, Henry?"

The old man looked wistful. "It has been years since I was on a good hunt. I would like to be a part of this one, Corcoran O'Connor. And who knows what it is that we track? Maybe the windigo itself."

Rainy and Louise Arceneaux stayed on at Crow Point, while Cork and English headed into Aurora. English dropped Cork at the house on Gooseberry Lane.

"Coming in?" Cork asked.

English shook his head. "Things to do. I've got to get Aunt Louise's insulin prescription refilled, and get this cooler cooled." He held the bag.

Cork got out of the pickup and leaned through the open window on the passenger side. "You'll be going back to Crow Point this afternoon then?"

"Yes."

"Your cell phone works out there?"

"I checked it, and yeah, it does."

"Give me a call tonight. We'll make a plan for tomorrow morning. I think we ought to head off early for Bad Bluff."

"Suits me," English said.

The big Shinnob looked toward the house. It seemed to Cork that the man's eyes lingered longer than a mere glance of curiosity would merit. And Meloux's words came back to him: *You are a turtle chasing the moon.* At last, English pulled away.

Jenny met Cork at the front door. She craned her neck to look down the street where English's truck had gone. "He didn't want to come in?"

Cork shook his head. "Things to do, he says."

She gave a shrug, as if it mattered to her not at all, but Cork had a feeling that wasn't exactly true.

He walked past her into the house. "Where's my grandson?"

"He's with Aunt Rose. They took Trixie for a walk. So? What happened with Henry and Louise?"

Cork sniffed the air. "Is that coffee I smell?"

"I just brewed a pot."

"Pour me a cup, and I promise to tell you everything."

In the kitchen, Jenny's laptop sat open on the table. Cork figured that in the few minutes she had while Waaboo was gone she'd been working on her manuscript. "How's it going?" he asked.

"It goes," Jenny said. And she closed the computer.

She poured them both coffee. They sat at the table, and Cork kept his promise. His daughter listened, her eyes burning with anger, her mouth drawn into a thin, bloodless line.

"Children," she said. "They prey on children. God, I'd love to get my hands on those sons of bitches."

"At the moment, we're focused on one thing: finding Mariah Arceneaux. The larger picture will have to wait."

"And do you know how to do that? Find Mariah?"

"I think I know where to begin. We're going back to Bad Bluff and talk to Lindy Duvall."

"She wouldn't talk to you before. What are you going to do differently?"

"Me?" Cork crossed his arms and sat back. "I'm just going to watch and listen."

"I don't understand."

"One thing I didn't tell you. Henry's signed on to this investigation."

"Henry? Dad, he's—well, who knows how old? He's really going to do this?"

"Try to keep him from it."

"It might kill him."

"I don't think that'll happen. He's a tough old goat. And he was a great hunter once. Probably still is."

"So, back to the Bayfield Peninsula? All of us?"

"If I told you not to come, would you listen to me?"

"Absolutely not."

"Then all of us," Cork said. "For now anyway."

He made some calls that afternoon, connecting with officers in Duluth PD whom he'd come to know while he wore the uniform of the Tamarack County Sheriff's Office. He got nowhere. Not only did no one recollect an Indian named Smiley but they were less than forthcoming whenever Cork approached the subject of the boats in the harbor and the possibility of sex trafficking there. In a way, it reminded him of the blindness of Captain Bigboy on the Bad Bluff rez.

That evening after dinner, he wrestled with his grandson on the living room floor. Waaboo got the best of him. Waaboo always got the best of him. When bedtime came, the little guy begged for his grandfather to put him down. Jenny got her son into his pajamas and his teeth brushed, and Cork took it from there. In Waaboo's room, he sat on the rocker with his grandson on his lap and read from a collection of fairy tales. Snow White and the Seven Dwarfs. The Three Billy Goats Gruff. Little Red Riding Hood. Waaboo nodded, nodded, and then was asleep. Cork carried him to bed, tucked him in, and kissed his forehead. Then he stood awhile, watching the sleeping child, the gentle rise and fall of Waaboo's chest, the flutter of his eyelids as he dreamed. And in his heart, Cork wanted every child everywhere to be this safe in sleep. He wanted the terrors of the world to be nothing more than fairy tales, the terrible creatures—the witches and wolves and windigos—nothing more than make-believe. But that was what growing up was all about. Understanding that there were monsters out there and that every story didn't end happily ever after.

Though one had, for the O'Connors. It was the story in which the little rabbit Waaboozoons was saved by Jenny. Like many stories, it began with a storm, freakish and terrible, that had ravaged a good deal of the beautiful wilderness in northern Minnesota and left Cork and his daughter stranded on a remote island. First they'd discovered the body of a young woman, little more than a girl, who'd been murdered. Then, hidden among all the debris, they'd found the baby she'd died trying to protect. When the people who killed the girl returned to the island, hoping this time to find and murder the child, Jenny and Cork had risked their own lives to thwart that dark purpose. Jenny had been a tiger, defending the baby as fiercely as if it had been her own. Cork had marveled at his daughter's resourcefulness and determination. And then he'd seen the fairy-tale ending happen. The evil had been destroyed, and the child had become Jenny's own.

He called Daniel English on Crow Point and discussed the plan for the next day. Then he found Rose and Jenny and Trixie on the front porch. The two women drank herbal tea that smelled of cinnamon and clove. The dog chewed on a rawhide bone. Above them, the sky held a pale purple light, the last of the day. The streetlamps had come on, and Gooseberry Lane was lit in circles with stretches of darkness between them.

Rose said to no one in particular, "I try not to feel hate, but when I hear about men who prey on children, it's a trial." Then she said, "What do you do tomorrow?"

"We leave early," Cork told her. "Daniel will swing by with Louise and Henry around five, and we'll drive back to Bad Bluff."

Rose said, "Are you going, Jenny?"

"Would you be okay watching Waaboo another day, Aunt Rose?"

"Or so," Cork added. "We don't know how long this might take."

Rose laughed. "Please don't throw me in the briar patch." She grew serious again. "Do you have any idea what's going on?"

Cork didn't answer immediately. Cicadas had begun to buzz in the trees, a long chorus that rose and fell, and though it was a natural sound of the summer, it put Cork in mind of the windigo, of that unsettling call that had come to him from across the lake in Bad Bluff.

He said, "I've been thinking about Carrie Verga."

Jenny said, "What about her?"

"If Raven Duvall took her and Mariah away from Bad Bluff, and if they were working the boats in Duluth, how did she end up on Windigo Island?"

Neither of the women offered an explanation.

Cork went on. "I've also been thinking about what Puck Arceneaux said, that people on boats often throw what they don't want into the lake."

"You're saying someone just threw her away?" Rose asked.

"According to the medical examiner's report, she was alive when she went into the water. And one of the things Louise told me was that girls who went on the boats didn't always come back. So I'm wondering if it's possible Carrie Verga was trafficked out to a crew who mistreated her and she jumped. Or maybe they just got rid of her, tossed her overboard thinking Lake Superior would hide what they'd done. If it happened that way, it had to be after they left the harbor and while they were passing the Apostle Islands."

Jenny said, "Wouldn't her body have sunk? I mean, it's Lake Superior, Dad."

"Despite Kitchigami's reputation, the bodies of men lost in shipwrecks have occasionally washed ashore, especially if there have been storms churning up the water. I'm not saying this is what happened, but it's something that might go a long way to explaining the unexplainable."

"So you're not looking at Demetrius Verga any longer?"

"I'm not closing any doors yet, Jenny. There's something dirty about that guy, but I haven't nailed down how he fits into any of this, if he does."

Trixie got up, trotted to Cork, sat on her haunches, and looked up at him.

"Once around the block," he said to her. "Then it's bedtime for both of us."

Rose excused herself, said good night, and headed to her room. Cork got Trixie's leash from the kitchen, and a little plastic baggie to clean up her litter. When he returned to the porch, Jenny was standing alone at the railing, staring up at the stars.

"You should get some sleep," he said. "I'm guessing tomorrow will be a long day."

She didn't move, didn't take her eyes off the stars.

"I'm a writer," she said. "Or I like to think of myself that way. A storyteller." She gave a deep sigh. "I want to write about the world as I think it ought to be. If I were writing Mariah's story, we'd find her in the end. She'd be alive, and we'd save her."

"What makes you think we won't?"

"Because more and more, I see the world as it is. And what's bad about it is worse than anything anyone could imagine."

She was right, but not completely so. Cork knew that hopelessness was not the answer. He dug deep inside himself, ignored the voice of reason that was part of what fed his own fear. "Know what Henry would say to that?"

"What?"

"The good things balance the bad, because there's also more good than any of us can imagine. And you want to know something else?"

"You'll tell me anyway, so go ahead."

"You're one of the very good things."

He kissed her forehead lightly. Then he said to Trixie, "Come on, girl. Let's get this business behind us."

CHAPTER 19

They pulled into Bad Bluff a few minutes after nine the next morning. Daniel English offered to drop Louise at her house so that she could see her boys and Red, but she wanted to be with Henry Meloux and Cork when they confronted Lindy Duvall. They parked on the street in front of the duplex they'd visited three days earlier. Jenny and English stayed in their vehicles. Louise walked with Cork and Meloux to the door, and it was she who knocked. Lindy Duvall answered, wearing gray sweats, no makeup, her hair an unbrushed tangle. Her face registered surprise.

"Louise." Her eyes locked on Cork. "You again." Then wordlessly she took in Meloux.

"Anin, noozhis," the old man said gently. Hello, my grandchild.

From the room behind her came the sound of a television, which, judging from the outlandish sound effects, was tuned to cartoons.

"We need to talk," Louise said.

Duvall shook her head. "Not a good time."

"My daughter's in trouble, Lindy. And your daughter's why. We need to talk."

"I'm not talking to anybody." Duvall tried to close the door.

Cork didn't let that happen. He put himself in the threshold, his body an unyielding doorstop. Duvall stepped back.

Meloux spoke. "Granddaughter, it is a sad thing when The

People turn their backs on one another. It is a hard world, and alone there is only fear in us. Give me your hand, child."

The old man reached out. The woman was clearly afraid. Of the man whose body kept her from closing her door. Of Louise Arceneaux with her ornate peg leg and the truth of what she knew about the pasts of them both. Of whatever it was hidden in her own heart. But clearly she was not afraid of the ancient Mide. Maybe because of his age. Or his size, small now, whittled away by time. Or his eyes, as soft as brown pillows. Or his voice, which promised understanding and acceptance and safety. She did as he asked, took his hand, and let them all inside.

Wade, the boy Cork had met on his first visit to the house, was in the living room, in front of the big, flat-screen television, watching Japanese anime and eating cereal from a bowl. His little sister, Shannon, was asleep in the playpen in the corner. The boy looked at them, and Cork could see that he was more curious than afraid.

"Lindy, could we go somewhere private to talk?" he asked.

"This is as far as you get in my house."

"Granddaughter," Meloux said. "We will not harm you. But what we want to talk about is not for the ears of children."

"What do you want to know?"

"About Duluth and the boats and Raven," Louise said.

"I don't know anything."

"What is your fear?" the old man asked.

"I'm not afraid."

"We are all afraid. Louise Arceneaux is afraid for the daughter she loves. Corcoran O'Connor fears that he will fail the people who have put their faith in him."

Which surprised Cork, though he knew it to be absolutely true.

"What about you?" Duvall asked. "What are you afraid of?"

"That I will not die a good death."

When Cork heard the old man say this, he knew it was a truth, one he wanted to think about, but now was not the time.

"Let us go somewhere and speak truth to one another. It may save the life of your daughter, too."

Lindy Duvall teetered, uncertain.

Then the old man said with great humility, "This I beg of you, granddaughter."

She breathed out deeply, as if expelling something foul, and she turned.

They followed her down a hallway to her bedroom. The bed was unmade. A pile of clothing lay in one corner, awaiting washing, Cork supposed. The walls were bare except for a big dream catcher above the bed and a photograph, cheaply framed, on the west wall. It was of Lindy Duvall with two children. The younger child was clearly Wade when he must have been about five. The older of the children was maybe twelve. She had long black hair and deep brown eyes and the lovely bone structure of the Ojibwe. The smile on her face looked as if it had been coerced. Behind them lay the blue of the lake and the sky and the green of one of the Apostle Islands.

"She is in danger," the old man said without preface.

"Mariah?" Duvall asked.

"Raven," the old man said. "You know this, and this is your fear."

"She's fine," Duvall insisted.

"How can you battle a wolf if you turn your back on it, grand-daughter? It will eat you for sure."

"I don't . . ." she began. "Raven's . . ." But under the steady gaze of the old Mide, she couldn't continue with whatever lies she was telling herself and was about to tell them.

"She's working the boats in the harbor, isn't she, Lindy?" Louise said. There was no accusation in it, just a statement of a sad truth.

"I don't know about the boats," Duvall said. Her strength seemed to desert her, and she sat down heavily on the bed.

Louise hobbled to her and sat beside her on the mattress. "She came and took Mariah and Carrie Verga. Is that what she does now? She brings in the young ones?"

"I don't know. I don't ask."

Louise took the other woman's hand. "Remember what it was like, Lindy?"

Duvall nodded.

"We never wanted that for our girls."

Duvall dropped her head as if ashamed of the tears that had begun to fall. She said in a small voice, "She tells me they're her family now."

"They?" Cork said.

"Men. I don't know who."

"How did she meet them? Do you know?"

"Her father."

"Your husband?" Cork asked.

"We never got married. He was an A-number-one asshole. Never cared about me. About us. Gambling and drinking, those were his loves. He got into trouble with some people. Owed them a lot of money. They threatened to hurt us all. One day I came home from working the casino—I cashier there. He was supposed to be watching the kids. Raven wasn't here. He said not to worry about her. He said the debts were all cleared up, and we didn't have to worry about that either. I screamed and called him a liar and plenty of other things. He laid into me good, beat me so I could barely move. He told me if I said anything to anyone, he'd beat me again, kill me the next time. Maybe Wade, too. I didn't know what to do. I didn't have no one to go to."

"Is he still here, in Bad Bluff?"

"No. He left real soon after that. I don't know where he is. I don't care."

"You've been in touch with Raven?"

"She finally called me, a little over a year ago. Said she was fine, not to worry. Had friends. Was working. Modeling, she told me. I asked her where she was. She said Duluth. Wouldn't tell me any more. Said she was thinking of coming home for a visit."

"And so she came," Cork said.

Duvall nodded. "But she was different. Grown up. Dressed

real good. Drove this nice car. And she wasn't even seventeen. Me, I was wearing things I got from the church thrift store. She was good, real loving to Wade, but she was real hard on me. Like I done something to her. I asked her about this family of hers. She said there were these guys who cared about her, took care of her. And she had sisters there. Wouldn't say nothing else. Spent most of her time with younger girls on the rez. They were all googly-eyed cuz of how she dressed and her car and all. Then she was gone. Not a word to me. And I haven't heard from her since. But she said one thing that scared me."

"What was that?"

"I told her I wanted to come down to Duluth sometime, visit her and this family of hers. She got real freaked. She told me I shouldn't ever do that. She said if I did we were both dead. That's why when you came asking about her, I didn't want to say nothing. I mean, there was Carrie Verga dead. I didn't want nothing like that to happen to my girl."

"Did she say anything to you about taking Carrie and Mariah with her?"

"She didn't say nothing to me about nothing. She just up and left. Then I heard that Mariah was gone and later that Carrie Verga was gone, too. I knew they both spent a bunch of time with Raven when she was here. I put two and two together, but what could I say? I'm sorry, Louise. I just kept thinking about what she said. Don't come looking for her or she's dead. I kept hoping I'd hear from her again. Maybe she'd tell me they were all right, her and the girls. I didn't want nobody hurting them."

"She hasn't called you since?"

"No. But she sends me money sometimes. She says it's cuz of Wade."

"How does the money come?" Cork asked.

"Money order in the mail."

"Any return address?"

"No."

"Do you have a photograph of Raven? Anything recent?"

She nodded. "I took a few pictures when she was here."

"Could I have one?"

The fear was in her eyes again. "What for?"

"We want to find her, Lindy."

"See, that's exactly what I was afraid of."

"Granddaughter," Meloux said gently. He walked to where she and Louise sat together on the bed, and he took the frightened woman's hands in his own. "I am an old man. I have seen much evil in this world. And what I know about evil is that it has no heart and its hunger is great. Sooner or later, because of this hunger and because it loves nothing, it will eat your child. We will try to find her before this happens. We need your help. Your child needs your help."

She was crying, her deep fear leaking out of her in a stream of tears. "You can do this?"

"I will try."

The distraught woman bowed her head. The old man didn't release his hold on her hands. Cork saw her chest rise and fall, and her body changed. Relaxed. She lifted her face and looked into the eyes of Meloux and said, "All right."

She stood, went to an old, beat-up dresser, and opened the top drawer. She pulled out a photograph and held it toward Cork. Before she gave it over, she said one final desperate word to him, to them all.

"Please."

CHAPTER 20

English drove Louise to see her children and her brother, Red, but Meloux asked a favor of Cork that would take them in another direction.

"Before we leave, I would like to visit this Windigo Island, Corcoran O'Connor."

"Why, Henry?"

"A place that calls the windigo to it, now that would be something to see."

"I don't think we have time."

"There is a reason the spirits of Kitchigami delivered the body of the girl to that place. I would like to understand the reason."

Cork knew it was pointless to argue with the old man. In the end, Meloux would have his way. "Let's rent a boat then, and get this over with."

At the marina in Bad Bluff, they hired out a small Lund with an inboard motor. Windigo Island was less than a quarter mile into the West Channel, due east of the reservation town. Basswood Island, vast in comparison, lay beyond it, a long shoreline of dense wood rising dark green against the azure sky. As Cork headed the little rented craft onto the water, a sleek sailboat slid past Windigo Island, its white sails cupping the wind, and Cork thought about Demetrius Verga, wondering how often the man had guided his own sailboat past that solitary landmark. Was he one of those who routinely threw unwanted things over the side?

"Bone," the old man said.

"What was that, Henry?" Jenny asked.

Meloux squinted against the bright sun and the blinding reflection off the water. "It is an island of bone."

Cork could see what the old man meant. By any standard, it was a tiny island, all rock broken into pieces by millennia of relentless pounding from the legendary storms that surged across Kitchigami. The rock was the gray of old bone. The only sign of life was the tall, ragged pine tree that rose from the island's center. It wasn't a healthy looking piece of timber, but somehow it had managed to put down roots in all that stone, and had held itself there long enough to have grown to a height of sixty or seventy feet. In its singleness and its unlikely existence on such unwelcoming ground, it stood out magnificently. And given that it rose up from what Meloux himself had seen as nothing but bone, Cork could understand why the Anishinaabeg of Bad Bluff thought of it as a beacon for evil.

As they approached, Cork spotted the message spray-painted on the flat face of a great rock: KYLE B + LORI D. He smiled, thinking, *The things we do for love.*

He slowly circled the island, and no one spoke.

Then Jenny said, "What's that?"

Cork saw it, too, a white donut wedged among rocks at the waterline. He carefully nosed the boat very near the rocks, spun the wheel, and brought them gently broadside, close enough that Jenny could jump ashore. She worked her way across boulders and broken stones, nabbed the item, and climbed back aboard.

It was a life ring, and there was a name on it: *Montcalm.*

"What do you think?" Jenny said.

"I don't know," Cork replied.

"Junk?"

"Maybe."

"Or maybe Carrie Verga thought it would save her."

"Maybe," Cork said. "But she wasn't wearing it when she hit Windigo Island. The cops would have taken it as evidence. I'm guessing it washed up afterward. Have you seen enough, Henry?"

The old man said, *"Mudjimushkeeki."*

Which Cork knew meant a place of sickness, of evil.

Then the old man said, "I am ready."

They motored back to the marina. When they pulled up to the dock, the kid who'd rented them the boat wasn't alone.

Cork said, "Morning, Captain Bigboy."

"Heard you were back in town, O'Connor." The cop stood watching as, one by one, they disembarked. "Morning, folks," he said to the others. His tone was business. "You know, we have a lot more picturesque scenery than the little island out there."

"I wanted to see it," Meloux said.

"Yeah? And why was that, old-timer?"

The Mide didn't flinch at the patronizing tone or the disrespectful appellation. He said, "It is a powerful place and fearful. But you know that."

Bigboy tried to match the stone in the old man's gaze, but he finally looked away, and his eyes settled with undisguised curiosity on the life ring Jenny held. "I'll take that."

Jenny made no move to comply. "We picked it up on the island," she said. "You think it could be evidence?"

"Doubt it. Things wash up on these shores all the time."

"Then you won't mind if I hang on to it."

"I mind. Like you said, could be evidence. Better safe than sorry."

Jenny still held on to the life ring. "You'll make sure it gets to the Bayfield County sheriff's people?"

"It'll get to the right people."

Cork said, "We'll check with Hammer, the detective down in Washburn, tomorrow and see what he thinks. Any objection?"

"Free country, cousin. You make all the calls you want."

Jenny glanced at her father. Cork gave a brief nod, and she handed over the ring.

"Something I didn't ask you the other day," Cork said, then added, "cousin. How many other girls have gone missing from the rez?"

Bigboy held the life ring in the crook of his arm. "Like I told you. Kids here run away. They usually come back. I don't keep track of every kid who decides to make it permanent."

"One more question," Cork said. "You like barbecued potato chips?"

"Is that a joke of some kind, O'Connor? Because I'm not getting the punch line."

"Forget it," Cork said.

The cop put a finger to the bill of his cap. "You folks be careful going back. We get some pretty mean fog here on occasion. Can swallow you like the whale did Jonah. I'd hate to lose you."

"Thanks," Cork said. "We'll keep that in mind."

Bigboy walked back to his cruiser, a black-and-white with the Bad Bluff insignia on the door. He threw the life ring in the backseat, got behind the wheel, gave them one more long look, then drove away.

"Why the question about barbecued potato chips, Dad?" Jenny asked.

"The guy who worked me over in the casino parking lot, his breath reeked of them."

"Bigboy, you think?"

"He's not the most welcoming cop I ever met. Could be a reason for it that has nothing to do with his less than sterling personality."

"Do you think he's involved in all this?"

"If not this, maybe something else no better, Jenny." Cork turned to Meloux. "Did you get all you wanted, Henry?"

"*Mudjimushkeeki*," the old man said, staring at Windigo Island. "A black mole on the face of all this beauty. I have seen more than enough, Corcoran O'Connor. It is time to go."

They drove to the home of Louise Arceneaux. She, her brother, and Daniel English were gathered around the dining table. It seemed to Cork that some progress had been made in cleaning the clutter from the house, but the place was still a masterpiece of disorder. In their bedroom, the two young boys, Cal and Denny, were already hard at their video games. The door to the room that Toby shared with Puck was closed. Cork introduced Meloux and Red to each other, then filled the Arceneauxs in on what they'd found on Windigo Island, and what he suspected as a result.

"You really believe that life ring is somehow proof that Carrie Verga jumped off a freighter, or was thrown off?" English asked.

"I know it sounds like an unbelievable coincidence," Cork replied. "And I'm the first to say I don't believe in coincidence."

"Why do you call it coincidence, Corcoran O'Connor?" Meloux asked.

"The only thing that makes sense to me, Henry, is that Carrie Verga went off a boat called *Montcalm* with a life ring, maybe hoping it would help her get to safety. Or, maybe she went over the side and someone threw it to her. In any event, the same current that brought her to Windigo Island must have brought that life ring. It's a stretch, but it's the only way I can account for them both ending up there."

"Corcoran O'Connor," the old man said with great disappointment, "do you not believe in *majimanidoog*?" Meloux used an Ojibwe word that meant evil spirits, or more loosely, devils.

"I'm willing to believe in almost anything, Henry."

"Then why not believe that place calls evil and the product of evil to itself?"

"The *majimanidoog*, the evil spirits? They had a hand in this?"

"Is that harder to believe than coincidence?"

Cork laughed. "I don't suppose so, Henry."

Red Arceneaux said, "You think Bigboy might be involved?"

"I have a feeling he's got things to hide, Red."

Louise said, "If he had anything to do with Mariah being gone, I'll kill him."

"That might not be what he's hiding, Louise," Cork said. "Let's figure this out before we challenge any guy wearing a badge."

"So what now, Dad?" Jenny asked.

"I think we should go to Duluth. I'm pretty convinced that's where Raven Duvall took the girls. And while we're there, we can check out this ship *Montcalm*."

"All of us?" English glanced at Meloux, who already looked weary.

"You up for this, Henry?" Cork said.

"To the end," the ancient Mide replied, then added with a broad grin, "Even if that end is my own."

"I'm not going to let that happen, Henry."

The old man weighed Cork's words. "You made that promise to me once when you were a boy. Do you remember?"

"No."

"We were hunting medicine herbs, you and me. A storm came on us suddenly, a very bad storm. The lightning was all around us, and the thunder hurt our ears. You told me not to be afraid. You told me that you would let nothing harm me. Do you remember what happened?"

"No, Henry."

"I found a cave to shelter us both." The old man wryly cocked one feathery white eyebrow. "In this trouble now, I wonder who will save who."

CHAPTER 21

Duluth, Minnesota, has been called the Emerald City, the Zenith City, the Gem of the Freshwater Sea. It's the world's largest inland port, at one time surpassing even New York City in the oceangoing tonnage it handled. Built on hills that rise steeply out of the vast, cold water of Lake Superior, it's a beautiful city in a beautiful setting, but its history is a harsh lesson in the reality of cultural friction.

The early inhabitants—the Gros Ventre, Menominee, Fox, and Dakota—were driven out by the Anishinaabeg, who found the area rich in resources, including an abundance of fur-bearing animals. The Anishinaabeg, in turn, were overwhelmed by the flood of whites, who were drawn to the area by all the economic possibilities there—the timber of the forests, the fur of the animals, the fish of the lake, the minerals of the earth. When the canal at Sault Sainte Marie opened the Great Lakes to the Atlantic Ocean and railroads opened the way to the Pacific, Duluth's geographic position and its enormous natural harbor made it an ideal transportation center. Vast fortunes were made, and by the turn of the century, Duluth was home to more millionaires per capita than any other city in the country. With every new enterprise, there arrived a multicultural work force to supply the labor—French, Scandinavians, Finns, Italians, Poles, Irish, African Americans. And with all this unwieldy mix, there came the inevitable clash of culture. In 1918 a group calling itself Knights of Loyalty hauled Olli Kiukkonen, a Finnish immigrant, from his room in a boardinghouse, tarred and feathered and then lynched him, this as a warning to those who, in the opinion of the Knights, were not American enough in their patriotism. Two years later, three black men accused of raping a white woman were dragged from their jail cells by an angry mob, beaten, and lynched from a lamppost in the center of the downtown.

Cork O'Connor knew about these things. But death and degradation unremarked upon had been occurring on a regular basis in Duluth from the beginning. In this part of the Emerald City's tarnished history, Cork and those with him were about to get a thorough education.

They passed over the Duluth–Superior harbor on the Blatnik Bridge. Spread below them along the harbor shoreline were rows of tall grain elevators and squat regiments of storage tanks and the hulking latticework of the iron ore loaders, and alongside these structures were the long fingers of the docks. Many of the docks lay empty, and Cork wondered if this was normal or simply the way it was in these days of economic uncertainty. They stopped for lunch at Grandma's, a local landmark eatery. Grandma's stood beside the shipping canal, which was a man-made passage between Lake Superior and the inner harbor large enough to accommodate the great freighters making port there. They sat under a big umbrella on the deck, where they could see both the Lift Bridge over the canal and the open water of the lake. It was a sunny Thursday afternoon. While they ate their walleye sandwiches and burgers, they watched a stream of small boat traffic traverse the canal.

Because he'd received no real help in his earlier contact with Duluth PD, Cork had called ahead and made arrangements to see an old friend, a homicide detective retired a couple of years from the city's police force.

"I'd prefer to talk to Dan alone," Cork told the others at lunch. "I don't want him to feel like there's a mob coming down on him."

"What do we do in the meantime?" Jenny asked.

"Why don't you see what you can find out about *Montcalm*?" Cork suggested.

"Any idea how to do that?"

"Your smart phone," English suggested to her.

"Maybe there's a harbormaster who would know what ships come and go here, or a port authority," Cork said.

Jenny shook her head. "Let's do this the old-fashioned way. Let's try the library. This is their territory. They probably have resources we wouldn't necessarily find on the Internet. And if they don't have what we need, I'll bet they know who does."

"Sounds like a plan to me," English said.

Louise looked as if she wanted to say something, but then decided to remain silent.

Cork asked, "You okay with this, Louise?"

She shrugged. There was something going on with her, Cork could see, but he decided to let it go for the moment. He checked his watch. "I'm meeting Dan at Fitger's at two. I'll give you a call when I'm finished, and we can figure out where to go from there. Okay?"

They agreed, paid their bill, and went their separate ways, Cork alone in his Explorer, and the others with Daniel English in his crew-cab pickup.

Fitger's was another Duluth landmark, one perched on a rise above the lake at the north edge of the downtown business district. A brewery for more than a century, it had long ago been converted to a hotel-retail complex with some pretty good restaurants. Cork found a meter out front and walked into the Brewhouse. His eyes took a moment to adjust to the dark, then he spotted Dan McGinty watching him from a stool at the bar. McGinty stood as Cork approached, and the men shook hands.

McGinty was compact and had been powerfully built in his days on the Duluth police force, but since his retirement, a lot of that muscle had gone soft. He was mostly bald. When he smiled, which was often, it was a gesture that involved his whole face, and his cheeks squeezed his eyelids nearly shut. His nickname was Squinty McGinty.

"Long time no see," McGinty said as he sat back down.

"You look good, Squinty. Retirement seems to agree with you," Cork said.

"Semiretirement," McGinty countered.

"Still working the good causes, huh?"

McGinty, who was an Eagle Scout, had always been deeply involved in that organization. In addition, he donated a lot of time and energy to a relief organization called Feed My Starving Children. Because he was that kind of man, he was also, Cork had always believed, the kind of cop you could trust.

McGinty smiled. "The hungry will always be with us. You still playing Philip Marlowe?"

"When a case interests me."

"And you've got one now?"

McGinty already had a beer. The barkeep asked Cork what he wanted. Normally Cork would have asked for Leinenkugel's, but he was in the Fitger's Brewhouse, so he ordered a pint of their North Country Pale Ale.

"Not a case so much as doing a favor for a friend," Cork said when the barkeep had moved away. "Missing person. And probably murder."

McGinty's eyebrows humped like little silver caterpillars. "Tell me about it."

Cork gave him the whole history. McGinty listened with the intensity of a guy used to keeping detailed mental notes. In the middle of the story, Cork's beer arrived, but he didn't touch it until he'd finished laying things out.

"You're about to open a can of worms, my friend," McGinty said.

Cork finally took a long pull on his beer. "How so, Squinty?"

"A lot of economic and political interest tied up in the boat traffic. Always been that way. Publicly, there's a periodic outcry over the prostitution that goes along with being a port city. But privately, the policy, more or less, is to look the other way. The department'll stage a sting now and then, nab a few johns, but they mostly pick up clueless locals. Generally, they don't touch the guys coming off the boats."

"Coming off the boats? I understood that the women went to the clientele, pretty much bunk to bunk on the boats."

"I've heard it used to be that way, but I can't really confirm it. Definitely not that way now. Since nine-eleven, harbor security's become way too tight. Getting women on and off the boats would be difficult. A lot of the prostitution now is done out of apartments near the water."

"How do the boat crews find the women?"

"They just walk the streets of downtown. Or they find them on Backpage or Craigslist. Or they go to a strip club."

"But Duluth PD doesn't touch them?"

"That's probably putting it a little strong. But think about it. These guys, a lot of them, come off salties. They're foreign citizens."

"Salties?"

"That's what we call the boats that come all the way up from the Atlantic through the Saint Lawrence Seaway. They're built different, designed, as I understand it, to take the beating the ocean can give a ship. All the other big boats are lakers, built specially to operate only on the Great Lakes. Those are domestic or Canadian. So imagine the red tape involved in arresting a bunch of sailors from places all over the globe. And imagine the ruckus. So there's a lot of pressure from above just to look the other way. I mean, prostitution's the oldest profession, right? Practically part of being human. So where's the harm?"

"The harm, Squinty, is that girls get used and knocked around pretty badly and sometimes killed."

McGinty shook his head. "You always were a backwoods cop at heart, Cork. The realities of urban life are different. In the grand scheme, prostitution is a fly, something circling around all the real shit you have to deal with as a cop, and you can't waste a lot of effort trying to get that fly because the honest-to-God truth is that you know it's never going away."

"I won't argue the big picture with you, Squinty. Right now, I just want to find one girl."

"Got a photo?"

Cork took it from his wallet and slid it across the bar.

McGinty looked at it. "Jesus, she's just a kid."

"Yeah, Squinty. But probably a prostitute, so who cares, right?"

"Okay, okay," McGinty said in a tone of contrition. "Can I keep this?"

"And do what with it?"

"I know the guy who heads up the Special Investigations Unit. They deal with vice, among other things. Let me show him, see if he can make an ID. Can I call you back at the number you called me from?"

"Yeah, that's my cell."

McGinty reached for his wallet.

"On me," Cork said.

The ex-cop nodded. "Tell you what. This crusade of yours pays off, I'll buy the next round."

They shook hands and McGinty left. Cork signaled the bartender for the tab, laid down payment, and walked away.

Instead of heading directly back to his Explorer, he strolled along the deck behind the big complex, which overlooked Lake Superior. Three great freighters, each longer than two football fields, all of them dark against the blue water, lay anchored outside the harbor. Cork had no idea if they were waiting for permission to enter, or waiting for some dock facility inside the harbor to become free, or simply idling for reasons only sailors would know. He watched a white yacht, large by most standards, glide past the nearest freighter, and the craft was dwarfed by the great monster. Despite what McGinty had told him, he couldn't help imagining Mariah on an enormous boat like that, a small child in the belly of a huge beast, and his gut fisted in an angry way.

His cell phone rang, Jenny calling.

"We came up empty, Dad," she said. "The librarian suggested we check the *Duluth News Tribune*. The paper reports all the comings and goings of the freighters every day. And not just here but in all the local commercial ports in the area. We checked issues as far back as the beginning of the shipping season and, like I said, came up with nothing. How'd you do?"

"Not much better. Why don't we regroup and figure what next?"

"Where?"

"I suppose the library's as good a place as any. I'll meet you there in ten."

Cork took one last look at the lake. The sun in its afternoon decline was at his back, and there was no wind that he could feel. A high, white haze hung on the horizon. Against it, the surface of Superior looked hard and cold as a sheet of steel. He couldn't help wondering if the body of a young girl lay somewhere below that unyielding surface, waiting for the spirits of Kitchigami to decide if she would remain there forever.

CHAPTER 22

The Duluth Public Library had been built in the shape of a great ore boat, a grand nod to the commerce that had helped establish the Zenith City. Cork found the others waiting in the shade of the enormous portico in front. Vertically down the huge central column that supported the portico roof were painted the spines of a quirky selection of literary offerings, from *Charlotte's Web* to *The Great Scandinavian Baking Book*. Jenny, Meloux, Louise, and English were all gathered in the shade in front of the spine for *The Catcher in the Rye*.

It was going on four o'clock, and Cork could see weariness in all their faces. They'd been on the road since well before dawn, and as nearly as he could tell, they were at a dead end. Until he heard from McGinty, he didn't have a good suggestion what to do next. He considered the possibility of simply waiting until dark, when according to McGinty, the girls came out on the streets near the harbor to sell themselves. If he showed Mariah's photo around or Raven's, maybe one of the girls would recognize them. Or maybe it would be better to hit the strip joints, wherever they were, and do the same. He suspected it would prove useless, and he was tired, too, and out of ideas at the moment. Reluctantly, he told the others so.

"If we offered the girls money for information, would that make a difference?" English asked.

Cork said, "There's no guarantee what they told us would be the truth. The other problem is that word'll get around, and if Mariah is being trafficked, whoever is handling her will make sure she disappears."

"Shelters?" Jenny suggested.

"Maybe," Cork said, but he had trouble being hopeful there, too.

"Corcoran O'Connor," Meloux said. "I think you should listen to her." The old man nodded toward Louise Arceneaux, who stood leaning her bulk wearily against the great painted spine of J. D. Salinger's classic story of a lost youth.

"Is there something you want to say, Louise?" Cork asked.

The woman's face, normally the color of wet sand, was red from all the exertion of the day, the struggle to move her large body on one leg and a wooden peg. But looking at Meloux, she seemed to gather strength. "Yes." She pushed herself from the column. "But I don't know if it will help."

"Go ahead, Louise," Jenny urged her gently.

"Forget about your cops, Cork," Louise told him bluntly. "All I ever got from them was trouble. And if you just go putting questions to the girls on the street, you're going to get nowhere. Don't take this wrong, but you look and sound and smell like a cop." She eyed English. "You both do."

"Okay," Cork said. "So what do we do?"

Louise said, "I've been thinking for a while now about something else. See, there used to be an organization here when I worked the boats. It was called Nishiime House. The people there helped women like me. Well, those who wanted help back then. I wasn't one of them, but some of the other girls went there. I heard they were very understanding and kept everything confidential and kept the cops out of it. Those people might have an idea how we can find Mariah. If they're still around."

"Let's find out." Jenny pulled out her iPhone and spent a couple of minutes accessing the Internet. "They're still here. On Fourth Street, at the edge of downtown."

Louise nodded and said, "Then we should go."

She turned toward English's pickup, which was parked at a

meter along the curb. Using a single crutch and with Jenny at her side, she made her way there.

Cork shrugged and said to English and Meloux, "I'm in. Let's go."

They drove a few blocks from the library and parked in front of an old brownstone on a block of old brick and brownstone buildings. A small sign on a wrought-iron stand set in the front yard bore the name Nishiime House. *Nishiime*, in Ojibwemowin, meant "little sister." Below that was a single word: *zahgidiwin*. It meant "love."

They entered through a heavy wooden door. Inside was a large room whose scuffed wooden floor was overlaid with a braided area rug. There were armchairs, a love seat, a table and a lamp, all looking like thrift store purchases. The windows were leaded glass, recalling a day when the building might have been the residence of an upper-class business family, before the Iron Range mines closed and the flow of ore stopped and the number of ships making port in Duluth dwindled to a fraction of what it had once been. A hallway angled to the right, and just beyond that was a stairway. A woman sat at a reception desk, typing into a computer. She was thin and young and had short hair the color of cotton candy. She looked up and smiled when Louise and Jenny came in. Her eyes flicked down to the carved wooden peg below Louise's right knee, but her expression didn't change. This was clearly a young woman who had seen much. But her smile faded when she caught sight of the men entering behind them.

"Yes?" she asked.

Cork and English hung back, but Meloux went forward and stood with the others. He said to Louise, "Go on, Niece."

Louise said, "I'm looking for someone. I'm looking for my daughter."

A long, pale white scar began at the right corner of the young woman's mouth and followed the jawline for nearly three inches. It looked as if someone had slit her cheek with a sharp knife. "I don't think I can help you," she said.

"Are you in charge here?" Jenny asked.

"No. That would be Bea Abbiss."

"Is she in?"

"Yes."

"Could we talk to her?"

The young woman looked beyond Jenny, at Cork and English, and it was clear that she was reluctant to agree. Cork thought about leaving, but Meloux spoke up.

"Granddaughter," he said. "You have been lost, too."

She eyed him. The muscles near her long scar flinched as if from an uncontrollable tic, but she didn't reply.

"And someone offered you their hand and that kindness brought you out of your lost place," Meloux said. "Yes?"

The young woman remained silent, but Cork could see in her eyes that Meloux had nailed it.

"All we are asking," Meloux went on, "is that you offer us your hand so that we can find our child and bring her home from the place where she is lost."

Her gaze once again swept them all, lingering on the two men near the front door. Then she decided. "Just a moment." She picked up her phone, punched a button, and said, "Some people are here, Bea. They're looking for their daughter. They'd like to talk to you." She listened and gave a nod to whatever was said. "All right." She put the phone back in its cradle. "Ms. Abbiss will be right out."

"*Migwech*," the old man said.

Cork heard a door open down the angled hallway. A moment later, a woman appeared, smiling cordially. She was a big woman with the features and coloring of a Native. She had black hair with little veins of gray, and dark, intelligent eyes. She wore a loose-fitting, light blue blouse and jeans, a turquoise necklace and earrings that matched. She came directly to Louise Arceneaux, extended her hand, and said, "How do you do? I'm Bea Abbiss, director of Nishiime House."

"I'm Louise Arceneaux. This is Jenny O'Connor, Henry

Meloux, Cork O'Connor, and Daniel English. We're looking for my daughter."

"So I understand," Bea Abbiss said pleasantly. "Why don't we go back to my office and talk?" She glanced at the young receptionist. "No calls for a while, Gina."

The hallway was long. There was a window at the far end with stained glass, and the light that came through fell across the worn beige carpeting in vivid splashes of color. Abbiss stepped through an open doorway, and the others followed. It was a neat office but comfortable, with several plants, shelves of books, and lots of Native art on the walls.

Abbiss slipped behind her desk and said, "I apologize. I only have two chairs for visitors. I hope some of you don't mind standing."

"Louise," Jenny said, indicating one of the empty chairs. "And, Henry, why don't you take the other?" She stood between them, and once again, Cork and English remained in the background.

"All right." Abbiss folded her hands on her desk. "Tell me what you need."

Louise told her story. She began with her experience as, in her own words, "a boat whore." She talked about her children, about Mariah. She confessed she hadn't been a very good mother. She began to cry but kept on with her story. She told about Mariah disappearing with Carrie Verga and about the girl's body washing up on Windigo Island. She told Bea Abbiss how scared she was for her daughter, how desperately she wanted to find her, to have another chance, to be a better mother this time.

Cork didn't know Abbiss's tribal affiliation, but her reaction to all this was not the stone face he'd seen so often among the Anishinaabeg. The woman's expression communicated compassion and understanding and empathy, and at the end, she left her chair, walked around the desk to Louise, bent, and gave Mariah's mother a long, warm hug. She took Louise's hands and said, "I'll help in any way I can. But you have to understand, some of what I'm going to tell you will be difficult to hear."

"I know, Ms. Abbiss," Louise said. "I know."

The woman seated herself again at her desk. She frowned a moment, as if trying to decide where to start. "The first thing is call me Bea. Everyone here does. The second thing, Louise, is that I want you to believe that you can let go of your guilt. What happened to you, what may have happened to your daughter, is an old, old crime, but you aren't the criminals. You are victims of the crime. When people of European descent"—here she glanced at Cork and Jenny, the only ones among those present who didn't look Ojibwe—"came to this area, they shattered our culture. Sometimes it was because of ignorance, but more often it was because of greed. And this brokenness, this wounding of our spirit as a people, has never been completely healed. We continue to struggle with it today. One of the terrible, terrible effects of that brokenness is violence, particularly against our women. Our men are sometimes a part of that violence, and white men are certainly a part of that violence. Our women have been sold from the beginning, traded as a commodity. We're dealing with decades of trauma forced on our people.

"What I'm saying, Louise, is that we have to heal ourselves, as women and as a people. And a huge part of that healing is to understand, to accept, to really believe that we have been victimized. We are not the criminals. Okay?"

"Okay," Louise said and nodded.

"We see a lot of women here who are caught in that deep net of trafficking. They want to get out of it, but it's not easy. And I'll be honest with you, there's only a certain amount that we can do. We're a nonprofit. We depend on the charity of others, so our resources are limited. To really break away from the trafficking, women need to be assured of good housing, a job, continued support in so many ways until they're able to stand on their own. We simply can't do that, though I'd give my right arm to be able to. So we do a lot of referring, a lot of advocating, a lot of hand-holding. But in the end, we often see the women simply disappear."

Abbiss took a deep breath. Cork suspected what she'd just told them was a truth she often had to deliver, but it was not one she wanted to accept. And he couldn't help but wonder if, as a Native woman, she'd experienced herself the horrible truths she was laying out.

"Okay, let's talk about Mariah," Abbiss went on. "I don't know a girl by that name. We see so many young Native women here, and very often they don't give us their real names. And that man you told me about—Smiley—the one who trafficked you when you worked the boats? That's not a name I know either, and I know a lot about the traffickers. Probably he got pushed out by the gangs—the Crips, the Bloods, the Native Mob. They all have a hand in it now. But back to your daughter. Do you have a photograph?"

From her purse, Louise took out two photos of Mariah, one before her transformation and the other the photo she'd posted on Facebook just before she disappeared. Abbiss looked at them both carefully. Then she shook her head.

"I haven't seen her here," she said.

Jenny reached into her purse and brought out another photo. "Here's a picture of Carrie Verga, the girl she left with, the one who's dead now."

Abbiss studied this photograph with the same result.

Cork said, "I have another picture, this one of the woman we believe may have been responsible for the girls running off in the first place."

He stepped forward with the photo Lindy Duvall had given him of her daughter Raven.

Bea Abbiss took the photograph in her hands, and the moment she looked at it her face changed. Darkness swept across it in a fury.

"Oh, Christ," she said. "Oh, dear Christ."

PART II

JENNIFER O'CONNOR:

"Can the Devil Speak True?"

CHAPTER 23

Men never talked. Not about themselves, anyway, not really. They talked about what they'd done, what they were doing, what they intended to do, but they didn't talk about what was at the heart of them, why they did these things. That's what Jennifer O'Connor believed, and she believed it in large measure because that was what she'd seen in her father all her life.

Her brother, Stephen, believed that everyone was born with a purpose to serve. Stephen was very Ojibwe in so many ways, and he believed that every human being was a part of the plan of Kitchimanidoo, the Great Mystery, the Creator. He believed that their father was born *ogichidaa*, which was someone who stood between his people and evil. Stephen himself was born *Mide*, a healer. Although in the Ojibwe clan tradition the O'Connors were *makwa*, or bear, Stephen claimed that Anne's spirit was that of a bird, or *bineshii*. The bird flew in the spiritual realm, and was the teacher of spiritual ways. Stephen firmly believed that Anne had been born to be a nun. And Jenny? She was always meant to be *nokomis*, which literally meant "grandmother." She was a nurturer, Stephen believed, and Jenny didn't argue.

So Cork O'Connor was a man born *ogichidaa*, chosen to stand against evil. Which he'd done time and again, often at great risk to himself. Yet he'd failed twice in this purpose, and although he never spoke of it in this way, Jenny believed these failures cut him to the bone.

It had been nearly half a decade since her mother had been

killed, an innocent victim in a grand and brutal plan intended to make a very few men very rich. As a part of that scheme, the charter plane she was on had been lost in a snowstorm in a wilderness in the Rocky Mountains of Wyoming. Jenny's father had gone searching for her. With difficulty and danger, he'd found the truth, but he'd been too late to save his beloved wife. And only seven months ago, a madman who bore a grudge against her father had, in revenge, tried to kill Stephen. In this instance, too, her father had uncovered the truth too late to stand between the evil of that man and his own son.

Jenny believed her father suffered because of what he saw as his failure, but she didn't believe this because he revealed himself by talking about who he was deep inside. In that way, he was like a stone. Instead, she saw it in his face, heard it in his silence, felt it sometimes in his touch. Across the course of her life, this was always how she'd known him.

In the small office in Nishiime House, she watched her father's reaction to all that Bea Abbiss laid out, and she never saw a flicker of emotion on his face. He probably would have told her wryly that it was the Ojibwe in his blood. Partly true, Jenny thought, but she was pretty sure that it also had a lot to do with the Y chromosome he carried in every part of him.

When Bea looked at the photograph of Raven Duvall, and fear and anger and fury exploded on her face, and she said, "Oh, Christ. Oh, dear Christ," Cork didn't bat an eye. Nor did Daniel or Henry. Jenny, on the other hand, felt everything inside her go cold and afraid, and she knew that her own eyes grew as huge as eggs.

"What's wrong?" she said.

Bea looked up from the photo. "I know this woman. What did you say her name was?"

"Duvall," Cork replied. "Raven Duvall."

"I don't know her by that name," Bea said. "To me, she's always been Sparkle. Just Sparkle."

"How do you know her?" Louise asked.

"Through our street workers." She laid the photograph on

the desk in front of her and shook her head. "We have staff here whose job is just to walk the streets looking for the runaways, the lost kids, the vulnerable ones. We try to get to them before the predators do. Our people go out with what we call Green Bags, full of things that someone on the street might need. Blankets, toiletries, tampons. We don't try to wrangle kids in here. They might be scared and desperate, but they've also been lied to and betrayed and used in so many ways that trust is an enormous issue. So, we just try to make sure they know we're here and that we want to help."

"And Raven? Or Sparkle rather?" Daniel said. "She's come to you?"

"No. But she has sent girls to us from time to time, ones ready to get out of the kind of life Sparkle leads."

"You were clearly shocked when you saw her photograph," Cork said. "What's that about?"

"It's not about Sparkle. It's about the men Sparkle works for. They're what, if you talked to her, she would call her family. And one of the most tragic things in all of this is that she would mean it."

"Tell us about her family," Jenny said.

"Most of the girls who are trafficked here are handled by men."

"Pimps," Cork said.

"That's not how the girls see them. It works this way. A girl runs away from home, from the rez, from a situation that's intolerable or threatening. Maybe it's parents who are alcoholics or addicts, or a situation of sexual abuse. She ends up here, or in some other city, a place where she's just another stranger. More often than not, she knows no one. So she's on the street. I don't know how they find her so quickly, but the predators are on her in no time. They offer her food, shelter, protection, all the things she needs. They're kind, like big brothers or good uncles. And for a while they do exactly as they've promised. They take care of her. This is what we think of as grooming.

"Then these predators begin with the real agenda. They point out that they've given her everything, and they need to have something in return. Sex is certainly part of that, which the girls are too often already familiar with and not so very reluctant to give to the men who've been, in a way, their saviors. Then it involves more. This new family might say that they need them to do some stripping. Nothing wrong with a little stripping. And their young bodies are so beautiful, they ought to be proud to show them off. And after that, it's maybe private parties and lap dances, and eventually it's sex for money, which is where all the grooming was meant to lead in the first place. And by then it's too late for the girls. Often, they've become hooked on drugs, another way for the family to control them. And they're emotionally bound, because they know their family loves them and needs this from them. But also they're afraid, because they've seen—or even experienced themselves— the punishment for refusing to do what's asked of them."

"They're beaten?" Jenny said.

"Oh, yes, and worse. But even though terrible fear has become a part of the whole dynamic, they believe that they only got what they deserved, because family comes first. It's brainwashing, and the men who do it are very good at it."

Louise said, "But Mariah didn't just run away. Raven brought her here."

Bea nodded. "That's another way this happens. Girls who are older—seventeen, eighteen, nineteen—become procurers. They go back to the rez, looking successful—nice clothes, nice car, jewelry—and like the Pied Piper, they get much younger girls to follow them."

"Why so shocked when you found out we're looking for Raven?" Jenny's father asked, coming back to that point. "What's so unusual about her family?"

Bea stood up and went to a file cabinet, pulled open a drawer, and brought out a folder labeled WINDIGO.

"What you're going to see is pretty bad," she warned them. "You might not want to look."

No one turned away. Bea opened the folder, pulled a photograph from inside, and laid it on her desk. The girl's face was a mass of bruises and swelling. Her lower lip was torn open, showing the white of teeth beneath. She was holding up a hand on which none of the fingers extended from the palm in a natural way.

"Her name is Melissa Spry. Windigo and his brother did this to her."

"Why?"

"One night she told them she was too sick to turn any tricks for them."

"Did she come here?"

"Yes. Sparkle dropped her off."

"Did you call the police?"

"She wouldn't let us. She said if we did, she'd just leave. She told us she deserved what had been done to her. She really believed that."

"What did you do?"

"We took her to a clinic and got her treated. She's Grand Portage Ojibwe. I returned her to the rez myself, delivered her into the hands of a social worker we have a relationship with there."

"She's okay?" Jenny asked.

"Within a couple of weeks, she'd run away again. We heard on the street that she'd gone back to this Windigo." She tapped the folder. "I have other photos of other girls just like this one in here if you want to see them, all girls that have been part of this Windigo's family."

"Windigo?" Henry spoke in a way that made Jenny think they were old enemies.

"That's what he calls himself and that's how many of the girls refer to him," Bea said. "You all know the story of the windigo, right? Once a man, then through dark magic he became a monster, a cannibal with an insatiable hunger for human flesh and a heart made of ice. We see girls who've been trafficked by Crips and Bloods and the Native Mob. But Windigo is the worst."

"Oh, dear God," Louise said. "You're not telling me that Mariah is part of this Windigo's family?"

"If Sparkle—Raven—is involved, that's probably the case." Bea spoke in an even tone, but couldn't disguise the concern in her voice. "I'm sorry."

"How do we find her? Raven, I mean," Jenny said.

"That would be very difficult. As I understand it, she's not actually out there being trafficked at the moment. She acts as a sort of big sister to the other girls."

"Some sister," Daniel said.

"I know. But understand where her head is at. She's deep in thrall to Windigo. And give her credit. She's taken chances sending girls who really need help to us." She nodded toward the file containing the horrible photographs.

"Do the police know about this?" Cork said.

"Yes, but there's not much they can do. The girls don't trust cops. Most of them have grown up believing law enforcement is their enemy. So they won't speak a word against Windigo." She started to say something more but hesitated, as if very reluctant to go on.

"What is it?" Jenny asked.

Bea's eyes flicked to Louise, then back to Jenny. "I've heard, only heard, that the girls in Windigo's family disappear if they talk to anyone about any of this. They're at risk even coming to us. I'm very afraid that might have been what happened to Melissa Spry."

"Disappear?" Louise looked frightened to death. "You mean they're murdered. Is that what was supposed to happen to Carrie Verga? Is that what's happened to my Mariah?"

"I don't know, Louise. I just want you to be aware of all the possibilities. I want you to be prepared."

In the quiet of the room, Jenny asked, "Do you know anything about this Windigo?"

Late afternoon light came through the window at the back of the office and fell across Bea Abbiss. The window mullions cut the light into squares the color of blood oranges, and it made her look as if she were a prisoner behind dark bars. She shook her head slowly. "There's not much anyone knows. We think he's a Shinnob. Some of the girls have called him Angel. I don't know if that's his real name or just something he calls himself, like Windigo. I've also heard that even the Crips and Bloods and the Native Mob keep out of his way. Apparently he has a brother, someone called Manny, who's also part of this family."

"You can find Raven," Jenny's father said. He spoke as if it was a truth, not speculation. Jenny was afraid he was too blunt, too confrontational, and they might lose the goodwill of Bea Abbiss.

"I haven't heard from Sparkle since Melissa Spry disappeared. So I don't know," Bea said. "But I'll try."

"How?" Jenny asked.

"I know the Native community in Duluth. I have a pretty good ear on the streets. I know who to ask. I can't promise anything, but like I said, I'll try."

"Thank you," Louise said. She looked in real pain.

Bea gave her a reassuring smile. "We call our house Nishiime—'little sister'—for a reason. We're family here, real family, and we do our best to help one another." She looked to Jenny. "This might take some time. If I find out something, how do I get in touch with you?"

Jenny gave her cell phone number and Cork gave his. Bea walked them to the reception area, where the thin young woman with hair like cotton candy and a long scar across her cheek was still at work on her computer. She glanced up, her face twitched, and she smiled as they passed, an encouraging smile, Jenny thought, and liked her for that. At the door, Bea said, "I don't want to give you false hope, but I think that hope is always a good thing to hold to. And please believe that I'll do my best to help."

Henry took her much younger hand between his ancient, ancient palms, and he smiled in the way he had that was as if he was offering dawn to a dark world, and he said, "One kind thing is the seed from which a great goodness grows. It is not hope we hold to, Niece. It is belief in the power of that growing goodness. *Migwech. Chi migwech.*"

The old man turned and began down the steps.

CHAPTER 24

Jenny had always loved Duluth, its hills, its great mansions, its sense of grand history, its cultural crazy quilt, its location there against the largest and most beautiful freshwater lake in the world. When she was a girl, she and her mother used to drive from Tamarack County and spend the day doing what girls did together—shopped, ate, strolled through Canal Park. They bought ice cream cones at the DQ and stood licking them at the edge of the ship channel, while they watched the Aerial Lift Bridge rise and the huge boats pass beneath. Sometimes when they were in the city, they visited a spa or had their nails done, just for the fun of it.

For the girls helped by Nishiime House, Duluth was a different place, and what they did there gave them no pleasure. After Bea Abbiss opened her eyes, Jenny realized how blind she'd been. The city seemed terribly different to her from what it had been before. She felt wounding all around her. She felt deceit, menace. And she might have succumbed to a sense of hopelessness in what they were attempting if it hadn't been for the indomitable spirit of Henry Meloux. She loved that old man.

The visit to Nishiime House had unwound Louise. Though all the activity of that day had clearly been exhausting, she'd held herself together well. When they left the brownstone, she was silent. She labored into the truck with Daniel and Henry and sat staring ahead, a distant look in her eyes. Jenny leaned in the window.

"You okay?"

"She's with the devil," Louise said in a small voice. "My girl is with the devil."

Which, in its way, was promising, Jenny thought. Promising because it meant Louise still held to the belief that Mariah was alive. Which was a tough thing for Jenny to do. In her own mind's eye, she couldn't help seeing Mariah's little body draped, like Carrie Verga's had been, across the broken rocks of Windigo Island.

"We'll find her," Jenny said. "We'll find her and take her from the devil." Then she repeated those wonderful words Henry had spoken. "One kind thing is the seed from which a great goodness grows. We have that seed now, Louise."

Louise gave a small nod and managed a smile.

They drove back to Canal Park and sat at a table in a little café on Lake Avenue. None of them seemed very hungry, but they ordered something to drink. Jenny ordered coffee, regular. She knew it would keep her awake that night, but she wanted to be alert. She stirred in cream and added Splenda and asked, "So what now?"

"We wait," her father said. He drank coffee, too. Regular, black.

"For what?" she asked.

"Something to break. Someone to call us. The dawning of an idea that hasn't occurred to us before."

"That seems so . . . impotent."

She knew immediately it wasn't the best choice of word in the presence of men, and she could tell that it needled her father.

"Do you have a better idea?" he asked, a little sliver of iron in his voice.

"I could try talking to the women on the street," she suggested. "I'd be less threatening than you or Daniel."

She could see that didn't sit well with him. She also saw something in Daniel's expression, but it didn't seem so much criticism as concern, maybe for her safety. She was beginning to like him, quite a lot. He was beautifully Shinnob. His cheeks were high. His eyes were the color of pecans. His skin reminded her of doe hide, soft and tanned. He was quiet, but when he said something, it was well considered and worth listening to. She was glad he was a part of this investigation, though she had no intention of telling him that.

"I think we risk word getting back to Windigo," Cork said. "And that strikes me as a bad idea on lots of levels."

"I don't know. Wouldn't it, like, flush him out?" Jenny had never been a hunter, but she heard herself use that hunting phrase—"flush him out"—as if what they were looking for was a quail or something. It sounded stupid, even as she said it, but she was trying to relate to her father on his terms.

It was Henry who answered. He said, "There are two important rules in hunting, Jennifer O'Connor. The first: you always stay downwind of your prey. The moment a hunted thing catches your scent, it will disappear. Or worse, if it is also an animal of prey, it may turn on you, and the hunter becomes the hunted."

He paused, and Jenny waited. But he simply continued to stare at her placidly, until finally she blurted, "And what's the second rule, Henry?"

"Patience," he said with a wry smile. "That is the second rule. It is also a hunter's best friend."

Louise came to her rescue. "The longer we sit, the more chance this Windigo might hurt Mariah. Or worse."

"Unless he feels threatened, there's no reason for him to do anything to Mariah," Jenny's father said.

He spoke as if it was an obvious truth, and Louise seemed to accept this perception. She closed her eyes, and Jenny could see her face melting into exhaustion.

"Should we think about a place to stay tonight?" Jenny said. "Because it doesn't appear that we're going to finish this business any time soon."

Cork said, "We're an hour and a half from Aurora. We could drive back and wait there."

"No." Louise's eyes popped open, and her voice was strong. "I don't want to leave here without Mariah."

Cork showed no reaction. He simply said, "Fine. Then we should get rooms somewhere."

Daniel nodded toward the north. "There's a pretty good hotel next street over, on Canal Park Drive. You're helping my family. The rooms are on me," he insisted.

"All right," Cork said without argument.

A short time later they found themselves checked in to the Canal Park Lodge. Cork, Henry, and Daniel shared a suite. Louise and Jenny took a room with two queen beds. It was early evening by then. Jenny stood at the window, looking out at the lake, which was only a stone's throw from the hotel. Behind her, Louise lay on her bed, her wooden peg removed and propped against the nearby wall, along with her crutches. She'd given herself an insulin shot, then exhaustion had overwhelmed her. She was already sound asleep. Jenny had called Rose and had talked with little Waaboo. He said he missed her. He wanted to know if she had found the girl who was lost and when would she be home. "Soon," Jenny told him, which was purposely vague, and what did *soon* mean anyway to a boy who couldn't tell time and kept no track of days?

The color of Lake Superior was changeable, and not just with the weather. Henry Meloux believed, and Jenny did, too, that everything had spirit. Kitchigami wasn't just a great hollowed bowl of rock filled with water. It was a living thing and had moods. She'd seen it silver and calm, black and angry, nearly turquoise and coquettish. That evening, under a sky laced with ragged clouds, it was like fabric washed so many times the blue had faded to almost white, and the lake seemed tired. In her hand, she held one of the copies they'd made of Mariah's photograph in order to show it around. She looked down at that young face, a child's face, and felt a deep stab of fear. How could a child stand against the kind of man Bea had described that afternoon? What chance did she have? Jenny thought of Mariah's Facebook postings, of her telling anyone who cared to read about it that she was learning to play her new guitar on the lakeshore of the Bad Bluff Reservation, telling of the eagle that had flown overhead, and that was a good sign, wasn't it? She knew so little of the world then, but, oh, Christ, she'd had an education since.

You save her. That's what Waaboo's murdered birth mother had said in Jenny's vision.

And now she thought of Waaboo and how she'd pulled him out of the reach of people as bad as Windigo, pulled him from the very hands of death. But she hadn't saved his mother, who wasn't much older than Mariah. Was that what she was supposed to do now? Save this child, this little girl in the photograph she held. Even if it was not what was meant in her vision, it was what she wanted. She wanted it for Mariah, and for Louise, whose exhausting fear Jenny understood so well, and for herself, too, because she cared so deeply now.

You save her.

"I will try," Jenny said, as if someone were listening.

There was a knock at the door. Louise didn't stir. Jenny opened up, and her father stood there. "We've ordered pizza," he said. "It'll be here in half an hour."

"Thanks."

"You two doing okay?"

She glanced back at Louise. "This is taking such a toll."

"She's strong," Cork said. "She wasn't, but she is now. She has to be." He smiled, genuine and happy. "By the way, I got a call from Stephen and Annie. They took a walk today. Not a long walk but a real one. Stephen thinks he'll be coming home within a week or so."

"That's wonderful," Jenny said, a bit too loud. On the bed behind her, Louise made a sound but didn't wake. Jenny whispered, "Let me know when the pizza comes. I'll see if Louise is up to eating."

Cork didn't turn away immediately. He looked deep into her eyes. "I don't think I've told you, but I should have. I'm glad you're here. I'm glad you're a part of this. At least for now."

He kissed her forehead, turned, and was gone.

CHAPTER 25

The sky all day had been relatively clear, but after dark, thick clouds stumbled over the hills above Duluth and obscured the stars. It felt like rain, though nothing came for the longest time. The hour was late and no word yet from Bea Abbiss or Dan McGinty. Sleep was out of the question for Jenny. At home when she couldn't sleep, she usually got up and wrote. And so now she sat at the desk in her hotel room with a small, opened notebook in front of her and a Bic ballpoint in her hand. She stared at her own reflection in the window glass of the room, at the face of a woman who thought of herself as a writer. She could see the lights along the boardwalk behind the hotel and, beyond them, the big dark of the water. She was thinking about this hunt they were on, and the terrible men who were a part of what they hunted. Her hand moved across the blank notebook page. She wrote: *Downwind of the Devil.* Which, according to Henry Meloux, if they wanted to hunt a windigo, was where they were supposed to stay. She wrote: *Mariah.* She wrote: *Lost, Alone, Afraid.* She wrote: *Child.* She wrote: *You save her.*

She studied her face in the window. What she saw now was a comfortable woman who knew nothing of what Mariah or the other girls enslaved by Windigo and his brother might really feel. What was it like to be alone on the street at night? What was it really like to have no one to turn to except monsters?

Her cell phone played the first few notes of Cyndi Lauper's "Girls Just Want to Have Fun." She took it from her purse and read the display. An unfamiliar number. She answered with "This is Jenny."

"I want to talk to the Shinnob woman." The voice was male, growly.

"Louise? She's sleeping at the moment."

"Wake her up. It's about her kid."

"Mariah?"

"Wake her up."

"Hold on." Jenny went to the bed where the woman lay in a dead sleep. She shook Louise gently, then when she got no response, more vigorously. "Louise," she said. "Louise, wake up. It's about Mariah."

Louise's eyes snapped open instantly, but they were unfocused. She said, "Huh? What?"

"Someone's on the phone for you. He says it's about Mariah."

"Okay," Louise said, drawing herself upright. "Okay." She blinked a few times, trying to become alert, then reached for the cell phone in Jenny's hand. She put it to her ear. "This is Louise Arceneaux." She listened, squinted as if to focus more intently, nodded. "Is she all right? Just tell me that." She listened. "Okay. I understand." She kept the phone to her ear a few moments more, lowered it, and stared at Jenny.

"What is it, Louise?"

"I have to go out."

"Now?"

"Yes. Now."

She swung herself around on the mattress and settled her good leg on the floor. She reached for the peg propped against the wall next to the bed, along with her crutches.

"Who was that, Louise? Where do you have to go?"

"No time. I have to go now."

"Wherever it is you're going, I'm going with you."

"No. He said alone."

"What else did he say?"

"He said he can tell me about Mariah."

"Wait a minute, Louise. Just wait a minute."

The woman was fitting the saddle of the peg leg against her stump. Jenny put a restraining hand on her arm. Louise shook it off and gave her a killing look. "Leave me alone."

"Think, Louise. Whoever it is, he doesn't have your best interest in mind. Or Mariah's. It could very well be Windigo. Hell, it probably is."

"I don't care who it is, I'm going to meet him." She finished strapping on her carved appendage and reached for her crutches.

"You're going out like that?"

Louise looked down at herself. She wore a big wrinkled T-shirt and gray sweatpants hand-cut into shorts. "Okay," she said, finally pausing to breathe. "All right. Will you help me?"

"Only if you'll let me go with you."

"He said alone."

"I don't think two women will scare Windigo off. And I definitely think it's safer."

"All right. But let's go. He said fifteen minutes."

Shortly after midnight, they walked out of the hotel and onto Lake Avenue. Jenny had tried to convince Louise to bring Cork, Daniel, and Henry into this, but the woman was iron in her resolve. The best Jenny could do was to take the extra set of keys she had for her father's Explorer, and while Louise waited impatiently, Jenny rummaged through the toolbox in back and grabbed a box cutter and a metal pry bar just over a foot long. She slid the box cutter into the back pocket of her jeans. The pry bar she carried at the ready in her hand.

The night seemed heavy with the anticipation of some dramatic change. A storm, maybe. Or something else. Jenny thought she could actually feel the colliding of two forces—the warm, moist air from the southwest and the cool wall that rose up from the deep, deep cold of the lake. She walked beside Louise toward Superior Street, less than a quarter of a mile from the hotel, their way lit by streetlamps. They crossed the overpass above I-35. Although most people didn't know this, that interstate route was a part of the Pan-American Highway, part of a road that began at the tip of South America and ran north all the way to Prudhoe Bay in Alaska. Jenny took a moment on the bridge to look south down the asphalt corridor, which was empty now. She couldn't help thinking that it was a long journey, indeed, from that place near the bottom of the world to the place near the top, but it was not as long a journey as Carrie Verga had made.

Much of the area they could see had once been, Jenny knew, filled with brothels and bars and flops, an area where all kinds of illicit trafficking occurred. It was still, according to Bea Abbiss, a place where men could buy almost anything they wanted from a woman. They continued walking until they reached the corner of Lake and Superior. A block north was the neon splash of the Fond-Du-Luth casino. Despite the cars along the curb, no one was on the street. Jenny wondered if maybe it was because they could feel the approaching storm.

"Here?" Jenny said.

"That's what he told me. Corner of Lake and Superior."

Jenny's phone sang again, Cyndi Lauper. Same number as before on the display.

"Yeah?" she answered.

"The girl's mother, I said. Alone."

"Not gonna happen," Jenny said. "You talk to us both. Or are you afraid of a couple of women?"

"Ha. That'll be the day. Move south on Superior. That's to your left." He broke the connection.

"That way," Jenny said, and Louise followed her.

They walked away from the casino glare, into a rising wind, one that brought with it the first drops of rain. This was stupid, Jenny knew, walking into some fierce and terrible unknown. But wasn't this exactly what Mariah and girls like her did? Walked into the dark time and time again, into horrific possibilities? The two women passed dark recesses where the doors were closed and locked against them, passed buildings deserted of life. Sometimes the pavement was lit by the splash from streetlights, and sometimes there was only the dark of that hour now long past midnight. The wind grew stronger. The rain began to fall more heavily, the drops big, hitting them like pellets.

Where was he? Jenny wondered, thinking they needed to seek shelter. Where was this Windigo?

And that's when she heard it. Heard it call her name.

They'd come to a corner where the wind funneled the rain between tall, dark buildings. Out of that storm came a high keening, a howl inside the wind. It was a voice filled with hunger, with hate, and it tore into her heart as if the sound itself had teeth. It was her name, only her name, but it was the most horrible sound she'd ever heard, and it shook her right down to her soul.

"Jenny." Louise looked at her with great owl eyes. "Did you hear that?"

"You heard it, too?"

"Hell, yes. Somebody screaming your name." She stared into the wind, her face beaten by the rain. "Who was that? What was that?"

"You bitches. You fucking bitches."

The man came at them out of an unlit recessed doorway, nearly faceless in the dark, big as a bear. He swung, and his fist caught Louise across the face. She went down hard against the sidewalk. He shifted toward Jenny, but the pry bar in her hand was already on its way. The steel connected somewhere near his right ear, and the big man fell back against the brick of the corner building. Jenny went at him again and again, raining blow after blow as he raised his arms in a feeble shielding. Then Louise was in the fray, using the end of her crutch to ram his gut. He retreated along the wall, and Jenny thought he would run, but he sprang at them instead, wrapped his enormous arms around Louise, and threw her against Jenny, knocking both women off balance.

"Police!"

The cry came from Superior Street, and Jenny caught sight of a running figure briefly illuminated beneath a streetlight. The big man saw it, too, turned and fled. A moment later the running figure passed, paused briefly, and said, "You guys okay?"

It was Daniel English.

"We're fine," Jenny said.

"Stay here."

Daniel was off and running again in pursuit. Down Superior Street, around a blind corner.

Despite the rain and the wind, the street seemed to drop into silence. Jenny stood breathing fast, the pry bar tight in her fist and the hammering of her own heart hard against her chest. Fire ran through her, the burn of adrenaline. Even though the man was gone and the danger past, she was still in the grip of a wild, mindless impulse to swing that pry bar again and again and again.

Beside her, Louise said, "Hope we killed him."

"We did a lot of damage anyway."

The women stood together in the downpour, but neither of them seemed to notice the rain.

"You okay?" Jenny asked.

"My cheek'll be sore for a while. Maybe a bruise. Won't be the first time. But I swear it's gonna be the last. You were pretty good with that pry bar."

"Terror," Jenny said. "Total terror."

"Windigo?" Louise asked.

"That would be my guess."

Louise stared down the empty street where the man had disappeared. "He wasn't going to tell us about Mariah."

"Probably just wanted to scare you off."

"Ain't gonna happen," Louise said. Her hair hung in her face and she blinked against the cascade of rainwater off her brow. "Think he'll hurt Mariah?"

Jenny wanted to offer comfort, but they both knew the probable truth.

"We gotta find her," Louise said. "We gotta find her real soon."

They saw Daniel jogging toward them, returning from the chase, empty-handed.

"He had an SUV parked next street up," Daniel said. Like them, he was soaked to the bone, rain streaming down his face. "Too dark even to get a plate number."

"Where'd you come from?" Jenny asked.

"Couldn't sleep. I was out on the boardwalk, trying to figure a few things. I saw you two come out of the hotel. You're hard to miss, Louise, with that leg and crutch. And you I'd know any-where," he said to Jenny.

She wasn't sure exactly what that meant, but she liked the sound of it.

"I thought maybe you were going to try to talk to some of the girls on the street," Daniel went on. "Whatever it was you were thinking, seemed to me Superior Street at midnight wasn't a great idea."

"So you followed us."

He looked like a kid caught with his hand in the cookie jar. "Yeah."

"We didn't see you at all."

"I'm a game warden. I get paid for watching people without them knowing." His eyes went to the pry bar in Jenny's hand and then to the crutch Louise still held like a battering ram. "Not sure you needed my help."

"*Migwech*, Daniel," Louise said. She put her hand on his shoulder, drew herself up, and gave him a kiss on the cheek.

They returned to the hotel. When they parted ways, Jenny made Daniel promise he would say nothing to Cork or Henry. Morning, she insisted, was soon enough for that. She wasn't look-ing forward to trying to explain to her father what she and Louise had believed they might accomplish. In their room, they changed out of their wet things and into dry sleep clothes. Louise propped her peg leg and her crutches against the wall. She eased herself under the covers, said, "Good night, slugger," gave a quiet laugh, and was very quickly lost in sleep.

Jenny wasn't quite ready to close her eyes. She lay in the dark, staring up at the ceiling, the vast cold of Kitchigami just outside the window. She pondered the whole experience on Superior Street, trying to make sense of it. They'd been set up, but how? Bea Abbiss? Bea had been the only person to whom Jenny had given her cell phone number. But she'd had such a good feel from Bea, such a sense of her dedication that Jenny was inclined to dismiss this possibility. Their assailant had come by this information in some other way. But how? And had scaring them off been the only motive? And what would have happened in the end if Daniel hadn't been there?

Daniel. She recalled what he'd said—*You I'd know anywhere*. It seemed a simple thing but was, she understood, so much more complicated. She closed her eyes and saw him again as he'd been on that dark corner, big and wet and chagrined to have been caught following them. Louise had given him a kiss in gratitude. Jenny wondered if she should have done the same, and then was sorry she hadn't. Except, would it have been another thing that seemed simple but was, in fact, much more complicated?

Finally she thought about what she'd been avoiding: a windigo had called her name. She tried to decide if it was something that, along with everything else about that night, she would have to tell her father. So far, he'd taken such a rational approach in their hunt that she figured he'd easily dismiss it as a phenomenon of the storm and her own vivid imagination.

But she knew what she'd heard. And she knew what it meant when the windigo called your name. And the only person she could think of who might understand was Henry Meloux.

CHAPTER 26

"Henry? Could I talk to you? Alone?"

The old man was eating oatmeal, one of the complimentary breakfast items the hotel offered. He also had a small glass of orange juice and a cup of coffee. He finished chewing, swallowed, looked at Jenny, studied her face, her eyes, and said, "You have seen something."

"No, Henry. I heard something."

Cork and Daniel were at the buffet area, dishing up eggs for themselves. Louise was still upstairs in their room, getting ready to come down. She'd told Jenny she could make it on her own and to go ahead. Which was a good thing, because Jenny wanted very much to talk to Henry and, as she'd told him, alone.

Outside, the morning was gorgeous, a sky full of sun. The storm of the night before had moved somewhere far to the east, over Wisconsin or Michigan by now. Beyond the hotel windows, the water of Kitchigami was a deep blue. Sunlight struck the surface in a broad silver band, and shattered in a splash like a million diamonds.

In reply to Jenny's urgent request, Meloux simply gave a nod and said, "When I have finished my breakfast, we will talk." He dipped his spoon into his oatmeal and resumed eating as if nothing had passed between them.

Cork and Daniel drifted over, plates of food in their hands. Daniel wore a blue knit shirt and khakis. He looked showered and refreshed. He sat at the table and glanced at her. His face showed no emotion, but as he began buttering his toast, he said, "I don't know about you, but I always have trouble sleeping in a strange bed."

She still felt unsettled from the night before, and she realized she must have looked it.

Cork set his plate on the table next to Meloux. "Where's Louise?"

"She's coming down on her own," Jenny said.

Henry Meloux went right on eating as if he were alone at the table, as if he and his food were the only two things in his universe. Jenny got herself a bowl of sliced fruit and a carton of yogurt and joined them. Louise came in, wearing her peg leg, a crutch under her arm. Although she'd had not much more sleep than Jenny, she looked better rested, as if she possessed the energy to face whatever this day might hold.

She came to the table and nodded to Jenny in greeting. "You tell them?"

"Not yet," Jenny said.

Cork stopped eating. "Tell us what?"

At that fortuitous moment, Meloux finished his meal, stood up, and said, "Jennifer O'Connor, I would like a word with you."

She was still eating her fruit and yogurt, but the old Mide left the table abruptly. She had no choice except to follow. At the door, she glanced back. The others were staring, watching them go.

Meloux walked into the sunlit morning. The double path along the lakeshore—one of asphalt, the other a wooden boardwalk— was already filling with walkers and joggers and skateboarders and strolling tourists. Meloux ambled along the boardwalk, in no hurry. Although he had to be nearing a hundred years old—Jenny didn't know anyone who knew his exact age; she wasn't sure if Meloux himself even knew—he walked with an upright gait, an almost regal bearing. She'd always thought that in his youth he must have been drop-dead gorgeous. He finally stopped and stood for a long time considering Kitchigami, which was radiant in the sunlight and in the diamond reflections off the water.

He finally said, "When I am in the presence of this great spirit, all that I worry about is like a pebble I can throw to that spirit and walk away."

"I can't forget about Mariah, Henry."

The old man smiled at her, as if she were a child. "Not forget. Accept. We do what we can, and then we let go and accept that the hand of Kitchimanidoo, the Great Mystery, is at work in all things. In you, me, Mariah, this shining big water. And even in this Windigo, though we may not understand how this is so. Tell me what you heard, granddaughter."

She told him about the phone call, about going out with Louise, about the storm and how, inside the howl of the wind, she'd heard the voice of a windigo. She told about their battle with the big man who'd come at them from the dark.

"You sent him running with his tail between his legs."

"With Daniel's help," she said.

He laughed. "That is something, Jennifer O'Connor, I would give my left thumb to see."

"I'm afraid, Henry. I'm afraid I'm not strong enough for this."

"For what?" Meloux asked.

"You save her," Jenny replied.

The old man studied her but made no reply.

"That's what you said to me, Henry. You knew about my vision, didn't you?"

"Your brother shared it with me."

"Is this what it means? Am I supposed to save Mariah? That's how it feels to me."

"The vision is yours, Jennifer O'Connor. Only you know the true meaning."

"Should I be afraid?"

"There is good reason to be careful. That does not mean you need to be afraid. The cry of a windigo is meant to strike fear, and then fear, too, becomes your enemy. But in calling your name, this windigo has revealed to you that you are the hunted. Surprise is no longer possible. This is, I think, a good thing, because you will be wary now. You will be vigilant. You will be ready."

Meloux closed his eyes, as if in sudden meditation. His ancient face was a stone fractured by a hundred lines, and there was something in it hard and, at the same time, yielding, an apparent contradiction that seemed to Jenny possible only with the old Mide.

His eyes opened again, and she knew he'd come to some decision.

"Your father, too, heard a windigo call his name."

"He did? When?"

"Early in this hunt."

"He didn't say anything to me."

"Just as you have said nothing to him."

"I will now."

"Yes," the old man said.

But when they returned, her father was no longer at the table with Louise and Daniel.

"Your dad got a call on his cell phone and took it outside," Daniel explained.

"Who was it, do you know?"

"The retired cop he talked to yesterday, I think. What was his name? McGinty?"

"News, maybe?" Jenny said.

"I guess we'll find out." Daniel nodded toward the door. "Here he comes."

She could tell already that the news from her father's acquaintance wasn't going to be good. Cork was frowning, deep, troubled lines across his forehead. When he saw them all looking, his face went unreadable.

"McGinty says his guy in Duluth PD has nothing. The photos of Mariah didn't ring any bells. As for Carrie Verga, that's Bayfield's jurisdiction. At the moment, of no interest here."

"Did you tell him about the man who calls himself Windigo?" Jenny asked.

"Yes. Didn't mean anything to him, but he said he'd check with his guy again. So, more waiting on that front."

"We should tell him," Louise said.

Cork eyed Louise, then his daughter, and waited.

"Sit down, Dad." When he had, Jenny related the events of the night before, everything except the voice of a windigo calling her name. That was something she wasn't ready to share.

She was glad that, when she finished, her father made no effort to chew her out. He did, however, eye Daniel unhappily. "You didn't say a word."

"I promised Jenny," Daniel said. There was no note at all of apology in his voice. "It had to be Windigo."

"Probably," Cork said. "But I've got bruises from Bad Bluff that'll keep me concerned about what might have followed us from there. Whoever it is, we need to be even more careful, because it's clear we're being watched."

"You think the woman from Nishiime House gave us up?" Daniel asked.

Jenny rose immediately to the defense of Bea Abbiss. "The only vibes I got from her were good ones."

"I got the same good feel from her," Cork said. "We could be wrong, but I'm with you, Jenny. I'm guessing she had nothing to do with last night. If she tried to pass along your cell phone number, it could very well have ended up in anyone's hands. When word goes out on the street, it's like throwing crumbs to pigeons. They all feed. Could I see your phone?"

She handed it to him. He checked recent phone calls, selected the number from which the call the night before had been made. He listened, broke the connection.

"No answer. I'll have McGinty check it out, but my guess is that it was a cheap throwaway. We'll get nowhere tracing it."

"So what now?" Louise asked. She didn't seem defeated in the least, and Jenny found herself taking courage from Mariah's mother.

"Let's think about that life ring we found," Cork said.

Daniel said, "What about it?"

"Once Louise told me her story of working the boats and about girls maybe going overboard, I got fixed on the idea that

that life ring must've come from a freighter, which was probably a mistake. Because other vessels have life rings, right? So I think we should widen our search."

"Widen to include what?" Daniel asked.

"Every possibility. Sailboats, powerboats, fishing boats, cruise liners. You name it."

Daniel didn't look convinced. "That sounds like a lot of territory to cover."

"It probably is. So our challenge is to figure how to do this most efficiently."

"Got a suggestion?" Jenny asked. Because she didn't think he'd go down this road without some idea of where he was headed.

"I do. We begin at the Coast Guard Marine Safety office. It's just down the street, next to the Maritime Visitor Center. I'm thinking they may keep a record of all the craft that use the harbor, commercial or otherwise. And if they don't, they may have an idea who does."

Before anyone could respond to this suggestion, Jenny's cell phone rang. She looked at the display, surprised to see that it was coming from Nishiime House. When she took the call, Bea Abbiss was on the other end of the line.

"I'd like to talk to you," Bea said.

"You have something for us?"

"Maybe. But I want to talk to you and Louise alone." Her voice sounded troubled.

"All right. When?"

"Are you free now?"

"Yes. We'll be right over."

"Thank you."

"That was Bea," Jenny said, slipping the phone back into her purse.

"What's up?" Cork asked.

"I don't know. She just said she wants to talk to us."

"Well, let's go," he said, rising.

"She wants to talk to Louise and me, alone."

"Like the guy who called you last night?"

"This is Bea, and it's broad daylight, Dad."

"I don't like it," he said.

Louise said, "We're going."

Jenny watched her father take this in and digest it. She could see that it didn't sit well with him. But she could also see that he knew what he was up against. "All right. But Daniel and I are going to park a block away. At the first sign that anything's fishy, you run, you understand? Deal?"

"Deal," Jenny agreed.

Meloux spoke quietly. "I will go with the women."

"I don't think that's such a good idea, Henry," Jenny said. "Bea wanted only me and Louise."

"An old man is nothing, Jennifer O'Connor. Just a shadow. You will see."

She started to protest again, but Louise stopped her. "*Migwech*, Uncle," she said.

And so it was decided. And, although Jenny didn't know it at the time, so also was their path toward the man called Windigo set with irrevocable consequence.

CHAPTER 27

Bea Abbiss greeted them at the door to her office. When she saw Meloux, she shot Jenny a worried look but said nothing. She invited them in and asked them to sit. The room seemed darker than the day before, when the late afternoon sun had poured gold through her window.

"You talked to Raven?" Louise said.

"Yes."

Jenny said, "We had a run-in last night with the man we believe is Windigo."

"I know. Raven told me."

"Did she set us up?"

"No. She couldn't do anything to stop it."

"Will Raven see us?" Louise asked.

"With conditions. But I'm not sure it's a good idea now, considering." Her eyes leaped to Meloux, then back to Louise and Jenny. "She's agreed to see you two. She wants no men there." This time she looked pointedly at Meloux. "Not even you, grandfather."

Meloux made no reply, gave no sign at all that he'd heard. He let silence sit between himself and Bea. Finally she seemed compelled to explain.

"You have to understand the situation these girls find themselves in." She spoke now to Louise and Jenny, as if they might need to interpret for Meloux. "They have nothing except what they're given by their family. They also have come to believe that their own self-worth is tied to that relationship. Even if they're scared to death, they won't desert the family. Because, honestly, being scared to death is their daily lot. These girls have been beaten, raped, tortured by the men who head the family, all because of some trespass, not even necessarily a big one. A word of complaint. A look of resistance. It doesn't take much."

She paused, maybe to let the horror of that reality sink in, especially for Meloux.

"I'm telling you this," she continued, "because you need to understand the chance Sparkle—Raven—is taking if she talks to you. And if she does talk to you, you need to be very careful in what you do afterward. Because a wrong move can have huge consequences for her. Do you understand?"

"Yes."

"Do you know where Erikson Park is?"

"North along the lakeshore," Jenny said.

"There's a rose garden there. She'll meet you."

"When?"

"As soon as I call her."

"So you have her number?" It may have sounded like an accusation, as if this was a piece of information she should have given them sooner, but Jenny didn't mean it that way.

"This is risky for everyone concerned," Bea shot back. "We have a relationship with the girls out there. We have street cred. I don't want that jeopardized."

"We understand," Louise said.

Bea looked again at Meloux. "Grandfather, I don't think you should be a part of this."

The old Mide, who'd not spoken before, replied, "Granddaughter, I am a shadow, nothing more."

"Even a shadow might scare her away."

"Then I will be less than a shadow."

Bea looked at Jenny, probably seeking support in dissuading Meloux.

It was Louise who spoke. "He'll be fine. I want him there."

Bea gave a little shake of her head, a clear indication she still thought it wasn't a great idea, but she gave in. She picked up her cell phone, punched in a number, waited. "They'll be there in ten minutes," she said.

She saw them to the front door. They stood in sunlight slanting from above the lake, and it seemed to carry a little silver with it, a bit of promise.

"I hope with all my heart that you find your daughter, Louise," she said, and the two women exchanged a hug, heart to heart.

"*Migwech*," Louise said.

"For God's sake, be careful," Bea said to Jenny, but gently. "Our Windigo isn't a myth."

"We will," Jenny promised and then echoed Louise's thank-you. "*Chi migwech*."

"Grandfather," Bea began, but she didn't seem to know what else to say.

The old Mide took both her hands in his. "I have seen much in my life, granddaughter. The windigo, I have met before. We are old enemies."

She seemed surprised by this. She studied him in the silver light. "This Windigo is still young and very strong."

"Where it counts," the old man replied, "so am I."

The roses in Erikson Park were in full bloom. Behind them the great lake, Kitchigami, stretched toward the horizon, where it met the sky. The green foliage and the red and white and yellow blossoms were like splashes of bright paint against a solid blue wall. The day was already hot, and the park was full of visitors dressed in shorts and shirtsleeves. Jenny didn't see Raven Duvall, the girl who now called herself Sparkle, but she wasn't sure if she'd recognize her, having met her only through a photograph. Louise walked beside her, using a crutch. Meloux followed at a slight distance, and Jenny figured Bea Abbiss's caution had finally sunk in.

After their meeting in Nishiime House, Jenny had spoken with her father, assured him that their meeting with Raven Duvall would be in a very public place, and that he and Daniel were free to do their own research with the Coast Guard. She felt a little vulnerable, knowing their backup was no longer a minute away. But the park was very public, and the sun was very bright, and their hopes were high.

They stopped near a wrought-iron fence. "Do you see her?" Jenny asked.

Louise shook her head. "But I suppose she's changed a lot since the last time I saw her on the rez."

"Would she recognize you?"

Louise shrugged. "I had both legs then." Her eyes scanned the roaming tourists and locals drawn to the garden and the park. "Is that her, maybe?"

She nodded toward a slender young brunette in white shorts and a turquoise tank top approaching them. The brunette wore sunglasses, and a white visor shaded her face. Although she didn't look particularly Native, Jenny knew that meant nothing. The young woman eyed them as she came, then walked right past and stopped at the wrought-iron fence. She pulled a thin camera from the pocket of her shorts and began taking photos of the lake.

They turned back and discovered that Meloux was gone. Jenny scanned the garden, the park, the street they'd just crossed. No Henry anywhere to be seen. He'd simply vanished.

"Mrs. Arceneaux," a voice said behind them.

When they turned, they found a young woman of seventeen with a face that looked much older. She sported a long blond wig, no makeup, dime-store sunglasses. She wore cutoff jean shorts, a purple Vikings jersey, Nikes.

"Raven," Louise said. "Thanks for coming."

Raven Duvall wasted no time. "I know what you want. I can't help you."

"Why are you here, then?" Jenny asked.

She felt the eyes behind those dark lenses assessing her.

"To tell you to stop looking for Mariah," Raven said. "You'll only get yourselves hurt."

"Windigo?" Jenny said. "Is that who'll hurt us?"

"Just leave."

"We saw Windigo last night."

"No, you didn't. If you saw him, you wouldn't be here to talk about it."

Louise reached out to grab her hand, but Raven took a step away, out of reach.

"What about Mariah?" Louise pleaded. "Is my girl all right?"

"I don't know." Her words were harsh. She looked around, her head swiveling as Jenny had seen certain birds do when the shadow of a hawk circled above their nests. She removed her sunglasses, and Jenny saw her eyes, a softer brown than she'd imagined. "Honest, I don't know, Mrs. Arceneaux. But if you keep poking around, even if she is okay now, she won't be for long."

"Where can I find her?" Louise asked.

"I don't know."

"Is she here? In Duluth?"

"Go away. Please."

Jenny jumped in. "We want to help, Raven."

"You can't. No one can. Just go away."

From behind them, a familiar voice spoke gently. "*Boozhoo*, granddaughter. *Anish na?*"

And there was Meloux, who as nearly as Jenny could tell, had materialized from thin air. Raven's eyes shot everywhere, taking in the park, everything, everyone around her. Jenny remembered how afraid she'd been alone in the dark the night before. This girl was with people and in broad daylight, and still she was scared to death.

"Who's he?" she said to Louise, accusing.

"I am no one, granddaughter. I am nothing to fear."

"I said alone. You were supposed to come alone." She looked as if she was about to bolt.

"Before you run away," the old Mide said in a voice that

held not a whisper of threat and yet was utterly compelling, "tell this desperate mother one thing. Just one thing. Is her daughter alive?"

Jenny could see the struggle in Raven Duvall, her head undoubtedly pulling her one way, her heart the other. Her eyes never left the ancient, wrinkled landscape of Meloux's face. Then she broke. "Yes," she said, barely above a whisper. "At least I think so."

"Can you get a message to her?" Louise leaped in.

The spell Meloux had cast was broken. Raven shoved her sunglasses back on her face, hiding her eyes. "No."

"Can you tell us where she is?"

"I already told you. I don't know. It's the truth."

"But she's okay?"

Now she seemed more annoyed than frightened. "She was. She probably is. But I can't say anything for sure now. Everything's changed."

"What's changed? Why?"

"I have to go. I really, really have to go."

"Do you want us to give your mother a message of any kind?" Jenny asked.

"Mom?" Jenny thought that if she'd been able to see the girl's eyes, a lost look would have been there. Raven thought for a long moment. "No," she finally said. The word seemed to hurt her. "Don't tell her anything."

She turned to leave.

"Granddaughter?"

Meloux's voice made her pause, but she didn't look back.

"I have fought the windigo before."

Now she turned. "You?"

"I can stand between you and this Windigo, if you will let me."

"You?" she said again, her voice full of disbelief, even derision. Then she said, "Right," as if it were nothing but a joke and a hurtful one at that.

She spun away abruptly and hurried off among the strolling, clueless tourists. Jenny watched her go, feeling as if she was letting something important slip through her fingers, as if there was so much more she should have been able to pull from the girl.

Tears streamed down Louise's cheeks. She smiled at Meloux and Jenny, her face full of sunlight.

"She's alive," she said. "My girl's alive."

CHAPTER 28

Jenny tried her father's cell phone and got no response. She left a voice message telling him they'd met with Raven Duvall and were heading back to the hotel.

Cork and Daniel were there already, waiting in the lobby. It was approaching checkout time, and as Jenny and the others walked in, several people were leaving, luggage in tow. Jenny's father gathered the group at a table in the breakfast area, which was deserted now.

"Got your message," he said to Jenny. "So, you talked with Raven? What did you get?"

"She thinks Mariah is alive."

"Thinks?" Daniel said. "She doesn't know?"

"That's what she said. She was also clearly scared."

"For herself or for Mariah?" Cork asked.

"Both, it sounded like. And for us."

"Because of Windigo?"

"Yeah."

"What else did she say?" Cork sounded as if he was certain there had to be more.

"She said it wasn't Windigo who attacked us last night."

"Who was it?"

"She didn't tell us that."

He looked disappointed—or that's how Jenny interpreted what she saw in his face—and she couldn't help feeling that she'd let him down. Again. Against his wishes, she'd insisted on being involved in this investigation, but so far, she'd contributed little. Knowing that her father would never have allowed it, she and Louise had gone out alone at night and had been attacked and could have been killed. Despite his objections, she'd gone without him to the meeting with Raven Duvall and had returned almost empty-handed. She wanted to do so much, felt such an obligation—not just to her father but to the girl they sought—and yet she continued to screw up. She was a total disappointment. That's how she felt, anyway, and she feared that this was exactly what she saw reflected in her father's eyes.

Meloux said, "The girl was like a bird, Corcoran O'Connor. She sang her song, a song of warning, and was gone."

Louise asked, "Did you guys find out anything?"

Cork's disappointment, if that was truly what Jenny had seen in his eyes, vanished. "I have only one thing to say. God bless the Coast Guard."

"You got something?"

"We got something," Daniel said.

Between them, they explained their visit. The officer who'd spoken to them was pleasant and helpful. He told them the Coast Guard didn't keep any record of all the boats that used the harbor, nor did he know of any agency or organization that did. Between the freighters, commercial boats, and pleasure boats that sailed in and out every day, there was just no way. But as for a boat christened *Montcalm*, there was a possibility. He explained that the owner of every vessel of at least five tons empty weight that plied the Great Lakes had to file papers of documentation with the Coast Guard. The information included the name of the vessel, home port, and ownership. Cork and Daniel had asked how they could get that information, and the Coast Guard officer had, quite agreeably, gone onto his computer, to a public website the USCG maintained that carried exactly what they needed. He'd found listings for three boats that included the word *Montcalm* in their names. One was a freighter whose home port was Toronto. It was called the *Louis-Joseph de Montcalm*, which, the Coast Guard officer explained, was the name of the great French general who died defending Quebec. The second was a towboat that operated in Lake Erie out of Cleveland and bore the name *Montcalm's Revenge*. The third was a sailboat named simply *Montcalm*, whose home port was Chicago. It was owned by a man named John Boone Turner.

"The towboat's out, I'd guess," Jenny said. "The freighter?"

Her father shook his head. "Based on what McGinty told me about port security, I'd say no. And when you looked at the shipping reports in the *News Tribune* you didn't find any indication that it had been in port here recently."

"Our guess is the sailboat out of Chicago," Daniel said.

"What would it be doing here?" Louise asked.

"I don't know," Cork told her. "But it's the best lead we have so far."

"And what do you do with it?" she asked. Although they were hearing promising news, Jenny could tell that Louise was already exhausted from the morning's expedition. She looked ready to drop.

Cork said, "Let's see what we can find out on the Internet about the *Montcalm* and Mr. John Boone Turner."

"While you do that," Louise said, "I need my insulin, and then I think I need to lie down."

Daniel glanced at his watch. "We ought to make a decision about staying here tonight or not. Checkout's just about now."

"I think we should keep our rooms," Cork said. "There's still a lot of work ahead of us here."

"I'll make the arrangements." Daniel stood up.

"Louise, why don't you go ahead and rest?" Jenny suggested. "When we have something, I'll let you know."

"Thanks," Louise said.

"Let me give you a hand getting to your room." Daniel helped her up and headed with her toward the elevator.

Meloux said simply, "I think I will sit in the sun."

He rose and ambled out the door on the lake side. Jenny

watched him make his way slowly toward a bench on the boardwalk. To anyone else he might have seemed just a frail old-timer in need of a resting place, but Jenny knew better. This was the man who'd offered to stand between Raven Duvall and this Windigo. She suspected that what the great lake and the bold sun offered him was not rest but strength. She was afraid that before all this was over he would need a good deal of that. They all would.

Jenny was left alone with her father. She didn't want to disappoint him anymore. "My phone or the computer?" she asked.

"If we use a real computer, we can look at the screen together," her father said.

Both computers in the business center were available. Cork stood behind Jenny while she logged on to the Internet.

"What do you want me to do, Dad?"

"Whatever you think will get us what we need."

Which felt good to her. Like trust.

First she keyed in "John Boone Turner," which yielded a mother lode of results related to a company called Solidified Investments. The first listing was, in fact, the company website. She clicked on it and saw right away that it was a brokerage firm headquartered in Chicago and owned by Turner. According to the site, there were several offices for Solidified Investments located in other cities across the upper Midwest. One of those cities was Duluth.

There was a photograph of Turner, a handsome man, who despite his silver hair, looked to be only in his mid-forties. Even in the still photo, he exuded a sense of power, a man who would fill a great deal of space in a room and suck up a lot of the air. His eyes were hard and dark as espresso beans. He wore a navy blue suit, white shirt, and bold red tie. Jenny took an immediate dislike to him.

There was also a Wikipedia entry for Turner, which she clicked on. It wasn't long, but it was informative. Born in Waco, Texas, son of an auto mechanic. Graduated La Vega High School, 1990. Enlisted in the Marines. Served in the first Iraq war. Honorable discharge. Enrolled in the Wharton School in 1994. Graduated cum laude. Began immediately working for Goldman Sachs in Chicago. Opened Solidified Investments in 2002. Named one of Chicago's top ten young businessmen in 2003. Married socialite Sylvia Burnhurst in 1999. Two children. Well known for his love of sailing.

"Okay, we know who he is," Cork said. "Now try his name along with *Montcalm*."

Which was exactly what Jenny had planned to do. Without any prompting. But she held her tongue.

She keyed in the search terms, with *Montcalm* as the first. Again, a wheelbarrow full of results. One of them was a very recent posting, a headline: "Racing Against the Wind." It was a link to a Chicago trade magazine, *Investment News*, and she clicked on it. The story was about something called the Grand Superior yacht race, which according to the article, was a biennial event that began at Sault Sainte Marie and ended in Duluth. It had been held two weeks earlier. The article focused on Turner, his sleek sailboat *Montcalm*, and its crew. In this particular race, the crew was composed of several men who worked in various branch offices of Solidified Investments across the Midwest and who were themselves sailors. According to a quote from Turner, "I love the team building that comes from this kind of race. It's us against the elements and the other competitors. In a way, it's like going to war."

A photograph accompanied the article, a shot of Turner and his crew standing in front of a big, sleek, elegant-looking sailboat. The names of all the crew members were listed below along with the cities in which they lived. They came from Minnetonka, Minnesota; Milwaukee, Wisconsin . . . and Duluth.

"Duluth," Cork said, bending over her shoulder and sounding as if they'd struck gold. Jenny couldn't see his eyes, but she would have bet they were shining. She could feel his body tensed, in the way she imagined a hunting dog's might be when, with a sudden and fierce rigidity, it struck a pose, nose pointing toward quarry.

There was another result on the search page, an article from the *Duluth News Tribune* published the day following the yacht race. She clicked on it and found the results of the race. The *Montcalm* had come in second in its class. The race had ended on Sunday, two weeks earlier. The following Tuesday, there was to have been a banquet at which trophies would be awarded. Jenny wasn't sure what this further information added that might be necessary but figured it couldn't hurt.

"Hand me your notepad and pen," she said. Her father always kept a notepad and a pen in his pocket. He'd done this when he was sheriff, and it was still part of his standard daily equipment.

He handed them over, and Jenny made a note of the dates and particulars.

"Look up the number for Solidified Investments here in Duluth."

"I was just going to do that," Jenny said.

"Good girl."

"Don't call me 'girl.'"

He put his hand on her shoulder. "You okay?"

"I know what I'm doing," she said.

"I know that."

"Do you?" She turned and faced him. "Or am I just a fuckup?"

He didn't answer right away, and she was afraid he was trying to come up with a diplomatic way of agreeing.

"Two wolves," he finally said.

"What?"

"It's something Henry once told me. There are always two wolves inside us fighting. One is fear and the other is love. The one you feed is the one that will win that fight. Don't feed the wrong wolf, Jenny. What you're doing is good and important, and I trust you. When it seems that I don't, that's not about you. That's when I'm feeding the wrong wolf inside me."

His eyes were soft and searching, and she knew the truth of what he said.

"We okay?" he asked.

"We're okay," she said.

"All right. We still have work to do."

In Solidified's website section on its branch offices, Jenny found contact information for the Duluth office. Included was a portrait photo of the president of that branch, a man in the photograph of *Montcalm*'s crew, named Simon Wesley. He looked to be in his late thirties, maybe early forties. He had sandy blond hair and a smile that appeared genuine and human, very different from the smile she'd seen on the face of his boss. Or maybe she was only seeing what she hoped to see, a little crack in all the darkness of this case, a small place for the light to shine through.

Cork said, "I'm going to call, make an appointment to see this Simon Wesley."

"What kind of appointment?"

He thought a moment. "I'll tell him I want to talk investments."

Her father wasn't poor. A few years earlier, he'd sold some landholdings for a tidy sum. Cork had invested well, and Sam's Place still brought in a nice chunk of change in season. Nor did he do badly at all in his business as a private investigator. So he knew something about money and could probably bullshit his way into Wesley's office. But Jenny thought there might be a better approach, one that could open the door to questions about Carrie Verga without necessarily raising a lot of red flags too early.

"It might be a startling jump from a stock portfolio to a dead girl on Windigo Island," she said. "Enough that he'd clam up."

"Clam up?" her father said. "You've been reading too much Mickey Spillane."

She smiled at that, then suggested, "What if I called, said I wanted to do an article on him for something like *Lake Superior Magazine*. Him and the yacht race and whatever else might stroke his ego and start him talking. Once he's opened up, we get down to the real stuff."

Her father spent a few long moments thinking it over. Jenny began to muster all the good arguments in favor of the plan.

Which proved unnecessary, because he finally said, "That sounds pretty good. Let's give him a call."

Before they did that, however, Jenny searched for more information on Simon Wesley, which wasn't hard to find. He was a very public figure in Duluth. He ran a charitable organization that taught handicapped kids how to sail. He was on the board of directors for the Great Lakes Symphony Orchestra. He was the face of Save the Lake, an organization aimed at keeping the water of Superior free from pollution. He was also a family man, married eighteen years, with two children.

She logged off the computer, and she and her father went outside. She pulled her cell phone from her purse and keyed in the number she'd written down. She could see the back of Meloux's head where he sat on his bench, no doubt communing with the spirits he seemed to see everywhere.

On the phone, Wesley's voice sounded even younger than the forty years Jenny had pinned him at from his photograph. She could tell he was pleased with the idea of the article she outlined in glowing detail: Lake Superior at the heart of his life and all the good that had come from that. When she told him she had a strict deadline and asked could they speak that very day, he was more than accommodating.

"I'm free most of the afternoon," he offered. "How about two o'clock?"

"That's fine," Jenny said.

"I'll tell our receptionist to expect you."

She ended the call, looked at her father, and gave him a thumbs-up. "We're in."

"Don't get cocky. It's just a foot in the door."

"What door?"

They both swung around, and there was Daniel, face smooth in the sunlight, eyes deep brown and quizzical.

Jenny told him everything. Gushed actually. She felt as if she finally had both hands around the throat of the situation. She realized that her body was tingling. Although she wasn't the hunter that her father and probably Daniel were, she wondered if this was what they felt when they were deep into the chase.

"So you'll be the magazine writer," Daniel said to her, then looked at Cork. "And you?"

"I just need a camera," Cork said. "Then I'm the official photographer."

Meloux rose from his bench and came to them. Jenny thought he would look serene from his communion with the sun and the lake and whatever else he might have perceived that they did not. But he was clearly troubled. She hoped to set his mind at rest and told him what they were up to.

He listened, but didn't look at all relieved. He said, "Have you told your father?"

"Told me what?" Cork looked from Meloux to Jenny.

She didn't think this was the time or place, but Meloux had put her on the spot. So Jenny explained to her father about hearing a windigo call her name the night before. She was ready to argue the reality of what she'd heard, and to ask Louise, who'd also heard it, to back her up. And she was ready to tell him she knew that he'd heard a windigo as well.

But no argument was necessary. Her father said, "That makes two of us. The windigo called my name, too."

"I know."

Cork glanced at the old Mide. "You told her?"

"On this hunt, there should be no secrets. A windigo understands the dark and uses it. In all this, as much as we can, we should stand in the light." Meloux squinted, but not because the sun was in his eyes. "One more thing to understand, Corcoran O'Connor. A windigo is already among us."

CHAPTER 29

The old Mide's statement caught Jenny off guard. "Here, Henry?" She swung her gaze in a full circle, scrutinizing every person she saw on the boardwalk or lounging on the hotel patio. She thought maybe she'd recognize the man who'd attacked her and Louise the night before. But she saw no one who looked familiar and menacing in that way.

"What the hell do you mean, Henry?" Jenny's father said. There was a brittle edge to his voice, one Jenny had never heard him use in addressing Meloux.

"How do you fight a windigo?" Meloux asked him.

"We don't have time for riddles."

"This is no riddle, Corcoran O'Connor. And you know the answer."

"Okay, Henry. The only way to fight a windigo is to become one."

"That is your head talking. Does your heart understand what that means?"

"Look, Henry, we don't have the luxury of a lot of spiritual consideration. These people already know that we're here and that we're looking for them. I don't want this man who calls himself Windigo—and he is only a man—to run for cover. So forgive me, Henry, when I say let's just get on with this."

"On this hunt, never stop listening to your heart, Corcoran O'Connor. That is all I have to say."

The old man fell silent. Jenny couldn't tell if it was because he had, as he said, spoken his piece, or if it was her father's unusually harsh response that had silenced him.

Daniel checked his watch. "We have better than three hours between now and your appointment with Wesley. What do we do in the meantime?"

Her father took a moment to gather himself. It seemed to Jenny that his exchange with Meloux had unsettled him in some significant way. "Okay, there's a question we need to consider. If Carrie Verga came off the *Montcalm*, and if she boarded it here in Duluth, how did her body get up to the Apostle Islands? The racecourse would have taken the sailboat past the Apostles *before* arriving in Duluth."

Jenny said, "Give me your notepad, Dad."

He took it from his shirt pocket and handed it over. She flipped to the page she'd used to write the information from the *News Tribune* article about the race.

"The sailboats that participated arrived in port on Sunday," she said. "The awards were given out at a banquet on Tuesday evening. They were in port for at least two nights, probably three. Maybe one of those nights they sailed back out onto Superior."

"A pleasure sail?" Daniel said.

"Why not? If you race, you must love sailing, right?"

Cork seemed to be rolling something around in his head. He finally said, "They had to dock somewhere here. Let's find out where."

They used Jenny's smart phone. There were only five marinas in the harbor area. Daniel took two, Jenny and her father the others. Meloux stayed at the hotel with Louise while she rested. He didn't want her to be alone, and he was, himself, looking tired. Daniel offered to stay, too, concerned about this Windigo, who seemed to know they were on his trail. But the old man was certain his own presence was enough. Meloux had fought and defeated a windigo once. If necessary, he was up to the task again. Jenny handed

Meloux her cell phone, just to be sure, and gave the old man a crash course in how to use it.

Jenny and her father began at the marina on Barker's Island across the harbor in Superior, Wisconsin. It was one of the largest and had lots of slips for guest dockage. They hit pay dirt right away.

Cork talked to the dockmaster, shot the breeze a bit, flew a story past him about friends in the yacht race, narrowed it down to the *Montcalm*, and the dockmaster spilled what they needed. The sailboat had, indeed, docked there the night after the race. But she'd sailed back out the following day, and didn't return until the morning of the awards banquet.

"Any idea where she went?" Cork asked. Jenny was amazed at how casual he was able to keep his voice.

"The skipper said he was setting sail for the Apostles. That's a destination for lots of the boats here. An easy day trip, and a number of good leeward anchorages in the islands if you decide to stay the night. Gorgeous place. You know it?" the dockmaster asked.

"Better and better all the time," Cork said.

He called Daniel, and they rendezvoused back at the hotel. Louise was awake and rested, and they filled her and Meloux in on what they'd found.

There was talk of lunch. Cork said, "You all go ahead. Jenny and I need to buy a camera, and then we need to keep our appointment with Wesley."

"What about us?" Daniel asked.

"Enjoy your lunch. And keep your eyes peeled for anyone who looks like a windigo." He glanced at Henry Meloux, but the old man's face showed no sign that he'd noticed.

They purchased a Nikon digital SLR at the Best Buy on Miller Hill. Cork had the same camera at home, which he often used in his investigations, so he knew his way around it and wouldn't look stupid or false handling it. Jenny's father also bought one other small piece of electronic equipment.

At two o'clock sharp, they were shaking hands with Simon Wesley.

"Sit down, please." He held out his hand toward two chairs on the opposite side of the desk from his own. They all sat, and he smiled, a genuine gesture.

"I'm pleased and flattered that you're doing another article so soon," he said.

"Soon?"

"It hasn't even been a year since your magazine did the piece on Save the Lake."

"Oh, that," Jenny said. "The range of this piece will be much broader. You're a man of many interests, and you contribute in so many ways to the community here."

He accepted this with a careless little shrug.

Jenny began with his family, and he was clearly proud on the home front. She moved to his work with the orchestra, and it turned out he was a musician himself, a clarinetist. He also liked the theater and had been asked to be on the board of directors for a community repertory company. He'd declined; lack of time. And then she asked about his love of sailing.

"I'm originally from California," he said. "Long Beach. I grew up with a tiller in my hand. I could tie a bowline before I could tie my shoes." He laughed, a very pleasant sound, and ran a hand through his sandy blond hair.

"You love to race, is that true?" she asked.

His brow furrowed a bit. "I'm actually not big on racing. Mostly I just love being on the water. The feel of the wind and the way, on a good day, the boat just seems to fly. Do you sail?"

"No," she said.

"If you'd like, I'd be happy to take you out." He glanced at Cork. "You'd get some great photos, Liam." Jenny had introduced her father as Liam McKenzie. Liam was his middle name. McKenzie was her mother's maiden name.

"I'm on board," Cork said and snapped a photo of Wesley.

"You don't like racing?" Jenny said. "But didn't you recently participate in the Grand Superior yacht race?"

"That's a horse of a different color," he replied. "It's only once every two years, and really I do it at the insistence of my boss. He considers it a morale builder. And you know how it is. Your boss says let's have some fun, you can't very well say no."

"You were part of a crew made up of other men who work for Turner, right?"

She thought she saw a little cloud come into his look, a little shadow of concern. But he held his smile when he answered, "Yes."

"You must work well together. *Montcalm* took second place in its class."

"Best result we've had in that race yet."

"Your skipper must have been pleased."

"He was pretty happy."

"Did you celebrate?"

The smile slowly faded, and it was clear that they'd entered dangerous territory.

"A little, I suppose."

"There was a banquet of some kind to give out the sailing trophies, wasn't there?"

He brightened again. "Yes. A couple nights after the race."

"Did your wife go with you?"

He shook his head. "She and the kids are out in South Dakota visiting her folks."

"Still?"

"They go every summer for two or three weeks. My in-laws own a ranch near Rapid City. The boys have a great time."

"They're not sailors?"

"Oh, they love to sail. But they also love to ride horses. What boy doesn't?"

They were back on easy ground, and he was relaxed. Jenny thought maybe it was time to surprise him. "You ever sail to the Apostle Islands?"

He hesitated too long. "Sure. It's a great trip."

"There and back in a day, yes?"

"Pretty much, yes."

"Do you ever stay overnight?"

"I have on occasion."

"A favorite anchorage?"

His face had gone slack, his blue eyes troubled. He said, "Is this all going to be a part of your article?"

"I ask a lot of questions, and then I sort through for the information that's relevant. When you finished the yacht race, did you sail back to the Apostles with your boss and the rest of the crew?"

He dropped any pretense of civility. "Who are you?"

Jenny glanced at her father, and he produced two photos. One was of Carrie Verga lying dead across the rocks on Windigo Island. The other was of Mariah Arceneaux. He put them on the desk in front of Wesley.

Jenny gave him time to study them well, then said, "When you and all your friends on the *Montcalm* headed off for a little celebratory sail after the race, you weren't alone, were you?"

"I want you to leave my office," he said. "Now."

"What happened on the *Montcalm*, Simon?" Cork said.

"Get out. Now."

"We know the *Montcalm* left its slip at Barker's Island the day after the race and was gone for a night," Cork said. "A couple of days later the body of a girl washed up on a little pile of rocks in the Apostles, a place called Windigo Island. Maybe you read about it. And yesterday we found a life ring on that island, a life ring from the sailboat you were on."

Jenny watched the man's face go ashen. He said feebly, "How do you know there's any connection?"

Which was not a denial.

Cork said, "This is how it's going to play, Simon. Either you talk to us, or we go immediately to the police with everything we know. It won't be hard to connect all the dots, and it will become public and ugly really fast. Do you want that? Or would you like some time first for personal damage control? Either way, it's all coming out. We're giving you a chance at the only measure of control you might have in this. The choice is yours."

Wesley's breathing had quickened. He took up a pen and tapped his desktop. He glanced out the window of his office. The view was across Lake Superior toward the long sand spit of Park Point, which stretched seven miles toward the east, creating the safe harbor that had made the port city famous.

"Who are you?" He could barely croak out the words. "Really, who are you? Because you're not from the magazine."

Cork brought out his license and flashed it and said, "I'm a private investigator. I've been hired by the family of that girl"—he put his finger on the photograph of Mariah Arceneaux—"to find her. I know she was on the *Montcalm* with you."

Jenny was surprised at this, then realized he was bluffing.

Wesley hooked his eyes on her with a desperate, pleading look. "I can't tell you anything. I honestly can't."

"But not because you don't know anything," she said, as coldly as she could. "You were there. You know what happened to Carrie Verga."

"Carrie Verga? I don't know who that is."

She jammed her finger onto the photograph of the dead girl. "That's her. Fourteen-year-old Carrie Verga."

"Fourteen? Oh, Christ. Oh, Christ." He sat back, as if exhausted. Beaten.

"What happened on the *Montcalm*?" Jenny said.

His eyes had fluttered closed, but now they opened, tired and scared. "I didn't have anything to do with it. I swear I didn't."

"Tell us what happened, Simon." The tone of her father's voice had changed, become almost comforting. He sounded like Father Green, their parish priest, when giving permission in the confessional to speak the worst of what was in your heart.

Wesley looked at them a good long while, then said, "It was J.B.'s idea. The whole thing."

"J.B.? As in John Boone Turner?"

He nodded, slack-faced. "When J.B. tells you you're going to do something, you don't say no. He called me up the day after the race and said we were going for a celebratory sail. I love to sail.

Mary and the boys were gone, so I said great. I didn't know about the girls until I climbed aboard at Barker's Island. Fourteen," he said and shook his head. "I would never have guessed."

"They were already on the boat?" Cork said.

"Yeah. J.B. had arranged it."

"How?"

"No idea. J.B. knows how to get what he wants."

"So you all sailed out to the Apostles," Cork said, a statement not a question.

Wesley nodded again. "We anchored off Oak Island, a place I know, a good, protected spot. We'd been drinking, sailing, enjoying the lake. The girls seemed to be having fun. J.B. had brought along a pretty good larder—caviar, pâté, cheese, champagne, really good stuff. Three of the guys, they disappeared belowdecks with her." He pointed toward Mariah's photograph. "J.B., he went below with her." He indicated Carrie Verga. "It was dark by then. I stayed up top because . . . well, because I didn't want to be a part of what was going on down below. I'm a family man." He drilled Jenny with a desperate look. "I *am* a family man."

"I understand," Jenny said quietly. "You were offended by J.B.'s actions."

"You better believe it. But like I said, nobody says no to J.B."

"What happened then?"

"I stretched out in a deck chair and fell asleep. Honestly, I figured I'd just spend the night like that. But about two in the morning, a storm came up, a big, thundering, howling thing. No rain, just wind and lightning. We were leeward of Oak Island, but the water was still pretty rough. I was checking the anchor line when I thought I heard screaming. I couldn't be sure because of the wind and thunder, and I was having trouble because we were dragging the anchor, so I was pretty focused there. When I got us secured again, I went back to my deck chair. J.B. was standing at the railing looking into the dark. I asked him if everything was okay. He said, 'She's gone.' I asked him who was gone. 'Misty,' he said," at which point Wesley nodded toward the photograph of Carrie Verga. "That was what she called herself. I panicked, yelled at him, asked him if she'd gone overboard. He said, and I apologize for the language, 'The fucking little bitch jumped ship.'"

"What did you do then?" Jenny asked.

"Hit our spotlight, swung it all over that wild water. She wasn't anywhere. I screamed at J.B. that we had to find her. I hollered to the other guys belowdecks, and we got to it. We hit the engine and sailed all over that lake in that wind. We never found her."

"You didn't notify the Coast Guard?"

"I wanted to, but J.B. forbid it. 'The scandal,' he kept saying."

"She was beaten before she died. Did you know that?" Jenny said.

"Oh, God." He seemed genuinely devastated. "I didn't."

"What happened to Mariah?" Jenny asked.

"Mariah?"

"The other girl."

"Oh, her. She called herself Candi. When we sailed back to Barker's Island Marina, some guy met us there and took her away."

"What did the guy look like?" Cork asked, taking up the questioning for a while.

Wesley shrugged. "Big."

"Indian?"

"Didn't look Indian."

"How was she doing? Mariah?"

"Upset. Real upset."

"Did she know what happened?"

"Yeah. She was on deck when we were cutting back and forth trying to find her friend."

"It was J.B. who arranged for the girls, right?"

"Right."

"And you don't have any idea who he contacted?"

"No. It's not the kind of thing I do. Ever."

"Has J.B. sailed to Duluth before?"

"Every other year for the Grand Superior."

"So if this is the kind of thing he does, he's probably done it here before."

"I don't know. This was the first time my family was away during the race, the first time he'd invited me on his little pleasure excursion. I didn't know it was going to be that kind of outing. Honest to God, I didn't."

Cork sat back, studied Wesley, then said, "Okay, this is what you're going to do. You're going to contact your boss and do your level best to get out of John Boone Turner the name of his contact in Duluth who arranged for the girls. And you're going to do that without tipping him off to what's going on here. Understand?"

"How am I supposed to do that?"

"You're a smart man, Simon. You'll think of something. I need that information this afternoon. If you get it, I'll make sure that when all this is in the hands of the police and breaks to the media—and it will, big-time—you'll be the one bright spot in the whole shitty mess."

"You can do that?" His eyes lit up, as if he was treading water in the middle of an empty sea and had suddenly spotted a life raft.

"I can do that," Cork promised. "But John Boone Turner goes down."

Wesley took a deep breath, looked away from us, let it out. "This'll ruin him."

"A girl's dead, Simon," Cork shot back. "She was beaten, and probably she jumped from that sailboat to get away from the man who was beating her. Hell, yes, his life is ruined. And, hell yes, it ought to be. But you? You can still salvage something if you do the right thing now."

Jenny's father stood, and she with him. He pulled out his wallet and plucked a card from it, which he laid on the desk. "Call my cell when you have what I need." Jenny turned to leave, but her father wasn't quite finished. "If you get cold feet, or if you think there's some way you might still weasel your way out of this, there isn't."

He took from his shirt pocket the small tape recorder they'd purchased at the same time they'd bought the camera.

"I have your full confession on tape, Simon. I own your ass."

They walked out, leaving Simon Wesley in his office, alone, staring out across the vast blue of Lake Superior and probably seeing nothing on the horizon but the end of his world.

CHAPTER 30

The sun was hot, the day sultry, the tourists on Canal Park Drive as busy and numerous as flies on a carcass. It was Friday afternoon. Only the previous Sunday, Daniel English had come to Tamarack County seeking help, but it seemed to Jenny like a good deal more time had passed than just five days, and she felt, too, that somehow they had all gone a great distance, though they weren't really far from home and never had been. She missed her son. She missed the routine of Sam's Place. She missed, in a sad and selfish way, the naïveté of her life in Tamarack County before that week. When they'd all risked their lives for little Waaboozoons, she thought she'd seen the darkest of spirits. But the more she learned about the world that Mariah Arceneaux and Carrie Verga and Raven Duvall were caught up in, the more she realized she was still just standing at the threshold to all the twisted corridors that wound their way through the human heart.

Her father was unusually quiet as they drove back from their meeting with Simon Wesley. His jaw worked and his face was held tense, as if he were chewing on something hard and bitter. She didn't know what to say. She was thinking they were making headway. Although they still didn't have Mariah safely in their grasp, they'd answered a lot of questions about her disappearance and knew much of the truth behind Carrie Verga's death. That seemed like progress. But she watched her father's hands choking the steering wheel, and she had the feeling she sometimes did when the sky above Tamarack County filled with clouds that were sick green and she listened for the tornado sirens.

Her father had always been a complicated man who seldom shared what went on deep inside him. Her mother had been the viaduct, the way internal knowledge had flowed from him to his children and from them to him. With her death, that natural channeling had ended, and they'd had to try to create something new. It wasn't always easy or infallible, and they weren't always on the same page, but what she realized was that at the heart of it was trust. Trust had always been there. And trust meant love. And love was the wolf to feed. So whatever was going on with her father, she told herself to trust that it was necessary for him, necessary for the way he worked, and she didn't push or pry.

They hadn't eaten since breakfast. They bought sandwiches at a deli on the way to the hotel and ate them quickly. At the hotel, they gathered with the others in the room that Jenny shared with Louise, and Cork filled them in on what they'd learned from Wesley.

"You didn't call the cops on him?" Louise said at the end. She sat on her bed, her back pillowed against the wall, her legs covered with the white bedspread. Her hands were balled into angry fists. "Him or his boss or those other bastards on that boat? You didn't call the cops on them?"

Jenny's father stood at the window, dark against the light beyond the glass pane. "We need one more thing from him before he turns himself in," he said.

"What?" Louise shot back.

"The name of whoever put Carrie and Mariah into the hands of a man like John Boone Turner. That name and a way to contact him. When we have that, I'll tell Simon Welsey to turn himself in to the police."

"Turn himself in? How the hell are you going to make him do that?"

"We hold all the cards, Louise. Or at least he believes we do. Most especially, we have his confession captured here." Cork held up the tape recorder.

"What if he can't get what you want from Turner?" Daniel asked. He'd turned a chair around and sat with his arms draped across the back. "Worse, suppose he tips off these guys, and they all go underground, including this Windigo."

"The men on the *Montcalm* won't run," Cork said. "They're too visible. They have lives they can't just drop and leave. They'll fight it, but in the end they'll go down. Windigo?" He cupped his hand like the claw of a raptor. "I've almost got him. I can feel it."

Jenny saw Henry Meloux studying her father. His eyes were dark and intent, but he said nothing.

Her cell phone rang. She checked the display. The call was coming from Nishiime House.

"Jenny, it's Bea Abbiss. I need you to come here as soon as you can."

"Just me?"

"Maybe you should all come."

"What is it?"

"Just come. You'll understand when you get here."

"We're on our way," Jenny said. "Ten minutes."

"What is it?" Louise asked. "Is it about Mariah?"

"I don't know," Jenny said. "That was Bea Abbiss. She wants us at Nishiime House, all of us. Now."

They took both vehicles and parked in front of the old brownstone. There was no one at the reception desk. The place felt deserted.

"Bea?" Jenny called into the silence.

They heard the boards on the second floor creak under the weight of someone's passage. All their heads turned toward the top of the stairway that led up from the reception area. A rhomboid of sunlight from a west-facing window fell on the wall there, pale yellow against the brown paneling. A sudden shadow cut the light in half, and Jenny felt a shiver of terrible anticipation run down her back. For a moment, nothing happened.

Then Gina, the young woman with cotton candy hair and the

long facial scar, appeared. She looked shattered, as if someone had struck her a blow. "Lock the door," she said.

Daniel stepped back and did just that.

"Up here." She motioned them to follow.

They went slowly, the stairway difficult for Louise and her peg leg and crutch. Both Daniel and Jenny helped. Cork went ahead. Meloux patiently brought up the rear. The sunlight through the window on the landing was intense, and Jenny found herself blinded as she mounted the stairs. She had no idea what they were walking into, but every indication at this point was that they were about to enter one of those dark corridors of the human heart she was becoming more and more acquainted with. Anishinaabe blood flowed in her veins. She'd been raised a stone's throw from reservation life, where poverty and violence were so often a normal part of life. And yet, she understood how shielded she'd been from the darkest realities, the kind that drove Mariahs and Carries and Ravens into the arms of men like Windigo and his brother. These were fearful steps she was taking, but she understood this was a journey that, for her, was long overdue.

At the top of the stairway, they turned right down a short, ill-lit corridor, and then they followed the young woman through an open doorway. It was a room with several beds, little more than cots. All the beds were empty save one. On that narrow mattress lay Raven Duvall, a girl now barely recognizable because of the bruising and distortion of her face. Her eyes were closed, and Jenny wasn't certain if it was voluntary or simply that she couldn't open them because the sockets were so swollen. Her lips were ragged, lopsided balloons. She was wearing the purple Vikings jersey she'd worn that morning when she'd met them in the rose garden of Erikson Park. The jersey was torn and darkened by what Jenny was certain was blood. Two emotions fought inside her. One was a deep, painful empathy for the battered young woman lying helpless on the bed. The other was a terrible, searing guilt because she knew why Raven was there in that horrible condition.

Bea Abbiss sat in a chair at bedside. In her right hand, she held a folded washcloth that had once been white but was now a mottle of red hues. She said, "Sparkle showed up an hour ago, like this. She was barely able to walk. We got her up here, and then I called you."

"You've called 911," Daniel said.

She shook her head. "Sparkle wouldn't let me. She'd have to tell the truth about this, and she doesn't want to do that."

Jenny understood. "She's afraid worse would happen to her."

Bea nodded. "And her family."

"Windigo did this?" Cork's voice was like lava, hot and seething.

Raven's head moved a little on the pillow, a shake indicating *No*. She managed a whisper: "His brother."

"She needs medical attention," Daniel said.

Raven gave a small gasp. "No. They ask questions." Her deformed lips barely moved. "He'd find me. Hurt me, my family. Kill us, maybe."

"We could take her to Tamarack County," Jenny's father said. "She'd be safe, and we could get someone to look at her there."

"*No-o-o.*" A hiss from Raven, like air escaping.

"I know a place, closer," Bea said. "A clinic near the Fond du Lac Reservation. They've helped us out in the past, discreetly."

"I can't see anybody," Raven moaned. "He'll find out. If he can't get me, he'll go after my family."

Louise touched Jenny's arm and said, "Help me down." She gave Daniel her crutch, and Jenny gave her a hand as she knelt beside Raven. "Sweetie, it's Louise Arceneaux." She leaned close and spoke gently. "We're going to help you. We're going to keep you safe. And we're going to keep your family safe, I promise."

Louise looked up at Cork for confirmation.

He said, "I swear to you, Raven, no one will lay a finger on you again or your family."

"He's a good man," Louise said, as if speaking to a small child. "You can trust him."

Then Meloux was beside the bed. In a voice that would have calmed an angry sea, he said to Raven, "You are safe now, granddaughter. You are safe. No one will hurt you anymore. No one will hurt your family. This, I promise." He laid his old hand, steadier than Jenny had seen in a very long time, upon her heart. "Say to me, 'I am safe.'"

She didn't respond. She lay still as death, and Jenny wondered if perhaps her ordeal had finally overwhelmed her and she'd passed out.

"Say to me, 'I am safe,'" Meloux gently repeated.

Jenny saw tears leak from Raven's swollen eyes. Her chest trembled. She caught her breath. At last she whispered, "I am safe."

"Say these words to yourself again and again, granddaughter, like a prayer. They are only words to you now. You do not believe them yet, but they are true. As long as we are with you, you will not be harmed. This is my promise. Our promise."

"And I'll promise this, too," Cork said. "The man who did this to you will pay."

Jenny looked at him. Her father had many faces, most of them shaped and colored by love, because he was a good and loving man. But the face he wore at that moment was like none she'd ever seen before. He meant, Jenny was certain, to offer Raven Duvall some hope of justice, but what she saw there scared her, and she was afraid that if Raven opened her eyes and saw it, too, she might be frightened enough that she would forget the healing mantra Henry Meloux had offered her.

Bea Abbiss made the call.

Cork's Explorer had three rows of seats. He folded down the back row into a flat storage area. He took a mattress from one of the cots in Nishiime House, spread it in the empty place he'd created, and dropped a pillow there. Daniel carried Raven down the stairs of the brownstone, cradling her in his strong arms with great tenderness. He laid her on the mattress carefully, in a way that struck Jenny as deeply caring, and she looked at the big, quiet Shinnob, seeing again his goodness. He was not particularly handsome, yet he was, at that moment, profoundly attractive. Even if he did like Hemingway.

Raven didn't protest. Either she was too deep into her pain and exhaustion to care or she'd accepted—even if she didn't necessarily believe them yet—the promises that had been made.

They stood on the street with Bea.

"Find yourself a safe place," Cork advised her. "Until I've dealt with Windigo."

"You have my number," she said. "Call me when she's been seen, okay?"

"That's a promise," Jenny replied.

They found the clinic just west of Cloquet, half an hour's drive from Nishiime House. It wasn't what Jenny had expected. It sat off the road in a stand of birch trees with its back to the St. Louis River. There were two parts: a nice log home and, next to it, a substantial business-looking structure sided in white aluminum. The sign over the door of the aluminum building read "Rollie's Large Animal Clinic." A wisp of a woman in jeans and a blue work shirt met them in the gravel parking lot. She introduced herself as Lenora Downfeather.

"You're a vet?" Cork said.

"No, that would be my husband, Rollie. I'm a physician's assistant. I work for health services on the rez. Where's the girl?"

"Here," Cork said and lifted the rear hatch on his Explorer.

Lenora Downfeather leaned inside and got right down to business. After a quick preliminary look, she said, "We'll need a gurney. My husband's in the clinic. Tell him what you want."

Daniel went inside and came out with a gurney and another Shinnob, who introduced himself as Roland Downfeather. "Rollie to folks around here," he said. He wheeled the gurney to the back of the Explorer. "How's she look, Lennie?"

"We'll need some X-rays."

"I'll get things set up," Rollie said.

Daniel and Jenny's father lifted Raven out of the vehicle, onto the gurney, and wheeled her inside. The waiting room, like the parking lot, was empty.

"Rollie cleared his schedule when Bea called," Lenora explained. "In this kind of situation, we don't need folks asking questions and spreading the word on the rez telegraph. You all stay here while Rollie and I get the X-rays and I do an examination."

She wheeled Raven down a short corridor and into a room.

Jenny sat down, and the others took seats as well, all except her father, who prowled the waiting area as if it were a cage.

"What now, Dad?" she asked.

"As soon as we can, we ask Raven where to find the man who did this to her."

"And go after him?"

"I made her a promise," Cork said.

What Jenny saw in his eyes was more than a desire to keep a promise. What she saw there looked very much like murder.

It was almost an hour before Rollie Downfeather returned and said that they could talk to Raven now, but to keep it limited in time and to one or two visitors at most. Cork went first, and Jenny said, "I'd like to come, too."

Her father made no objection.

Lenora met them in the corridor. She explained that despite how bad Raven looked, the X-rays had shown no evidence of broken bones or internal bleeding. She'd given the girl something to help with the pain, which Raven would probably be experiencing for quite a while. She said it would be all right to talk to her but to take it easy.

Raven lay on a cot in an exam room. She was covered with a sheet and blanket. She was awake and turned her head when Jenny and her father walked in.

"He'll hurt my family," she said. It was still mostly a mumble through those distorted lips, but it was understandable.

"We'll make sure they're safe," Cork said. "I promise."

That seemed to comfort her more than any painkiller.

Cork took her hand. "Who is Windigo?"

She shook her head. "Don't know his real name. Nobody does. When I first met him, he told me it was Angel. But it's not."

"You said he didn't do this to you. It was his brother. Does his brother have a name?"

"Manny. Short for Maiingan."

"Wolf," Cork said, translating the Ojibwe word.

"Yeah. Wolf."

"Why did he do this to you?"

"Word came down Bea was looking for me. Manny heard. Bea's always trying to help us girls. Manny knows. Usually he ignores it. Thinks he has us too scared. He said I should call her, see what she wanted. She told me you were looking for Mariah. Gave me phone numbers. Manny said he'd take care of it. He came back last night beat up and pissed as hell. I thought if you kept at it, he might get mad enough to kill somebody." She looked at Jenny. "What I told you in the park was true. I thought if you and Mrs. Arceneaux went poking around you'd get killed or Mariah would. Better if you just left."

She was quiet for a few moments, maybe collecting herself, her strength.

"Manny followed me to the park," she went on. "Said he'd been watching me since Misty—Carrie—died. That I'd been different. He grabbed me after I talked to you, wanted to know what you said. I told him you were religious people trying to save my soul. He called me a lying bitch. Said you were the same ones he went after last night. He took me back to our crib, started on me, made the other girls watch. Said he was going to give me the face a lying bitch deserved. A lesson, he called it. He likes giving lessons."

"How'd you get away?"

"A couple guys off one of the freighters wanted company for the weekend. Manny took Krystal. Before he left, he said if I ever talked to anyone again, he'd kill me. He meant it."

"But here you are."

"They say we're family. We're not. Carrie's dead. They didn't care. Mariah didn't do nothing, but they blame her."

"What about Mariah? Is she with Manny?"

Raven shook her head. "Don't know where she is. Angel took her. Her and another sister. Haven't come back."

"And you don't know where they went?"

"He takes girls all over. Don't know where he went this time."

"Would Manny know?"

"He'd know."

"Where can I find him?"

"Apartment. In Duluth." She gave a street and number, which Cork wrote down on his notepad.

"Who else is in the apartment?"

"Just Manny, one other sister. Like I said, Krystal's with the guys off the boat for the weekend."

"No other men?"

A shake of her head. Jenny could see she was tiring. So could Lenora Downfeather. She said, "I think that's enough for now."

They stepped into the small corridor and spoke in whispers.

"Can she stay here?" Cork asked Lenora.

"How long?"

"Just until after dark."

"She really needs to go somewhere she can get constant care. I've pretty much done what I can for her. And I know how this will sound, but I'm not eager for the man who did this to know I help these girls."

"I understand," Cork said. "The man who did this? When it's dark, I'm going after him."

Lenora Downfeather looked back at the girl lying beaten on the cot.

"Godspeed," she said.

CHAPTER 31

They wouldn't be staying in Duluth that night. In the early evening, while the others kept watch over Raven Duvall, Jenny and Daniel English drove to the hotel to retrieve the things they'd left behind. It was deep twilight when they returned to Rollie's Large Animal Clinic. Jenny's father was in the parking lot, talking on his cell phone.

"That's disappointing, Simon," Jenny heard him say. "I expected more."

Cork paced back and forth, his voice taut, bordering on anger.

"No," he said. "Tomorrow morning will do. But I'll be keeping tabs on you, Simon, so don't get cold feet. This won't simply go away. Tomorrow morning will be the only chance you have to salvage something from all this, the only chance you'll have at saving your good name. When you've done what you need to do, have your lawyer call me. Understand?"

Jenny didn't hear him say good-bye.

"Simon Wesley," he explained to her. "Says his boss arranged everything over the Internet. Met the guy who delivered the girls, but got no names. His boss said that's the way it always works." Cork's face was a stone mask, but his eyes were cold. "By the time this is over, it won't work that way anymore for John Boone Turner. Not ever again."

Inside, in the waiting room, her father said to everyone, "It's time to do this."

He'd outlined earlier what would occur, and his plan had

included only him and Daniel. This didn't sit well with Jenny, though she'd said nothing at the time. Now she said, "I'm going."

"We've already decided how this will be," her father said.

Once again, she found herself in a position of defiance, a place that, so far, hadn't turned out to be particularly good. And she knew that once again she was at risk of screwing up a construct that her father, with years of experience in this kind of thing, had designed. But she was damned if she was going to be left behind.

"Not we. You. You decided."

"You're not going, Jenny."

"I am."

"When you came along in the beginning of all this, it was with the understanding that I gave the orders."

"Things are different now."

Louise said, "Let her go, Cork. If I could, I'd go. I'd help."

He put up a warning finger. "Not your call, Louise." He turned back to Jenny. "If things go south, and there's no guarantee they won't, I don't want to have to worry about your safety."

"And I can't worry about yours?"

"How will you being there help?"

"We won't know unless I am, will we?"

His eyes were iron, and he spoke with slow deliberation: "Think about Waaboo."

"And what do I tell my son as I raise him? That he should stand up for what he believes only if it doesn't threaten him? That's certainly not how you raised me."

"There's no logical reason for you to do this. Daniel and I can handle it."

It was like hammering against a locked door, but she kept trying. "I need to do this for me."

"Why? This isn't part of the vision."

He was right. Somewhere along the way it had become about something much more substantial than a vision. The girl they were trying to save had left home long ago, had walked through a door into the world and been lost. To find her, and in a way, to find herself, Jenny believed that she needed to leave the safety of her own life and follow into that world where Mariah had gone. She understood her father's resistance. This was a journey no parent wished for a child.

"Maybe all of this is a part of the vision," she said evenly. "Or maybe none of it is. All I know is that it feels right for me to go. It feels right here." She put her fist against her breast, over her heart.

Her father opened his mouth to make a reply, but Daniel spoke first. "If we get in too deep, Cork, it wouldn't be a bad idea to have someone on the outside of things to call for backup. If she promised to stay clear of the action."

Cork shot Daniel a look that said *traitor*. He took a deep breath. "Would that satisfy you, Jenny?"

"That would satisfy me."

Cork turned away from her, turned away from them all, and was silent a long time before he finally faced them again. "All right. But you do exactly what I say, understood? If trouble comes and I say run, you get the hell out and you don't look back. Are we clear?"

"We're clear."

"Fine," he said, though his tone said otherwise. "Let's go."

The crib, as Raven had called it, turned out to be in an old brick apartment building not far from downtown, the kind a rat might call cozy. It appeared to be a fourplex, two apartments up and two down. There was a wide porch on the first floor and above it a balcony. An alleyway bordered it on one side. On the other lay a great patch of weeds with one tall sunflower making a proud showing near the center. The neighborhood was a sad collection of residential buildings that had probably once been large family homes but had been carved up into tiny, forgettable units, and everywhere Jenny looked, the face of neglect stared back. The saving grace of the old fourplex was that anyone sitting on the front porch or on the balcony would be able to see the calming blue of Lake Superior far down the hill. Jenny imagined this would be a blessing to a girl constantly under the eye of men like those who called themselves Wolf and Windigo.

They'd taken Daniel's truck and had parked across the street and a few houses down, where they could check out the place without being seen. The moon was climbing, everything beneath it painted in either silver or shadow. Far down the hill, Jenny could see where the moonlight spilled like mercury across the dark surface of the lake. She could see the tall sunflower and the shadow it cast across the weeds, a sort of black reflection of itself. She could see the glow behind drawn shades in the apartments. What she didn't see, none of them saw, was any kind of vehicle parked near the building.

"You two stay here," Cork said. "I'm going to do a little reconnoitering. Daniel, you got a crowbar in that toolbox of yours?"

"Yeah." Daniel handed him the key.

Cork climbed into the bed of the truck, rummaged around in the big toolbox, came back with a crowbar, and returned the key to Daniel. Without further explanation, he left the truck, slipped across the street, kept to the shadows, and disappeared down the alley around the back of the apartment building.

For a little while, neither Jenny nor Daniel talked. Then Jenny said, "Thanks for backing me up."

Daniel, whose attention seemed to have been totally on the building across the street, angled his face toward her. He smiled gently in the dark. "I was beginning to think we might be there all night arguing the point. He can be stubborn, can't he?" He waited a beat and said, "Kind of like you."

"Both cut from the same cloth," Jenny said.

"Good cloth," Daniel replied.

They waited fifteen minutes. Jenny's father didn't come back.

"I'm getting a little worried," Jenny said.

"He's just doing a thorough lookover is my guess. Never good to walk into a situation you haven't scoped out well."

He sounded as if he meant it and wasn't just trying to reassure. Like her father, he knew this kind of business better than she. So she believed him.

A dark SUV pulled into the alley and parked next to the apartment building. Two figures got out. One was tall and powerful-looking. The other was small, a walking willow branch. Female, Jenny thought. And probably just a kid. The two entered the building through a back entrance. Lights came on in one of the upper units.

"Where is he?" Jenny said after another few minutes had passed. "Shouldn't he have had a good idea of things by now?"

"Every situation's different," Daniel said. "But I think I'll go see if he needs a hand." He reached across Jenny, opened the glove box, and took out his sidearm and a pair of handcuffs.

"I'm coming, too," Jenny said.

"That's exactly what you promised him you wouldn't do."

He was right. She said, "Don't be long. Call if you need me." She held up her cell. "You have my number."

"On speed dial." He smiled that gentle smile again, then left his truck and crossed the street. Like Cork before him, he stuck to the shadows cast by the moon. Jenny watched him slide around the back of the building, where the big man and willow-stick girl had gone.

Minutes passed. A lot of minutes. In the dead silence, Jenny tried to keep judicious counsel with herself. There was good reason both Daniel and her father had disappeared. Good reason she hadn't heard anything. Good reason to keep her promise to her father.

This was the part of the hunt that Henry Meloux had said was the most important. The patience. But Jenny knew she was no hunter.

"Screw it," she finally said aloud and got out of the truck.

She stepped into the street just as a car rounded the corner behind her and caught her full in the glare of its headlights. The blast of a horn came loud and long, and Jenny jumped back.

"Watch where you're going, crazy bitch," the driver hollered and drove on.

Jenny stood on the curb, catching her breath, settling herself.

She studied the apartment building to see if any shades had been raised at the sound of the horn. As near as she could tell, no one gave a damn. That kind of neighborhood.

She crossed the street and entered the alley and came to the SUV parked there. Minnesota plates, she saw. Tinted windows that, in the dark, were like ink bottles. As she stood in the shadow of the building, amid the foul garbage smell that poured off a big trash bin in the alley, trying to decide what her next move was, the back door opened, and Jenny froze.

The man who stood in the drizzle of light from the overhead bulb was big, well built. He made Jenny think of the WWE wrestlers she sometimes caught a glimpse of when she surfed the television channels looking for something interesting to watch. His face, or what showed of it in the dull light, didn't look Indian, but Jenny knew that meant nothing.

"Okay, Ember boy, do your stuff."

Jenny now saw that the man had a dog with him, an Irish setter. The dog looked old, and when it descended the back steps it moved gingerly. It wandered into the weed patch next to the building, sniffed around the single sunflower stalk, and lifted its hind leg. The guy watched from the porch, and Jenny took the opportunity to ease herself behind the cover of the SUV.

The man reached into his shirt pocket and brought out a joint. He dug into the pocket of his khakis, pulled out a lighter, and lit the joint. He drew smoke deep into his lungs, held it, then exhaled. He repeated the process, and it wasn't long before the scent of burning weed drifted down to where Jenny hid.

"Come back here, you worthless old hound." The words themselves were not gentle, but the man spoke them as if they were. The dog laboriously climbed the steps, and the two of them sat side by side, the man running his hand lovingly down the length of the animal's body, the dog's tail sweeping contentedly across the porch floorboards.

A girl stepped through the door behind them and came out onto the wooden landing. She was young, probably early teens, blond, willowy. Maybe the girl Jenny had seen earlier, but she couldn't be sure. She wore a white tank top, clearly no bra beneath, and tight jeans. She stood beside the man, who paid her no mind.

"Sharesies?" she said.

Without replying, he held up what was left of the joint. She accepted it, took a couple of tokes, handed it back.

"Thanks, Manny," she said. "I needed that." Then she said, "I'm hungry, Manny."

"Food in the refrigerator," he said.

"It's all crap."

"Guess you'll have to eat crap, then."

"There's a twenty-four-hour McDonald's on London Road."

"I'm not taking you to no McDonald's."

"Sparkle—" she began.

He turned on her. "You say that bitch's name again, I'll break your face."

"I was just going to say that she used to go get food for us there at night sometimes. Maybe she's there now. I mean, if you really want to find her."

"I find her, I kill her," Manny said.

"You already came pretty close."

"McDonald's," Manny said, as if thinking. He shook his head and said, "She'll come back. You bitches always come back."

"If she's there, you could bring her back. That would be good, wouldn't it?"

"I told you, Cherry, I'm not taking you nowhere. Get back inside."

Cherry didn't move. Manny stood, lifted his arm as if to slap her face, and the girl said, "I'm going, Manny. I'm going."

The man was left alone with his dog. He eyed the last little bit of the joint he held, tossed it in his mouth, chewed a couple of times, swallowed.

"Come on, Ember boy," he said, standing up. "Let's call it a night."

After the man and dog had gone back inside, Jenny waited a full minute before she dared to move. Slowly, she rose from the crouched position she'd held, despite her aching knees.

The hand on her shoulder made her jump. She spun, fists raised, ready to defend herself. Daniel held a finger to his lips, begging silence.

"You," she whispered in relief. "Dad?"

Daniel said nothing but crooked his finger in a sign for her to follow. He made his way around to the other side of the building, where a short flight of steps led down to a basement doorway. The door was open a crack. Jenny saw splintered wood along the doorframe, and the hasp and padlock hung there, useless. She followed Daniel into the utter black inside. She felt his hand on her arm and let him guide her blindly for a dozen steps, then another door opened, this one onto light and a stairway that headed up. Daniel led the way, and again she followed. They came into a long hallway suffused faintly with the odor of mildew and fried onions. The floor was bare, the old boards worn to gray. The hallway ran straight to the front of the building, where doors on either side opened onto the two lower units and another stairway led up. Daniel went ahead and began to climb. Jenny started up after him, but when she put her weight on the first stair, an old board let out a screech. She held still. They both held still. Nothing else happened. They moved on, but after that, Jenny followed exactly in Daniel's footsteps.

On the second floor there were two doors, just as there'd been on the lower level. From behind one came the sound of a television turned too loud. Jenny had yet to see her father. She looked to Daniel for explanation, but he only pointed, his finger indicating a set of hallway windows that overlooked the long balcony in front. The panes were up to let in the night air. Jenny saw that one of the window screens had been cut, a long slash down the center. Daniel slipped through the cut screen and signaled Jenny to follow. Outside, Jenny found that each of the upper units had a door that opened onto the balcony. Her father was standing at one of the doors. He put two fingers to his eyes, then indicated a window beside the door. Daniel eased himself to the window frame and took a look. He drew back so that Jenny might look, too. The window was curtained, but the curtain wasn't completely closed. Jenny could see an old green couch, and on it was seated the girl who'd earlier been on the back porch with the man she'd called Manny. She wore only the white tank top and shiny, lime-green bikini underwear. She was idly turning the pages of a magazine. Manny was nowhere to be seen.

Jenny's father motioned Daniel to him but raised his hand like a traffic cop, warning Jenny to stay where she was. Daniel slid his Glock from where he'd nested it in the waist of his jeans. He worked the slide and nodded to Cork. In one hand, Jenny's father held the crowbar. With the other, he gripped the doorknob and turned it gently. The old piece of hardware gave a rusty little cry, and Cork shoved the door open fully and rushed inside.

She was supposed to stay back, but Jenny could no more do that than she could stop her heart from beating. She bolted to the doorway.

Inside, the girl had jumped from the couch. She stood staring at Cork and Daniel, her eyes big as apricots, her mouth opened, as if for a scream that hadn't yet come. From a doorway behind her, where Jenny could see a refrigerator and half a stove, the big man, who'd also been on the back landing, appeared, wiping his hands with a dish towel.

"Police. Hold it right there," Daniel shouted and leveled the Glock.

The big man looked at Cork. He looked at Daniel and the side-arm Daniel held. Jenny had a sense that he might be calculating the distance between himself and the intruders and the intruders' gun. But he did as Daniel had ordered. Until the girl finally let out her scream and charged.

She came at Daniel and threw her whole self onto him, wrapping as much of her thin body as she could around his gun arm. As soon as she'd made her move, the guy in the kitchen doorway charged Jenny's father. He knocked the crowbar from Cork's hand, and the two of them tumbled in a sprawl of limbs. The man made wild beast sounds and went at her father like rage sheathed in flesh, as if murder pumped through his veins instead of blood. Daniel was doing his best to shake off the girl, but she was like glue and was trying to sink her teeth into his arm.

Both of the men Jenny cared about could use a hand. She chose Daniel. She caught the girl around the throat in the crook of her arm and squeezed to cut off air. It was a move that her father had shown her once, but that she'd forgotten until this moment. The girl let go of her hold on Daniel to claw at Jenny's arm. Daniel used his sudden freedom to club the back of Manny's head a good one with his sidearm. The wild man pitched forward and rolled to the floor.

The girl in the crook of Jenny's arm had begun to ease up in her struggle.

Jenny said, "If I let you go, will you behave yourself?"

The girl nodded rapidly.

"Sure?"

"Uh-huh," the girl managed to grunt.

Jenny released her. The girl stumbled away and stood feeling her throat as if to be certain it was all still there.

From somewhere in the back of the apartment came a barking, but the dog didn't appear.

The girl lunged for the door to the hallway. Daniel cut her off.

"We're not here to hurt you," he said. "We came for that one." He nodded toward the man who called himself Wolf and who lay groaning on the floor. "Who else is here?"

"Nobody," she said. "Just him and me right now."

Jenny's father rose slowly from the floor. He gave his head an experimental turn to the right, to the left. He looked down at the man lying prone at his feet, then at Daniel. He said, "Thanks."

"What's your name?" Daniel said to the girl.

She glared at him and didn't answer.

"Cherry," Jenny said, then added more softly, "But that's not your real name, is it?"

"Fuck you," the girl said.

"You know someone named Sparkle?" Daniel asked.

Her mouth was silent, but her eyes said everything. *Fuck you.*

"She's okay," Daniel told her. "Sparkle's safe."

The girl's face changed. She'd been like a cornered animal, angry, maybe afraid she'd end up like Wolf, or worse. But now she seemed surprised. Amazed even.

"Okay?" she said.

"Yes. Safe. We can make you safe, too, if you let us."

It was clear she didn't believe him. She stared down at Wolf and shook her head. "There's no safe now."

"We're after the one who calls himself Windigo," Cork said. "We'll get him, you can be sure of that. And you'll be safe then, I promise."

"Windigo? I don't think so."

"Can you tell us where he is?"

She shook her head again, harder this time.

"You can't or you won't?"

"I don't know who you are," she said, "but I know him and I know what he'll do if he finds out I said anything. I mean anything."

"Just tell us this: Do you know where he is?"

"I don't," she said. "I swear to God I don't."

"Does he?" Cork gave a nod toward Wolf, who was just now beginning to rouse himself.

She didn't answer, and that in itself was an answer.

The dog somewhere in a back room had stopped its barking. Daniel pulled his handcuffs from where he'd hung them on his belt. Wolf tried to push himself up from the floor, but Daniel kicked his hands out from under him, and the big man went down again. Daniel knelt with his knee in Wolf's back, grabbed an arm, cuffed the wrist, then cuffed the other. He rolled Wolf over, so that the man looked toward the ceiling. Wolf blinked a few times, and his eyes began to focus.

Cork leaned over him. "Where's your brother?"

Wolf took a moment to reply. When he did, it was cold and quiet. "I'll kill you. And then my brother'll kill you."

"Where's your brother?" Cork asked again.

Wolf glared up at him. "We'll both kill you," he said. His dark eyes traveled across Daniel and Jenny. "And then we'll kill you and you." He looked at the girl who'd done nothing but try to help him. "And what the hell. We'll kill you while we're at it."

Cork spoke to the girl. "Do you have any duct tape?"

"In a kitchen drawer."

"Jenny?" he said.

She went to the kitchen. The barking began again, from behind a door next to the refrigerator. She ignored the sound, found the duct tape, and brought it back. Her father took a strip from the silver roll and pressed it over the mouth of the man called Wolf.

"Let's get him out of here," he said.

"What about me?" the girl said.

"Do you want to stay here?" Cork asked.

She considered that possibility and gave a faint shake of her head.

"Do you have someplace to go?"

Another slight headshake.

"I'll take you somewhere, to someone who'll help you figure what your next move will be."

"Not the cops," she said.

"Not the cops," Cork assured her. He waited, but received no response. "So, do you want to go with us?"

She looked at Jenny's father in the same way she probably looked at every man by then. There was no trust left in her. Why should there be? And why should she trust Cork O'Connor or Daniel or even Jenny? All she knew of them was violence, whose proof lay at her feet. Although that violence had been directed at Wolf, her keeper, her own experience probably told her that sooner or later it would be visited on her. But there was also a look on her face that seemed to Jenny old and beaten and must have been simply the realization that in her life she had no real choices.

She said, "I'll go."

Cork and Daniel hauled Wolf to his feet.

Jenny said, "What about the dog?"

CHAPTER 32

They walked into Rollie's Large Animal Clinic, and Louise looked at them curiously. "Where'd you get the mutt?"

"His name's Ember," Jenny said. "He belongs to Manny, but don't hold that against him. He's a sweet pooch."

The old Irish setter trotted forward as if Louise were very familiar. He nuzzled the hand she held out to him. He went to Rollie Downfeather, who was keeping Louise company, and did the same.

"Where's Henry?" Cork asked.

"Him and Lenora are sitting with Raven," Louise said. "She wanted Henry there."

At that moment, Meloux came from the exam room where Raven lay. When Ember spotted him, it was as if the dog had found someone lost to him long ago. He bounded to the Mide and, if he'd been smaller or Meloux larger, would have leaped into the old man's arms.

Meloux was clearly taken with him. "Who's this?"

"His name's Ember," Jenny said.

"Ember, eh? Good name." Meloux worked his hands lovingly across the dog's coat. "You're old like me, but I can tell that you, too, have a lot of fire in your heart."

"What about the man?" Louise said. "Maiingan?"

"Under a blanket in Daniel's pickup," Cork said. "We've got him trussed up like a mummy with duct tape so he can't move or talk. We're taking him back to Tamarack County."

"Why so far?" Louise said.

"I want to question him in my own way. Best I do it there."

"But what if Windigo is here, in Duluth?"

"According to Raven and the girl who was with Manny to-night, Windigo's been gone awhile."

"Another girl?" Louise said. "Where is she?"

"We put her in the hands of Bea Abbiss," Jenny said.

Louise seemed satisfied. "So, we're going to Tamarack County?"

"Not all of us," Cork told her. "You and Daniel are heading back to Bad Bluff. I told Raven we'd protect her family. I can't do that if they're in Wisconsin. Lindy Duvall doesn't know Daniel, but she knows you, Louise. You have to convince her to come to Tamarack County with her children until we've taken care of Windigo."

Louise said, "I can do that."

"Good. It's settled. Let's get Raven into the Explorer. The sooner we start the better."

Lenora Downfeather brought them a wheelchair, and Jenny and Daniel helped Raven into it. Daniel wheeled her out to Cork's Explorer. He lifted her from the chair as gently as if she were his own sister and laid her on the mattress they'd put in the back at Nishiime House.

"My family?" she asked.

Jenny watched Daniel lean over the girl, big and gentle and protective, and when he spoke, it was with such tenderness that Jenny's heart seemed to crack. "I'm going to get them, Raven. I'll keep them safe, I swear to you. Just rest. You'll see them soon."

He drew back and stood up. To Jenny, in the moonlight, he looked armored in silver.

They transferred the man who called himself Maiingan to the Explorer. He sat in the backseat, his mouth and feet taped, his hands in cuffs. Ember jumped into the vehicle, too, and made himself comfortable at Manny's side on the broad seat. They said good-byes and thank-yous to Lenora and Rollie Downfeather.

Cork said to Louise, "You make sure you bring Raven's family back."

"What about my family?" she asked.

"Let your brother know what's up. You have lots of relatives in Bad Bluff. It's time they started looking out for one another. Once we have a fix on Mariah, we'll make sure they're all well protected."

Jenny touched Daniel's arm. "Before you go, I owe you something." She lifted her face to his, intending to give him that kiss on the cheek she believed she'd owed him since the incident on Superior Street the night before. Instead, her kiss landed full on his lips. She stepped back, surprised—though not completely—by what she'd just done. "I'll see you in Tamarack County."

The big Shinnob, whose face had so often been a desert of expression, looked absolutely stunned. He said, "Okay." He got into the truck with Louise and drove away.

Cork handed Jenny the keys. "You drive. And Henry, you can sit up front."

"I'd rather sit beside the old dog," Meloux said. "It will put me closer to the girl, if she needs me."

"Your choice, Henry," Cork said.

"You're sure you want me to drive, Dad?"

Her father gave a curt nod. "I've got calls to make. A lot of wheels to set in motion. The clock's ticking, and we don't have much time."

With that, they took their places in the Explorer and headed north.

It was nearing one in the morning when they pulled into the garage on Gooseberry Lane. Rose was expecting them. Rainy was there, too, something Cork had arranged. Jenny's little Waaboo was in his bed, sound asleep. Cork carried Raven into the house. He took her to his own room and laid her down on his bed. Meloux had followed them inside the house, accompanied by the old Irish setter.

"Who's this?" Rose asked, when the dog padded into the kitchen.

"His name's Ember. He'll be staying with us for a while," Jenny said.

Trixie came from the living room, and the two dogs spent a moment nose to nose, then noses to other places. In the end, they seemed just fine with each other.

Meloux and Jenny went upstairs, where her father had taken Raven. The girl on the bed looked up at the old Mide, pleading in her eyes.

"Don't leave me," she said.

"Granddaughter," Meloux replied, "that is not even a possibility."

Cork pulled an armchair to the side of the bed, and the old man made himself comfortable in it.

"Grandfather," Raven said, addressing Meloux for the first time in this way.

"What is it, child?"

"This is my fault," Raven said. "It's all my fault. Carrie's dead. Mariah? I don't know. I'm to blame. I lied to them."

Behind Meloux, Cork spoke. "How did you lie to them?"

Tears ran from the corners of her bruised, swollen eye sockets. "Carrie was already messed up. Her son of a bitch stepfather was already using her. Mariah was going to be part of that, sooner or later. That asshole Verga was working on her. I told them it would be different with me. They could model. They'd have nice clothes, cars, bling. And no one like Demetrius Verga to worry about. They'd be free of all that crap, that's what I told them. I'm a liar, grandfather. A liar and worse. So much worse."

"What you did is done," Meloux said gently. "What you were is not what you are and not what you will be. Rest, child. You are safe now."

Cork said, "I have to go, Henry."

The old man nodded. "Maiingan."

"And after him, Windigo."

Because he sat, Meloux had to look up at Jenny's father, who was standing. The old Mide studied him a very long time. "You will take me on that hunt."

"If that's possible, Henry, I will."

"Do not hunt this windigo without me, Corcoran O'Connor."

Meloux's voice was sharper than Jenny had ever heard it. This was no request. This was an imperative. If it had been said to her, Jenny would have knuckled under in a flash and done whatever it was Meloux wanted. But her father gave the old man—his friend, his mentor of a lifetime—a long, steely-eyed look.

"I began this hunt without you, Henry. If I need to, I'll finish it that way."

"What does it take to kill a windigo?" the ancient Mide asked.

"The balls of a windigo," Cork replied. Without another word, he turned and left the room.

The only light came from a small bedside lamp. Meloux sat in the dim glow, staring at the empty doorway Jenny's father had just passed through. He said, very quietly, "No, Corcoran O'Connor. The heart."

Jenny followed her father downstairs and into the kitchen, where Rainy intercepted him.

"Cork?"

"What is it?" Not harsh words, but impatient.

The door was open at Rainy's back, the black of night impenetrable beyond the screen. Moths and night insects buzzed against the mesh, trying to get inside, get to the light.

Rainy spoke carefully. "I know you made me a promise in the beginning of all this, and I love you for that, but I won't hold you to it, Cork. What you're about to do, you don't have to. You know that."

"I keep my promises, Rainy. But this isn't about a promise anymore. These men need to be taken down."

"And you're the only one who can do that? It won't bring her back, Cork. It won't change what already is."

Jenny knew what she was saying, knew that Rainy wasn't talking about Mariah Arceneaux or what had happened to her.

Her father didn't answer. He stared at Rainy a long time, then turned, shoved the screen door open, scattered the flying insects, and was eaten by the night.

Rainy watched him go. "Did you see?"

"See what?" Rose asked.

But Jenny had seen it. She said, "Murder in his eyes."

CHAPTER 33

It had been a long time since Jenny and Henry Meloux had eaten. Rose reheated lasagna she'd made the night before and threw together a tossed salad. Rainy took a plate up to her great-uncle. She returned and reported that Raven was sleeping soundly. After they ate, Jenny cleared the dishes, and Rose made good coffee. She always made good coffee. She had cookies in the jar shaped like Ernie from *Sesame Street*, which had occupied its place on the kitchen counter as far back as Jenny could remember. They sat at the table, drank coffee, ate cookies, and while the night lay deep around the house on Gooseberry Lane, gave themselves comfort in talking.

At first they talked about Raven and the whole awful situation with the man who called himself Windigo. And then they got onto the subject of how a young girl could fall into that kind of mess.

Rainy said, "Try to imagine what it's like growing up Indian. You're part of a culture that white people have, from the beginning, done their best to eradicate. The whole smallpox on a blanket thing. Bounties on our scalps. The government schools, which were really an attempt to drive the Indian out of us and to get free labor in the bargain. Even in today's enlightened times, if you're Indian and you walk into a store up here, you're noticed and you're watched."

Rose said, "Even you?"

"No one who's clearly Ojibwe hasn't experienced that up here, Rose." Her face went troubled, and for the first time Jenny could remember, Rainy looked at them as if they were strangers. "Being Indian is living with a wound that's never healed. The violence, the alcoholism, the unemployment—White people think that's who we are, who we've always been, that somehow we deserve this. No matter how many of us they see who don't fit that image, they continue to believe it. And you want to know the worst thing? A lot of Indians believe it, too. So is it any wonder that a girl growing up Ojibwe or Lakota or Cree on a reservation sees no hope for herself there and falls into the hands of someone like Windigo?"

"What do we do?" Rose asked. "How do we help?"

"You don't. It's something we need to do for ourselves. And we are, Rose. It's going to take time, but it's happening. Believe me, it's happening."

Hearing her say this and hearing the certainty in her voice, Jenny believed it, too. Even so, there was a girl out there named Mariah who, unless she was found soon, would never benefit from the hard work so many of her people were doing.

Then Jenny caught herself. *Her people.* Those were the words she'd thought, although she, too, had Anishinaabe blood flowing in her veins. Her great-grandmother Dilsey had been true-blood Iron Lake Ojibwe. One-eighth of her genetic makeup had come from The People. Still, despite the powwows she'd attended, despite the fact that she had blood cousins on the Iron Lake Reservation, and even despite having adopted a son who was fully Anishinaabe, she'd never truly thought of herself as anything other than white. Most of her ancestry was Irish. She was blond and blue-eyed, just like her mother had been. It was Stephen who looked Ojibwe and who had somehow ended up with a profound Ojibwe sensibility. Jenny had always been fine with that. Now she was angry at what she understood had been her willing disregard for an important element of herself, her family, her heritage, and with Waaboo, her maternal responsibility. She felt like a traitor. Or worse, a coward. And she knew that changing this was a part of the journey she was on, and maybe a part of the vision that had begun it.

They'd fallen quiet, the weight of so many awful realities

pressing down on them. It was Rainy who jumped to another subject, one she'd clearly been thinking about.

"So what's between you and Daniel?" she asked.

"What do you mean?" Jenny said.

"I heard you kissed him." She smiled and said, "Uncle Henry just happened to mention it to me when I took his dinner up."

This was a place Jenny wasn't certain she wanted to go. She was still trying to figure out her feelings for Daniel. Where men were concerned, she'd not been particularly judicious in her choices or wise in her actions. At eighteen, she'd been in love with a poet. They'd dreamed of living together in a garret in Paris, both of them struggling to write works of greatness. But she'd become pregnant, and her gallant young poet had turned out to be a scared kid who wanted no part of caring for a child. A moot point in the end, because Jenny had miscarried. The young poet had abandoned his dream of Paris and settled for becoming a druggist in his father's pharmacy. Her next love had been a more intellectual choice, another writer, but a man who made sense to her in her own plans for a future. Then she'd stumbled upon Waaboo, and her life changed. But her fiancé had not loved the child as she did, and she'd shoved him away because of it. In the end, he'd sacrificed himself, died trying to save the child and her, and her guilt was still something she hadn't put behind her. She believed that she'd been the catalyst for the bad that had befallen these two men who'd loved her. And if there was a possibility of another man in her life, maybe only bad would come to him, too. So she'd been content with the company of her son, her father, her brother, and Henry. What more did she need?

"I kissed him," Jenny said. "One kiss. No big deal."

"No big deal?" Rose's eyes were huge and curious. "When?"

"Just before we split up in Duluth tonight."

"Well, there you go," Rose said.

"There you go what?" Jenny said. "It was just one kiss."

"The first kiss," Rose said. "I remember the first time Mal kissed me. You want to know something? It was the first time any man had ever kissed me. There I was, thirty-nine years old, and I'd never been kissed by a man. Let alone anything else with a man."

"A good kiss?" Rainy asked.

"How was I to know?" Rose laughed. "But I'll tell you this. I will, to my dying day, remember that kiss, because I knew my life had changed. And what a change it's been."

Jenny envied her aunt, her obvious love of her husband. She'd loved before, or thought she had, but never with the depth that seemed to flow between Rose and Mal.

"What about you, Rainy?" Rose asked. "First kiss?"

"Johnny Blumenthal," Rainy replied. "At the homecoming dance, sophomore year."

"Good kiss?"

"A little sloppy, but it was pretty sweet. We went steady for six months. Then I found out he was two-timing me with Holly Knowles, one of the cheerleaders. Johnny was my first in a series of very bad choices in men."

"You were married once," Rose said. "One of your bad choices?"

"The worst. I had my head up my ass with that one. Good-looking, Lord yes. But a snake underneath. I finally learned my lesson with him. It's not what's on the outside that counts."

"I agree. Men are like M&M's," Rose threw in. "What's on the outside is just a thin cover. It's what's underneath that counts."

"Ain't it the truth. You've got to watch out. What looks like chocolate under that candy coating might be nothing but bull-shit," Rainy said with a laugh.

"You think Dad's like that?" Jenny asked.

"Of course not. But the truth is I didn't much like him at first."

"Cork?" Rose said, surprised. "But he's such a sweet guy."

"I know that now. When I first met him, though, I found him . . . aggravating. He was so sure of himself."

"He can be that way sometimes," Jenny said.

"All men can be that way sometimes," Rose put in. "Even my precious Mal. It's in their DNA, I think. The know-it-all gene."

Rainy said, "Jenny, did you know that Daniel's a writer?"

Jenny looked at her as if she'd spoken Swahili. "What?"

"It's true," Rainy said. "Poetry mostly. He's kind of well known in the Ojibwe community."

"He didn't say a thing about it," Jenny said.

"He didn't talk about books? He's a passionate reader. Did you tell him you write?"

"I don't tell anybody I write."

"I think Daniel would understand," Rainy said.

The kiss had confused Jenny. Now it frightened her. Maybe Daniel didn't want to be kissed by her. He hadn't told her he was a writer. He hadn't wanted to share himself with her in that way. Maybe what she'd seen, what she connected with, that gentleness of spirit, was all in her own imagination, out of her own loneliness or desperation or some other pathetic need. She thought that maybe her relationship with Daniel would, in the end, consist of one kiss. And would that really be so bad? Because, really, wasn't she happy with the way her life stood at the moment? And based on her past experience with men, which had been mostly disappointing or tragic, did she really want to go through all that again? It made her tired thinking about it, so she decided she wouldn't.

She hadn't seen her little guy since she came home. She stood and said that's what she intended to do. Rainy got up as well and said she'd go up and give Henry a break. Rose said she would make another pot of coffee so she could offer the old Mide something fresh and hot. They all parted ways for the moment.

In Waaboo's room, Jenny found her son asleep, tangled, as always, in his bedding. He was a restless sleeper, though his restlessness seldom woke him. She didn't know if it was part of who he was and would always be, or if, considering the harshness of his very early existence, it was something that came at him from his subconscious. She wanted so much for him to grow up happy and free from fear. But did anyone? And, of course, there were degrees of fear. She thought about what must have driven Mariah Arceneaux and Carrie Verga and Raven Duvall to abandon their homes and families for the likes of the man called Wolf and his brother, Windigo.

She straightened the covers over Waaboo and sat in the rocker near his bed. This was the place that she and her father and Aunt Rose and Rainy and anyone else who offered to put her little guy down for the night did what needed doing—read to him, or made up a story for him, or listened as he made up his own. She'd grown up with much the same experience. At night, her father or mother would sit with her and Anne and Stephen, and read a story. The comfort in that sharing—with the dark outside the window but, inside, the little circle of light in the room, and all of them safe in that circle—Jenny wished every child in the world could have.

She rocked and listened to the crickets and heard the breeze stir the branches of the elm with a gentle, liquid rustle, and before she knew it, the long day caught up with her, and she was asleep.

It was Rose who woke her later. She touched her shoulder, and when Jenny opened her eyes, Rose said, "They're here."

CHAPTER 34

Her watch told her it was 4:47 a.m. The dark outside didn't seem as profound as it had been when she nodded off. Dawn wasn't far away. She followed Rose downstairs. Those who'd arrived were just now coming into the kitchen through the side door. It was Daniel, along with Louise and the Duvalls. The children looked sleepy and bewildered. Lindy Duvall looked worried.

"Where's Raven?" she asked the moment she was inside.

"Upstairs," Rainy said. "She's fine. She's with Uncle Henry."

"Henry?"

"The old man who talked to you in Bad Bluff," Jenny said.

"Can I see her?"

"Of course," Rainy said. "But I think that maybe we should wait a bit before her brother and sister see her."

"She's . . . ?" Lindy didn't finish, but her face said it all.

"She'll be fine," Rainy assured her. "But these children look pretty beat. How about we get them squared away?"

Rose said, "I've got Waaboo's old crib set up in the office, and I've put a cot in there as well. Why don't you all come with me?"

The Duvalls followed Rose out of the kitchen. When they were gone, Daniel asked, "Where are your father and Manny?"

Jenny shrugged. "Dad took off a long time ago. Didn't say where he was taking Manny or when he'd be back."

"Got a cup of coffee?" Daniel asked. "It's been a long night."

"Everybody sit down," Rainy said, "and I'll make a fresh pot."

They took chairs at the table. Meloux walked in, relieved of his vigil at Raven's bedside, and he sat down with the others. When the coffee was ready, Rose poured mugs for them all.

The sky had begun to hold the promise of light. Outside the kitchen windows, the birds had launched into a noisy chorus. Jenny heard the newspaper hit the front porch. It was Saturday morning, a day she'd always loved. She should have felt promise in that dawn, in the jubilant song of the birds, in the possibility of a return to normality that the clunk of the morning paper signaled. She should have been looking forward to a glorious summer day. Instead, the world felt oppressive, and the only promise it seemed to hold was of more worry, more waiting.

Meloux, who'd probably had little sleep at Raven Duvall's bedside, looked drawn, emptied. That concerned Jenny a lot. She didn't know how much he could take. They'd been on this hunt for nearly a week and still didn't have Mariah safely in their grasp. Jenny knew that the uncertainty ate at Louise's strength. She looked exhausted, too. And something had changed in Daniel. When they'd set out, there'd been a freshness in him, almost a boyish excitement in the hunt. Now he seemed old, hardened, a constant wariness in his eyes, as if he wasn't sure that anything he saw could be trusted.

Rose offered them hope. As if she'd sensed the depth of their despair, she said, "I think we need some breakfast. I think we'll all feel better if we eat."

Rainy stood up to help. Jenny came to her feet as well and offered, "More coffee, anyone?"

No one had a chance to answer. They heard the front door open and close, and a moment later Cork appeared in the kitchen doorway.

He was Jenny's father, and he was not. He had the face of her father, and his eyes were her father's eyes, but it was not her father behind those familiar features. He stood in the doorway, looking at them as if they were the strangers, not he.

Meloux spoke first. "*Anin*, Corcoran O'Connor. Will you have some coffee?"

The man in the doorway thought about that, then said, "Thanks."

"Sit down, Cork," Rose said. Although Jenny was standing, it was Rose who filled a mug and brought it to him. Jenny couldn't seem to move.

Her father took a chair, sat with the mug in his hands, stared at the coffee and did not drink.

"Nothing," he said, as if in answer to a question none of them had asked.

"Nothing?" Louise said.

"I got nothing from him," Cork said.

Jenny spotted what appeared to her at first to be a red rash across the front of his blue work shirt, then she realized she was looking at a tiny spray of blood.

"You didn't . . ." The words caught in her throat. "You didn't kill him, Dad?"

"Kill him?" He thought about that. "I wanted to." Jenny watched him work through something difficult in his own mind; then he continued. "Our children disappear. They run away or they're seduced away. Some never come back. I know why now. He told me things. Things he's done to girls. As if he was proud of it. He told me what he'd do to Raven, to Mariah, to me if he ever gets free." He lifted his bloodshot eyes to them. "To all of you. But he didn't tell me anything I wanted to hear. No matter what I did." He finally sipped a little coffee. He looked at Louise, and for the first time in all this, there was defeat in his face. "I'm sorry. I tried."

Rainy walked to him and stood at his back and put her hand on his shoulder. He tensed, as if her touch had been fire. Or maybe the coldest ice.

"Corcoran O'Connor," Meloux said. "Inside this Maiingan, there is still a man. A man is a human being. Every human being, even the darkest of hearts, has two wolves fighting in him."

Cork gave the old man a flat look. "I haven't seen any fear in him, Henry. And I can't believe there's any love in him either. I'm not convinced he's human at all."

The ancient Mide stood. "Come with me."

They followed Meloux upstairs to the bedroom where Raven lay. Her mother sat beside the bed in the same chair that Meloux had occupied. When they stepped in, Lindy Duvall was sleeping, her chin resting on her chest. Raven was awake however. She watched them enter, Meloux in the lead. The old man came to her side.

"Good morning, granddaughter," he said.

She didn't smile, but she looked relieved to see him.

"Granddaughter, I want to ask you a question. Is that all right?" She nodded.

Lindy roused and blinked and looked at Raven and then the others. She said nothing, just straightened in her chair and listened.

"This man, this Maiingan, what does he love?"

"Nothing." She said it without even a second of consideration.

"Think, granddaughter. Has he ever shown a kindness toward anything?"

She closed her eyes for a moment, then opened them, and they held a little flame of understanding. "Ember."

"Ember," the old man echoed and nodded.

"Sweet old thing. Manny's had him forever. He won't take any of us to a doctor, but he's spent a fortune on Ember. Angel, he's always ragging on Manny because of that old dog. Always saying that one of these days when Manny's not around he's going to slice Ember up and throw the pieces into the weeds for the crows to eat. Would never say that to Manny's face, but I think he means it." Her face took on a pained look, Jenny thought maybe from her injuries, but she said, "Pepper, a girl I brought over from Red Lake, left the door open once, and Ember got out, ran off. Manny beat the hell out of her for that. But when Ember came back a few hours later, Manny cried. The son of a bitch actually cried. Never thought I'd see that day."

"Thank you, granddaughter." Meloux turned to Cork. "The wolf is ours."

* * *

Downstairs, in the kitchen, Cork said, "Daniel, you mind coming with Henry and me?"

"I'm coming, too," Jenny said.

Her father started to reply, and Jenny could tell it was going to be in the negative. But Daniel cut him off. "All right, Jenny."

Cork shot him a look, not a pleasant one, but voiced no objection.

Cork drove his Explorer and Meloux rode with him. Jenny rode with Daniel in his truck. The dog settled in on the seat between them. They'd put one of Trixie's old collars around the dog's neck and had brought a leash.

They hardly spoke. For Jenny, that kiss in Duluth seemed to have opened a big crack between them, a dangerous chasm, and she, for her part, had decided not to go near the edge. If she said nothing, if Daniel said nothing, maybe they'd be safe.

They headed onto the reservation and east along a dirt road that ran past the old mission, with its graveyard in back. The sun had risen above the hills, and the day was already feeling hot and sultry. The road wound through a section of the rez Jenny had never been on before, but her father clearly knew where they were going. The Explorer kicked up a big rooster tail of yellow dust, and Daniel stayed well back.

Cork stopped suddenly, and Daniel stopped, too. Jenny's father got out and went to the side of the road. He moved a blind constructed of heavy brush, revealing a narrow, barely visible track that led into the trees. He returned to his vehicle and drove onto the track. Daniel followed. When they were inside the trees, Cork stopped again. He got out, jogged back to the opening of the track, and returned the brush blind to its original position. They continued on.

After fifteen minutes of slow progress, they came to a tiny log structure, dilapidated and abandoned-looking, an old trapper's cabin, Jenny thought. It stood in the shade of tall pines at the edge of a small lake. Parked in front was a dusty brown pickup with Iron Lake Reservation plates. Two men stepped from the cabin. Jenny knew them both: Tom Blessing and Elgin Manypenny.

The men were roughly Jenny's age. Earlier in their lives, they'd been part of a gang on the Iron Lake Reservation. They'd called themselves the Red Boyz. When he was sheriff, Cork had dealt with them in an official capacity. A few years later, well after he'd given up his badge, he'd dealt with them in a different way, one that he never spoke about. They'd all been a part of something significant, something that had changed them, something that Jenny understood she would never know the truth of. The gang had dissolved, and the young men had gone on to more productive lives. Blessing and Manypenny ran the Wellbriety program and worked with at-risk tribal youth. In their days as Red Boyz, each had branded an *R* into his skin, part of the initiation ritual, and the raised scar tissue was still there. When necessary, they could bring back the swagger of those days and the cold, stone faces they wore. On rare occasions, when he needed them, they turned out to help Jenny's father.

With no greeting, Cork asked, "How's he doing?"

To Meloux, Blessing said, *"Boozhoo, nimishoomis."* Then he shook his head and answered Jenny's father. "Still playing dumb. This is one hard nut, Cork. I don't think he'll crack."

Jenny came from the pickup with Daniel. She brought Ember, who padded at her side, held by the leash. She also brought a baggie full of dog biscuits.

"Who's that?" Blessing asked, nodding toward the dog.

"The nutcracker," Cork said.

They went inside the cabin. The floor was dirt. There were no windows, and it was dark and smelled of rot and animal leavings and, somewhere in its not too distant past, something dead. Wolf sat against the far wall, at the end of the long, narrow fall of light that came through the doorway. His face was bruised and puffed, not unlike Raven Duvall's had been. He was shirtless, and Jenny saw what looked like cigarette burns on his chest. He lifted his head and watched them enter, and even in that dark, she could see the fire of defiance in his eyes.

"Brought something you might be interested in, Manny," Cork said.

Wolf leered at Jenny and said, with a kind of growl of satisfaction, "Another girl for me to have some fun with. Thanks."

"But see who this girl has brought with her?"

The brightness of the light from outside seemed to blind him a bit, and he squinted. Then his face went ashen.

"Go ahead, Jenny," Cork said. "Let Ember and Manny get reacquainted."

She allowed Ember to trot to the man called Wolf, and the old dog's tail went crazy. He licked Wolf's battered face and nuzzled a bound arm. Jenny saw the weakness in Wolf's eyes, which she understood would be his undoing. But when he looked back up, those eyes had gone hard again. A show, Jenny knew. They all knew.

"What are you going to do?" he asked.

"Kill Ember," Cork said.

"He's just an old dog."

"He's your old dog, Manny. That makes him special. Jenny, give Ember one of the dog biscuits you brought along," Cork said.

Jenny took a biscuit from the baggie. She held it in her palm, bent down, and called, "Here, Ember. Here, boy."

The trusting old canine came to her, grabbed the biscuit, gave a few chews, and swallowed. Jenny patted his head affectionately. "Good dog. Such a good dog."

"Daniel," Cork said. "Give me your Glock."

Daniel handed over the sidearm.

"Give me a biscuit, Jenny." She did, and Cork knelt and held it out. "Come here, Ember. Have a last meal."

The dog padded over and ate out of Cork's palm. Cork put the Glock to Ember's head.

"On three, I shoot him, Manny."

Jenny had thought whatever they did with Ember would be for show. But she could see that her father wasn't bluffing. She knew absolutely that he would kill the dog. He seemed to be a man she'd never seen before, a man she didn't know, a man who, if he did what he was threatening to do, she would hate, hate forever. She glanced at Meloux, hoping he might intervene, but his face showed no expression. His eyes were hard, dark pebbles. She stood frozen with horror and disbelief as her father began his countdown.

"One. And consider this, Manny. After Ember, I'll begin on you again. I'll shoot your right kneecap, then your left."

The dog was licking Cork's hand, licking off biscuit crumbs. Manny watched, but his eyes gave away nothing.

"Two," Cork said. "And by the way, you know what your brother says about old Ember here? Says he's going to cut him up and let the crows eat the pieces. At least, that's what Sparkle told us. You willing to let Ember die for a man like that, Manny? You willing to lose both your kneecaps over him?"

Manny's face didn't change. Jenny was sure he wouldn't crack. She tried to dart at her father, to save Ember, but Daniel caught her and held her back.

"Three." Cork worked the slide on the Glock and settled the muzzle against the back of Ember's head.

"All right," the man called Wolf screamed. "All right. Don't hurt Ember. What do you want to know? I'll tell you. I swear I'll tell. Just don't hurt Ember."

"Where's your brother?" Cork said.

"Williston."

"North Dakota? What's he doing there?"

"Man, you don't know about Williston?"

"Tell me."

"Fucking Wild West. In Williston anything goes. We have some girls there, my brother, me. We got a partner."

"Is Mariah there?"

"Mariah? She calls herself Candi. With an *i*."

"Is she there?"

"She's there."

"You have an address?"

"You really think you can take down my brother?"

"Give me the address, and we'll see."

The man called Wolf suddenly seemed not so eager to talk.

"Ember," Cork said and once again leveled the sidearm at the old dog.

"A trailer south of Williston." Wolf gave a highway number and the name of another road that, he said, branched off. "It's in a stand of cottonwoods, sits up on a kind of bluff. You can see the Missouri River from the back."

"You'll draw me a map?"

"You let Ember go, I'll take you there myself."

"The map'll do," Cork said.

But the map wasn't all Jenny's father got from the man called Wolf. He got a real name—Samuel Leland French—and a real name for the man called Windigo—Robert Wilson French. He also got a brief history. Both born on the Red Lake Reservation. Mixed-blood alcoholic father, alcoholic mother, white. "She was Irish, like you, O'Connor," he said with a sneer. Raised mostly in foster homes, sometimes placed together, sometimes separately. Didn't matter, all the homes were bad. "But what the hell," Samuel Leland French said, "that's just what it is to be Indian, right, cousin?"

Elgin Manypenny was the one who responded, his voice ice-cold. "I grew up in foster homes. I don't traffic girls or torture and kill them."

"Then you've missed out on some fun, cousin."

"What do we do with him?" Tom Blessing said.

Jenny saw murder in the eyes of the ex–Red Boyz, and as much as she hated the man called Wolf, she was horrified that, when she left, they might exact their own kind of justice. It was Meloux who, in his usual way, eased her mind. He said to all present in that small, smelly trapper's cabin, "Keep him, but harm him no more. We will find his brother, this Windigo, and then we will decide what is just."

"What about the dog?" Manypenny said.

"Let them be together," Meloux replied. It sounded to Jenny less like a moment of generosity than like the granting of a final wish before execution. But Meloux had spoken, and Jenny knew that he would be obeyed and that Wolf and Ember would be there—alive—when they returned.

They gathered outside and said their good-byes to the ex–Red Boyz. Before they divided into their vehicles, Daniel drew Cork aside. Jenny saw something in his face that she hadn't seen there before. A deeply troubled and distrustful look.

Daniel said, "Would you have killed that dog, Cork?"

Jenny's father replied, "If the sacrifice of the dog might save the girl, what choice would you have made?"

Daniel said, "You didn't answer my question."

"And you didn't answer mine," Cork replied.

CHAPTER 35

Jenny called ahead and asked a hard favor of Rose and Rainy.

When she and the others returned to the house on Gooseberry Lane, the two women had fed all the children breakfast and had taken them to play in a park. This was because Jenny couldn't bear to see her precious little Waaboo again only to say good-bye once more.

It was, according to MapQuest, an eleven-hour drive from Tamarack County, Minnesota, to Williston, North Dakota. What Jenny knew of Williston was what most folks in Minnesota knew. It was an oil boom area. Men had flooded there to work the oil fields, where drilling companies seemed to be putting holes in the ground faster than a town of prairie dogs on speed. They'd seen the reports on the nightly news: the high wages, the wave of workers, the lack of adequate housing to meet the needs of this influx, the rising crime rate. Jenny remembered seeing a waitress at a restaurant there interviewed about the change in her hometown. The waitress said it was a place she barely recognized anymore. She'd grown up in a safe, small town. That was not Williston anymore. She was afraid to walk the streets at night. The men she served looked at her as hungrily as they looked at the food she delivered to their tables. They worked hard all day and had few comforts when they left the job, and she understood their loneliness and their needs. But they scared her. They scared her a lot.

Louise wanted to go with them, but Jenny's father pointed out that they didn't really know what they were getting themselves into and would probably have to move quickly. He didn't make any reference to her leg, but it was clear what he meant, and she accepted the situation. Jenny almost argued her case, because she understood how it would be staying back, waiting, wondering, worrying. But she saw Daniel nod his agreement with Cork, so she held her tongue.

Meloux said, "I will go."

Cork studied the old man a long time, and Jenny figured that she knew the variables he was weighing: Meloux's age and health and the likelihood of the old man somehow holding them back. Finally he said, "All right," but with obvious reservation.

They planned to take two vehicles—the Explorer and Daniel's pickup. Cork said he wanted lots of flexibility in Williston. He also said, "I don't like the thought of going into this blind."

"Maybe we don't have to," Daniel told him. "I know a guy. Shinny Fox. He's Mandan, out of Fort Berthold. Met him at the United Tribes International Powwow in Bismarck a couple of years ago. We both drum, and we played against each other in the three-on-three basketball tournament. We've stayed in touch."

"You'll give him a call?"

"Sure, right now."

"This needs to stay unofficial, Daniel. No law enforcement, at least not yet."

"No cops? What Indian would object to that?"

Raven and her mother came downstairs. Raven moved gingerly, but she was clearly feeling better. The girl took Jenny's hand and gripped it tightly.

"Angel's worse than Manny," she warned. "He's smarter. Real smooth, you know. He can make you believe anything. Don't listen to him. Under his skin, he's nothing but ice."

"We'll be careful," Jenny promised. Then she turned to Louise and made another promise, one that felt sacred to her. "We'll bring Mariah home."

It was almost noon when they left Aurora. They hoped to reach Williston by midnight.

Meloux accompanied Cork, and Jenny rode with Daniel. They drove all afternoon, passing through the Leech Lake Reservation and skirting the edge of White Earth. At Grand Forks, shortly before five o'clock, they crossed the Red River of the North and left Minnesota behind. Because it was such a long journey and she was uncomfortable with silence, Jenny finally decided to talk about books, a safe middle ground, she figured. She was blown away by the extent of Daniel's knowledge, which was even broader than her own. He spoke quietly and never at length, but he was clearly passionate about the written word. She didn't ask him about his writing, nor did she mention her own. That was something still too personal.

Finally he said, "About that kiss."

"What kiss?" Jenny said.

"Oh." He seemed willing to let it go. But not without reluctance, it also seemed.

"Look, maybe I should apologize," Jenny said.

"For what?" He stared at the white lines firing at them down the middle of the highway. "I liked it."

"Really?"

"Really." He offered her a smile out of that broad, honest face. "When all of this business is behind us, could we think about doing things in a more normal way?"

"I'm not sure what normal is, but, yeah, I'd like that."

"Me, too," he said.

They were among rolling fields of sunflowers when the moon rose at their backs. They had not stopped except for gas, sandwiches, coffee, and restroom breaks. Jenny and Daniel had traded off at the wheel, but her father had driven the whole way. Now Jenny followed his Explorer in the growing dark, wondering about him and worrying. There was a word that kept running through her head: *ogichidaa*. She believed that about her father, that he'd come into the world already chosen for a hard and dangerous duty, to stand between evil and his people. She knew he'd killed three men. She couldn't say why exactly, but she had a sense there

were others she didn't know about. This wasn't something her
father spoke of, ever, and it wasn't something she intended to ask,
ever. Everyone had their terrible secrets. But as she followed his
taillights, which seemed to stare back at her like little red demon
eyes, she wondered about the toll it took, what it cost her father
to be the man he was, to do the duty they all expected of him and
that he expected of himself.

She'd thought Daniel was sound asleep, but in the darkness
somewhere in the middle of nowhere, he said something that
made her think he'd read her mind. He said, "Your father."

She waited.

"He's . . . intense," Daniel said cautiously.

"I've never seen him quite like this before," she admitted.

A hawk rose up suddenly from some mutilated roadkill along
the shoulder of the highway, a bright flash of gold feathers in the
headlights, then it was lost in the night.

Daniel said, "In the woods, I face guys carrying rifles who
don't appreciate the laws I'm paid to enforce, but even they don't
worry me like your dad does at the moment. Today in that cabin?"
He shook his head. "A helpless old dog."

Jenny felt as if she should defend her father, and she pointed
out, "He got what we needed."

"But a little something died there. It wasn't Ember but
something. Maybe you'd call it faith or trust. I'm concerned
about where he might draw the line. There are places I won't go,
Jenny."

"You don't know him like I do."

"You just said you've never seen him like this before."

He was right, but she trusted her father, didn't she? Wasn't
that what you did with people you loved? You gave them more
rope than you'd give others?

"You know the word *ogichidaa*?"

"Yes."

"Henry Meloux says that my dad was born *ogichidaa*."

"Okay."

"Has Rainy or anyone else told you about my mother or my brother?"

"No."

"My mother was killed several years ago, collateral damage in a scheme that involved a lot of money. Long story. I'll tell you the whole thing someday. But I think my father has always believed he should have saved her, although there was no way he could have."

"And your brother?"

"He's in the Twin Cities, at the Courage Center. He's struggling to walk again."

"What happened?"

"Last Christmas, a crazy man put two bullets in him. One of those bullets damaged his spine. We were afraid he'd never walk again."

"I'm sorry. I didn't know."

"I think my father believes he should have been able to keep that from happening, too. I could be totally wrong because it's not something he'll ever talk about. But I'm thinking that maybe he's come to see Mariah as a way to atone."

Jenny stared where the headlights illuminated only a microscopic part of the dark around them.

"I understand," Daniel said.

"There's more," Jenny said. "I remember my mother used to argue with Dad about the risks he took. I thought maybe it was just because she was worried about him being hurt or killed. But now I think there was more to it. I think she saw the toll it took on him, what it did to his spirit, and I think that any risk he took worried her."

"And it worries you," he said.

"My father almost killed the guy who fired those bullets into my brother. He would have except for my sister, Annie. She pretty much put herself between that madman and the barrel of the gun my father held. I've never talked to Dad about this, but I've talked to Annie. She told me she saw something in him, something absolutely cold and emotionless. The killing he was contemplating wasn't motivated by anger or vengeance, but was simply the answer."

"To what?"

"How to deal with someone like that man. When Annie told him she wouldn't let him commit murder—that's what it seemed to her—my father told her that if he didn't, the guy would find a way to come back and finish what he'd started. Someday he'd return and kill Stephen. Or Annie or me or Waaboo."

"Do you think that's true?"

"I don't know. But I don't think you ever kill someone because of what they might do in the future. Do you?"

Daniel didn't answer immediately. They approached a field that ran north away from the road. There was a moving light in the middle of it, a piece of machinery. Jenny wondered what a farmer would be doing among his crops so late at night. She knew nothing about farming. In all that black land, she wasn't sure she knew much about anything.

"I don't know," Daniel said. He stared out the window and watched as they passed the solitary light in that big field. "If I really believed it, maybe."

"No," Jenny said and couldn't help feeling disappointed in him.

"It's a hypothetical," he said. "Honestly, in your dad's shoes, I don't know what I'd do."

"You wouldn't kill a dog, would you? Not like that. No one in his right mind would."

Daniel seemed to think it over but, in the end, didn't respond.

They were in the dark again, following Cork and Henry. Jenny thought about what Daniel had said. *Maybe.* Although she'd given him a knee-jerk reaction, she wondered if she was being naïve and he was right. If she really believed someone was going to kill one of the people she loved, what would she do? And taking that a step further, if she really believed someone was going to kill a child like Mariah Arceneaux, really believed it, what would she do?

"Life Saver?" Daniel held out a roll of the candy.

"No, thanks."

He took one for himself. "Why are you doing this?"

She knew what he meant.

"Because I started," she said. "Because I'm in the deep of it. Because I want to see it to the end."

"Why do you care so much? Mariah isn't family to you. And forgive me for saying it, but even though you've got Shinnob blood in you, you're not really Shinnob."

"Mariah's not just a name to me, Daniel. I know her now. I know her mother, and I know what Louise is going through as a mother. I'm as deep in this as you or anyone else, and I'll be damned if I'm going to be left behind."

Daniel said, "You've got a son back in Minnesota. Things might get rough out here."

"I've been in some pretty rough situations before."

"I know. I was there on Superior Street."

"Long before that."

She told him the whole story of how she'd found little Waaboo hidden in a hole on an island destroyed by storm, of fleeing desperately from people who wanted to kill them both. She told of holding a knife in her hand, prepared to kill to defend the abandoned child, whom she'd instantly fallen in love with. She told of rappelling down a cliff face with the child bundled to her and with a killer above.

He listened, rigid and intent, and at the end he sat back. He was quiet for a long moment, then said, a little amazed, "And I thought I'd been through a lot."

They drove and drove, tunneling through the huge dark, keeping themselves awake with talk. Looming over it all was the uncertainty of what awaited them in Williston. And following her father deeper and deeper into that night, Jenny wondered if there might be more than just Windigo they needed to fear when they arrived.

CHAPTER 36

They reached New Town, North Dakota, just shy of Williston, a little past midnight. It was a small community on the Fort Berthold Reservation and was where Daniel's friend Shinny Fox lived. They found the address on Eagle Drive, a cozy frame house with a welcoming light burning on the porch. When they pulled up to the curb, a tall, slender figure in a snap-button Western shirt, faded jeans, and cowboy boots pushed open the front screen door and called, "*Boozhoo*, Minnesota."

Jenny liked Shinny immediately. He wore his hair in a graying braid. His face was long and angular, and the laugh lines at the corners of his mouth and eyes were deep. He had coffee and beer waiting, along with a big bowl of Cheetos. They brought in their bags and sat around his kitchen table and filled him in. He listened without interrupting, his face implacable.

"Fourteen," he said at the end. "I have nieces who are fourteen. What do you need from me?"

"You've already given it," Daniel said. "A place to stay. We understand that's hard to find here."

"A hotel room that would go for a hundred bucks anywhere else goes for three times that around here. If you can even find one that's vacant." He took a swallow from the bottle of Fat Tire in front of him. His fingers were orange from the Cheetos. "So, this Windigo, what are you planning on doing about him?"

They all looked toward Jenny's father.

"I don't know yet," Cork replied. "I need to do a little reconnoitering."

"Maybe I can help there," Shinny said. "After Daniel called, I went out to have a look at the trailer myself. It's isolated. You drive up to it, and whoever's inside can see you coming for a mile. I watched for a couple of hours. Saw two SUVs coming and going."

Cork frowned. "You did that without being spotted?"

"There's another rise a quarter mile east. I hunkered down there with my field glasses, the ones I use when I'm bird watching. The windows on the SUVs were tinted, so I couldn't see inside, but from what Daniel told me, I figured whoever it was, they were ferrying girls back and forth."

"Back and forth where?" Jenny asked. She sipped her coffee. It was good and strong and made her like Shinny even more.

"There are whole housing communities the oil companies have thrown up here. Mobile homes, little shanties, prefabs, you name it. Anything that'll put a roof over an oil worker's head. You look at some hillsides, and it's like a tiny military base. People are turning their garages into temporary housing, renting out vacant rooms. Little food operations, mom-and-pop diners, opening up out of home kitchens. There's so much money to be made here. I mean, these guys, they get paid a shitload for what they do, and they've got nothing to spend it on."

"But they can buy a fourteen-year-old girl for a while," Cork said.

"Yeah," Shinny said soberly. "My guess is the girls get ferried to these workers' communities. Maybe they've got one or two guys lined up, or, hell, maybe they go from trailer to trailer. I don't know."

Jenny thought about the stories they'd heard from Louise, about the days she'd worked the big boats in Duluth, going from bunk to bunk. She thought, *Things never change.*

There was a cuckoo clock on the kitchen wall, and the little wooden bird gave one call. Shinny looked up at it and said, "The real birds'll be carrying on in a few hours. Maybe we should all get some shut-eye and figure this thing out in the morning."

He had a spare room with a twin bed, which they all insisted Meloux take. He was looking more and more worn-out. Jenny was given the living room sofa. Daniel said he'd roll out his sleeping bag on the floor. Cork said he'd sleep in his Explorer.

When the house was dark and quiet, Jenny lay thinking about the man they'd come looking for, thinking that everything they knew about him was frightening. Worse than Wolf, Raven had cautioned. That was hard to imagine.

"Daniel?"

"Yes?" His voice came from the floor, sounding wide awake, like her.

"There's something else."

"Something else? What do you mean?"

"A selfish reason I came. It's not just because I'm concerned about Mariah."

He fell silent, waiting patiently for her to continue, in the way Jenny had come to expect of him.

"Downwind of the devil," she said.

"I don't understand."

"I've been trying to write a book about what happened to me and my family when we found Waaboo. It's not working. I don't know why. But I've been thinking about Mariah, about her story and the story of girls like her. This is a story I can write, Daniel. I know I can. But to do that, I need to see this through to the end. I know that sounds mercenary."

In the dark and into the quiet, Daniel said, "No, I get it." Then he said, "Downwind of the devil?"

"A title maybe?"

"I like it," Daniel said. "The hunting motif and what we're hunting. Sounds very Hemingwayesque to me though."

She laughed softly. "May I read some of your poems one of these days?"

"I think that could be arranged."

Later, when sleep still eluded her, she said, "Did you bring your gun?"

"My Glock? It's locked in my truck."

"Is it a powerful gun?"

"Standard issue. It's durable, does the trick. Why?"

"Have you ever shot anyone?"

"I've only fired warning rounds."

"Do you think you could?"

"Shoot someone? I'm trained for it."

"That's not what I asked."

He didn't answer for a while, and Jenny appreciated this, appreciated that he didn't give her some bullshit macho reply.

"I don't know," he finally said. "I'd like to believe I'll never have to find out. But if it came down to it, I'd like to believe I wouldn't hesitate. Lives might depend on it."

Another period of quiet followed. She could feel him lying awake, like her, in that long, dark night. Finally she asked a question that had been bothering her from the moment they'd set out for Williston.

"Shouldn't we let the police here know what's going on?"

"Do we know what's going on?"

"Aren't we pretty sure?"

"And what do we tell them when they ask how we know this? That the information came from a man your father worked over?"

"We could lie."

"The point I'm making is that law enforcement is just that. It enforces laws. All laws. Some of what we've done has already crossed a legal line. Things are complicated now."

"And they'll only get more complicated."

Daniel said only one more thing to her that night and clearly with a measure of regret. He said, "Yeah. They will."

Morning came too early, after much restless dreaming. Jenny woke to the smell of brewing coffee. She got up from the sofa, tiptoed past Daniel in his sleeping bag, and went to the kitchen, where an early, golden light poured through the windows and flooded the room. Shinny was there, his braid undone, his hair hanging long and loose down his back. He wore gray sweatpants and a yellow T-shirt with a big dream catcher on the back. He was barefoot. When she walked in, he was pulling mugs from the cupboard and setting them in a line on the counter near the coffeemaker.

She said quietly, "Good morning."

He turned and smiled. *"Boozhoo. Anish na?"*

"Good, thanks," she said.

"Slept well?"

"Not long enough."

"I get that. Coffee'll help. Be ready in a minute. Have a seat."

Jenny sat and took in the kitchen, which the night before she'd been too tired to appreciate. The room was done in retro. The cuckoo clock on the wall. The dining set—red Formica tabletop, shiny, steel frame chairs with red vinyl seats. Kitschy salt and pepper shakers shaped like Dutch windmills. On the counter, a vintage radio of yellow and red plastic. Even the mugs he'd set out were retro, each bearing an image of a Warner Bros. cartoon character—Porky Pig, Foghorn Leghorn, Wile E. Coyote, Tweety.

Beyond the windows she saw rolling hills, seared brown by the summer heat and the dryness of the high plains. Among those hills, great rock bluffs thrust up, dark and volcanic-looking. From where she sat, the whole landscape appeared torn and rugged and bare. But the air outside was full of the promising song of birds. She wondered was there a place on earth that had no birds? If so, she never wanted to go there.

She scanned the kitchen again, marveling at the care with which it had been decorated. "Are you married, Shinny?"

He poured half-and-half from a carton into a little ceramic server. "Was," he said. "Not anymore. Maybe never again."

She didn't want to pry, but failed relationships were so much a part of her own history that she was always—a little morbidly, she sometimes thought—curious about that experience in the lives of others.

"Children?"

"Nope. Part of the problem. I'm sterile."

"You couldn't adopt?" Prying again, but in for a penny, in for a pound.

He opened the refrigerator and put the half-and-half back on a shelf. "Fine by me, but my wife—ex-wife—wanted children of her own. I get that. She married a guy must be a sperm fountain. She's got six kids now. You have kids, Jenny?"

"One. He's three. His name is Aaron Smalldog O'Connor. We call him Waaboo. Short for Waaboozoons."

"Little rabbit," he said with approval.

"You know Ojibwemowin?"

He opened a bread box on the counter and took out a loaf of something heavy-looking. "Some," he said and pulled a serrated knife from a block of knives. "Also some Arapaho, some Dakota, a little Crow. Mandan, Arikara, and Hidatsa, of course. This is the reservation of the Three Affiliated Tribes, after all. Pays to be able to talk with your neighbors, you know."

"If you don't mind me asking, what does Shinny mean? Is that your real name? Is it Mandan?"

He smiled broadly. "It's an old Plains Indian game. Kind of like hockey. I did a research project about it when I was in high school. The name stuck. My given name is Clarence. I like Shinny a lot better."

"What do you do here? When you're not playing shinny."

"I'm in charge of waste management on the rez. But my real interest is in the health of the land here. We're in trouble, let me tell you."

"The oil drilling?"

He slid a cutting board from a drawer, set it on the counter, placed the loaf in the center, and began slicing the bread. "We sit right on top of the Bakken Formation. That's about two hundred thousand square miles of oil- and gas-bearing shale. Current estimates are that the formation contains more than two billion barrels of recoverable oil. But it's deep underground, and to get it out of the rock requires fracking. You know about fracking, of course."

She told him she did.

"Nobody really knows the ultimate effect of fracking on an environment. Or that's the official stance. Me, I believe it's going to be absolutely devastating. We've already had the largest oil spill on land in U.S. history here. And those communities thrown together to try to house all the workers, God, are they a blight. You can't go anywhere without hitting road construction. All this in the name of the almighty dollar. Jesus, they rape our women, they rape our land, and they call us the savages." He'd been slicing the bread with a kind of vengeance. Now he stopped and stared outside the kitchen windows at the distant brown hills. "I know a lot of people see this area as nothing but wasteland. To me it's infinitely beautiful. I'd love to keep it that way."

"I'm sorry," Jenny said. Feeble, but she didn't know what else to say. "It must be difficult."

He shrugged it off and went back to slicing bread. "If I didn't have my music to fall back on, I'd probably go crazy. That's how Daniel and I first got together, you know."

"Drumming, right? At powwows?"

"There's that, but we jam together, too."

"Daniel's a musician?"

He looked up from his work. "He didn't tell you?"

"He hasn't said a thing."

He laughed. "I can guess why. The accordion's his instrument."

"The accordion?"

His laugh was rich and deep. "Yeah. An accordion-playing Shinnob. Go figure. But he's damn good. You should hear him when we do zydeco."

"Zydeco?"

He eyed her with curiosity. "You and Daniel, there's something there, right?"

"Maybe."

"He's a good man. You could do a lot worse."

"Now there's a ringing endorsement." Daniel stood in the kitchen doorway, running his hand through a head of unkempt black hair.

Jenny smiled at him, and the first thing she said was "The accordion?"

He gave Shinny a cold glare. "You told her?"

"Time you came out of the closet, amigo."

"Why the accordion?" she asked.

Shinny said, "You want coffee before you answer that one, Daniel? It's ready."

He poured them all mugs, and they sat together at the table and sipped the good brew in silence, while the birds sang outside the windows and morning sunlight gilded the room.

"The accordion," Shinny finally said, smiling at Daniel. "This is a story I haven't heard."

"Okay." Daniel sounded as if he was settling into a tale he'd told before, but not one he particularly liked telling. "My grandmother loved Lawrence Welk. When I spent weekends with her, we watched his show, which was in reruns by then. So it started out being something I did because I loved my grandmother and to be, you know, a good grandson. Funny thing was, I ended up liking it, especially the guy who played the accordion. His name was Myron Floren. For my ninth birthday, my grandmother gave me an accordion and money for six months of lessons. A couple of weeks later, she had a heart attack and passed away. What could I do? I learned to play."

"That's lovely, Daniel," Jenny said.

Shinny laughed. "I told you you could do worse, Jenny." He took a sip from his mug and glanced toward a window. "By the way, where's your father?"

"Sleeping in his Explorer."

"Explorer's gone," Shinny said. "Was gone when I got up this morning."

Jenny stood and went to the kitchen window above the sink,

where she could see the street out front. The place her father had parked the night before was empty. "I don't know where he went." She looked back at Daniel. "Did he say anything to you?"

"Not a word."

She returned to her seat. Her gut began to knot. She stared into her coffee, into the little world reflected on its dark surface. "I still think we should bring the police into this."

Neither of her companions spoke immediately. Then Shinny said, "You don't look Indian."

"My grandmother was true-blood Iron Lake Anishinaabe. I'm one-eighth."

He nodded. "Around here, looking the way I do, the way so many of us do, being Indian pretty much defines how we're perceived. You walk into an off-rez community, and you get looked at. You get watched. You get judged. On the basis of your genes alone. Most of us have been stopped by white cops for no other reason than we're driving a truck with reservation plates. We've had altercations with white people, and more often than not, the guy who shows up wearing the badge, a white guy, doesn't much bother to see our side. Not all cops out here are like that, but enough that you just never know. So trusting law enforcement runs against the grain."

"So does vigilantism," Jenny said. "Look, I want to help Mariah, I really do, but I'm concerned about going at it on our own. I have this overwhelming sense that people are going to get hurt."

"Someone has already been hurt, Jennifer O'Connor."

They all turned and found Henry Meloux walking slowly into the kitchen.

"That coffee," the old man said. "I would pay gold for a cup."

"Have a seat, Henry," Shinny said, rising. "And the cost is your company."

"*Migwech*," the old man said. He looked at Jenny. "You slept better than your father."

"You knew he was gone?" she said.

"I heard him drive away. It was very dark."

"Black, Henry?" Shinny asked. "Your coffee?"

"Yes."

Shinny brought Meloux the mug with Wile E. Coyote on it. The old man studied the image and said, "Thin. Not a good hunter, I would guess."

"Abysmal," Shinny said with a laugh.

The old man drank his coffee and closed his eyes, savoring the flavor, the warmth, the caffeine promise.

"You meant Raven Duvall?" Daniel said. "Already hurt?"

Henry lowered his mug and opened his dark eyes. "Before that girl, they hurt others. Hurt is what they know, all they know."

"So hurt for hurt, Henry?" Jenny said. "And we do the hurting?"

"When we walk the Path of Souls, Jennifer O'Connor, we leave the hurt and the hurting behind."

"You're advocating killing these men?"

Meloux cupped his mug as if warming his old, blue-veined hands. He looked deeply into her eyes and spoke softly. "If you kill a wolf for the pleasure of it, that is one kind of killing. If you kill a wolf because it has attacked you, that is another kind of killing. If you kill a wolf that has been caught in the jaws of a trap and injured beyond healing, that, too, is a different kind of killing."

"There are good killings, Henry?"

"There are necessary killings."

"And who decides what's necessary?"

"That is always a matter of the heart."

"I can't accept that, Henry."

"You have never killed."

"And I hope I never have to."

"Granddaughter, I hope that, too."

"Look, we're not going to kill anybody," Daniel said. "If I thought that, I wouldn't be here. There's a way of getting Mariah away from Windigo without resorting to bloodshed."

"You brought your gun," Jenny pointed out. "Are you familiar with Chekhov?"

"What's Chekhov got to do with this?" Shinny asked.

Daniel stared at Jenny while he answered Shinny's question. "Chekhov said that if you hang a gun on the wall in the first act, you have to use it by the third."

They all heard the sound of the Explorer returning, the sudden cutoff of the engine, the thud of a door closing, then another. They heard the little cry of hinges as the front screen door opened and shut. They heard the tread of footsteps across the floor of the living room. They waited for Jenny's father to come into the kitchen. When he finally appeared, he wasn't alone.

CHAPTER 37

The girl with him was no older than Mariah Arceneaux, but she was not Mariah. She wore a tight yellow skirt that barely covered her butt, a tight red top, red heels with straps. A little white purse hung over one shoulder. Her face was a mask of heavy, but carefully applied, makeup. She was Indian. And she was pissed.

"Got a chair for our guest, Shinny?" Cork said.

"Take mine." Daniel stood up.

The girl eyed the vacant seat as if it were the electric chair and made no move to fill it.

"Sit down, Breeze," Jenny's father said.

"Fuck you."

"You're going nowhere. You might as well be comfortable."

"Coffee?" Shinny asked.

Breeze swung her gaze toward him, appraised him, and said, "What the hell." Then she did, in fact, flop down into the chair Daniel had offered. She clutched her purse in her lap and stared at the Formica tabletop.

"Everybody, this is Breeze," Cork said. "Breeze, these are the people who've come a very long way to help you."

"Fuck your help." She spoke toward the red Formica.

"Where have you been, Dad?" Jenny asked.

Cork said, "Could I get a cup of that coffee while you're at it, Shinny? Black?"

"Sure thing, Cork."

Jenny's father stood directly behind Breeze, as if to block her escape should she try. "I couldn't sleep, so I decided to drive over to Windigo's place and check it out for myself. I no sooner get there than one of the SUVs loads up and takes off. I decided to follow it."

Shinny brought Cork a mug and then one for Breeze. "Black?" he said to her.

"You got cream and sugar?" A sulky request.

"Coming right up."

Cork stood sipping from his mug. He looked dark, haggard, but the coffee seemed to brighten him some. He went on: "The SUV drove to one of the thrown-together workers' camps Shinny told us about. Dropped Breeze off there at a place hardly bigger than an outhouse, then took off. I peeked in a window—Christ, the place didn't even have curtains—and saw what was about to go down, knocked on the door. Guy opens up. I flash this at him." He took a badge wallet from his shirt pocket and flipped it open. Jenny had no idea what it actually was, but it looked like official law enforcement. As fast as he'd opened it, he flipped it closed. "I tell him I'm working for Williams County Social Services. I tell him the girl's a runaway, underage, I'm taking her with me. I tell him if he doesn't want to be cited for soliciting sex from a minor, he'll just step aside and let me do my job. He bought it, and here's Breeze."

"And here's Breeze's cream and sugar," Shinny said, setting before her on the table the little ceramic pitcher, a small, matching sugar bowl, and a spoon.

She fixed her coffee, stirred, took a sip. They all watched in silence, as if this was some exotic ritual.

"They'll kill you," she said.

"They might try," Cork replied.

She put her mug down and finally looked at each one of them carefully. "Who are you? What do you want?"

"We want to know about Windigo and that trailer," Cork said.

"Windigo? I don't know anything about anyone named Windigo."

"Maybe you know him as Angel," Cork said.

It was clear that she did, but it was also clear that she wasn't going to give them what they wanted.

"What's your name?" Cork asked. "Your real name?"

"Fuck you," she said.

"Sounds Chinese," Shinny said.

Jenny smiled, but the joke didn't register with Breeze. She drank more coffee, sullen and silent.

Cork moved to the kitchen doorway and leaned there, casually. "I want to know about the men who keep you in that trailer."

"They don't keep me there. I stay because I want to."

"Of course you do. Who are your roommates?" When she didn't reply, Cork said, "Let me show you something, Breeze." He disappeared into the living room and came back a moment later with a photograph in his hand. He laid it on the table in front of her. It was a photo of Raven Duvall, taken at the clinic on the Iron Lake Reservation, as she lay beaten and bruised on the examination table. "One of Angel's girls when he didn't need her anymore."

"She did something to deserve it," Breeze said.

Jenny said, "There's nothing anyone could do to deserve this."

"Fuck you, bitch."

Henry spoke for the first time since the girl had joined them. "Are you hungry, granddaughter?"

"I'm not your granddaughter."

"Are you hungry?" he asked again, unfazed.

She didn't look particularly well fed, and the idea of food seemed the most agreeable thing suggested to her since she'd arrived.

"I guess I could eat." As if it nearly killed her to admit it.

"How about scrambled eggs with cheese, some Canadian bacon, toast with huckleberry jam?" Shinny suggested brightly. "Best breakfast in all of Indian country, I promise."

Jenny gave him a hand, and in a short while, the kitchen smelled wonderfully of the meal. Shinny filled a plate and set it in front of Breeze. As he did this he said, *"Haw mushkay. Doe ksh kay ya oun hey?"*

The girl looked up at him, startled.

"Lakota," he said to her with a smile. "Rosebud?"

She lowered her eyes and concentrated on her food.

They all put breakfast on their plates, and eating seemed to bounce their spirits up a bit.

Then Daniel said exactly what Jenny had been thinking. He said, "They probably know about us by now."

Cork set his plate on the counter. "Probably. I made a play a lot sooner than I would have liked. I hoped maybe it was Mariah in that SUV. When I saw what was going to go down out there in that camp, even though it wasn't Mariah, I just couldn't let it happen. Sorry, Breeze."

Oddly, she didn't appear upset. The food seemed to have had a positive effect on her disposition. She said offhand, "I've done him before. I'll probably do him again." She'd eaten her food, every last crumb. Jenny wondered if she might be thinking of licking the plate.

"There's more, Breeze," Shinny said. "If you'd like."

"Hell, yes. I don't eat this good ever."

"Who cooks?" Jenny asked.

"Me or one of the other girls. Mostly we make Hamburger Helper, pizza out of a box, shit like that."

"None of the men cook?"

"Right." She rolled her eyes. "Who are you guys? Not cops, I can tell." She glared at Jenny's father. "Well, you, maybe."

"Not anymore, Breeze," Cork replied. "We're just people trying to find a lost kid. Know any?"

"Like a little kid, you mean?"

"Like you."

"Right," she said and gave a hoarse laugh, full of derision.

"Her name's Mariah," Jenny said. "Mariah Arceneaux. But she probably goes by another name. Candi, maybe. I've got a picture of her."

Jenny dug in her purse and pulled out the shot of Mariah they'd been showing everyone. She put it on the table in front of Breeze.

The girl glanced at it, and Jenny could see recognition register on her face.

"She's with you and the others at the trailer?" Jenny asked.

Breeze stopped talking. Shinny set another plate of food in front of her, but she didn't make a move to eat.

"Those men won't hurt you," Cork said. "We won't let them, I promise."

She mumbled something.

"What did you say, Breeze?" Jenny asked.

"I don't need your fucking promises."

Because promises have been made to you before, and they've been broken, Jenny thought. And she wondered, had it been that way all her life?

"All we want is to take Mariah home," Cork said. "If you want to go home, too, we'll take you."

"Home?" The very word seemed poison. "Are you fucking kidding me? Home is why I ran away."

Meloux said, "Granddaughter, if you could go anywhere, where would you go?"

She stared at the old man as if he'd spoken a foreign language.

"Dream a little," he said gently. "Where?"

She looked out the window at the distant, dun-colored hills. She was quiet a long while, then she said, "Denver."

"Why Denver?" Meloux asked.

"An aunt there. I visited her a couple of years ago. She has a nice place. You can see the mountains."

"What does she do in Denver?" The old Mide's voice was so soothing it made Jenny want to curl up in his lap.

"Works in a hospital. Like a nurse's aide or something. A real good job."

"If we got you to Denver," Cork said, "to your aunt's place, would you help us?"

She came out of her dream. "I don't even fucking know you."

Meloux said, "Every promise I have ever made I have kept, granddaughter. If you help us, we will help you go wherever you want. This, I promise."

She looked into Meloux's soft brown eyes, and her own eyes became windows to the terrible struggle going on inside her. A lifetime of broken promises pitted against a child's deep desire to be safe and to be free.

Please let her believe this old man, Jenny prayed. *Please let her believe this one promise.*

But in the end, her history killed her hope. Her answer was still "No."

That tiny word took the air from the room.

Then Cork's cell phone rang. He glanced at the display and left the kitchen to take the call.

"So," Breeze said, "I suppose you're going to turn me over to social services, right?"

"No," Jenny said. "We'll just keep you safe until this is over, then we'll let you go."

"Just go?"

"That's what you want, isn't it? And no matter who we turned you over to, in the end, you'd just run away, wouldn't you?"

"Well, yeah." Something seemed to come to her suddenly. "You're really going to fuck with Angel?"

"We're going to get our friend away from him, whatever that takes."

"You know about the cops, right? That's why you're not just turning us all in?"

"What about the cops?" Jenny asked.

"Angel's got 'em in his pocket. Don't you know how it is out here? Everybody's making money, so why shouldn't the cops? That's how they figure it, anyway."

Jenny glanced at Daniel. The argument for doing this on their own had just become immeasurably stronger.

Cork came back in. "That was Duluth PD. Simon Wesley

turned himself in this morning, spilled everything about Carrie Verga and John Boone Turner and the *Montcalm*. Duluth PD wants to talk to me at my earliest convenience." He leveled a look at Breeze, one Jenny couldn't read. "We're going to take your friends down," he said. "You can go down with them, or you can buy yourself a ticket to freedom. The choice is yours."

"You really aren't cops?"

"We really aren't."

"And you really would get me to Denver?"

Cork gave a nod toward Henry Meloux. "I've never known this old man to lie. He's made you a promise. You can believe it."

She looked again at the barren hills all around them, thought about it a long time, and finally said, rather wistfully, "Denver."

CHAPTER 38

They moved quickly after that.

Breeze told them about the situation in the trailer. There were two men—Windigo, whom she knew as Angel, and a guy called Brick. That was the only name she knew him by. She said he was mixed, Lakota and white, but not from Rosebud like her. She thought he might be from Standing Rock. There were three other girls, and Mariah was one of them. One of the other girls was also from Minnesota, White Earth, maybe. The other was from Pine Ridge. Because the men in the oil fields worked crazy hours, the girls had crazy, unpredictable schedules. They could be called out anytime, night or day. Like her, they were all under fifteen.

Breeze was clear: if they were really going to take down Angel and Brick, there was no way she was going back to that trailer. They didn't want to leave her alone, so Shinny called his sister. He explained that he had an emergency and would she mind coming over to his place for a little while. She was there in ten minutes. Her name was Vonda Fox. She looked to be in her late forties, a big, commanding woman. Shinny had told them that Vonda pretty much raised him, worked now for the Three Affiliated Tribes social services, in their Child Care Assistance program, and could handle a girl like Breeze. He introduced them all and gave her a thumbnail idea of what was going down. She looked them over skeptically. "I think you need a bigger war party" was her only comment. Then she eyed Breeze. "That all you got to wear?"

"Yeah."

To her brother, she said, "You go do what you gotta do. Breeze and me, we're going to dig through some old clothes down at the office, find something decent to cover this girl's ass."

Shinny was a hunter. He took two rifles and a box of cartridges from a gun case in his bedroom. Jenny remembered that early on in their search for Mariah her father had said that he didn't like the idea of firearms being involved, that he didn't want anybody hurt. But when he saw the rifles now, he nodded and said to Daniel, "Bring your sidearm."

When they left New Town, Jenny could hear the bell of a church calling the faithful to worship. It was Sunday, a day for rest and for reflection on the divine. Their day, Jenny suspected, would hold something entirely different, and she felt her gut already twisting at the dangerous unknown ahead.

It took almost an hour to reach the trailer. They drove through Williston on the way. Even though it was Sunday morning, the place felt like an anthill of activity. Dust everywhere, coating cars and buildings, choking the air. It was kicked up by a constant stream of trucks rumbling along the highways that intersected the town. All the roads seemed torn up, undergoing construction. The big rigs rolling over them hauled long pipes and great cement pre-fabbed structures and spider webbings of steel. They passed hotels, whose lots were completely filled, the spaces taken up by pickups and SUVs wearing coats of red dust. The town was eating into the prairie like an ugly cancer. The thrown-together communities that housed the men working the oil fields reminded Jenny of photos she'd seen of the spare, platted bases at the South Pole, and she couldn't help wondering what became of human beings who lived too long without beauty.

South of Williston, they turned off the highway and took a dirt road east through hills still untouched by the blight of the town's sprawl. After fifteen minutes, they mounted a crest and Jenny saw the Missouri River below. The river itself was a lazy, red-brown flow between hills covered with the baked, brown grasses of a late, dry summer. Along the banks there were green stands of cottonwoods and other thriving vegetation. In the distance, tall bluffs exploded out of the ground along the river's course, dark against the broad, pale wash of the sky.

On top of the rise, the road divided and Cork braked to a stop at the fork. He pointed along the branch that headed southeast, toward a long, elevated finger of land nearly a mile distant, a promontory above the river, crowned with a copse of cottonwoods.

"It's hard to see without binoculars," he said, "but the trailer's in those trees. If we come at it from this road, they'll spot us long before we get there." He nodded toward the southwest branch of the road. "Up there is where I parked last night and watched."

Cork took the right fork, which climbed a slight ridge that paralleled the Missouri. The trees on the wooded promontory below them moved in and out of their sight line. After nearly a mile, he stopped again.

"My binoculars are in the glove box, Jenny. Will you hand them to me?"

She did as he asked, and he left the Explorer. They all got out with him, Meloux and Daniel and Shinny Fox and Jenny. They walked through the dry ground cover off the road, sending grasshoppers flying before them. The air smelled parched, and the dirt under their feet felt soft and dry as ash. Her father hunched and moved ahead a dozen yards and, with a gesture of his hand, signaled them to keep low. He brought the binoculars to his eyes and studied the scene below. From her vantage, Jenny could now see the clearing in the trees where the trailer sat. It was a good-size mobile home. Two dark SUVs were parked in front. There was a long, white, pill-shaped tank off to one side, which she figured contained propane. In Tamarack County, a lot of the rural homes used propane for heating and cooking, and those white tanks were a common sight.

It was going on ten o'clock by then. The sun was already high, the day hot and dry. Except for the buzz of the grasshoppers, there wasn't a sound in the hills around them.

"Steel grates across the windows. To keep people out or to

keep them in?" Cork said. "Both SUVs are there. I think we have them all corralled inside. I don't know how long that'll last, so we should move fast."

Shinny pointed toward a shallow fold that ran down the hillside below them. It was studded with rock outcrops that provided modest cover. "We could make our way down that little gulley there. They might not see us."

"But if they did, they'd know exactly what we were up to."

"What about coming at them from the back?" Daniel suggested. "The trees'll provide ample cover."

"That'll take too long," Cork replied. "One of them might head off by then, maybe with Mariah."

"What do you suggest?" Shinny said.

Cork lowered his binoculars. "We drive up to the front door, and I knock." He turned back toward the Explorer.

His plan was to play the same card he'd played earlier at the oil workers' camp when he'd taken Breeze into his custody. That would get his foot in the door. The rest of them were to stay hunkered down out of sight in the Explorer. When he'd ascertained that Mariah was inside, he'd give the word, and Daniel and Shinny would come running.

"And how exactly are you going to give us the word?" Daniel asked. It was clear he wasn't entirely on board with the plan.

"I'll have my cell phone on and in my hand. You'll be able to hear everything."

"I think there should be two of us inside," Daniel said.

"Why?" Cork had reached the fork and was preparing to turn onto the branch that led to the tree-capped promontory and the trailer.

"Better logistics," Daniel replied. "Someone to make sure the door's unlocked and open if you're otherwise occupied."

Cork glanced in his rearview mirror. "That would be you, I suppose?"

"That's what I'm thinking."

"Two men'll scare them for sure. And if they have firearms inside, they might be prone to use them. One guy alone won't be such a threat."

"How about one guy and a woman?" Jenny said.

"No." Her father shook his head. "Not you."

He said it firmly. Jenny didn't know if it was because she was a woman or if it was because she was his daughter. Either way, she could tell it was useless to argue.

"Nobody fears an old man," Meloux said.

"I don't know how I'd explain you, Henry," Cork said.

"If necessary, I will explain myself, Corcoran O'Connor. Seeing me will confuse them, and it is always a good thing, is it not, to confuse your enemy? If you are, as my nephew has said, occupied, even an old man can hold open a door."

The Explorer was stopped where the road forked. Behind the wheel, Jenny's father eyed the distant cottonwoods and considered the old man's offer.

"All right, Henry," he finally said. "Everyone else in back and out of sight. Daniel, I'd like your weapon."

Daniel handed over his sidearm and said, "You're going in with it?"

"I like the leverage." He pulled out his shirttail, leaned forward, and wedged the gun into the waistline of his pants at the small of his back. He tugged his shirttail down to cover it.

Daniel, Shinny, and Jenny lay down in the back of the Explorer. Cork left the rear door ajar so that they could exit quickly when necessary. Meloux sat up front. Cork called Jenny on his cell phone to open the line. "Can you hear me?"

"Loud and clear," she said.

"Okay. Here we go. Everyone stay cool."

From where she lay, Jenny could see only sky that was indigo through the tint of the rear windows. The road was rough, and they bumped along, and she could smell and then taste the dry grit the tires kicked up. They were leaving a pretty good rooster tail of dust, and she thought this was intentional. She figured her father wanted to be seen. He wanted there to be no sense of ambush.

She looked at Daniel. His face was intense, focused. She thought about what he'd told her the night before, about confronting men in the woods who carried rifles, and she wondered how you prepared for that. How did you make your heart stop galloping, slow your breathing, quell the fear? Until this moment, what they were doing had been a kind of hypothetical. What if they did this or that? Now they were doing it, and there was no going back.

The Explorer turned left and pulled to a stop. Out one of the windows, Jenny could see the upper branches of tall cottonwood trees.

"Let's do this," Cork said, and Jenny heard his door open.

Then she heard Meloux speak to him. "Corcoran O'Connor, there is something I want you to think about."

Cork's voice, in his reply, was terse. "Make it quick, Henry."

"The windigo is a creature of darkness. Darkness feeds on darkness."

Cork was quiet a moment. "Okay," he finally replied, but his tone was a dismissive *Whatever.*

Meloux could often be a mystery, but one thing Jenny knew was that you never dismissed lightly something he'd told you. She wanted to believe that her father had heard the old Mide, really heard him, but she suspected that he had not.

Meloux's door opened, and both doors slammed shut simultaneously. Jenny put her phone to her ear. She heard the knock on the trailer door, a hollow sound. She also heard music, faintly, the whine of a slide guitar. A few moments passed, then another knocking.

"Williams County Social Services," her father announced.

She was beginning to think the men inside simply wouldn't respond, and what would they do then?

She heard the click of a latch and the sound of the door creaking open. The music was louder, and she recognized the Allman Brothers, Duane Allman doing licks on "Statesboro Blues."

294   WILLIAM KENT KRUEGER

"Yeah?" A gruff, unwelcoming voice.

"Williams County Social Services," her father said. Jenny heard the flap of a wallet and figured he'd flashed the same ID he'd used early that morning. "I'm following up on a report of runaway minors being housed in this trailer."

"No one like that here." Then, "Who's that?"

"My granddaughter is in there," Meloux said. "I just want to talk to her."

"Your granddaughter ain't here, old man. Buzz off."

"I can come back with sheriff's people, if you prefer," Cork said. "All I want to do is talk to the girls."

"And say what?"

"That we're available to help them if they want help."

"They don't want your help."

"So they're here?"

"Get lost."

Jenny heard the sound of a human collision, of a banging door, of a painful exhalation. Then her father spoke breathlessly, "Come on in, Jenny."

They piled out the back of the Explorer and ran for the trailer. Meloux stood holding the door open. They rushed inside and found Cork looming over a man who lay sprawled on the floor. Cork held Daniel's gun trained on the downed man.

On a green sofa on the far side of the room sat a girl. Jenny saw immediately that it was Mariah Arceneaux.

CHAPTER 39

Mariah stared at them and didn't seem at all surprised or frightened. Jenny thought maybe everything she'd suffered had made her numb to fear, numb to all feeling, perhaps. She wore next to nothing—a purple camisole over tight white shorts. Her feet were bare, her toenails painted a garish magenta that matched her lipstick. Her hair was long and black and, at the moment, in need of washing. Her eyes were calm, a little unfocused, and her lips hinted at a smile. A Raggedy Ann doll sat in her lap.

Here she was, the girl they'd been searching for, for whom they'd risked so much, risked everything. Jenny wanted to run to her, wrap Mariah safely in her arms, call her child, because with that doll in her lap that's exactly what she looked like. Everything in Jenny that Stephen would have called *nokomis* urged her forward to save this lost little girl, which, for Jenny, had been the whole point of this hunt at first. But the hunt wasn't over, she knew. It wouldn't end until Windigo was taken or Windigo was dead.

The music inside was blaring, and Jenny's father spoke loudly to be heard over it. "Where's your partner, Brick?"

He was small and weasel-looking, not at all how the man who called himself Windigo had been described to them. Like her father, Jenny figured this was the guy Breeze had called Brick. Manny, in saving the life of his dog, had told them his real name was Bob Two Bears.

"I don't know what the hell you're talking about," Brick said. "Who are you?"

"Robert Wilson French, that's who I'm talking about. Aka Angel, aka Windigo." Cork signaled to Daniel and Shinny. "Check the other rooms."

They split off with their rifles in hand and moved through the trailer.

Mariah spoke: "Angel." She said it as if she were speaking to the doll in her lap. The sound of the Allman Brothers almost drowned out her voice.

"Turn that off, Jenny." Cork gestured toward an iPod docked in a compact speaker system.

She did as he asked. The trailer got quiet and, in an odd way, seemed somehow larger and more threatening.

"Yes," Cork said to Mariah. "I want to know about Angel."

"Angel comes, Angel goes," she said, again to her doll. "Chop, chop, chop."

Daniel came back. "Nobody."

Shinny returned, accompanied by two girls no older than Mariah. They both wore T-shirts and skimpy underwear and nothing else. They were clearly Native and were clearly scared and confused.

Cork said, "Why don't you two sit down?"

They did as he'd suggested and perched on a brown leather love seat. Their eyes jumped from him and his gun to Daniel and Shinny with their rifles, to the man on the floor, and finally to Jenny and Henry Meloux. They reminded Jenny of small birds ready to fly at the first opportunity.

"Chop, chop, chop," Mariah said dreamily and to no one in particular.

Daniel laid his rifle down and seated himself on the sofa beside her. "Hello, Mariah."

She studied him a long time and seemed confused. "Danny?"

"Yeah, it's me."

She shook her head. "Dreaming."

"Not a dream, Mariah." He reached out and gently took her hand. "I'm real. I'm real, and I'm here, and I'm going to take you home."

"He won't let you." Her eyes drifted to the man on the floor.

"He won't stop us."

"Angel will."

"Where is Angel?"

"He was here." She looked around, her eyes studying each of them as if they might prove to be Angel. "Gone now."

"Where did he go?"

"Chop, chop, chop," she replied and smiled.

Cork spoke to the girls. "Do you know where Angel is?"

From the floor, the man they knew as Brick said, "Keep your mouths shut, you know what's good for you."

The two girls said nothing.

"Is he hiding somewhere?" Cork asked.

"He just goes," Mariah said. "Comes and goes. Like the wind."

"Or like a windigo?" Cork said. He watched her closely for some reaction, but either the name meant nothing to her or she was too far gone in what Jenny had come to believe was a drug-induced state of disconnection to be able to respond coherently.

Cork glanced at Shinny. "Check outside. Be careful."

Shinny nodded and left through the front door.

"Do you want to go home, Mariah?" Daniel asked.

"Too far," she said. There was at last some emotion in her voice, a distant sadness, as if she were speaking of something lost to her a very long time ago.

"Not too far," Daniel told her. "I'll take you there."

She closed her eyes and smiled and said, "Basketball."

"Yes, Mariah. You can play basketball again."

Cork spoke to the two girls. "Where do you want to go?"

Their eyes grew huge with surprise. They looked at each other in bewilderment.

"We won't leave you here," he said. "Where do you want to go?"

They gave him no reply, and Jenny couldn't tell if they were too scared or if they simply had no answer to his question.

"No matter," Cork said. "We can sort that out later."

Shinny returned from outside. "Nothing," he said. "I checked everywhere."

"Okay." Cork addressed the girls. "Gather your things. We're leaving."

They made no move to comply.

"Now," he said sharply. "Shinny, go with them. Make sure they come back."

The two girls rose and, with all the enthusiasm of people being marched to execution, headed off with Shinny at their backs.

"What about him?" Daniel said, gesturing to the man on the floor.

"Cuff him. We'll take him with us."

Daniel got up. "Roll over," he said to Brick.

"Fuck you."

"I said roll over."

Daniel gave him a good kick in the ribs, which made Jenny wince, but it did the trick. Brick rolled over. Daniel took his cuffs from the belt where he'd hung them and cuffed the man's wrists behind his back.

"Check his pockets," Cork said.

Daniel frisked him and came up with a set of vehicle keys and a wallet. He opened the wallet. "And we thought his name was Brick or Two Bears," he said. "According to this ID, he's Benjamin O. Baker. Which do you suppose it is?"

"Could be none of them," Cork said. "Take him outside, put him in the Explorer."

Daniel hauled him off the floor none too gently and shoved him out the front door.

Shinny came back with the girls. Each carried a black plastic bag stuffed with her belongings. Neither bag was very full. They'd put on jeans and sneakers.

"Take them outside to the Explorer," Cork said.

"Let's go, girls." Shinny herded them out.

Which left the rest alone with Mariah. And that's when Jenny realized Henry Meloux had disappeared.

"Where's Henry?" she asked.

They looked at one another and around the trailer, what they could see of it. The situation reminded Jenny eerily of the meeting she'd had with Raven Duvall in the park in Duluth when Meloux had mysteriously vanished.

She called out, "Henry?" but got no reply. "He must be outside."

Her father said, "I'll check the rooms again."

He left, and Mariah and Jenny were alone. She started toward the girl. Just as Jenny reached the sofa, Mariah seemed to spot something, and her eyes went huge with fright. At the same moment, Jenny heard the front door close and lock. She spun, and a great bear of a man loomed before her. He held an enormous pistol in his hand, pointed at her chest.

He was no more Indian-looking than Jenny. Reddish blond hair, a plain face, maybe a little broad because of his Anishinaabe genes, eyes the same indigo color of the sky she'd seen through the tinted windows of the Explorer. There was something about those eyes, though, that made them like none she'd ever seen. They were bottomless and absolutely empty. Nothing showed in them, not hate or love or fear or excitement. They were windows on a vacuum, an inhuman void. She was looking at a creature that she truly believed had no soul. And she understood why the girls—why anyone—would be terrified to cross him.

"Windigo," she said, although it was more of a gasp.

He put a finger to his lips. A moment later, Cork returned and stopped dead in his tracks. He still held Daniel's sidearm in his hand and, as if he'd practiced the move a thousand times, quickly trued the barrel on the heart of the man called Windigo.

"You shoot, I shoot, she's dead," Windigo said, as if it were a simple equation. He gave a slight nod to the gun he held. "Desert Eagle, forty-four Magnum. Hollow-point rounds. Hair trigger. Put a hole in her the size of Iowa. I may or may not be dead at the end, but she doesn't stand a chance."

"There are others outside," Cork said.

"The important ones are right here."

"You knew we were coming," Cork said. "How?"

"I'm mythic. I know everything."

"Where were you?"

"Doesn't matter. I'm here now. And I'm curious about you."

"Family," Mariah said dreamily from the sofa.

Windigo nodded. "Yeah, I know that. But it's unusual. My girls, their families generally don't care. Sell them to me like unwanted furniture."

Jenny was becoming aware of an unpleasant odor in the trailer, so faint that its true nature didn't yet register.

"How'd you find me?" Windigo asked.

"Your brother, Samuel," Cork said. "Aka Manny, aka Maiingan. I made him an offer he couldn't refuse."

"What? Give me up or you'd kill him?"

"I just threatened to kill his dog."

"Ember? He dropped the dime on me for that old bag of bones?" He digested this, and it didn't seem to sit well with his stomach. "We'll discuss that next time I see him."

The look in his eyes and the coldness in his voice made Jenny think of sharp icicles. She figured that conversation with Wolf, should it ever occur, would be one-sided and brutal.

The front doorknob rattled, followed by knocking. "Cork?" Daniel called.

"Tell him to stay outside," Windigo instructed.

"Or what?"

"She's dead. Then probably I'm dead. Which is neither here nor there for me. But you're out a daughter."

So he knew things about them. But how? At that moment, Jenny was more perplexed than she was afraid.

"Our Windigo has materialized," Cork called to Daniel. "We're having a conversation. You just stay where you are."

"I'm here," Daniel called back.

"We're taking Mariah," Cork said to Windigo.

"I should have killed her when she came back from the Apostles and told me what happened on that boat. Knew that whole thing would bite me in the ass eventually." He shrugged. "Water under the bridge. As for taking her, be my guest."

"I don't suppose you'd come, too?"

"Not at the moment. I've got damage control to worry about. Then I'll get things up and running somewhere else. Not hard. Kids like her, dime a dozen. After that, I'll be along to deal with you. In my own good time."

"I don't like leaving that particular door open."

"Then shoot me."

They faced each other across that narrow width of flimsy aluminum housing. Jenny thought of mountains standing on either side of a valley. Neither man moved.

But something else did. Left of Windigo came movement so swift that Jenny couldn't make sense of it at first. A blur of human form. In that same instant, she saw the arm holding Windigo's .44 Magnum drop, and the big handgun fell to the floor. Then Henry Meloux—now she could see and understand—swung again. Windigo reeled backward, spewing blood from his face as he fell. The old Mide stood above him, a four-foot section of iron rebar in his fierce grip, poised to strike another blow.

"No more," Windigo cried and held up a palm in surrender.

"His gun," Cork said.

Meloux kicked the heavy piece of hardware across the floor, out of Windigo's reach. He didn't loosen his grip on the rebar.

"Where the hell did you come from, old man?" Windigo asked. He didn't appear angry, just curious. Despite the blood streaming from the wound across his forehead, he didn't seem much affected by the blows Meloux had delivered. He flexed his left hand, trying to assess, Jenny imagined, the damage the old Mide had done.

"You can always smell a windigo," Meloux said, not really answering the question.

"Up." With Daniel's gun, Cork motioned for the man to rise, which he did. "Open the door, Henry. Let Daniel in."

As big as he was, Daniel, when he entered, still had to lift his head to look into the face of the man called Windigo. Then he sniffed the air, and his own face took on a peculiar and startled look.

That's when Jenny realized what she'd been smelling all along, the odor that had become stronger during their confrontation with Windigo, and that was now almost overpowering. Because she'd been focused on the gun barrel leveled at her chest and the standoff between her father and Windigo, she had ignored it. She couldn't ignore it now. The odor of rotten egg, of sulfur, filling the trailer.

"Gas," she said. She remembered the white tank she'd seen off to the side of the trailer. "Propane."

"Outside." Cork waved his pistol toward the door.

"Nope," Windigo responded. "And I wouldn't think about coercing me with that sidearm of yours. The muzzle blast'll blow us all to smithereens."

Before Meloux could move to hit him again with the rebar, Windigo pulled a Bic lighter from his pocket and held it out, his thumb on the striker.

"Like I said, you're free to go. Me, I'm staying."

"Jenny, Mariah," Daniel said. "Let's go."

Mariah remained on the sofa, and Jenny couldn't tell if she had any idea what was happening. She took Mariah's arm and tried to ease her up. The girl pulled away.

"Danny?" Mariah said.

Daniel walked to her from the doorway. "Give me your doll, Mariah, and I'll take you both outside." He said it gently and without any hint that her life might depend on it. Or everyone's, for that matter.

Mariah put Raggedy Ann into his hands and eased herself up. Daniel took her arm and led her toward the door. As she passed the man that she knew as Angel and that Jenny and the others called Windigo, she said, "You promised it would be nice."

"Heaven is what I promised. In a while, little squirrel, I'd have got you there."

She went out with Daniel. Jenny followed, but hesitated at the door. "Dad? Henry?"

"You go," Windigo said to her father. "But the old man, he stays. I have something to say to him."

"We go together," Cork replied.

"Fine. We all go together." Windigo held up the lighter.

"You won't," Jenny said, but it was more hope than certainty.

Meloux looked into those empty eyes and gave a nod. "He will."

"Get out, Jenny," her father ordered.

"Dad—"

"Go!"

She went and heard the door of the trailer close behind her. She walked into the sunlight where Daniel and the others waited.

"Give me the key to the Explorer," Daniel said.

She looked at him, uncomprehending.

"We should move it." He meant a safe distance, in case the trailer blew up, but he didn't say it.

Inside the vehicle, in the backseat, still cuffed, sat the man whose driver's license identified him as Benjamin O. Baker. Next to him were the two girls. Because of the heat, the windows were down. She gave Daniel the key. He backed the Explorer nearer to the road and got out. Jenny led Mariah there, and Shinny joined them. They waited.

Fear, that hungry wolf, had come, and it gnawed at Jenny's gut now. Her father and Henry Meloux, two of the people she loved most in this world, were inside that trailer with a man who, if Meloux had read him correctly, was entirely capable of carrying out his threat to blow them all to kingdom come. She could hear nothing from inside. Outside, in the slightest of breezes, she heard the leaves of the cottonwood trees rustling with a lovely, liquid sound. She smelled the dry grass of the hillsides that bordered the river, and mixed with that scent was the fragrance of sage. She touched her face, hoping the feel of her own flesh might bring her out of this terrible dream.

The door opened, and her father emerged. The door closed again at his back. He walked toward them. The flesh of his face was pulled so tight over the bone beneath that it seemed to Jenny she was looking at a skull.

"Henry?" she asked.

Her father turned and stared back at the trailer. She could see that he'd wedged Daniel's sidearm in the waistband of his jeans. As powerful a weapon as that Glock probably was, Windigo had rendered it useless.

Her father spoke as if pronouncing sentence: "Henry said a hundred years was enough for any man."

"What do we do?" The panic rising. "There must be something we can do."

"We do what Indians have always done well." Her father's voice was leaden, dead. "We wait."

But they didn't wait long.

The sound was not what Jenny would have expected. It was not a cataclysmic explosion. It was, instead, a powerful *whooomp*, a blast of air and fire that blew out the trailer's windows and door and sent some of the roof flying in embered pieces into the branches of the cottonwoods. Jenny fell back, more from the shock of the moment than from the shock of the blast itself. The others fell back, too, and they all watched as arms of yellow flame and black smoke reached through the empty openings and groped for sky.

Jenny stood paralyzed, but her father leaped into action immediately.

"Call nine-one-one," he yelled and shot for the trailer opening where the front door had once been.

Jenny fumbled the phone from her pocket, where she'd slipped it when they rushed from the back of the Explorer. Her hands were shaking so bad she dropped it in the dirt. She bent, and when she came up with it and looked toward the trailer, saw her father falling back from the flames. A hell of fire and smoke lay beyond the gaping doorway inside the trailer. Daniel was right behind him, reeling back, too, his arms raised to shield his face from the intense heat. The odd quiet of the initial explosion had been replaced now by the roar of the burn and the groan of metal remolding or melting in the blast-furnace heat. Shinny joined them, and they stood yelling to each other over the sound of the trailer fire. Jenny couldn't make out their words. She was trying to find those three simple numbers on her phone pad, but her fingers kept hitting the wrong keys. She focused. Nine. One. One. Phone to her ear. When she looked at the trailer again, she saw that Daniel had grabbed a hose connected to an outside spigot. He'd turned on the water and was soaking her father.

"Williams County Dispatch." A woman's voice. "What's your emergency?"

"There's a fire," Jenny yelled into the phone. "A trailer fire."

"Where's the fire, ma'am?"

"South of Williston. A road. I don't know the name of it." She ran to Shinny and grabbed his arm. "Does this road have a name?"

"The Old Garrison Road. Three miles east of the split from Highway Eighty-five."

She repeated it into her phone.

Her father, dripping water from every part of him, once more attempted to enter the trailer. He ducked low beneath the black, billowing smoke and disappeared.

"Fire personnel are on the way, ma'am. Is anyone injured?"

"Yes," Jenny yelled.

"Are you hurt?"

"No. No."

"What's your name?"

She gave it.

"Stay on the line, ma'am."

"I can't," Jenny said. "I have to help." And she ended the call.

Daniel stood in front of the doorway, shooting a stream of water inside, in the direction her father had gone. Shinny, who no longer held a rifle, leaned close and said something to him.

Daniel handed over the hose, and Shinny soaked him, too, then Daniel headed toward the doorway. He didn't make it inside. Jenny's father stumbled out, coughing, hot vapor rising from his wet clothing. He fell into Daniel's arms. Daniel helped him away from the trailer, then turned to go back. Jenny's father grabbed his arm.

"It's no good," he yelled, then coughed a good ten seconds. "Can't see a thing inside. All smoke and flame."

Jenny was beside him, holding him as the coughing continued and racked his body. "Henry?" she said.

He'd doubled over from the exertion, but now he came up slowly. His eyes lingered on the trailer, then followed the black roil of smoke pouring upward from it, smudging the washed blue of the sky. One of the traditional beliefs of the Anishinaabeg was that the embers of a fire carried prayers to the Creator. Jenny looked up where her father looked, and understood.

Grief doesn't come in the moment of loss. It comes in the quiet of the aftermath. As she stood watching the trailer burn, and that beautiful old man Henry Meloux with it, she didn't feel grief. In a way, what she felt was simply emptiness. Her mind told her Meloux was dead. Her heart was not there yet.

"They're gone," Shinny said.

At first, Jenny thought he was stating the obvious, speaking of Meloux and the man called Windigo. She said, "We know."

"I'm talking about that scumbag from Standing Rock and the girls," Shinny clarified.

Jenny turned from the fire that had kept her attention and saw what Shinny had already seen. The Explorer was empty. The girls and Brick were gone. There was no sign of them on the road or on the barren hillside.

"What now?" Daniel asked.

Cork spoke without looking away from the conflagration, and he spoke without feeling. "You still have the keys you took off Brick?"

"Yeah," Daniel said.

"Take Mariah and Jenny and Shinny. Go back to New Town and wait for me there. I'll deal with this mess."

"You got that," Shinny said. "We're outta here. Which vehicle?"

Daniel tossed him the key. "See which it fits."

Shinny jumped into the nearest SUV, where bits of debris lay burning on the hood. The engine turned over.

"Let's go," he called. "I don't want to be here when the uniforms arrive."

"We can't just leave you, Cork," Daniel tried to argue.

Jenny's father turned bloodshot eyes on him. "You really want Mariah to be a part of what's going to happen here next?" Daniel didn't reply; the answer was obvious. "Go on," Cork said. "Get out of here. All of you."

"Dad—" Jenny began.

"Now," he said.

"Go, go, go," Shinny called out.

Daniel ushered Mariah into the backseat of the SUV and got in beside her. Jenny walked to the front passenger door and opened it. She looked back at her father, who stood alone, framed by fire, and she knew she couldn't leave him.

"Go on," she said to Daniel and the others. "I made the nine-one-one call. If I'm not here, they'll ask all kinds of questions."

"Are you sure, Jenny?" Daniel said.

"We came to save Mariah. So save her."

Daniel looked at her through the open window, and Jenny knew it killed him to leave. But what she said made sense, and he knew it. "I'll be waiting in New Town."

"I'll be there," she promised.

They pulled away, onto the dirt and gravel of what Jenny now knew was the Old Garrison Road, and sped off, trailing a long cloud of dun-colored dust. She went to her father and stood with him. They watched the trailer being consumed. The smoke was an ugly color and smelled nothing like the good fragrance that came from a campfire. These flames were fed by poisons, by all the unnatural elements that had gone into the manufacture of that cheap construction. But as she watched the foul, black cloud crawling toward the blue vault of heaven, she understood that at its heart was the purest soul she'd ever known.

"Henry," she said and could not now keep back the tears.

A moment later, her father looked toward the sky and echoed, "Henry."

PART III

CORCORAN O'CONNOR:

"To Be That Which We Destroy"

CHAPTER 40

The trailer was still burning when the fire engines screamed down the Old Garrison Road. Much had been consumed by then, but it still stood intact as a structure. Cork wondered how a thing so shoddy in its construction could hold itself together in the face of such fervent destruction. But logic had gone to hell when the man called Windigo blew himself to smithereens and Henry Meloux along with him.

There were no hydrants in that remote location, and the engines brought portable water tanks. Cork had moved his Explorer well away from the blaze and out of the way of the firefighters. He and Jenny watched as the long white blasts of water reached into the burned-out shell and quelled the flames.

The sheriff's department had dispatched a deputy in a cruiser, a Chevy Tahoe coated in red dust. Cork and Jenny together told the story they'd prepared: how they'd been hired to find Mariah Arceneaux and had traced her to the trailer; how Cork had confronted the two men inside; how they'd smelled the gas, which Robert Wilson French, whom the girls knew as Angel and Windigo, had purposely allowed to pour into the trailer; how they'd run outside, all but French and the old man, Henry Meloux; how they'd watched as the trailer exploded and burned; and finally how the trafficked girls, all of them, had fled, along with French's partner, Bob Two Bears, aka Benjamin O. Baker, aka Brick. Cork gave the deputy the wallet Daniel English had taken from the man but made no mention of English or Shinny Fox.

"How'd you get his billfold?" The deputy was a lanky, sun-browned guy, maybe Cork's age. His name was Seekins. "I don't imagine he just handed it over."

"I was persuasive," Cork said.

"Uh-huh." The deputy wrote something in his notes. He studied what he'd written, glanced at the firefighters who were mopping up, and scratched a mole on his upper lip. "So the two of you and an old man got the jump on a couple of pimps, that's what you're telling me? And one of the men blew himself up, along with the old guy? And everyone but you two ran off?"

"In a nutshell," Cork said.

Jenny nodded her agreement with that simple assessment.

"What was the old man doing with you?"

"He was a healer," Cork said. "A traditional Ojibwe healer. He came to help the girl we were looking for, if we found her."

"But she ran off, you say?"

"Yes."

"So she wasn't interested in being healed."

"The explosion," Cork said. "It sent everyone running."

In addition to Cork's driver's license, the deputy had taken his PI license. He'd taken Jenny's driver's license, too. Cork had given him the name of Marsha Dross, the sheriff in Tamarack County, and the names of several of the deputies there, in case he cared to check on Cork's credentials and character. Seekins said, "You folks just wait here a minute."

He went to his cruiser and spoke for a while on his radio.

The fire had been extinguished, but there was still smoke rising up here and there from the trailer. A couple of firefighters were making their way carefully through the ash and char inside.

Jenny seemed to have collected herself, but she was quiet. Cork understood. He didn't feel much like talking either. What he felt like was climbing one of the hills above the river all alone and giving himself over to the deep sadness that kept trying to break through the wall he'd put up to contain it. He'd held Jenny while she wept, and the truth was he wanted to weep, too. But now was not the time.

Jenny's cell phone rang. She took the call. Cork heard her say, "Yeah, a deputy's here. Asking questions. Lots of them. You got our girl to New Town?" She listened, head down, staring at the dirt. "At least we have what we came for," she said. "I need to go. We'll talk later."

She leaned to her father and spoke quietly. "Breeze is gone. Vonda took her down to her office, where she keeps a supply of donated clothing on hand. While Vonda was gathering up clothes possibilities, Breeze slipped away. Vonda caught her making a phone call. To her family, Breeze said, to let them know she was okay. She took the clothes Vonda gave her, went into the bathroom to change, was there a long time. Vonda finally knocked, got no answer. She went in to check. The bathroom window was open, screen off, Breeze nowhere to be seen. Damn. I thought we'd convinced her."

"Too many broken promises," Cork said. "Or just way too scared of our Windigo. Or maybe misplaced loyalty. Who knows? They've all been so damaged, is it any wonder they end up confused?"

"I wondered how Windigo knew so much about us. I'll bet the call she made was to him."

"Couldn't have been much before we came. We sure seemed to catch Brick by surprise, anyway." Cork wasn't certain how to put those pieces together, and he was too tired and too distracted at the moment even to try.

The deputy finally returned. "Warrants out on both the men you say were here in the trailer. The office made a call to Aurora, Minnesota, talked to your sheriff there. She's vouched for you. Says you used to be law enforcement, too. Sheriff. That right?"

"A while ago," Cork said.

"Then you'll understand if I ask you to come back into the office in Williston and give us a full statement and maybe go through this interview again. Both of you."

"We'd be happy to," Cork said.

"I'd like your cell phone number, too." He glanced at Jenny and said, "Got yours from the nine-one-one call."

Cork gave him his number. As Seekins wrote it down, one of the firefighters approached. He greeted the deputy with a nod. "Tommy."

"What'd you find, Walt?" Seekins asked.

"Well, I'll tell you what we didn't find. We didn't find no bodies."

"What?" Jenny had been leaning against the side of the Explorer, but this made her stand upright.

"My guys went through that whole damn trailer. Some hot spots still there, but nothing burning. They checked real careful. No bodies."

The deputy said, "You sure, Walt?"

"I been fighting fires as long as you been giving tickets, Tommy. When I say there's no bodies, there's no bodies."

Seekins looked at Cork and at Jenny. "You folks sure those two didn't get out without you seeing them?"

Cork said, "Bars on the window, Deputy. And I checked the back door after the gas blew, thinking maybe I could go in that way. Locked. No way anyone could've got out of there."

"Then you care to tell me where those two bodies went?"

"I don't know." Cork looked toward Jenny, but he could see that she was just as baffled as he was.

Seekins said, "We'll impound this SUV, and I'll have the office put out an APB for French and Two Bears. We'll get them."

"And Henry?" Jenny asked.

"No warrants on him. Don't know what to tell you. Man old as you say he is won't get far. He'll turn up." He gave them back their licenses. "Where you folks staying?"

"Friends on the Fort Berthold Reservation," Cork replied.

Seekins eyed him curiously. "You Indian?"

"Anishinaabe."

The name clearly didn't register with the deputy.

"Ojibwe," Cork said. "Chippewa."

"Oh, like Turtle Mountain."

"Yeah," Cork said. "Like Turtle Mountain."

"Well, could've fooled me, name like O'Connor, the way you look and all."

"Fools a lot of people," Cork said.

"All right, then. You coming into Williston now?"

"We'll be along shortly," Cork said. "Any problem if we stay here awhile? Got a few things to process, emotionally."

"No hurry. I've got to track down who it is owns this place. That'll take a while on a Sunday. Walt and his guys have got some cleaning up to do. Just see that you stay out of their way."

The deputy returned to his Tahoe, made a U-turn, and headed north, back toward Williston.

Jenny said, "No bodies. How could that be?"

"I'm thinking," Cork said.

By the time the fire engines finally pulled away, leaving the blackened, burned-out hull of the trailer, he had a thought. He waited until the big trucks were out of sight and the dust from their passing had settled and he was certain that he and Jenny were alone. The sun was high, the air still. Cork watched a couple of hawks circling high on the thermals that rose above the tree-capped promontory where the trailer—what was left of it—sat. The hawks reminded him of all the ash that had been aloft and scattered God knew where. He walked to the trailer through mud created by the water that had been sprayed in putting out the fire. He stood in the center of the destruction, in the wet char inside the gutted shell, and studied the floor.

"What are you looking for?" Jenny called from the safety outside the burnt shell.

"Remember what Mariah said about our Windigo? He comes and he goes. He was gone when we got here. And then suddenly he showed. Where did he come from?"

Moving carefully, Jenny joined Cork in the trailer.

"He was hiding," she said.

"Where?"

"I don't know."

"Think about it. No bodies. Grates on the windows, doors locked, but he and Henry got out somehow." He began walking slowly, kicking burnt debris clear of the floor as he went.

"You think there was some kind of trapdoor?"

"I think there was another way out, and I think the floor is the most reasonable consideration."

"Meloux came from there," Jenny said, pointing to the north end of the trailer. "So wouldn't it make sense that Windigo came from there?" Now she pointed south.

Cork began in the kitchen area, which was where Jenny had pointed last. He walked a grid across the bubbled, curled linoleum but found nothing that seemed promising. He moved out of the kitchen, down the short hallway to the bathroom. He came up empty there, too. He went to the bedroom. There'd been carpeting on the floor, but that had burned away. He slowly walked the perimeter, then worked his way across the rest of the room, around the blackened bed and mattress. The closet door stood open. A few shreds of clothing still hung from the metal hangers. A pair of leather shoes, cracked and hardened from the heat, sat in one corner. The carpeting had somehow remained mostly intact. Cork stepped inside. Immediately, he felt the floor give just a little under his weight. He bent and found a seam in the carpet. He pulled at the edge, and a flap curled back in his hand. Beneath lay the trapdoor of Jenny's speculation. Cork grasped the steel pull and lifted the door, revealing a crawl space below. He peered into the hole. Along the back wall of the cinder blocks that were fitted as a skirting between the foundation and the bottom of the trailer, he saw a gap where sunlight shot into the dark.

"They got out this way." Cork stood up. "Come on."

Jenny followed him outside. He hurried to the rear of the trailer, where he found four cinder blocks lying beside a two-foot gap in the trailer's skirting.

Cork said, "He crawled out here. See the handprints there.

And those deep, round indentations behind them, they've got to be knee prints."

"What about Henry?" Jenny said.

"He dragged Henry out. See those shallow ruts? Plowed by Henry's heels is my guess." He walked away from the trailer into the sparse, dead grass of the clearing. "And then he carried Henry."

"Why?"

"Only one set of footprints."

"No," Jenny said. "I don't understand why he would carry Henry."

"Most likely because Henry was unconscious." He looked at her straight in the eyes. "Or Henry's dead."

"But, Dad, why would he cart off a dead man? It doesn't make sense."

"I think you're right. So I think Henry's still alive, though probably unconscious."

"Why take him in the first place?"

Cork looked at the line in the dead grass Windigo had trampled in his flight. He looked toward the cottonwood trees a couple of dozen yards distant, where the footprints led. He closed his eyes, trying to imagine the mind of a man like Windigo.

"Two possibilities," he finally said. "He took Henry as a hostage, in case we followed. Or he took Henry as bait, so that we *would* follow."

"A trap?"

"Let's take a look at the lay of the land."

In the backyard was a gray chimenea with four canvas chairs nearby. There was also a stack of wood to burn in that outdoor fireplace. Not far away stood the stump of a cottonwood, cut flat with a chain saw. The surface of the stump carried dozens of scars where wood had been split for feeding to the fire, and the blade of the long-handled ax responsible for the splitting was sunk deep into the stump. Cork tried to envision Windigo or Brick chopping wood, preparing a fire so they could sit with their girls and enjoy one another's company under the broad, starlit North Dakota sky.

It was impossible. That kind of domesticity in the sort of hellish relationship that must have existed in Windigo's "family" Cork simply couldn't imagine.

Then he realized the kindling around the stump was freshly split, and he thought he had the answers to a couple of questions that had puzzled him: Why did Windigo know they were coming but Brick didn't?

"Chop, chop, chop," he said to Jenny.

"What?"

"That's what Mariah told us when I asked her where Angel was. 'Chop, chop, chop,' she said. He was out here, cutting wood for a fire tonight. That's when he must have got Breeze's call. But it came too late for him to do anything about it. He probably only had enough time to pop under the trailer before Shinny came around in back to check on things."

"Enough time for that and to fill the trailer with propane gas." She eyed the nearby cottonwoods. "Let's find him."

They followed the single set of prints into the trees. They made their way to the edge of the promontory, easily reading the trail Windigo had left in his passage. They stood looking down a steep slope covered, like the hills around them, with dry grass. At the bottom, a quarter mile distant, lay the silty brown flow of the Missouri River, bordered on the far side by a broad stretch of pale green wetlands.

"What do you think?" Cork said.

"He'll stick with the Missouri," Jenny replied. "Away from roads. There's no cover on these hillsides, but there's plenty along the river."

"Where will he go?"

"Williston, probably."

"Why?"

"Resources there."

"That's a long way to carry Henry. And what if he's followed? How will he know? Remember, that may be exactly what Windigo wants."

She thought, her blue eyes hard, focused. Finally she said, "He's down there somewhere we can't see, but he can see us."

"Where would that be?"

She scanned the near bank of the river, squinting. "In one of those clusters of trees."

She wiped a fist across her jaw, a pointless gesture, but it signaled to Cork the intensity of the moment for her, which was a good thing.

"If it's the police who follow," she went on, "he can dump Henry's body in the river. He might even go in with it, let the current carry him to Williston. If it's us he sees coming down this hill, he's got what he wants."

Cork was pleased. She'd learned a great deal on this hunt, how to think like the prey you hunted. If things went south, she wouldn't be unprepared. "Stay here."

He left Jenny at the edge of the cottonwoods and went back to his Explorer. Before the fire engines and the Tahoe from the Williams County Sheriff's Office had arrived, while he and Jenny were getting their story straight with each other, Cork had put Daniel's Glock under the Explorer's front seat. Now he pulled the sidearm from its hiding place. He leaned across the driver's seat and opened the glove box. From inside, he took his field glasses and a folded hunting knife.

When he returned to Jenny, she looked at the Glock. "What are you going to do, Dad?"

"Give him what he wants."

"We're going after him?"

"*I'm* going after him."

"Not alone."

"You need to stay here."

"Why?"

"You fulfilled your vision, Jenny. You saved her. Your part in this is finished."

"No."

"Yes. You've got a son back in Tamarack County to think

about. Take this." He held the sidearm out to her, but she refused it. "Look, we may be wrong," he said. "Windigo may double back, return to the trailer when he thinks it's safe. Until they actually send someone out to impound it, his SUV is still here. Maybe he has money stashed somewhere nearby, operating funds. I've seen it before. If he does come back, you'll need this."

"To do what?"

"Shoot him. Don't talk to him, don't hesitate, just shoot him."

"In cold blood?" she said.

"Can you do that?"

"I don't know."

"He won't give you time to think."

"You're talking about killing a man, Dad."

"I'm talking about saving your own life."

"Keep the gun. When you find him, you'll need it."

He held up the knife he'd taken from the glove box of the Explorer. "My Buck Alpha." He opened it. "Three-and-a-half-inch blade. I keep this razor-sharp. I find our Windigo, I intend to cut his throat and skin him."

His heart was ice, and it wasn't an idle threat. All his logic, all his clear reading of the signs had one purpose: to find the man called Windigo and kill him.

Jenny stared at him, stared nails. "I don't need a vision to tell me what's going to happen. Windigo's big gun wasn't anywhere in the trailer. He probably took it with him. He's hoping you'll go down there, Dad. If you do, I won't lose just Henry. I'll lose you, too."

"All right," he said. "I keep the gun, but you get out of here." He dug in his pocket and brought out the keys to the Explorer.

"I'm not leaving," she said.

"You're not going down there with me."

"Then you're not going down there."

Cork's whole body was iron, his hands like forged steel, white around the weapons he held. Below his thin sheath of human flesh was a beast hungry for vengeance. He could already taste blood.

"Dad," Jenny said, her voice quiet, amazingly calm. "Dad, listen to me. You march down there, that won't save Henry. It will only get you killed. I love you. Waaboo and Annie and Stephen and Rainy, we all love you, and we don't want to lose you."

"I left Henry to die once today. I won't do that again."

"There's another way. There's got to be."

"I don't know what that is, and we're running out of time. It may already be too late."

She reached out and put her hand gently against his chest. Her light, loving touch made him realize how tense he was, how hard he held himself, how bound up in his desire for blood he'd become.

"Listen to me, Dad. Remember what Henry told you? The windigo is a creature of darkness. Darkness feeds on darkness. Our Windigo wants you to do this. He wants you to blind yourself the way he's blinded. That's how he'll beat you in this hunt. There's got to be another way. And Henry would say look for it here." She tapped his chest above his heart.

They stood among the cottonwoods at the edge of the promontory. Cork lifted his field glasses and followed the trail Windigo had left through the tall, dry grass, so clear an idiot could have followed it. The hillside was uneven. Here and there, the slope was cut by swales and dips, and the trail dropped out of sight. He lost it eventually but could see that, more or less, it headed northeast, toward the largest growth of trees along the bank of the Missouri. There was something wrong with the cottonwoods there. The copse appeared ravaged, as if a violent storm had swept through, knocking trees down right and left in its rampage. If a man—or windigo—were looking for an ideal place to lie in wait unseen, this would be it. He knew it in his heart.

Cork lowered the glasses. Something had slipped in to replace the fear, the anger, the vengeance. A small glimmer of light had appeared, exactly what Meloux had said the windigo wanted to extinguish. And that light was simply hope.

"Maybe there is a better way," he said.

CHAPTER 41

From where he lay in the tall, wild grass, Cork watched Jenny emerge from the trees atop the promontory and begin, in a halting way, to follow the trail Windigo had left down the hillside. She moved slowly, pausing periodically to look about her, as if uncertain which way to proceed. Cork's field glasses hung around her neck, and every so often, she lifted the lenses to her eyes and scanned the riverbank. Alone on the tip of that high finger of land, which pointed toward the Missouri, she stood out like a black fly on a scoop of caramel ice cream.

Cork had descended the south side of the promontory, which was hidden from the ravaged copse of trees where he believed Windigo had taken Henry Meloux. He'd entered one of the swales that followed the contour of the hillside. As he'd hoped, he'd been able to get within a hundred yards of the riverbank without revealing himself to anyone who might have been watching from below. He'd taken his cell phone and had told Jenny that as soon as he was in position he would call her. That's when she needed to begin making her own way down the hillside, but in plain sight. If Kitchimanidoo and luck were with them, her descent would distract Windigo while Cork made his dash for the river.

He watched his daughter's great show of uncertainty. But it wasn't just hesitancy she played out. She moved oddly, one leg stiff, in the same way that Louise Arceneaux walked when she wore her peg leg. It was a brilliant piece of misdirection, he thought. It reminded him of how the little killdeer pretended to be hurt in order to lure away predators who neared its nest. He hoped desperately that Jenny's charade would attract and hold Windigo's eye.

Cork had kept the Glock, but had done so with one condition: as soon as he began to make his way along the riverbank toward the damaged trees, she would return to the trailer, drive the Explorer a safe distance away, and await his call. If she didn't hear from him within half an hour, she would phone the Williams County Sheriff's Office and explain her situation. Under no circumstance was she to put herself in jeopardy.

He allowed her a few minutes of playing out her charade before he made his run. When he was ready, he hunched low and shot for the river, trying to keep as much of himself as he could hidden by the thigh-high weed cover. Grasshoppers buzzed away at his coming, and not far from the river, he flushed a pair of grouse. When the birds hit the air, he dropped and waited, pressing his body against the dry earth, breathing dust. He gave himself a full minute before he pushed up and loped on. When he was finally inside the safety of the riverbank vegetation, he looked up the hillside and found Jenny still moving haltingly, awkwardly down the slope. He pulled his phone from its belt holster and made his call.

"I'm good," he said. "You go."

"Not until you reach those trees where we think he's got Henry."

"No, you go now. That's what we agreed to."

"I'll keep you in sight with my binoculars. When you get there, I'll turn back, that's a promise."

He didn't have time to argue. The bottom line was that he wanted her out of harm's way. So long as she was gone before anything went down with Windigo, he could live with it.

"Ten-four, kiddo. Wish me luck."

He turned the cell to vibrate so that the ring from an errant call wouldn't give him away. He reholstered the phone and eyed the landscape downriver. A hundred and fifty yards away lay the place he believed Henry was being held. He chose his next hiding place—a thicket of sumac sixty yards distant—and made a dash.

A strong breeze had risen, skating over the Missouri, shaking the leaves of the trees and underbrush along the riverbank. The wind was both friend and foe to Cork. It helped to mask his approach, but it also drowned out any sound that might give away Windigo's position.

Safely inside the cover of the sumac, Cork glanced up the slope. Jenny had descended halfway. She'd paused and was scanning the river north to south, as if checking all the possibilities before her. When she swung the glasses in Cork's direction, he eased himself into the open just enough to give her a wave. She kept scanning, and he couldn't tell if she'd missed him or was continuing her charade. She lowered the glasses and moved downslope again with that stiff-legged gait.

Cork chose his next sanctuary, a grouping of cottonwoods not unlike the one that was his final destination. He shot for the cover and, when he entered the trees, found not only wind damage—trees down, trunks splintered—but also evidence of habitation: old char from a campfire, rusted food tins, a stained, striped mattress that had disgorged its stuffing and had clearly become the abode of vermin. There was no sign of Meloux or Windigo. He felt this was a good indication that he was, in fact, thinking like the prey he hunted.

At the north edge of the cottonwoods, Cork used a broad trunk as shield and eyed the final copse. It had been thick with upright trees at one time, but whatever tempest had swept up along that river and across the hills and bluffs had razed a good quarter of that timber. Trunks lay uprooted or in great splintered sections on the ground. Between Cork and his goal, there was little cover along the bank. Mostly what he had to work with was the tall, dry grass.

The day was sweltering, and the effort of this hunt made him sweat profusely. Salty drops stung his eyes. His soggy shirt clung to his back. He was thirsty, and his mouth was dust dry. He eyed what seemed like an interminable stretch of impossibility, and knew he had no choice but to crawl those final fifty yards using the grass as cover. He pulled the Glock from where he'd shoved it into the waist of his pants, released the safety, and gripped the firearm in his right hand. He went down on his belly and began to slither ahead like a lizard. He wondered if Jenny could see him from her high vantage. He didn't dare risk lifting his head to look. The grass hid him, but it also obscured everything that lay before him. Blind, he made his way toward the damaged stand of trees.

He'd gone halfway when he heard the gunshot. It came from the cottonwoods in front of him. His first thought was *Meloux*. He had a sudden vision of the old man's execution, Meloux's long white hair dripping blood. His second thought was *Jenny*. He raised himself and looked up the hillside. She was gone. She'd been so far down the slope that if she'd headed back to the trailer she should still have been visible to him. But she was nowhere to be seen. There'd been the gunshot, and then she'd simply vanished.

Something happened to Cork that had seldom happened before: he panicked. He lost it. All his careful planning fled. He stood and began a wild race for the cottonwoods. He hit the copse at a dead run, crashing into and through the underbrush, leaping one fallen tree after another. No amount of wind could mask the sound of his coming. He glanced left and right, finally spotted a small clearing ahead. Sitting upright in the center, bound to a sapling with what appeared to be clothesline cord, was Henry Meloux. His head was down. His chin rested on his chest. Just as Cork had seen in his dark vision, Meloux's long white hair was stained with blood.

Call it training. Call it instinct. Call it a little of the wisdom Meloux had passed to him over all their years together that was now innate. Whatever it was, the next thing Cork did, he did without thinking. He was running headlong into a situation he had not reconnoitered but was so obviously a trap. Between him and the clearing where Meloux sat bound lay the trunk of a huge fallen cottonwood whose roots, at its thickest end, were like long, ragged claws. Cork had already leaped several very like it, but this one he did not. Instead, he dove for the cover that downed tree provided him.

Two quick shots sent splinters of the trunk into the air above Cork. The reports came from ahead and to the left. Cork hunkered down and kept himself shielded from what might come next from that direction.

What came was a voice: "Cork O'Connor. I hear you're part Mick, part Shinnob, like me. That true?" When Cork didn't answer, Windigo went on. "Your friend there, he's not dead. I just gave him a tap on the side of his head, just enough to keep him quiet. A lot of blood, but you know about head wounds. Bleed buckets. Look a lot worse than they are."

"What was the gunshot about?" Cork called.

"To flush you out. I saw your girl coming down the hill, but I didn't see you. Only a coward would send a woman in his place. I don't peg you as a coward. Your girl, though, when she heard that shot, she dropped out of sight like a prairie dog. Lucky for her. If she'd been a little closer, I might've tried to cap her."

"So what now?" Cork hollered.

"Now we negotiate."

"For what?"

"The old man's life."

Though he still trembled from the adrenaline that coursed through his body, Cork's panic had subsided. Two pieces of information that he'd needed he now had: Henry was alive—if Cork could believe Windigo—and Jenny was safe. A calm descended, once again Meloux's wisdom, in a way. Cork understood that a man sometimes had to enter the dark, but he did not have to become a part of the darkness.

Ogichidaa, he thought. To stand between evil and his people. This was what he was born for. If necessary, this would be the way of his death.

The wind had grown stronger. The cottonwood leaves above

him and the dead branches of the fallen trees around him rattled and clacked. Cork had to raise his voice even more to be heard.

"The old man's not moving," he cried. "How do I know he's still alive?"

"You don't," Windigo called back. "But if I don't like our negotiation, I can always pop a couple of rounds into him from here. That'll make things pretty certain."

Cork had a better sense of the direction now. He eased himself toward the clawlike roots of the blown-down trunk and risked a peek, trying to pinpoint Windigo's exact position.

The shot that came was high of Cork's head and to the right. It missed him but sent splinters of the trunk into his scalp and temple. He jerked back, stung and bleeding. He'd got what he wanted, however. He'd glimpsed his Windigo. The big man was protected behind a V formed by a couple of toppled trees thirty yards away, just beyond the clearing where Meloux lay.

"I don't think you want a negotiation," Cork said.

"No?"

"I think you just want blood. Mine."

Laughter, long and deep, came from Windigo. "My God. Finally, someone who gets me. Oh, I'm going to enjoy this, O'Connor."

Cork was safe where he was, but he didn't like the idea of Meloux trapped in the middle of what was taking place. He needed to draw the muzzle of Windigo's Desert Eagle away from his old friend. A dozen yards to his left was the shattered stump of a tree that had snapped. It stood five feet high and was nearly as big around as the fallen tree that currently sheltered him. Unless Windigo was a crack shot, Cork believed that, on the run, he would make a poor target.

He fired one shot from the Glock in Windigo's direction and launched himself toward the stump. He zigged and zagged as he crossed the dozen yards, and none of the three rounds that Windigo fired hit their mark. Breathing hard, heart hammering, he reached the protection of what was left of a once great tree, where he spent a few moments gathering himself.

Seven rounds. Cork had counted seven rounds from Windigo. Although he'd long ago given up his own firearms, Cork knew weapons. Year after year, when he'd worn a badge, he'd had to qualify on the range. So the Glock in his hand didn't feel alien at all. And what he knew about the Desert Eagle .44 Magnum was that the magazine carried eight rounds. Unless Windigo had brought an additional magazine or more cartridges, he had only one left to him. Cork ejected the magazine on his Glock. Except for the shot he'd fired, it was full. Windigo had the advantage of mobility. Cork, if he was lucky, had the edge in firepower.

"I know what you're thinking, O'Connor," Windigo hollered above the wind through the trees. "I know you. I'll bet you're a cop. Or you were a cop once. Am I right? I knew it back there in the trailer. I could smell cop on you like dog shit on a shoe."

His voice still came from the same direction. Windigo hadn't moved. He was counting on Cork to come to him, which was not exactly what Cork was doing. Not yet.

Windigo fired three shots in quick succession.

"Reloaded," the big man called. "That's what you were thinking, wasn't it? That I was expending all my ammo?"

The laugh came again, a sound that, within the whoosh of the wind and dull rattle of the cottonwood leaves and scrape of branches and groan of strained limbs, reminded Cork of a Halloween sound, something meant to scare children.

It didn't scare Cork, but it concerned him. He had no advantage now. Except that Windigo wanted his blood. Windigo's hunger was all-consuming. In the darkness of his soul, Windigo was blind to everything but Cork. Was there a way to use that blindness?

"Tell you what I'm going to do, O'Connor. Your friend there, the old man? He's safe only so long as you make this interesting. Once I'm bored, he's dead. Then I come for you. And you know what? After that, I might just go after that girl of yours. And when I'm done with her, I'll go back to Minnesota and find Mariah and take care of her and her family. Yeah, her family. I'm really warming to this, let me tell you."

Cork moved again, this time darting to the cover of yet another fallen tree, half a dozen yards away, an easy distance. But luck, if he had any, deserted him. His right foot caught in a snarl of root, and he went down hard. He felt the painful twist of his ankle. He knew without thinking it consciously that he had to keep moving, and he rolled. At that same moment, he heard the double crack of the Desert Eagle. Two dull thuds and a spray of dirt came from the place he'd fallen. Still on the ground, he scrambled to the cover of the downed cottonwood. Windigo expended two more rounds that burrowed uselessly into dead wood.

Cork checked his ankle. He didn't think it was broken, but there was no way he could put weight on it. It wasn't swelling yet, but it probably would. He thought about Kyle Buffalo, who'd twisted his ankle, too, in his own encounter with a windigo. Was it some black magic of the creature?

"Remember the rifle booths on the midway at the state fair, O'Connor? Remember those little metal rabbits that used to run across the back? That's what you remind me of. I was pretty good at popping those critters."

Cork looked around him, trying to figure his next move. Nothing offered itself. A good ten yards lay between him and the next reasonable cover, a tangle of branches where two broken trunks lay across each other in a lopsided X. He could pull off a round or two in Windigo's direction and try to make it across that open distance. But he suspected his damaged ankle wouldn't be much help. Also, it was the same direction he'd been moving, and Windigo would be expecting that. He could go back to the shattered stump he'd just abandoned. But that was a retreat of sorts, and in this game—as Windigo saw it—that might be a breach of some kind, and the penalty might well be Meloux's death. He could also do nothing and see what Windigo's reaction might be and play off that.

He chose the last option, which was very Ojibwe: to be patient and to wait.

This was Windigo's response: "We don't have much time,

O'Connor. I'm guessing the cops'll be coming sooner or later. So I'm going to change the game. If you don't make a move real soon, I'll plug the old man."

Cork again considered the crossed, downed cottonwood trunks ten yards ahead of him. It was a long, hopeless distance. And if he was trying to circle, it was the most obvious move for him now. That was exactly where Windigo would be aiming.

He tried to buy time. He brought his Glock up, swung into the open for a second, pulled off two rounds, and returned to cover. Three shots came in reply, buried themselves with reverberating force in the trunk that shielded Cork, reminders of the damage those hollow-point bullets could do to flesh and bone.

"I don't like stalemates, O'Connor. Never believed in that Mexican standoff shit. I think it's time I send that friend of yours on the Path of Souls and we really get things rolling here."

Cork hollered back, "You believe in the Path of Souls?"

"Grew up Shinnob. That doesn't mean I believe it. But the old man told me he's a Mide. So I'm guessing he believes it. Either way, he's about to find out."

Cork had no choice now, no time to think through another move. He gathered himself and launched, tried to sprint across the open ground, tried to ignore the agony of his injured ankle, tried to use that bad foot. Because it was his only chance at keeping Henry alive. Because he loved the old man. Because he was *ogichidaa*.

His spirit was strong, but his body—that damaged ankle—betrayed him. He went down almost immediately. He heard the shot and saw dirt kick up in front of his face. He scrambled in the dead leaves and the dry underbrush, which gave no cover, expecting any moment to feel the .44 Magnum hollow points explode in him. He rolled and crawled and finally limped across the stretch of open ground and threw himself behind the lopsided X of broken trunks. He lay there, breathing hard and fast, amazed still to be in one piece. For the moment, he lay shielded and completely bewildered.

He waited to hear more from the big man, but nothing came. He heard only the roar of wind among the trees, dead and living. He risked a glance toward Windigo's little stronghold.

He saw movement there. He lifted his Glock and sighted.

Then he lowered his weapon. He watched as Jenny stumbled out of Windigo's hiding place. He watched her faltering walk—no charade this time—as she made her way to where Meloux sat tied to the sapling. Once she was there, her legs seemed to give out under her, and she slumped beside the old man.

"Jenny," Cork called.

She didn't look up. He couldn't be certain that she'd heard him above the noise of the wind.

Cork studied the place Windigo had been and from which Jenny had come. He saw no indication of life there.

"Jenny," he hollered again.

She still didn't respond. She sat next to Meloux, her eyes open and unblinking. She seemed to be fascinated by the desiccated leaves on the ground in front of her.

Cork eased himself up and risked a step away from his own cover. No response from Windigo. He hobbled toward the little clearing where two of the people he loved most in the world sat together, unspeaking. As he neared, he could see that the pale blue T-shirt his daughter wore was spotted with blood.

"Are you all right, Jenny?" He eased himself down beside her. "What happened, sweetheart?"

She turned her face to him, and he saw that it was empty of color, and her eyes, in a way, were empty, too. "I killed him. I didn't mean to. But I killed him."

Meloux made a sound, a low groan, and moved a little.

"Henry?" Cork said. "You okay?"

The old man lifted his head. "Corcoran O'Connor. It is good to see you." The ancient Mide managed a weak smile. "But then, it is good to see anything."

"Let me cut you loose, Henry."

Cork pulled his Buck Alpha from his pocket. He cut the cord

that bound Meloux, then turned his attention back to his daughter. "What happened, Jenny?"

She stared at the ground in front of her and spoke in a dead voice. "I killed him. That's all. It wasn't part of the vision, but I killed him."

"I'll be right back, Henry." Cork put his hand softly on his daughter's shoulder. "I'll be back, sweetheart."

He found a broken branch that reached to his hip and used it as a crutch to help him hobble to Windigo's sanctuary. He climbed one of the toppled trees that formed half of the protective V. Behind it lay the man whose real name he knew to be Robert Wilson French, a Red Lake Shinnob of mixed heritage, a product of the foster care system, a man feared even by Crips and Bloods and the Native Mob and as empty of humanity at his core as anyone Cork had ever known. The right side of his head bore a terrible-looking wound. Beside him lay the long-handled ax, the blunt end covered in blood.

Cork checked for a pulse, found none. His daughter had spoken the truth.

Later, when she could talk, this is what Jenny would relate to her father, and then to the Williams County sheriff's people. While Cork had made his way down the promontory, she'd returned to the trailer's backyard and had grabbed the ax from the cottonwood stump near the chimenea. She'd slid the long handle down the leg of her jeans so that it would be invisible to anyone watching from below—which accounted for her stiff-legged gait as she descended. On the slope of the promontory, when she'd heard the first shot ring out, rather than running, as her father would have insisted, she'd dropped into the nearest swale and brought out the ax. She'd crawled in the tall grass to a place where she could use her field glasses and had located Windigo. She could see him crouched in the protective juncture of the fallen trees. As the exchange of gunfire had gone on, with Windigo distracted and that mighty wind covering the sound of her approach, she'd come at him from behind. And when he'd fired that final round at her father, she'd sprung on him and had swung the blunt end of the ax. To disable him, she said. To knock him out, maybe. She never meant to kill him. Yet that's what she'd done.

Although she didn't say it, this is what Cork understood: She had heard the windigo call her name. She had done battle. And she had won.

But at what cost, her father would forever wonder. At what terrible cost?

When Cork returned to the little clearing, the wind still shoved its way through the damaged stand of cottonwoods on the bank of the Missouri River. Meloux, old and tired and beaten but alive, held Jenny in his arms. Cork stood in the net of shadows cast by the sun through the leaves of those tall cottonwoods, those ancient survivors of an unknown tempest. He knew the worst was over. But there was so much healing to be done now. So much that he wondered if it was even possible.

He pulled out his cell phone and made the 911 call.

CHAPTER 42

Fear is who we are. But only part of who we are. It is the wolf we choose to feed, or not. It is powerful and hungry and always there. It would consume us, but for the other wolf also inside us, also part of who we are. This other wolf, of course, is love.

Cork knew this well, and a good deal of the healing that Henry Meloux and Rainy Bisonette undertook at the end of that hot, deadly summer was predicated on this understanding. Healing was sometimes a private experience, but often it involved family and the larger community. In those weeks following the return from Williston, North Dakota, there was much healing to be done.

As summer ended and fall began, Crow Point became a gathering place. Tents were pitched in the meadow. The air was often scented with burning sage and red willow and cedar. The deep rhythm of sacred drumming was as familiar as the call of crows. Cork sometimes spent whole days there, playing with Waaboo, the two Arceneaux boys, and young Wade Duvall, while Jenny and Mariah and Raven—and Louise and Lindy, too—did the work of their healing. He was happy to help in this way. He enjoyed introducing the kids to fun that had nothing to do with video games or television cartoons. They fished Iron Lake, swam in its clean water, played hide-and-seek in the shadows of the woods. According to Rainy, this was the *nokomis* in him, the nurturing spirit. He was not all warrior; no one was. If he were, she told him with a gentle kiss, she wouldn't love him half so much.

Stephen and Anne O'Connor were also often present. They'd

returned from the Courage Center in the Twin Cities. Stephen was walking again, though with a cane and with a limp that might well be with him for the rest of his life. Anne planned to stay until Christmas and then return to the Sisters of Notre Dame de Namur and resume her preparations to join that activist order. Even Rose was a frequent visitor, adding her own prayers to the great healing mix.

Daniel English took a leave of absence from his job as game warden and was a constant presence and help to Meloux and Rainy, splitting wood for the many fires in Meloux's sacred ring or to heat the Grandfathers for the sweats in Meloux's lodge. He made frequent trips to Allouette on the Iron Lake Reservation or to Bad Bluff in order to ferry friends or relatives to Crow Point for the ceremonies. In the healing of Jenny, whose spirit had been torn badly by her killing of the man called Windigo, Daniel was an important presence, a source of a kind of balm that neither the old Mide nor Cork could offer. He helped with Waaboo and the other kids, too, and Cork saw in this good man so much to admire. He hoped that beyond this season of healing they would see more of him.

The damage done to Mariah Arceneaux and Raven Duvall ran deep. It was a ravaging of spirit that had, in many ways, gone on most of their short lives. The ceremonies were a strong part of the healing—Meloux believed deeply in the power of these ancient traditions—and the benefit was obvious.

The deposed testimony of Mariah was an element in the arrest and eventual prosecution of John Boone Turner in the death of Carrie Verga. She also helped nab Carrie's stepfather, Demetrius Verga. In the warranted search of Verga's home in Bayfield, Wisconsin, Joe Hammer of the Bayfield County Sheriff's Department found a plethora of child and teen pornography, including incriminating photos of his sexual relationship with Carrie. The investigation also uncovered a list of prominent business associates who'd been guests on his sailboat and to whom Verga had probably prostituted his stepdaughter. The testimony of Raven

Duvall would help the Minnesota Bureau of Criminal Apprehension investigate and, eventually, aid in the successful prosecution of Samuel Leland French, aka Maiingan, aka Manny, for a number of criminal activities. These included the murder of a young girl named Melissa Spry, who'd run away from the Grand Portage Reservation more than a year earlier and had never been seen there again. Robert Two Bears, who'd called himself Brick, and who'd run from the scene at the trailer with his hands cuffed behind his back, hadn't been hard to locate. Within a day of the incident at the trailer, the Williams County sheriff's people had him in custody. Ultimately, the convictions resulting from his numerous outstanding felony warrants ensured that, for a very long time, the sky above him would be only a small patch of ephemeral blue framed by the obdurate gray of stone prison walls. As for the girls who'd been in the trailer with Mariah, they'd simply vanished, in the way of all small, frightened creatures.

By the time the leaves had begun to turn in Tamarack County and the morning air was brisk, the ceremonies had become less frequent and the visitors fewer. Meloux called for a final gathering of those whose lives would forever be bound by the deaths that summer. Daniel and Jenny and Mariah and Raven helped to build the fire. When the daylight had gone completely and stars became like frost against the windowpane of the night sky and the moon poured silver over the great Northwoods, they gathered around the sacred fire ring on the shore of Iron Lake.

When all was ready, Henry and Rainy and Cork walked together from the old man's cabin and across the meadow. Ember, the old Irish setter, whom Meloux had adopted, trotted after them. He'd proven to be a good companion for the Mide, and the affection that flowed between the two of them was obvious.

This should have been a time of peace for Cork, but lately he'd found himself brooding on his failures, worrying particularly about the fate of Breeze and those young, lost girls who'd fled Windigo's trailer and had ended up God knew where. Meloux, in that mysterious way he had of divining one's thoughts, said,

"There is a heaviness in you tonight, Corcoran O'Connor. What is it that weighs on your spirit?"

Cork looked up at all those stars, and although he knew that between them lay millions of miles of empty space, they still seemed to be one great company of light.

"I feel like I've left so much undone, Henry. There's a crooked cop in Bad Bluff, I'm sure of it. But what he's into and how to bring him down, I don't know. Maybe I never will."

"There are others to fight these battles," Meloux said.

"I'm also thinking about the kids, Henry. I'm thinking about the ones we didn't save. What about them?"

In the light of the stars and the full moon, Meloux's face was brilliantly illuminated. The blood from the blow Windigo had delivered had long ago been washed away, and his hair lay in a smooth white flow over his shoulders and down his back.

"We save the ones we can, Corcoran O'Connor," he said. "The others we include in our prayers so that we do not forget. Can you live with that?"

"I'll have to think about it, Henry."

"Come on, *niijii*," the Mide said, using the Ojibwe word for friend. He rubbed the old dog's head gently. "The spirits call us."

Meloux walked ahead with Rainy and the dog, but Cork hung back.

Although Mariah Arceneaux and Raven Duvall had been returned to their families and were healing, Cork couldn't stop thinking about the children who were still at risk. He couldn't help believing there was more he should have done, should be doing. But there were so many. How did you stand between them and men like Windigo and Maiingan? How could you protect them all? He had no answer for that, and because he could not entirely embrace Meloux's advice on the subject, it felt to him like yet another of his failures.

He thought, as he had endlessly in recent weeks, about Jenny. In all that had occurred, he'd believed himself to be *ogichidaa*. But it had been Jenny, in the end, who'd saved both him and Meloux,

Jenny who'd stood between evil and the people she loved. The violence she'd done wasn't a part of her nature and had required a significant sacrifice, a deep wounding of her spirit from which she might never fully recover. Although Jenny had insisted on being a part of the hunt for Mariah Arceneaux, Cork felt responsible for the way that hunt had ended and the damage that had been done to his daughter. Someday, he knew, he would have to talk with her about this. Someday when the right words came to him. When he'd found a way to forgive himself for his failures. When he felt ready to ask for and accept the forgiveness of others. Someday.

There was no wind that night, and the smoke from the great fire rose up in twining strands of gray and white, filled with the brief glow of embers. In the belief of the Anishinaabeg, the smoke carried prayers upward. Meloux burned sage in a clay dish and smudged those who'd gathered, cleansing them. He sprinkled tobacco as an offering to the spirits. Daniel English, Red Arceneaux, and Stephen drummed and sang. Meloux thanked the Creator for life, for family, for the safe return of the beloved children. Some of this was said in the language of his people, Anishinaabemowin, and some in English. He invited those who felt moved to rise and speak. Louise Arceneaux stepped forward first and stood on her carved peg leg. In the shifting light of the fire, she wept and expressed gratitude and made promises to Mariah and to all those present that the future would be different, and not just for her. Her work, she said, was to help open the eyes of all those who would not see, to do her best to make sure there were no more Mariahs or Ravens or Carries. She was a woman changed. Cork saw clearly that her own journey had brought her to a place he understood well. She had become, in her way, *ogichidaa*.

Others spoke and the night went on long and the moon rose like hope above them, and when it was fixed directly overhead, Meloux brought the gathering and the ceremony to an end. He stood and opened his arms to the last of the sacred flames and the thinning smoke that rose from the dying fire, and he offered this prayer in parting:

Grandfather, sacred one,
Teach us love, compassion, and honor,
That we may heal the earth
And heal one another.

They rose together and, strengthened, went back to the work of their lives.

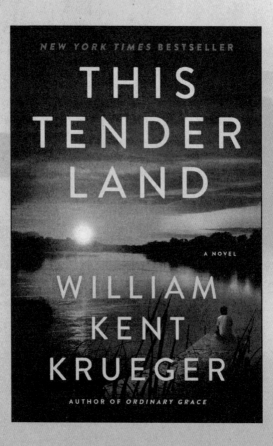